QUEEN'S PERIL

QUEEN'S PERIL

THE PAWN STRATAGEM BOOK II

DARIN KENNEDY

Charlotte, NC

FALSTAFF
BOOKS
WWW.FALSTAFFBOOKS.COM

To John Hartness and the team at Falstaff Books,
for giving this series a chance
and for making it shine so bright.

The middle game is real chess.
Whereas the opening is
an initial development of the forces
and the end game scientific calculation,
the middle game embodies every conceivable principle
of the sixty-four squares,
strategical and tactical, simple and profound.
The middle game is the art of chess.
I. A. Horowitz

1

LOST & FOUND

W*here the hell am I?*

Steven Bauer wiped blood from his swelling left eye and stared up into the swaying canopy of pine treetops above his head. Though night had yet to fall, the sky appeared dark through the waving branches. The balmy air smelled of ozone.

Wherever this is, there's a storm coming.

"Steven," groaned a voice from across his shoulder. A few feet away, Niklaus lay sprawled, his left ankle turned at an odd angle.

"Nik!" Steven rolled onto his side to get a better look and immediately regretted the decision. Every inch of his body throbbed as if he'd just gone ten rounds. "Are you all right?"

"I've been better." Niklaus pulled himself into a seated position. The pain in his features told Steven all he needed to know. "You?"

"Same." Steven forced himself into a low crouch and pressed the heel of his hand to his brow to staunch the flow of blood. "Any idea where we are?"

"Not a clue." Niklaus attempted to come to his feet but collapsed back to the ground with the first hint of weight on his injured ankle. The thirty seconds of grunted Polish that followed sounded like so much gibberish, but the message came through loud and clear.

"Here. Let me give you a hand." Despite the pain, Steven rose from the ground, pulled Niklaus up onto his good leg, and helped him hobble over to a fallen tree.

"Do you think the others ended up...wherever this is?" Steven peered around the dimly lit evergreens and let fly a shouted "hello?" but other than a quiet echo and the sound of rising wind whistling through the trees, the forest remained silent.

"Grey?" Undeterred, Steven climbed up onto the massive tree trunk and called for the rest of his team. "Archie? Emilio? Lena?" His voice cracked. "Audrey?"

"Looks like it's just us, Steven." Niklaus clenched his teeth in agony as he worked gingerly at the laces of his left sneaker, easing first shoe and then sock off the injured foot. Between the obvious swelling and the deep purple hue that had already set in, Niklaus would be lucky if he'd only sprained his ankle.

Truth be told, he's lucky to still have a leg.

With a pained grunt, Niklaus popped his foot back into something resembling normal alignment, all the while attempting to hide the agony behind his trademark grin. The bruising and swelling suggested Niklaus would be limping for a while.

"What do you think happened to the others?" Steven slid down from his perch and leaned against the fallen tree at Niklaus' side. "Where could they be?" An all too familiar fear rose in his chest. "You don't think they're—"

"Don't go there, man." Niklaus clasped Steven's shoulder, the friendly gesture sending a twinge of pain down his spine. "The two of us made it out of there. We have to assume the others did as well." He peered across his shoulder into the darkening forest. "As for where *they* might be, the truth is we don't even know where *we* are. Trees as far as the eye can see, blue skies, hot as hell: welcome to Anywhere, USA." Niklaus' voice dropped. "And that's assuming we're still on the continent."

"Don't worry, Nik." Steven forced a quick smile. "We'll figure it out."

"There's a far more pressing question, anyway." His fingers clamped down on Steven's shoulder as he adjusted the weight away from his injured foot. "How the hell are we going to get back? Unless I missed something, we've lost the pouch."

Steven groaned, the pain of the lost magical artifact that had become all but another appendage still fresh at his sore fingertips.

"Don't remind me." Steven gritted his teeth. "I suppose there's no use in worrying about the others until we get ourselves out of the woods, both literally and figuratively." Audrey's face flashed across his mind's eye, sending a pang straight through his chest. "And without the pouch's magic to get us around, looks like we're hoofing it until we get back to civilization."

"You, maybe." Niklaus winced as he massaged his rapidly swelling ankle. "I'm not going to be walking anywhere anytime soon."

"Why don't you just marble up? Doesn't becoming the Rook usually fix everything?"

"Maybe," Niklaus grunted, "though the circumstances last time were very different."

Steven shuddered as the image of Niklaus falling from the King tower in Atlanta, his flailing form riddled by no fewer than seven black-feathered shafts, replayed for the thousandth time in his mind. Niklaus joked about it now, but behind his perpetually laughing veneer lay a hint of anxiety and more than a little fear.

"No time like the present, I suppose." Niklaus fished the rook icon from his pants pocket and held it before him. "Here goes nothing."

His jest proved more accurate than he could have imagined.

"What are you waiting for?" Steven raised an eyebrow. "Go all Ben Grimm so we can get the hell out of here."

"Nothing's happening." Niklaus' eyes narrowed in concentration. "It's weird, but for the first time since you drafted me into this mess, I don't feel it. The power, it's...not there."

Steven drew the pawn icon from his pocket and held it up to the sky. "Pike," he whispered. "Shield." He focused his mind's eye on the attire and accoutrements of the White Pawn, emptying his mind of any other thought. "Cloak."

Nothing.

"See what I mean?" Niklaus flipped the rook into the air and caught it in his outstretched hand. "It's like they're out of gas."

"Come on." Steven shook the pawn icon. "It's got to work."

Their frustration growing with each attempt, both Steven and Niklaus worked to trigger their respective transformations. Still, no matter what they tried, their icons remained silent and dark. Though mere weeks had passed since Steven's first encounter with Grey and his induction into the wizard's Game, it felt as if someone had cut off one of his hands.

"Looks like we really are on our own." Steven surveyed the deepening purple around Niklaus' swollen ankle. "Which leaves the question of how in the world we're going to get you out of these woods."

Niklaus shot Steven an amused grin. "You could always carry me."

"Right." Steven let out a well-needed laugh at the thought of hoisting Niklaus' muscular six-foot-four form across his shoulders. "Then we'd both have broken ankles."

"Never were truer words spoken." Niklaus shifted to pull his good leg beneath him. "Honestly, with a little help, I think I'll be able to walk. Give me a hand getting up and we can get moving."

Steven scoffed. "Are you sure you're in good enough shape to travel?"

"I'll be fine." Niklaus managed to pull his shoe back onto his foot despite the swelling. "Once we get back to civilization, we can doctor it up right." He looked skyward as the low rumble of distant thunder echoed through the woods. "For now, though, we need to move."

With some help, Niklaus managed to get to his feet, and after a few minutes practicing using Steven as a human crutch, they began to make their way through the dense underbrush.

They followed the brackish flow of a small creek as the wind and storm continued to grow in strength. Oblong balls of raw electricity jumped from cloud to cloud in the darkening sky, the violent discharges of energy so distant the resultant thunder sounded like muffled gunshots from another world. The hair on Steven's neck stood on end as he recalled the last time he encountered a storm with such power.

"Funny thing." Steven broke the silence in an effort to distract himself from the dread swirling in the pit of his stomach. "You spend a few weeks being a superhero and hanging out with a guy who can heal injuries just by laying on hands and you forget how much the human body can hurt."

"Even if Archie were here, his Bishop mojo would probably work about as well as ours." Niklaus shook his head. "What is it Audrey always says? 'If wishes were fishes?'"

Just the mention of her name took Steven's breath. They'd come so far, and now, he had no idea where she was.

Or if she was even still alive.

The pair of them hobbled along, their awkward three-legged-race slowing their progress to a crawl. Other than a few close calls on the exposed rocks by the creek, however, Steven managed to keep the both of them upright and moving.

After about half a mile, Niklaus indicated with a raised hand and a quiet grunt that he needed to sit.

"Sorry. Ankle's killing me." He flopped down on an uneven stump. "And I'm sure you could use a break too."

"Might as well." Steven leaned against a tree. "For all I know, we're headed in the wrong direction anyway." He peered up through the evergreen canopy. "With all the cloud cover, I can't even tell where the sun is in the sky."

The creek they'd been following had gone underground ten minutes back. Since then, Steven had studied the terrain, doing his best to keep him and Niklaus on as straight a path as possible. Walking in circles wouldn't get them anywhere and would only make Niklaus' ankle worse.

"We've got to run into something soon." Niklaus loosened the laces on his shoe. "Maybe a house or a trail or…" A low rumbling echoed through the forest. "Wait. Do you hear that?"

Steven perked up his ears. Different than the repeating peals of thunder, which were nowhere near as quiet or distant as they had been an hour before, the low-pitched roar grew louder with each passing second.

"Sounds like a car." The sound quickly faded, but a minute or so later, they heard it again: the mechanical purr of an automobile. "We must be near a road."

"Help me up, then." Niklaus offered Steven his hand. "Let's go check it out."

They continued their slow trek through the dense underbrush. After about fifteen minutes, Steven noticed a break in the canopy ahead. The unmistakable sound of a third engine filled the air as they hurried their way across the last bit of uneven terrain, but as the pair stepped out onto an old two-lane asphalt road, there wasn't a vehicle in sight.

"Well," Niklaus said as the first raindrops fell, "another car has got to come along sometime. I guess we wait."

Steven peered up into the still-darkening sky. "I've got a feeling this is going to be more than just a light shower."

"What's the saying?" Niklaus laughed despite the pain etched in his features. "When it rains, it pours, right?"

For someone who had only spoken English for the better part of seven years, Niklaus' command of the language routinely amazed Steven, especially in the realm of humor. He had taken Spanish for years and couldn't pull off so much as a knock-knock joke with Lena and Emilio, much less the clever punnery Niklaus often spouted.

"True. Still, I can't believe there's no traffic." Steven peered up and down the two lanes of black asphalt. "I mean, I get that a big thunderstorm is brewing, but this looks to be a major road. Where are all the cars?"

"You've just gotten used to living in San Antonio." Niklaus motioned to the thick forest encroaching upon both sides of the road. "I'm guessing there are no major cities nearby."

"San Antonio." Far from any of their homes and with a million-plus population in which to hide, the sprawling Texas city had served as Steven and the others' base of operations for almost a month. Strangely, despite the constant fear of attack and all the stress of keeping the ragtag group together and focused, they had been some of the best weeks of Steven's life: Lena's infectious enthusiasm, Emilio's sardonic humor, Archie's sage though often off-putting advice, Niklaus' jokes, even Grey's infrequent but always poignant visits.

And above all, Audrey and those hazel eyes that peered through him as if she could see into his very soul.

"Here comes another one." Niklaus' announcement jerked Steven back to the present. In the distance, the low growl of an engine approached from what he guessed was the west. "Sounds like they're headed our way."

A few seconds passed before the top of a bright blue pickup popped above the next hill. As the truck grew closer, Steven found himself growing nostalgic. His grandfather had been an aficionado of classic cars and trucks, the two acres behind his Virginia home more junkyard than backyard. During the summer before he started high school, Steven had spent a couple of months helping his father's father restore an old '55 Chevy BelAir Coupe. He could still picture its weathered turquoise paint, the chrome grille he had polished for the better part of a day, the roar of the old V8 engine.

The approaching truck represented an even older vintage.

Royal blue from stem to stern and glistening in the rain, the truck was an unblemished specimen of one of the rusted-out automobile carcasses his grandfather had kept in his fleet of vehicles for "sentimental value." A silver chevron emblazoned with the word "FORD" decorated the area between the round headlights above the truck's twin grilles. As the vehicle drew close and decelerated, Steven could appreciate even more its unbelievably immaculate condition. Several touches like the authentic-appearing tires, old style wiper blades, and vintage Florida plates completed the pristine look.

The truck slowed to a halt as the driver leaned over and rolled down the passenger side window. The man behind the wheel looked to be in his mid-sixties with the leathered skin and wrinkles of someone who had spent most of his life out beneath an unforgiving sun. He wore denim overalls, a short-sleeved plaid shirt, and an old straw hat. The dirt under his fingernails suggested he had spent the day hard at work in the fields.

"You boys lost?" The man's drawl hit Steven as almost comical.

"Understatement of the year." Steven shot a glance in the direction the man was traveling. "Can you give us a lift?"

"Where you headed?" the man asked.

Niklaus, his hand firmly on Steven's shoulder for support, took one faltering step forward. "Any place that will keep the rain off our heads."

The man stared quizzically at the both of them for a long second before opening the door. Steven and Niklaus piled inside and the man bolted back out onto the road, quickly shifting the truck into high gear as he rocketed down the winding asphalt.

"Name's Ron," the man offered. "Ron Springer."

"Steven Bauer." He glanced over as Niklaus tried to pretend like having his ankle crammed between all the junk littering Ron's floorboard wasn't killing him. "My friend here is Niklaus Zamek."

"From Poland," Niklaus added with a bit of a groan, "in case you were wondering about the accent."

"Ah. You must have made it out ahead of the blitz." Ron shot Niklaus a friendly smile. "Good for you."

Steven and Niklaus shared a puzzled glance, but neither said a thing.

At the next stop sign, Ron studied Steven's injured brow. "If you don't mind my asking, son, what the heck did you do to your eye? Must have hurt something fierce."

"You don't know the half of it." Steven grimaced as his thoughts skimmed across the events of the preceding hours. "Guess I need to watch out for those eye-level tree branches."

"What are you two doing out in these parts anyway?" Ron pulled through the intersection as the rain continued to pick up. "We're miles from anything except trees and more trees, and neither one of you looks particularly dressed for the great outdoors, especially on a day like today."

"Car broke down a mile or so back," Steven said. "We were hoping to find a service station."

"You'd have been out of luck then. Nothing around here for miles." Ron studied Niklaus, perplexed. "Funny. I didn't see a car anywhere along the road."

"We pushed it off the shoulder so it wouldn't get hit." Steven shot Niklaus a sidelong glance. "You must have missed it."

"Must have." Ron huffed. "So, you two in Florida on business?"

"Actually," Niklaus said with an ironic grin, "this is more like an unplanned vacation."

"We're hoping to catch some of the sights." A stickler for honesty most of his days, Steven hated how naturally lies rolled off his tongue since his induction into the Game.

"Well, you two sure picked a hell of a day to visit southern Florida." Ron punched the gas as the first bit of hail hit the windshield. "And there's not too much in Homestead for tourists." He glanced up at the rearview mirror. "That is unless you've come to see the Castle."

Steven felt a pinch at his left chest.

"The Castle?" Niklaus asked, his question echoed by another pinch at Steven's pec. A glance down revealed Ruth's dragonfly pendant protruding from his front shirt pocket, a green glint flashing off its iridescent eyes.

That's funny. Steven pulled the dragonfly out of his shirt pocket and studied its green eyes. *That's the first time Amaryllis has done a thing since Atlanta.*

"Only thing worth seeing around here," Ron answered. "Rock Gate Park's a few miles down the road. Other than the beach, Old Ed's place seems to be the big draw to our little corner of the world."

"Old Ed?" Steven's question prompted a third pinch to the palm of his hand.

All right, Amaryllis. Message received already. Steven caressed the cool metal of the pin, his fingertips tingling as wings that had no business moving fluttered beneath his touch. *On the bright side, at least this little bit of magic is still working.*

Four weeks had passed since the dragonfly clasp Ruth called Amaryllis had somehow turned Steven's desperate leap of faith from the King tower into the first step in their miraculous victory in Atlanta. Since that day, the pendant had been quiescent, and Steven had wondered more than once if he had imagined all that the old keepsake had done for him.

"Ed Leedskalnin," Ron continued. "A little off his rocker, as you'll see if you visit his place. His Castle's something to see, though. Made all out of big hunks of coral. He built the whole thing himself, or so he says. I just hope it doesn't get taken out by the storm. My grandkids love to go visit when they're in town."

Steven caught Niklaus' questioning stare and raised a brow in answer. "Maybe we'll get a chance to check it out while we're here. For now, though, do you think you could drop us off in town? Maybe at the emergency room or an urgent care? My friend here has twisted his ankle pretty badly and might need an x-ray."

"An x-ray, huh?" Ron crinkled his nose. "That stuff will melt your skin off is what I hear." Steven and Niklaus shared yet another confused look as Ron turned onto a smaller two-lane road and accelerated back to his previous breakneck speed. The rain picked up a bit and Ron flipped on the windshield wipers. "Anyway, nearest hospital's up in Miami. I suspect they're gearing up for the hurricane, but I can take you there if that's what you want."

"If you think we can make it," Steven said. "Now, what was that about a hurricane?"

"You boys been living under a rock?" Ron asked. "It's been in the news for days. That big storm out in the Atlantic hit hurricane strength Tuesday and has been getting stronger every day. The radio says it hit Key Largo just a few hours back. Supposed to be on top of us any time now. I was trying to get home and get the truck covered up before everything hits the fan." As if in answer, the rain began to pelt down in earnest. "Looks like that plan just flew out the window. It's twenty or so miles to Miami, and there's bound to be wrecks on a day like today."

Steven had no recollection of any news about a hurricane, though that wasn't particularly surprising. With the multitude of strange occurrences brought on by the coming correction—the cataclysms Grey and Zed created the Game to prevent—it seemed only natural for the approaching storm to get lost among all the other catastrophes.

As they hit the edge of town, a surreal undercurrent began to play at the back of Steven's mind. From all appearances, Homestead was one of those quaint little places that had never fully entered the twenty-first century. He and Katherine had made a point one summer of traveling the eastern seaboard via a sequence of backroads in a quest to tour the best of small-town America. Homestead, in just the first few seconds of their impromptu tour, had most of the places they'd visited beat hands down. Each and every building they passed wove a spell of yesteryear, an understated yet undeniable quality that hearkened back to older, happier times, almost as if they were driving through a movie set rather than an actual town. Even the cars...

A strange realization washed across Steven's consciousness, a realization confirmed a moment later as they passed a small mom-and-pop service station. Outside the building, two red and gold pumps stood sentry, vainly awaiting customers who, in all likelihood, wouldn't set foot out of their storm cellars for at least a day or so. Seven feet tall and slender, the twin pumps had old-style analog dials that only went up to $9.99. Each crowned with a circular sign that said "ROAR with GILMORE" below a leaping lion, the pumps themselves advertised "GILMORE RED LION GASOLINE plus TETRAETHYL." Just past the pumps, parked outside the darkened station, Steven spotted a '43 Plymouth, a '39 Hudson, and a '40 Studebaker, all in the same pristine shape as Ron's truck.

So either Homestead is a town full of vintage car collectors, or...

"Ron, stupid question, but what's the date?"

"September 15th. Why?"

"No, the whole date." Steven lowered his eyes at Ron's incredulous stare. "Please."

"You're serious?" Ron asked.

"As a heart attack." Steven's face grew blank as he awaited an answer a part of him already knew all too well. "What day is it?"

"It's September 15th, 1945." Ron pulled to a stop at the next intersection. "All day long, as far as I know."

2

DIVIDE & CONQUER

"What do you mean you think we ought to stay put?" Lena's passionate glare burned with a potent mix of anger and desperation, a look Steven had seen on more than one occasion. "If someone doesn't do something fast, all of those people are going to die!"

"I'm sorry, Lena, but I'm not convinced running off after yet another disaster is the best idea right now." Steven searched the San Antonio hotel room he and the others had been using as a base of operations in a vain hunt for support. Emilio, Niklaus, and Audrey all avoided his eyes while Archie met his gaze with an unnerving, almost detached stare. "Last time, you and Archie both got hurt and—"

"I wish you'd leave that whole thing alone." Lena's cheeks flushed hot pink. "Archie and I—hell, all of us—have come through a lot worse."

"Still, I think—"

"We're fine, Steven, which is a lot more than you can say about them." Lena pointed a shaking finger at the old Panasonic television resting on the hotel room dresser. There, a nightmarish drama played out as line after line of silent words marched across the bottom of the screen.

MAGNITUDE 5.7 EARTHQUAKE HAS HIT NEW YORK CITY DURING RUSH HOUR - EPICENTER JUST SOUTH OF BROOKLYN BRIDGE

TREMORS FELT ALONG EAST COAST AS FAR AS SOUTHERN MAINE AND EASTERN VIRGINIA/MARYLAND

PARTIAL COLLAPSE OF BROOKLYN BRIDGE HAS HUNDREDS TRAPPED - STRUCTURE IS FEARED UNSTABLE

"Unstable." Lena's hands went to her hips. "Do you seriously expect us to sit on our hands and watch as cars and people start to fall into the river?"

"Not to sound callous, but it's not our responsibility to play coast-to-coast park ranger while the world goes to hell." Steven's guts twisted inside him, half because Lena wouldn't let it go and half because, at some level, he knew she was right.

"You know as well as I do this earthquake is just another sign of the coming correction." Lena crossed her arms. "Grey said the catastrophes were going to start coming harder and faster every day. I say the first major earthquake to hit New York City in over a hundred years definitely qualifies. That alone makes this our responsibility." Her voice cracked with emotion. "Those people are counting on us."

"Those people don't even know we exist." Steven's tone came out more than a little bitter, and though a part of him felt shame at his words, he didn't back down. "Not one of them."

"So?" Lena shot back, as fired up as Steven had ever seen her. "Does that mean we ignore what's happening? Just leave those people to die? That's not what you thought last week. What's changed? Better yet, what would Grey say if he were here?"

The last question hit Steven like a roundhouse kick to the gut. Lena's words regarding what his absent mentor would think about the situation made one thing imminently clear. Something *was* different this time, something subtle Steven couldn't quite place. He knew good and well he should be arguing the other side as the people flashing across the screen desperately needed help only they could provide. Despite that, his every instinct screamed to stay as far from New York as possible. The fact that both Audrey and Niklaus refused to meet his gaze while Emilio sat staring at him with a tortured mix of righteous anger and disillusionment only made things worse.

"Lena, please. I can't explain it. It just feels...wrong."

Hundreds of lives had been spared by their timely, albeit anonymous, interventions in what appeared to the rest of the world as a rash of natural disasters.

The floods in Houston.

The wildfires in Kansas.

The landslides along the California coast.

Steven didn't have the first clue what was different this time or why he felt so strongly against going to New York, but the feeling sat there in his gut and wouldn't go away.

"We've been lucky so far." He paced the room. "But how long do you think that luck's going to hold out? We're supposed to be saving ourselves for the Game, remember?"

"How can I forget?" Lena answered. "It's all you've been talking about for weeks." Her entire body shook in frustration. "Look, we can argue this all day, but there's one thing you can't deny. If not for Grey's stupid Game, those people wouldn't be in danger in the first place."

"Girl's got a point," Archie interjected. "Like always."

"Listen to her, Steven." Audrey approached him from behind, the usual comfort of her hand on his arm replaced with a hint of betrayal. "You know she's right. Even if this had nothing to do with the Game, we owe it to those people to try to help them. Just because we can."

"But..." The words caught in his throat.

Steven and Lena had spent many an hour over the preceding weeks debating books, movies, politics, religion. Even in the midst of this, their first actual argument, the fight remained familiar territory. With Audrey, however, things were different.

Since her near fatal wound at the hands of the Black Pawn, Steven had been on eggshells with this woman who captivated far more of his thoughts than he cared to admit. They had become fast friends over the last few weeks and flirted enough that Niklaus had called him out on it more than once. Archie often watched them with an amused eye, and Emilio usually found a reason to make himself scarce if he ended up alone with the White Queen and Pawn. Still, circumstances being what they were, their relationship had not yet progressed to the point that they knew how to fight.

And Steven couldn't bear to see even an ounce of disappointment in those hazel eyes.

"Not going to win many arguments that way, Steven." Niklaus crossed his arms and let out a quiet laugh. "What would your father say?"

Niklaus' vain attempt at lightening the mood accomplished the exact opposite and all conversation ground to a screeching halt. Realizing what he'd said, he rose from his chair and walked to the window, his cheeks as flushed as Lena's.

Donald Bauer, Steven's father, had been missing for nearly a month, and for all they knew, the man was dead.

Or worse.

"I'm sorry, Steven." Niklaus' usually boisterous voice dropped to a whisper. "You know I didn't mean anything by that."

Steven's thoughts wandered as Niklaus' apology droned on, his mind flashing like a slideshow through the events of the weeks since his father dropped him off in Roanoke to rejoin the others a month back.

The elder Bauer's last words to him that night as he rolled up the driver's side window and dropped the truck into reverse—a quiet reassurance that everything would be all right.

Sifting through the burned-out remnants of Audrey's house for any clue of her mother and grandfather's whereabouts and finding nothing.

An uncontrollable shudder as he stood silently in the rain at Emilio's brother's funeral, the majority of mourners at the sparsely attended event standing in that very room.

And then, the thousandth reiteration of Audrey all but bleeding out in the no man's land between the King and Queen towers in Atlanta.

"Look." Steven sidestepped the issue of his father completely. "I'm not saying we shouldn't help. You all know my heart on this. It's just that sometime in the not too distant future, we're going to have to stand and fight for our lives against a well-prepared team of killers, not one of whom gives a rat's ass about any of us, much less any of the people on that bridge. They'll exploit any weakness they can find and go straight for our collective jugular. On that day, I want us to be ready. On that day, we have to be ready." Steven's head dropped. "A lot more than just our skins are counting on it."

"Believe it or not, for once, I'm with Steven." Emilio's gaze didn't leave the ground at his feet as he avoided Lena's icy stare. "If we don't draw a line somewhere, one of us is eventually going to get hurt or worse. We've barely survived the first few skirmishes of this Game of Grey's. God help us if we're not ready when the main event finally comes around." Braving Lena's glare, he drew close to the only person on the planet outside his family he'd ever loved. "As much as I'd like to help those people, we can't be everywhere for everyone, *mami*."

"I don't want to be everywhere, Emilio." Lena's whispered words filled the room. "I want to be *there*."

"Look." Audrey stepped to the middle of the circle. "I'm sure Grey would know the right answer, the correct thing to say to rally the troops, but he's not here, and by the time he gets back from wherever the hell he's gone this time, it'll be too late to make a difference. It's up to us." She bit at her lip. "I think we should put it to a vote."

"All right." Steven retreated to one corner. "Though I'm going to have to sit this one out."

"You're out?" Frustrated lines formed at the corners of Audrey's eyes. "You're that dead set against this?"

"Just the vote. Despite everything I've said, I'm split on this one. You five decide, and I'll abide by the wishes of the group. Fair enough?"

"Fair enough." Audrey crossed her arms, relief spreading across her features. "I say we go. See what we can do to help."

A sharp pang hit Steven's side, the pain so intense, he reflexively glanced down at the pawn icon in his palm to ensure its white marble surface remained dark.

Not even a glimmer.

"My vote is to stay here." Niklaus shrugged, his head tilting to one side. "I feel for the people on that bridge, but I've grown to trust

Steven's instincts, perhaps more so than even he does." Niklaus glanced in his direction, and Steven answered with a subtle nod.

"I guess you all know my vote." Lena pulled up next to Audrey, glaring at Emilio who immediately raised his hands in exasperation.

"I don't know what you want me to say, *mami.*" Emilio's fists shook with frustration. "We've been playing junior league Super Friends for almost a month now and saved a whole bunch of people. Doesn't change the fact that Steven's got a point. We've got these powers for one purpose and one purpose only. If we screw things up before the Game begins and show up in anything other than tip-top shape or even, God forbid, lose somebody, that's it. We're done. Not to mention, if we lose, Zed wins, and God only knows what he's got planned." Emilio took Lena's hand. "Sorry, but I have to vote no."

"I guess that leaves it up to me." Archie stared at the television screen, his face turned up in that whimsical smirk that always set Steven's hair on end. "So, which way is Archie going to go this time?" His eyes cut in Steven's direction. "That's what you're wondering, isn't it?"

Running neck-and-neck with his constant suspicion that Archie could somehow read minds, Steven's thoughts revolved mainly around an even bigger question that had bugged him since they'd first met: Which Archie would be showing up today?

For weeks, the six of them had barely spent a waking hour apart, yet while Steven felt a certain closeness and familiarity with the others, Archie still posed more than a bit of a mystery. Most of the time, he seemed comfortable in his role as the "wise old man" of the group, regardless of his current outward appearance. He would entertain Lena and Audrey for hours with stories of his life growing up poor in New Orleans, talk motorcycles with Emilio, or discuss aspects of the Game with Steven. He'd even spent some time alone with Niklaus not long after they'd met to discuss a "spiritual matter" and, Steven suspected, taken his confession. He couldn't confirm that last bit, but kept secrets had become a rare commodity in their little four-bedroom rental. Whatever had transpired between the two men that night, Niklaus had seemed far happier and more at peace since the encounter.

That being said, of them all, Steven watched Archie in a way he didn't the others. His counsel could be on point one day and seemingly counter to their best interests the next. Kindness could fill his gaze one moment; an instant later, mischief. As it had been since the beginning, nothing ever happened that Steven could put his finger on, but he knew one thing for certain: Whatever agenda rested behind those dark eyes, only one person knew.

"Okay." Steven's eyes narrowed at the priest. "I'll bite. What do you think, Archie? Do we get involved or do we sit this one out?"

Archie studied him intently, his mouth flirting with a smile before settling into a subtle grimace. "I understand your trepidation about the days to come, Steven, but I'm afraid I must side with the ladies. As Audrey pointed out, our moral duty is to do all we can to help, though the issue at hand goes far beyond that." Archie's eyes glazed over, a phenomenon they had seen time and again when the priest received or recalled one of his visions.

"I've had flashes of this discussion for days, but until now they were like pieces of a puzzle that only now are coming together sufficiently to see a pattern. I can't speak to the outcome or even what our purpose there might be, but I am certain of one thing: we are meant to stand on that bridge." Archie's chest rose and fell three times as Steven and the others awaited his next cryptic words.

"We are likely all that stands between those unfortunate souls and a watery grave, but in the grand scheme, even that is unimportant." He pointed a trembling finger at the flickering television screen. "I believe our presence there is yet another step in preparing us for what is to come, a second trial by fire, if you will, an inexorable prelude to the Game." Archie's eyes returned to normal as he met Steven's frustrated gaze. "The choice is out of our hands. We must go, and soon. If we don't, many more than the hundreds trapped on that bridge will suffer."

Steven surveyed the room and found every eye fastened on Archie's quivering form and knew his cause was lost. The final vote had been cast, and soon, he'd be obligated against his better judgment to transport the six of them almost two thousand miles northeast to again face the fire.

How could he have gotten it so wrong? No one, not even Grey, understood the Game the way Archie did. In such matters, he rarely made mistakes, and Steven had learned to take his interpretation of his various flashes of the future as all but fact.

Still, as Steven brought out the pouch and crossed the door of their apartment to open a mystic doorway from Texas to New York, his inner Han Solo bubbled to the surface.

I've got a bad feeling about this.

3

LIVE & LEARN

"We're here." Ron pulled his truck into the hospital parking lot and stopped by a set of double doors marked with a small sign that read EMERGENCY. "Now, you boys stay put till the storm passes, you hear?"

Niklaus stepped gingerly from the blue pickup onto his good leg, a Polish curse falling from his lips as his injured ankle grazed the bottom of the door.

"Watch that ankle." Steven hopped out and slid under Niklaus' arm before he could fall. "We're almost there." He glanced back into the cab of the truck. "Thanks for the ride, Ron. We owe you big time."

"Yeah." Niklaus pivoted on his good foot and shot Ron a pained grin. "Thanks a mil."

"No problem." Ron hit the clutch and shifted the truck into gear. "Time for me to go. Rain's picking up again, and it's going to take me an hour to get back to the house."

"Be careful out there." Steven pushed the heavy door closed and muttered, "Last thing I need is another person on my conscience."

"He'll be fine, Steven." Niklaus took one faltering step forward. "Unless this thing blows up in the next hour, this is his turf. Not to mention, last I checked, we're the ones who just hit ground some thirty years before either of us was born."

"Time travel." Steven let out a long sigh. "And I thought horses moonlighting as motorcycles would be the strangest thing I'd ever see."

"Hate to break it to you, Steven, but till this is all over, anything goes." Niklaus took another cautious step and despite Steven's support, his bad leg nearly buckled beneath him.

"You all right?" Steven grunted as he did his best to support Niklaus' massive frame.

"Not even close." The White Rook's laugh came out as a groan. "Help me inside?"

Steven supported Niklaus as he limped the last few feet to the door of the hospital and hobbled inside. Flopping down into a chair, he peeled his shoe off, revealing an ankle twice again as swollen and purple as Steven remembered. Who could have guessed a mile-long hike over uneven terrain on a likely broken ankle would be a bad idea?

The waiting room sat vacant other than a gurgling water cooler in the corner. Steven strode over to a large desk at the far wall and pressed the plunger on a bell marked "Ring for Service." He suppressed a chuckle as a solitary morbid thought tickled his brain.

We sure spend a lot of time in hospitals.

A moment later, a round-faced woman in her fifties dressed in a blue sweater and a full-length plaid skirt came through the door behind the desk. She carried an old-timey radio, no doubt state-of-the-art in 1945, that looked like a set piece from *The Andy Griffith Show.*

"Be right with you," she said as she set the radio on the desk and plugged it into the wall. "Trying to get the latest on the hurricane and…" Her voice trailed off as she looked up into Steven's bloodied face. "Good Lord. I'm so sorry. You're hurt." Her gaze shot over to Niklaus' hulking form seated by the door and the swollen mess at the end of his leg. "Both of you. My goodness. I'll get the doctor."

"We'll be all right for the moment." Steven rested a hand atop the wooden box radio. "Let's see what this has to say about what's going on with the storm."

Her eyes narrowed for a moment, and then she sat at the desk and fiddled with the four knobs beneath the large analog dial that sported the cursive logo *American Overseas*.

"Still getting nothing but static," she whispered after a frustrated few seconds. "Just like in the back."

"Maybe the static *is* the latest on the storm. I imagine a radio tower would be one of the first things to go in a hurricane."

"Last we heard, the forward edge of the storm was about to make landfall." The woman grabbed a pair of clipboards from her desk. "In any case, you two didn't come here for the latest weather report. Fill out these forms, and we'll get you back to see the doctor as soon as possible. I just pray the electricity holds out. If you're right about the radio, the power lines won't be far behind."

"Curious." Steven's brow furrowed. "I'm not from around here. How far inland are we?"

Her lips turned up in an enigmatic smile. "Not nearly far enough."

As the woman disappeared behind the door, the wind outside screamed and the rain began to come down in buckets. A green awning ripped from its moorings rolled like tumbleweed down the abandoned street, followed soon by a pair of road signs and what Steven hoped was an empty baby carriage.

"I hope Mr. Springer is able to get home all right." Steven handed Niklaus a clipboard and pen. "He could've just come in with us to wait out the storm."

"Quit worrying about him." Niklaus scrawled his personal information onto the paper. "If the rain gets too bad, he can just hunker down."

"And get squished by a falling tree."

"Come on, Steven. You're supposed to be the team optimist, remember?" Niklaus let out a half-bitter chuckle and held the clipboard up to his face. "Funny. Even in 1945, these stupid forms are unreadable. Guess some things never change."

"I guess we use our real names." Steven's mouth shifted to one side. "But make your birthdate something believable."

"Of course." Niklaus put pen to paper. "How's 1915 sound?"

"Right on target." Steven filled in the same line on his form. "And, what do you know? Looks like we were both born during The Great War."

The howling wind outside gusted as a middle-aged man in a long white coat entered from behind the nurse's desk and motioned for them to follow him.

"Come with me, gentlemen." The doctor straightened his coat and adjusted his glasses. "Away from the windows."

Steven helped Niklaus to his feet, and the pair followed the man through the door.

"Do you think we'll be all right in here?" Steven asked. "Storm sounds pretty bad."

"They built this hospital pretty sturdy, but we should probably stay near the center of the building." He shot Steven a raised eyebrow, his lips turning up in a slight smirk. "Not our first hurricane, you know."

Miniscule by twenty-first century standards, the ER consisted of a single space divided by curtains into four small treatment areas, two on either side of a narrow hallway that culminated on a double door marked "AMBULANCE" at the opposite end.

"Wow." The lights flickered as Steven helped Niklaus onto one of the two gurneys. "We're really the only ones here?"

"To be honest, we weren't expecting much business today other than true emergencies as everyone is home preparing for the storm." The doctor pulled over a chair and rested his hands on the back. "Make no mistake, we'll more than make up for the lull later today." He extended his hand. "I'm Dr. Jim Bolton."

"Steven Bauer." Steven accepted the man's firm handshake. "And this is—"

"Niklaus Zamek." Niklaus gave the doctor a jaunty salute, though the sudden movement left him wincing with pain. "Glad you were open today."

"You two are lucky. In a few hours, the storm will be on top of us. After it passes, this place is going to be packed." Bolton's voice dropped. "God only knows what the death toll will be this time." He sat in the chair and took Niklaus' foot in his hands, shaking his head.

"Well, I hate to tell you this, Mr. Zamek, but this ankle is going to need an x-ray."

"Does it look bad, Doc?" Niklaus asked.

"Could be just a bad sprain." Bolton rested his fingers on the most swollen part of the ankle, and Niklaus answered with a quiet groan. "What the hell did you do?"

Niklaus flashed Steven a hesitant look. "I zigged when I should've zagged."

Bolton's eyes narrowed at the comment. "And you, Mr. Bauer? What in the world left such a gash over your eye?"

"Got whacked by a tree branch." Steven's cheeks grew hot at the lie.

Bolton's mouth turned up at one corner. "That was one angry tree, young man."

Steven shook his head and let out a half-chuckle. "You have no idea."

"What were you two doing out and about today anyway?" Bolton's gaze shot to Niklaus and then back to Steven. "It's been all over the radio for days for everyone to stay put till after the storm passed."

"Being in your hospital today was the last thing either of us had planned." Steven massaged the bridge of his nose. "Trust me."

A nurse entered from the hallway. "Do you need anything, Dr. Bolton?"

He glanced down at his clipboard. "Please bring me a suturing tray for Mr. Bauer's brow and then wheel Mr. Zamek down the hall for an x-ray of his left ankle."

Bolton stepped out of the room with the nurse, but before Niklaus and Steven could resume their conversation, she returned with a wheelchair and took Niklaus away, leaving Steven alone in an emergency room from another time. Rickety gurneys, wooden tables covered with bottles and bandages, and a smattering of medical equipment that would have looked right at home in a Humphrey Bogart film filled the space.

1945. Steven's scalp crawled. *We're really in 1945.*

Bolton returned with a rolling tray outfitted with a metal syringe and a suturing kit.

"Ready, Mr. Bauer?"

Steven laughed. "Depends on how long that needle is."

"Don't worry. Nothing but a little medicine to help lessen the pain."

"If it's all the same, can you just clean it up and put in the stitches without the shot?"

Bolton raised an eyebrow, shaking his head dubiously. "That's going to hurt."

"I can take it."

"Very well." Bolton set aside the syringe and grabbed a towel from a pan filled with hot soapy water. "Shall we begin?"

Steven gritted his teeth as Bolton cleansed the wound and put in seven stitches. The process hurt like hell, but when the doctor had finished, the cut had all but vanished save the few knots of black suture holding it closed.

"Bobbi?" Bolton called. "Can you please bandage up Mr. Bauer here while I attend to his friend?"

The nurse from before returned with a roll of gauze in her hand. Bolton gave her a few whispered instructions and vanished down the hall.

"You're looking a lot better." Likely a good ten years younger than her sunbaked skin would suggest, the nurse's name tag read "Bobbi Southern, RN" though her inflection marked her as a New Yorker. "I must ask, what in the world were you and your friend doing out on a day like today?"

"Just trying to get from Point A to Point B. We...had a little car trouble." *Pick a lie and stick with it*, Steven thought. "We'd still be out in it if it weren't for this guy named Ron. He really saved our bacon."

"Would that be Ron Springer?" she asked. "Old guy from down in Homestead? Face like a worn-out saddlebag?"

"That's him." Steven let out a quiet laugh. "I can't believe you know him."

"I may work up here in the city, but I drive in from Homestead every day." She shook her head. "Ron never did have the good sense to come in out of the rain."

25

"You two don't talk anything alike." Steven raised an eyebrow. "I'm guessing you're not from around here."

"Queens, born and bred." Her eyes narrowed at Steven. "And you? I'm guessing east coast? Maybe North Carolina?"

"Virginia, up in the Blue Ridge Mountains."

"Never been there. Heard it's pretty, though." Bobbi applied some ointment to Steven's wound and covered it with a bandage. "Me and the husband got tired of all the snow a few years back and headed south. Never looked back."

"Traded blizzards for hurricanes, huh?"

She smiled. "We all pick our poisons in this life, Mr. Bauer."

As Bobbi continued to dress his forehead, Steven's eyes slid shut allowing his mind to wander. Images, welcome and otherwise, washed across his consciousness as he continued to process the events of the preceding hours.

Unbelievably, he and Niklaus were alive and walking the earth some thirty years before either of their births, and without the magic of the pouch, Steven didn't have the first clue how to get them back to where and when they belonged.

And that was only the beginning of their problems.

What about the others?

Lena and Emilio. Archie. Grey.

Audrey.

All of them likely scattered to the four corners of the earth, stripped of their powers, and as out of their time as he and Niklaus were.

And the worst part, overshadowing everything else: the inescapable fact that back in their own time, seconds continued to tick away until the advent of the latest iteration of the Game, an iteration now primed to be played uncontested.

Zed's ploy had played out perfectly.

And Steven knew in his heart of hearts he had no one but himself to blame.

4

BAIT & SWITCH

The middle span of the Brooklyn Bridge dangled precariously above the East River's slow current, its entire length twisted like an airplane propeller blade. Torn loose from the Brooklyn tower and hanging askew some fifteen feet below its usual mooring, the deck rested atop an intricate series of rocky buttresses that rose from the river like the ivory tentacles of some impossibly huge octopus. The main suspension cables remained intact, but the majority of the vertical cables along the entire span had either snapped or pulled loose from the bridge. The few that remained appeared stretched beyond any reasonable limit of integrity.

"All right, Steven," Niklaus shouted, his voice like shattered granite. "I've secured the bridge, but I don't know how long I can hold it."

In his rocky form, Niklaus cut an impressive figure. Twelve feet tall and as broad as a locomotive, he resembled one of Michelangelo's marble masterpieces, yet moved as fluidly as the Grecian athletes the legendary sculptor once immortalized.

Steven had never seen him like this.

Hunched over like Sisyphus at the stone, the Rook stood rooted to the concrete surface of the bridge deck, his legs like twin tree trunks and his hands and arms melded with one of the Brooklyn tower's upright columns. His body now essentially a part of the architecture, the strain etched in Niklaus' rocky features made plain the toll of such a juxtaposition of man and mortar. That one man's will alone kept the fragmented middle span of the bridge from plunging into the river below left Steven in awe.

I just hope Nik can hold on till we finish this.

The earthquake had struck at the bottom of the five o'clock hour and, as such, had left the fractured bridge strewn with hundreds of stranded vehicles and terrified commuters. A few of the bravest had managed to negotiate the ever-widening gap at the base of the Manhattan tower and escape onto the intact segment of bridge to the north. Several more had risked life and limb and jumped for the turbid water below. Even so, over two hundred men, women, and children remained on the ruined structure once considered a pinnacle of human engineering.

"What now, Steven?" Audrey scanned the panicked throng teeming below her vantage atop the Brooklyn tower. "There are just so many of them."

Remember what Grey said. Steven took a breath. *You've got to lead.*

"Nik's supports seem to be holding, at least for now. That should buy us a little time." Steven caught Emilio's gaze. "You and Rocinante try grabbing two or three people at a time and bring them back here. If the bridge starts to go, get out of there."

"Roger that." Emilio shot Steven a quick salute and grinned, the ivory and chrome motorcycle beneath him revving to life of its own accord. "Just leave me some room."

In a flash, they were gone. A proud smile found its way to Steven's lips. Despite Emilio's litany of complaints, when push came to shove, you could count on him like no one else.

Next.

"Archie." Steven worked to keep the hesitation from his voice. "Stay here with Nik and prepare to take casualties."

Archie winked at Steven, a wicked grin flashing across his face. "You got it, boss."

The bizarre grimace set the hair on Steven's neck on end, the seemingly innocuous statement cutting him like a subtle blade slid between his ribs.

It wasn't the first time.

And, as usual, none of the others seemed to notice.

A new sound pulled Steven's attention to the water below. A small tugboat had made its way to beneath the bridge, its crew working feverishly to rescue the dozens of men and women flailing in the East River's churning expanse. Though his heart surged with hope, Steven couldn't banish the image of all the floating bodies below of those who hadn't survived the initial jump.

"Audrey." Steven pulled close to the woman whose eyes had captivated him for weeks. "Head down to the river and help the tug crew get those people out of the water."

Audrey nodded and motioned to Lena. "Care to join me?"

Lena stepped to Audrey's side, a thick white mist playing about both their feet. "That's why we're here, isn't it?"

"Be careful, you two," Steven murmured. "That bad feeling I had hasn't gone away."

"We've got this." Audrey lifted both hands before her, palms up, and the bank of fog beneath her and Lena's feet answered, lifting them both into the air. "The rest of you focus on clearing the bridge." The silver crown of the White Queen shining, Audrey inclined her head to one side, and the cloud carried her and Lena over the side of the bridge and out of sight.

A moment later, Emilio reappeared in a flash of brilliance atop Rocinante. Two small girls, neither long out of diapers, sat huddled together behind him on the gleaming motorcycle, the older holding onto Emilio's shirt for dear life and the younger clutching her sister's dress with white-knuckled fists.

"Two down." Emilio gently coaxed the girls off Rocinante and onto the deck of the bridge. "Two hundred to go." And with that, he disappeared in another flash of silver.

No sooner had he vanished than the older girl fell to her knees and began screaming for her mother. The younger of the siblings, however, merely stood on wobbly legs and stared silently in awe at Niklaus' colossal form.

"Don't be afraid," Niklaus grunted to the girl. "Everything's going to be okay."

"Are you an angel?" The girl's eyes grew wide in wonder.

Niklaus forced his grimace into something approximating a smile. "Something like that."

"Come to me, children." Archie beckoned to the pair of girls. "You're safe now."

The younger sister shot Niklaus a questioning glance and at his gentle nod, took her sister's hand and pulled her to Archie's side. The Bishop, in turn, welcomed the pair with open arms.

Steven shook his head as self-doubt regarding his suspicions about Archie weighed heavy on his soul.

One simple fact remained: Moments like these were where Archie shined.

Doom and disaster? Injured humanity? Children in danger?

No one did it better.

Still, none of that quieted the questions at Steven's heart.

"Niklaus," Steven shouted. "How are you holding up?"

"I'll manage." Niklaus' stony eyes slid shut as another ivory bulwark rose from the river to fortify the collapsing bridge. "How is everything looking?"

"Another tremor and the bridge is going to go." Steven brought his open hand to his brow to block the sun from his eyes. At the far end of the crumbling span, the White Knight loaded an elderly woman onto the back of his motorcycle. "And Emilio bringing folks back one or two at a time isn't cutting it." Steven stepped to the edge of the fractured steel and concrete deck and peered down at the frightened mob below. "Any way you can bring the bridge deck back up level with us so we can evacuate everyone at once?"

"Sorry, Steven." Niklaus' already gravelly voice cracked under the strain. "It's taking all I've got to keep the bridge out of the water. If I push it any more, we might lose everything."

"Dammit." Steven ran his fingernails across his scalp. "We're running out of time and... Wait." An image from Steven's lone college architecture class flashed across his memory. "You may not be able to bring the bridge back up to plum, but do you think you could reconfigure our end into something that might help?"

"I can try." Niklaus cocked his head to one side and gritted his teeth in a half-smile. "What did you have in mind?"

One harried plan later, the Rook's marble eyes closed tight in concentration. At his feet, the steel and concrete warped and folded into a trio of stony tendrils that shot from the fractured bridge deck, braiding together like a colossal coil of rope as they rocketed toward the huddled mass below.

"Stand back," Steven shouted over the edge. "We're trying to save you."

Ignoring Steven's command, the entire mob screamed as the stone battering ram swept down at them, their wailing quickly shifting into a collective gasp of wonder as the tongue of concrete and steel configured itself into a crude but functional spiral staircase.

"Will that do?" Niklaus asked, the ever-present sarcasm in his voice cutting through the strain.

"Perfect." Steven sighed. On face, the comment stood equal to Archie's barb from before, and yet, even as the priest sat playing patty cake with the two girls Emilio rescued moments before, Steven couldn't ignore that something with the priest was terribly wrong.

That's it. He answered Archie's sidelong smile with one of his own. *Once this is over, Archie and I need to have a little chat.*

"Out of the way!" Escalating shouts from below brought Steven back to the situation at hand. The panicked mob surged toward the miraculous set of stairs, climbing over each other in desperation as millennia of ingrained fight or flight instincts overpowered anything resembling civility. Steven's mind flashed back to the chaos that ensued weeks before during his first encounter with the Black Queen.

Time to save these people from themselves.

"I've got crowd control, Nik." Steven fished the Pawn icon from his pocket, shaking his head at the recognition of how little it took to turn even the best among humankind into so many rats on a sinking ship. "You just keep this bridge out of the river."

At Niklaus' nod, Steven held aloft the small hunk of carved marble that had all but become a part of him over the preceding weeks. The Pawn icon shone at his silent command, and then, with a quiet chuckle and a flash of silver, his one became eight. The charging mob, despite the cacophony of stomping feet and anguished cries, didn't hold a candle to a band of Blackfoot Indians armed with tomahawks forged of mystic steel.

"Here goes everything."

The eight Pawns raced down the spiral staircase against the rushing tide of humanity. Steven did his best to direct the charging mob while his seven doppelgangers helped the young, the old, and the infirm to safety. Despite Grey's many admonitions, Steven chose not to bring up his cloak of anonymity. The shock value of the Pawns' collective attire lent credence to their commands, not to mention twisting the perceptions of a panicked mob as they tried to negotiate a narrow stairwell didn't seem the best plan. He had little doubt the tabloids would be filled with tales of rocky giants, magic carpet clouds, and rescuers straight out of a Renaissance festival, but at the moment, he didn't care.

Steven continued to help the rushing crowd navigate Niklaus' crude staircase, Emilio skirted the rear of the mob continuing his two-by-two rescue service, Archie cared for the many injured and frightened that came his way, and all the while, Lena and Audrey worked the river below. In the end, they achieved barely controlled chaos, but within minutes, the Brooklyn end of the bridge sat clear as the octet of Pawns commenced searching the deck for other survivors. A car-by-car sweep of the fractured bridge revealed a few frightened stragglers Steven directed toward the Brooklyn end of the bridge. In minutes, the Pawns gathered beneath the Manhattan tower with the two remaining survivors: a white-haired gentleman still behind the wheel of a wrecked hatchback, his leg malformed and turned at a strange ankle, and a young bike courier who refused to leave his side. As Steven knelt by the older man, the entire bridge shuddered.

Hold on a little longer, Nik. Just two more to go.

Other than the brief mental contact Steven shared with Audrey after her abduction weeks before at the hands of the Black Knight, he'd experienced no more evidence of any sort of link with the other members of his team. Still, at his silent request, the vibrations along the bridge decreased in amplitude and then stopped altogether.

Good. No time to waste.

Steven and three of the Pawns worked to extricate the man from his wrecked vehicle while keeping stable what appeared to be a broken femur. The man screamed with their every attempt to move him, leaving their ears ringing, but they eventually freed him from the car and carried him slowly to the ever-widening fracture at the Manhattan end of the deck. As they lowered him to the bridge's surface, the man grasped weakly at Steven's tunic. "Don't let me die," he whimpered. "Please."

"No one else is dying today." The two Pawns closest to the edge leaped across the tear in the bridge and summoned their pikes. The two pole arms, one held high and the other low, spanned the gap and allowed the bike courier to scramble across.

That left the old man. Steven didn't have the first idea how to get him across the gap without making his leg worse. Still, they couldn't just leave him there.

"We'll get you across," Steven said, "but this is going to hurt."

"Maybe I can help." Astride Rocinante's gleaming chrome, Emilio appeared in a flash. "Load him up."

The motorcycle roared as Steven and his complement of doppelgangers helped the elderly man onto the seat behind Emilio. As Rocinante and his two riders disappeared in another shimmer of silver, he allowed himself a rare moment of pride.

Holy shit. We did it.

Steven recognized that Niklaus couldn't hold out much longer and that the Brooklyn Bridge had seen its last day, but that didn't change the fact they'd saved hundreds of lives, their mission accomplished with none of the White the worse for wear. Despite his every reservation, they had come. And not just that. They had won.

How could he have gotten it so wrong?

His answer wasn't long in coming.

As the phalanx of Pawns marched the five hundred yards to rejoin Niklaus and the others, one of the few remaining vertical cables caught Steven's attention. Near its connection with the deck of the bridge, the metal smoldered, the flames surrounding the steel wire as dark as a starless night. A moment later, the braided steel snapped, and its entire length shot upward like some impossibly long rubber band, the tip sizzling with black flame like a child's sparkler. The entire deck shook at the cable's sudden release, but Steven's sudden apprehension had little to do with any concern about the bridge's stability.

No. With eight pairs of eyes, he cast his gaze in every direction. *Not now.*

As his mind struggled to deny what his heart knew was coming, a wave of all-too-familiar nausea hit Steven, sending him and his seven doppelgangers into a full sprint.

And he was far from the only one who sensed the presence of the enemy.

Audrey and Lena floated above the East River less than a hundred feet away atop a cloud bank the size of a small bus. Lena's mace, drawn from wherever it resided when its services weren't required, shone like a small sun above its mistress' head as she cast about for any sign of the Black. Audrey, on the other hand, stood stock-still atop the cloud, her imploring eyes asking a question that Steven desperately didn't want to answer.

They're here. Another wave of nausea passed through Steven. *And close.*

The eight Pawns summoned pikes and shields and formed a tight perimeter at the center of the bridge as the one nearest Audrey raised an arm high in a prearranged signal. Wiping a solitary tear from her cheek, Audrey answered with a resigned nod. Her hazel eyes slid shut, and eight spheres of silver-white energy began to revolve around her body like an octet of miniature stars. Lena dropped into a crouch as Audrey moved the cloud-barge to join the circle of Pawns.

Shifting his attention to the far end of the bridge, Steven could just make out the remaining three of their party. The sight left him filled with dread.

Though a giant of stone, Niklaus stood defenseless, his rocky form still fused to the Brooklyn tower. Regardless of the danger, Steven knew one thing about his friend: he wouldn't budge an inch until he knew every last person had been evacuated.

He hoped his friend's unyielding resolve didn't end up getting him killed.

Archie stood beneath the tower and continued to minister to the small crowd that had formed around him, the silver flashes from his healing touch just visible from three football fields away. As with previous rescue missions, the old man had likely given more of himself than was healthy. Yet again, Archie's undeniable selflessness, made plain time and again in a dozen different scenarios, flew full in the face of Steven's fears.

Still, Steven's instincts about the day had proven true.

Emilio sat astride his chrome and ivory steed, his skyward lance shining like a magnesium flare as he stood guard over Archie and the priest's newest set of parishioners. Of them all, Emilio had changed the most since his induction into the Game. The death of a brother and having the fate of the world laid upon his shoulders had forced the boy to grow up fast. Though still the first to complain when things went south, Emilio's spunk and zeal were hard to deny, especially when coupled with the new confidence evident in the young man's dark eyes.

Regardless, he, Archie, and Niklaus remained the very definition of sitting ducks.

"Steven." Audrey brought the cloud carrying her and Lena to rest just above the gathered eight Pawns. "Get yourself together. We've got to go."

Steven focused for a moment, his seven doppelgangers fading into thin air as he merged back into the singular entity of the White Pawn. His eightfold perspective coalescing back into one set of eyes and ears, Steven pondered which of the two states now felt more normal.

No time for philosophy. We've got to move.

A tendril of palpable mist shot down like a frog's tongue and scooped Steven from the deck of the bridge. Before he could take a breath, Audrey's tractor-trailer-sized cloud took off at breakneck speed with Steven trailing like some fog-bound water-skier. With every inch closer they came to the Brooklyn tower, the stabbing pain in his side intensified, and though he'd already shifted into the garb of the Pawn, Steven had to stop himself from retching.

Dear God, the Black must be here in force.

"They've got to be somewhere close." Audrey's words echoed Steven's thoughts. "I haven't felt this bad since— Oh my God! Steven! Look!"

Steven's tether of mist brought him up to the main body of the cloud just in time to see a shimmering rectangle of black energy appear behind Emilio and Archie. A dozen fingers of pure darkness erupted from the doorway in space and grabbed the priest, pulling him in. With Archie out of the picture, the void in space turned its attention on Emilio. Two enormous tentacles of the ebon energy encircled Emilio and Rocinante, pulling them apart and holding them aloft, helpless.

Lena's screams drove home the spike of ice in Steven's chest.

"No!" The girl's entire form trembled in fear and rage. "*Dios mío!* Emilio!"

The crowd that previously had surrounded the Knight and Bishop scattered, leaving Emilio and his chrome horse dangling like forgotten puppets at the whim of an insane puppeteer.

"Dammit." Steven stepped to Audrey's side. "Can't this thing go any faster?"

"I'm trying!" Audrey's tear-filled eyes narrowed in concentration. "I'm trying!"

Her efforts were all for nothing. A breath later, the dark tentacle holding Rocinante hurled the ivory-and-chrome motorcycle into the East River while the other sucked Emilio into the void's shimmering surface.

And then, in a blink, the dark doorway vanished as if it had never been.

"They're gone, Steven." Audrey's shoulders slumped. "Dear God, they're gone."

"*Dios mío.*" Lena's gaze went blank. "Emilio."

"Lena," Steven shouted, waving his hand in her face. "Snap out of it. We need you."

"It's all my fault." Her eyes shot to Steven. "I made us come here today."

"We'll find them, Lena." Steven rested a hand on the girl's shoulder. "I swear it."

Far from comforted, the girl trembled like the last leaf of a tree in a December storm.

"Steven," Audrey interrupted. "Eyes forward. Nik's in trouble."

Steven peered up from Lena's tear-filled gaze. At the base of the Brooklyn tower, one of Niklaus' hands remained bound to the masonry and steel while the other waved frantically for assistance. His shouts incomprehensible over the groan of the collapsing bridge, the terror on his face told Steven all he needed to know.

"Come on, Audrey." Steven seethed with anger. "Nik needs us."

Audrey's eyes slid closed and her hands balled into fists. In answer, the barge of mist carrying them flew even faster. As they drew close, though, one thing became quite clear.

Niklaus wasn't waving for help.

He was waving them off.

"It's a trap," Niklaus bellowed. "Get out of here."

"Not a chance." Audrey brought the bank of mist to rest a few feet from where Niklaus' feet were rooted to the bridge deck. "We're not leaving you."

"They've already taken Emilio and Archie," the Rook grunted. "And I'm all that's keeping this thing out of the river. Save yourselves."

"The bridge is clear." Steven leaped down from the bank of mist. "You can let it fall."

"It's clear?" Niklaus scanned the far end of the bridge. "You're sure?"

Steven nodded. "Not a soul remaining."

"But the bridge itself. I can't just let it—"

"Stop, Niklaus. The bridge is a loss." Steven's voice dropped to a whisper. "Now. Let...it...go."

"It's not just the bridge, Pawn, but your entire cause that is lost."

The all-too-familiar voice from above their heads sent ice up Steven's spine: sultry and feminine with a hint of Irish lilt and dripping with venom. "Now, be a good boy for once and accept your fate." A quiet laugh echoed down. "Or don't." The air crackled with ozone. "Either way, the outcome will be the same."

5

REST & RECOVERY

Steven and Niklaus weathered the hurricane well into early evening from the relative safety of the small Miami hospital. The gash above Steven's eye had proven more ugly than dangerous, and other than the large hunk of gauze taped across his forehead, he remained none the worse for wear.

The same could not be said for Niklaus, who'd nearly lost his foot the day before.

The archaic x-ray films showed an ankle broken in two places and three fractured bones closer to the toes. Back in their own time, Niklaus would most likely already be in surgery, but in the Florida of 1945, Steven doubted that was even an option.

Instead, Dr. Bolton had put Niklaus in a simple leg splint with instructions to come back in a couple days for a recheck. "No cast till the swelling goes down," he had ordered with a raised eyebrow. The entire process had taken the better part of three hours, but in the end, and with some trepidation, Bolton cleared Niklaus to leave once the storm let up.

Steven and Niklaus now sat in the ER waiting area, the room packed to the brim unlike the nearly empty space they'd found upon their arrival hours before. The brunt of the hurricane had passed, and, for the first time that day, a ray of sunlight shone between the curtains of a nearby window. The storm's passing, however, had brought people—the injured, the homeless, the suffering—all leaving Steven feeling more helpless than ever.

"We still have a few beds upstairs." Bolton handed Niklaus a pair of wooden crutches. "At least for the moment. If need be, both of you can stay the night. I'm not kicking anyone out who doesn't have a place to go."

"Actually, I think we'll be heading on if you think we're all set." Steven peered around at the packed ER, the hurricane's aftermath bringing almost certainly the busiest day of Bolton's career. "Looks like you need all the room you can get."

"I'm good to go, Doc." Niklaus struggled to his feet, wincing at even the slightest weight on his bad ankle. "Yeah." His voice dropped to a low grunt. "Should be running marathons again in no time."

"I gave you those crutches for a reason, Mr. Zamek." Bolton stooped at Niklaus' side and inspected his splint. "I don't know how you could possibly make that ankle any worse, but I suspect you'd find a way."

"Doc, I'm—"

"No weight bearing on that side for at least a week and, like I said, I want you back here in two to three days to check on you, understood?"

"Roger that." Niklaus grinned through the pain. "Thanks, Doc."

Steven peered out the window. The winds still gusted from time to time, but nothing like the Old Testament scene that had unfolded earlier. After weeks of stepping into the boots of his favorite super-heroes from childhood comic books and cartoons, sitting by helpless as an entire city weathered a hurricane had been hard to accept.

"Hey, Nik." Steven headed for the door. "I'm guessing we've got about an hour or two of sunlight left. We should probably try to find lodging before it gets dark."

"Ready when you are."

An elderly woman two seats down perked up at Niklaus' words. "Young man," she said with a similar accent. "May I ask where you are from?"

"Poland." Niklaus turned in her direction and kept his smile despite the pain. "Krakow, to be specific."

"I thought so. As for me, I was born and raised in Warsaw, though I haven't seen my home in many a year, times being what they are." Her lips spread wide in a grandmotherly smile. "You remind me so much of my Ludwik when we were young."

"He must have been quite the handsome man." Niklaus shot the woman a mischievous wink. "Is he..."

The woman shook her head sadly. "No. Ludwik died three years ago, just days after our 44th anniversary." She looked away, a hint of moisture at the corners of her eyes.

"I'm so sorry to hear that." He leaned on one of the crutches and stretched out his massive hand. "I'm Niklaus."

"Dorota." She squeezed his hand. "It's so nice to run into someone from the homeland."

"Agreed." Niklaus gripped both crutches and stood as straight as he could. "At least something good came from our shared trip to the doctor today." His gaze followed a beam of sunlight trailing from the open window behind the woman's head to its final destination on the waiting room floor. "And now that the storm has passed, everything should be coming up aces."

"Careful." Dorota waggled a playful finger in warning. "My mother always said to never bless a day until the sun has set." A quiet laugh escaped her lips. "Still, this once, I believe I agree with you, young man."

"So," Steven asked, "you're here alone?"

"I'm just waiting for my son to pick me up." She stretched out her leg, covered knee to ankle in bandages. "I fell onto some broken limbs trying to cover the windows at our home just before the storm hit. It left a pretty bad cut, but the doctor stitched me up and gave me some medicine for the pain." Her gaze flicked to Steven and then back to Niklaus. "I'm curious. Do you and your friend need a place to rest your heads tonight?"

The gears in Steven's head began to turn in earnest. He'd been considering their dilemma for hours and hadn't been able to come up with a solution. Lodging would likely be scarce after a natural disaster, and even if they managed to find a hotel, how would they pay? A wallet full of cash that wouldn't be good for sixty years? A debit card not worth the plastic on which it was printed? A mobile phone that might as well have been a prop from an old *Flash Gordon* serial?

Penniless. Literally.

"We couldn't possibly impose—" Steven's words stopped short at Amaryllis' pinch.

"There they are!"

Steven spun around reflexively at the gruff voice, the pawn icon in his hand before his brain could register why the intonation seemed so familiar. His moment of panic, however, subsided as he met Ron Springer's gaze, the weathered lines about the man's eyes turned upward in a smile.

"I thought you boys might still be here." Ron rested a hand on Niklaus' shoulder. "How's the ankle, kid?"

"Hurts like hell, but the splint is helping."

"And your eye?" Ron turned to Steven. "Looks like they got you all fixed up."

"Seems that way." Steven's hand went to his stitched brow. "Doctor Bolton says I'll be good as new in a few days."

Ron knelt before Dorota. "And who might you be, lovely lady?"

A faint pink rose in the woman's plump cheeks. "My name is Dorota Nowak."

"Ron Springer." He wiped a hand on his pants leg and offered it to her. "Pleasure."

Dorota gave Ron's hand a firm shake. "A pleasure, indeed."

"Glad to see you made it through the storm all right." Steven took his turn greeting Ron. "And thanks again for picking us up earlier. You really saved our bacon."

"No problem." Ron smiled, his kind eyes dancing between the three of them. "After sixty-seven years in Homestead, it'll take more than a little wind and rain to slow down this old codger."

"Did your house survive the storm?"

"For the most part." Ron gave a noncommittal shrug. "A little damage to the roof, a few broken window panes, about what you'd expect."

"And your...family?" Dorota's face went another shade pinker. "Are they all right?"

"Oh, it's just me these days," Ron answered, a twinge of sadness in his voice. "My wife, Marjorie, died back in '42 of pneumonia, and the kids are all married and moved on to bigger and better than what you can find in good old Homestead."

"Who cooks for you, then?" Dorota raised an inquisitive eyebrow as she studied Ron's callused hands. "You don't strike me as a man that spends much of his day in the kitchen."

"You might be surprised, my dear." Ron cracked his knuckles. "I was a cook in the Army for four years. Used to feed hundreds every day. Cooking for one may be boring, but it's nothing I can't handle."

"How...interesting." Dorota's voice grew low, her lips pursed in thought.

"If it really is just you at the house, Mr. Springer," Steven glanced at Niklaus, "then I may have a proposition for you."

🍂

R on Springer's house, a one-story ranch with a brick foundation, remained miraculously standing, unlike many of the homes they'd seen upon their difficult sojourn to Homestead the previous evening. Night had fallen by the time Ron, Steven, and Niklaus finally pulled into the old man's gravel driveway, and the veil of darkness had left his rather cheery view of his home's condition intact.

The light of day told another story entirely.

The room where Steven and Niklaus slept, once the Springer children's shared bedroom, was the only one left with the windows mostly intact. The remainder were all missing at least a pane or two if not completely shattered. Half the shingles from the roof had blown off to God knows where, and water damage to the interior left half the house just this side of uninhabitable. Where the front porch had been, only splintered two-by-fours remained, all connected to a trio of brick stairs that now led to nothing. The house had no power, and the water came out of the tap brown. Still, the humble house still had four walls and most of a roof overhead, which was more than many of the neighbors could say.

"She sure needs a lot of work." Ron sighed. "You boys sure you're up for this?"

"Just tell us what you want us to work on first," Steven said, "and we'll get started."

Steven and Niklaus had negotiated the previous evening with Ron for a few weeks' lodging in exchange for helping the man rebuild. Though they were desperate for a place to stay, the arrangement allowed them to repay the kindly old man for rescuing them from the hurricane's fury. Not only that, Steven suspected Ron's part in their drama was neither accidental nor finished, an intuition supported by yet another pinch from the mystical dragonfly clasp that resided over Steven's heart.

"First things first. We clean up all the glass and mop up as much water as we can." Ron choked on his words. "For all the good it'll do with no shingles on the roof."

"What is it?" Steven joined Ron by the front corner of the house. "What's wrong?"

"Sorry about all the blubbering." Ron shoved his hands in his pockets. "It's just a lot to take in. You see, I built this place for Marjorie with my own hands. To see it this way breaks my heart."

"Don't worry, Ron. It'll all get done." Steven cracked his neck. "So, any place in town we can pick up shingles, nails, and some tools?"

Ron thought for a second. "We passed the hardware store on the way back into town yesterday. They survived the storm, thank God, though I imagine they're packed to the gills today." He pulled a ring of keys from his pocket. "We can take the truck."

"Nik," Steven asked, "you mind staying here and watching the house?"

"No problem." Niklaus turned and sat on the brick stairs that led to the three square feet of remaining porch. "Any looters come by, I'll swat them with one of my crutches."

"You do that." Steven shook his head with a quiet chuckle. "We shouldn't be long."

"Might as well eat whatever's in the icebox," Ron added. "Everything in there'll go bad by tomorrow if they can't get the electricity back up soon."

"I'll get right on that." Niklaus glanced across his shoulder at the debris that used to be Ron's porch. "That is if I can manage to get back inside with this bum foot." He raised an eyebrow. "Save you something?"

"There's a big bowl of Marjorie's famous chicken salad and what's left of a loaf of bread on the top shelf," Ron said. "Eat what you need and Steven and I will fix up some sandwiches with what's left when we get back."

"We'll score some groceries while we're out as well." Steven patted Ron's shoulder and motioned to the truck. "Ready?"

The drive to the hardware store somber and quiet, the roads sat empty for the most part. The radio picked up either static or stations so far out, they might as well have been. The lucky stood in their yards making repairs to houses left more or less intact while the less fortunate sifted through splinters that had been their homes just hours before.

"Must be tough." Steven tapped at the window.

"What's that?" Ron glanced in his direction.

"Seeing a place where you've lived for six and a half decades torn apart like this."

"We've been hit before." Ron huffed out a quiet laugh. "Heck, when doesn't southern Florida take it on the chin?" He shook his head as they passed a family of four squatting by a demolished house. "Doesn't look to be as bad as the one that hit up north back in '28, but there's no doubt it's going to be tough around here for a while."

"Do you have enough money to take care of this? Or insurance?"

Ron smiled even as he brought a sleeve across his eyes.

"If there was one thing Marjorie made sure of, it was that we'd always be taken care of." Ron turned into the hardware store parking lot. "Some of my friends thought I was crazy letting the wife handle all the money, but let me tell you, when everybody else went hungry back in the winter of '29, we had food on the table and wood in the stove." Ron parked the truck as close to the door as possible. "I still miss her, Steven, and that's no lie."

"I can relate." Twin flashes of Katherine and Audrey's faces vied for top billing in Steven's mind. "Believe me."

The pair exited the truck and stepped to the rear of the long line awaiting entrance to Hal's Hardware. Thirty deep or so, the queue encompassed people of all ages, races, genders, and incomes. *Mother Nature*, Steven considered, *the great equalizer.* Though the store remained mostly dark, a few flashlights shone inside.

"Man," Steven muttered, "I never thought I'd miss Home Depot."

"What's a Home Depot?" Ron asked.

"Oh, nothing." Steven contemplated how many buildings like the one before him would fit inside a single Walmart. "Just thinking about home."

"It's funny. I may be the one who just weathered a hurricane in a house with no roof, but you're the one who looks like you're about to fall over." Ron gave Steven a thorough up and down. "You want to wait in the truck?"

Still exhausted and aching from the battle atop the Brooklyn Bridge, Steven gave serious thought toward taking the man up on his offer. The broken night of sleep at Ron's place hadn't helped much, the sweltering humidity of the windowless house coupled with his worry over Audrey and the others making even minimal rest impossible.

Where could they be? Steven ground his teeth. *And more importantly, when?*

"Steven?" Ron waved a hand before his face. "You still with me?"

"Sorry." Steven faked a grin. "Just a bit distracted." He shot Ron a quizzical glance. "So, different subject. You going to take that nice lady up on her offer to cook you an authentic Polish dinner?"

"Mrs. Nowak?" Ron's already ruddy complexion went a shade darker. "Don't see why not. If those *pierogi* dumplings are half as good as she says…"

A solid forty-five minutes passed before Steven and Ron finally made it inside to peruse the picked-over offerings at Hal's Hardware. Fortunately, the well-constructed building had taken only minor water damage, leaving most of the stock in serviceable shape. Steven grabbed a wagon and began to sift through a hodgepodge collection of mismatched shingles while Ron assembled several large flat sheets of wood meant to cover the windows until he could work toward more permanent repairs. Half an hour later, they reconvened at the front of the store where Ron produced a thick roll of bills to pay for the various building materials along with a sundry collection of tools and hardware. The wad of cash like something you would expect to see in one of the Godfather movies, Steven wondered how much of Ron's life savings the man held in the palm of his hand.

The two of them loaded the truck in silence, fatigued with nothing but hard labor to look forward to for at least a week. Unfortunately, the grocery store hadn't fared nearly as well as the neighboring hardware store, so they got back on the road for Ron's place with plans to scrounge for food the next day. No more than a minute into the trip, Steven drifted into a fitful sleep, his dreams haunted by images of their latest encounter with the Black atop the destroyed Brooklyn Bridge. He relived the horror of Emilio and Archie each disappearing into dark holes in space and Rocinante's own watery fate. As his mind turned another corner, he sprang awake gasping.

"Audrey!" Steven shouted just as Ron pulled his truck into the debris-strewn gravel driveway beside his house.

"Bad dream?" Ron asked.

"Sorry." Steven attempted to play off his embarrassment. "Didn't mean to drift off."

"Not a problem." The old man grinned. "After all, I was the one driving." He shifted the truck out of gear and set the brake. "So, who's Audrey?"

"Audrey?" Steven found himself at a loss for words. "She's…"

Though he and the woman fated to be the White Queen in this iteration of Grey's Game had yet to venture beyond the boundaries of friendship, Steven felt a bond with her matched only once before in his few years on the planet. Circumstances being what they were, he'd been hesitant to push the envelope into romance, a decision he now regretted.

What if he never got the chance to tell her…

But it was more than just the Game. In every conversation, every look, every moment alone, Steven got the impression Audrey was holding something back. An underlying sadness he'd not been able to penetrate even on the best of days kept them apart, even during the best of times. She worried over her family, as did they all.

But this was something different. Something Audrey was choosing to face alone.

"It's a long story." Steven looked away. "Accompanied by a lot of unfinished business."

"I know that look." Ron clasped Steven's shoulder. "She's the one that got away."

"I certainly hope not." Steven pulled in a deep breath. "For all our sakes."

6

COMINGS & GOINGS

A square of dark energy ten feet across descended from above, its lone occupant a muscular man armed with a drawn ebon bow. A full-length breastplate fashioned of black leather, bleached bone, and buffalo horn protected the archer's torso and groin, and his dark headdress resembled the charred skull of an enormous raptor.

Vulture. Steven tensed. *Definitely vulture.*

Any exposed skin painted black, a single line of white crossed his face, accentuating his hate-filled eyes. At his side rested a small axe fashioned of intricately carved wood and dark steel, the sun reflecting off the blade's finely honed edge. Nocked and aimed directly at Steven's chest, the Black Pawn's arrow shimmered with darkness, its tip barbed and cruel.

"Wahnahtah." Steven stepped forward as the shimmering platform of darkness touched down opposite Niklaus on what remained of the bridge. "Didn't think we'd be seeing you again so soon."

"Greetings, Bauer." The Black Pawn descended from his perch onto the hot asphalt and offered a slight bow in response, though his black eyes never left Steven's. "Zamek, Richards."

From the corner of his vision, Steven noticed Lena bristle at the snub and smiled despite the fear eating at his soul.

Good. She's coming around.

Steven's eyes narrowed. "What have you done with Archie and Emilio?"

Answered with nothing but a silent grin, Steven struggled to put it all together.

How did they know we'd be here? And where the hell is the Black Queen? That was Magdalene's voice before, not to mention the whole floating platform of darkness is her shtick.

As if in answer, a self-satisfied sigh from across his shoulder set the hair on Steven's neck on end. Lena spun around, her gleaming mace held high above her head while Audrey crouched atop her misty bulwark, the eight silver orbs revolving about her body slowing in their orbits as she narrowed her eyes in concentration. Even Niklaus, his feet still melded with the grey stone and black asphalt of the bridge deck, hunkered down as if bracing for impact. A wave of déjà vu nipped at Steven's subconscious as he turned to face the two figures before them.

"Zed." Steven spoke the name of the Black King with at least a measure of deference, a measure notably absent in the next word that fell from his lips. "*Magdalene.*"

"*Bauer.*" The Black Queen spat the word as if it were the foulest oath.

"Now, now, Magdalene." Zed steepled his fingers beneath his aquiline nose. "No need to antagonize the opposition." With a flourish, the Black King stepped to one side to address the small group of curious onlookers that remained on the bridge.

"I would advise all of you to leave now and return to your homes." Zed's voice echoed as if amplified, though his words remained calm and even. "Your esteemed rescuers and I have business to discuss, and I cannot guarantee your safety should you choose to remain."

"Leave them alone!" A man in a flannel shirt and hard hat at the front of the pack shook a fist at Zed.

"They saved us!" A pregnant woman, clearly due any day, picked up a loose piece of stone and held it aloft. "Just back off and let them be!"

"Magdalene." Zed's eyes slid closed. "If you will."

The Black Queen raised her scepter. Though the Black Pieces' collective cloak of anonymity twisted the perceptions of all present, the fan of black flames that spread across the asphalt sent the remaining two dozen survivors fleeing for their lives.

"Leave those people alone!" Steven leveled his pike at the Queen. "They have no part in this!"

"Calm yourself, Pawn." Zed raised a hand. "In honor of White's gallant efforts today, I am merely ensuring the cattle are removed from harm's way before we conclude our business." He turned his mouth up in a mockery of a beneficent smile. "Wouldn't want anyone to get hurt, now would we?"

"This is war." Black fire danced between Magdalene's eyes. "Casualties are unavoidable."

The King silenced his Queen with a cutting glance. "I must confess, Bauer. I'm impressed. Disaster averted, hundreds rescued, national landmark salvaged. Bravo." The King clapped his hands three times in succession. "Yet again, the forces of *good* have saved the day."

Steven's fingers tightened around the pike's smooth poplar. "What do you want?"

Silent, the Black King studied each of the remaining White Pieces in turn, his dark eyes piercing them with their cold intensity. His attire unchanged from their previous encounter, the intricately designed platinum breastplate gleamed from within the dark fur of his regal robes while the jewels adorning his crown cast a deep purple glow that pulsed ominously about his head. Though his arms remained folded across his chest and his dark-steel broadsword sheathed at his side, one thing remained clear.

The Black King had not come on a social call.

"The six of you have been quite busy the last few weeks." The King paced before them, his voice an unpleasant mix of amusement and disdain. "Racking up the 'frequent flyer miles,' as the saying goes."

"For the last time," Steven grunted. "Where are Emilio and Archie?"

His blood boiled at the King's quiet laugh.

"Oh, they are far, far from here, and quite safe, I assure you. At least for the time being. Much safer than if they were here. Wouldn't you agree, my Queen?"

Magdalene's clenched fist erupted in dark flame, though the Black Queen continued to hold her tongue.

"What do you want with us, Zed?" Steven strove to keep the attention on him. "Nothing has changed since we last crossed paths. The Game has yet to begin, and as I understand from Grey, that puts us firmly in the 'off limits' column. Aren't you afraid of the repercussions of breaking the rules you created with him all those years ago?"

"You will address the King with proper respect, Bauer," the Black Queen seethed.

"And *you* are going to learn to get over yourself, bitch." Audrey's eyes glowed, the silver light faint beneath the New York sun. "Seriously, come off it, Mags. You talk a big game, but you know Steven's right. You would never have left us alive in Atlanta if he weren't."

"Our presence here today violates none of the precious rules you and your pathetic little band cling to." The Black Queen smiled. "In fact, you could almost argue that we're...enforcing those very rules. Quite aggressively, in fact."

"By killing us?" The tremor in Lena's voice betrayed her fear despite her firm grip on the shining mace. "Before the Game can even start?"

"Kill you?" Zed laughed. "Child, whatever gave you the idea we came here to end your lives?" The King drew his sword and passed it before him, pausing briefly on each of the remaining quartet of White. "I've had more than ample opportunity over the last month with the lot of you gallivanting from coast to coast sticking your noses in everyone's business to be rid of you once and for all. Yet all of you still breathe." A long sigh passed his lips. "Even were I not limited by a ridiculous set of rules I helped create in my more naïve youth, simply killing you would seem a most inelegant solution to the matter at hand."

Steven took a step in Lena's direction. "Didn't seem so 'inelegant' a month ago."

"A month ago, you were sheep." Zed rested a hand on the hilt of his sword. "Wandering through your meaningless lives, herded here and there by forces beyond your ken, never knowing if the blade that awaited you each day was the master's shears or the butcher's knife. You still walk among them, look like them, act like them. You may even risk your lives for theirs, but know that each of you is different now. With the power of the coming correction flowing through your veins, you walk as gods among insects. Do you not understand that simple fact?"

"Good to know that correspondence course on how to deliver melodramatic archvillain speeches is paying off." His limbs liberated from the tower and bridge deck, Niklaus lumbered over in his marble form and took a position to Steven's forward left. "Sort of Kurgan meets Vader with just a touch of…Christopher Walken?"

Despite the absence of Niklaus' mighty frame from the tower's base, the buttresses and supports he created beneath the fallen bridge deck held. The sound of wrenching steel and stone grew quiet, at least for the moment.

"So," Audrey interjected, a potent mix of anger, exhaustion, and adrenaline in her voice. "If you're not here to fight, then why are you here?"

"And why all the destruction?" Steven waved a hand in the direction of the fractured span. "I suspect summoning an earthquake lies beyond even your skills, Zed, but the cut bridge cables are clearly Maggie's handiwork."

The Black Queen answered Steven's taunt with a wry smile.

"People died here today." Steven's voice grew quiet. "And a lot more would've joined them if we hadn't intervened."

"Suffice to say, having you here today is of utmost importance to my cause." Zed's eyes filled with resignation. "You see, the tectonic disturbance that left this bridge in shambles merely represents the latest in a long series of events leading up to the coming correction. For weeks, my forces have tracked your progress as you've insinuated yourselves into one catastrophe after another along this massive continent. When the earthquake struck this afternoon, it seemed a foregone conclusion that you six would not be far behind."

"The King, however, leaves nothing to chance." A ball of flame materialized above the Black Queen's outstretched hand. "Therefore, I ensured this little disaster was of sufficient scale to capture your full attention." She smiled, clearly pleased with herself. "And here you are."

"The air in this place is thick with power." The King studied each of them in turn. "Cannot all of you feel it?"

Steven had indeed noted several differences since their arrival. Apart from a subtle buzz in his head he'd attributed to the rush of danger, Niklaus' rocky form had seemed more massive than he remembered. Lena's mace more brilliant. Audrey's powers more potent than ever before.

And whatever madness resided behind Archie's faux innocence, as bad as he'd seen it.

"All right." Steven brought the pike to his shoulder, offering a momentary olive branch. "There's lots of spare mojo flying around. I get that. Why bring us here now with the Game almost at hand?"

"No doubt he hopes to utilize the energies at hand against you in some fashion." At this latest voice, a wave of relief washed across Steven. "I suspect, that my erstwhile associate believes he has found yet another loophole in the rules we fashioned so many years ago."

Grey stepped from the shadows of the Brooklyn tower dressed in his usual fashion. A wide brimmed fedora sat atop a head of black locks streaked with silver, the hem of his grey duster kissing a pair of highly shined sharkskin boots as he strode toward the gathered forces of White and Black. His steel grey eyes surveyed the crowd one by one.

Here comes the cavalry.

Steven's moment of hope evaporated half a second later when he caught Zed's eye. Though the Black King's features remained inscrutable, Steven expected to see there at least an iota of concern. Instead, he saw only satisfaction and maybe a hint of a grin.

"At last, old friend." Zed offered Grey a subtle bow. "I feared you might not be joining us today."

Steven had held out hope as well that his mysterious mentor would make an appearance, as he felt more out of his depth than at any time since his first encounter with Magdalene.

Now, he fought the instinct to scream for Grey to run.

Since the grand confrontation at the King and Queen towers in Atlanta and their team's subsequent recovery in Roanoke, Grey's visits had become increasingly scarce. There seemed little rhyme or reason to the White King's frequent sabbaticals, only his continual reassurance of their necessity.

Had it been to avoid this very scenario?

And by coming here, had Steven and the others led Grey into a trap?

"Regardless of how different you wish the circumstances to be, this iteration of the Game is not yet upon us." Grey continued his slow approach toward the Black King. "To remove any of my Pieces from the Board before the Game proper commences would be tantamount to forfeit, an outcome I would guess you seek to avoid at all costs. Certainly, killing any of them is not an option, and a second attempt at capture would, no doubt, result in casualties on both sides."

As if on cue, Niklaus cracked the knuckles of his massive marble fist. The sound, like exploding boulders, drew the Queen's attention for half a second, the momentary trepidation in her eyes giving Steven a flash of hope.

"Regardless of whatever advantage you think the rampant energies surrounding this bridge affords you," Grey continued, "the situation remains unchanged, and the rules you and I put into place so many centuries ago remain in force."

"Good points all, old friend." Zed stroked his beard. "But there exists a third possibility that neither you nor your errand boy has considered." The corners of the Black King's mouth turned up into a wicked leer. "While I do concede that further conflict at this time would be ill-advised, a novel solution to your figurative thorn in my paw has presented itself, one that involves no weapons, no bloodshed, no pointless conflict."

Grey shot Steven a wary look as Zed continued.

"You see, I am not nearly as interested in the energies that surround this ruined bridge as I am the instability left in their wake." From beneath his royal robes, the Black King produced a small bag fashioned of black leather covered in similar runes and sigils to the white pouch that rested at Steven's side. It pulsed like a dark heart in his hand, its rhythmic drone both like and unlike its brighter counterpart's. Grey's eyes grew wide.

"So, it is to be today," Grey whispered. "Gods be with us all."

"What is it, Grey?" The pouch pulsed at Steven's side. "What is he—"

"Fare thee well, Steven." Without another word, Grey drew a silver dagger from beneath his coat and charged the Black King. In response, Zed raised the dark pouch before him, its drone growing louder with each molar-shaking pulse. A single word fell from his pursed lips.

"Door."

A portal of scintillating darkness opened directly in Grey's path, catching him midleap. Before any among the White could so much as take a breath, both wizard and door were gone as if neither had ever existed.

"Grey!" Steven locked eyes with the Black King. "What have you done?"

"Fear not." The King laughed. "You will understand soon enough." Holding the pouch before him, Zed cast his gaze upon the occupants of the floating bank of mist that rested just beyond the bridge's jagged edge.

"Door."

Another portal opened behind Audrey and Lena. Before either could utter a sound, countless wisps of black energy swirled from the dark doorway and pulled them inside.

"No!" Steven screamed as this latest hole in space disappeared as well. "Where did you send them, you bastard? What have you done?"

"Mind your tongue, Bauer. Name calling won't bring back your friends." Zed ran his fingers along the mouth of the black pouch as the Black Queen and Pawn looked on with dark zeal. "As for their whereabouts, I have simply asked the *Svartr Kyll* to deposit them in a place where they can no longer interfere with my plans."

Steven tensed but held his tongue.

"Fear not, little Pawn." Zed's expression shifted to one of mocking concern. "They live. They all live. In fact, your friends have been granted a truly rare opportunity, the chance to begin anew, as it were. Truth be told, I expect most of them will thrive in their new circumstances. They are quite a capable lot, though I suspect it won't be easy for any of them in the beginning." He crossed his arms, his lips curling into a smug smirk. "I even went so far as to ensure none of them would be alone. The women have each other to keep themselves company, as should the priest and the boy. Quite the equitable outcome, wouldn't you agree?"

"And Grey?" Steven asked. "Where have you sent him?"

"Somewhere you cannot follow." The Black Queen flashed a devil's grin. "Pawn."

"Like hell I can't." Dropping his pike, Steven grabbed one of Niklaus' stony fingers, ripped the pouch from his belt, and held its cool white leather above his head. "Take us to—"

Air whistled past dark fletchings as a lone ebon arrow tore the pouch from Steven's hand, sending it over the edge of the bridge and into the river below.

"It is done, your Majesty." Wahnahtah watched from the shadows, all but forgotten in his silence. "There will be no escape for you this time, Bauer."

This was all about the pouch. Steven cursed himself for a fool. *Dammit. Played twice in the same day.*

Steven kept his silence as the Black King shifted his attention in Niklaus' direction.

"And now for their Rook." Zed raised the dark pouch before him. "Door."

A fourth portal opened behind Niklaus. From the hole in space, innumerable tendrils of dark energy swept out to enmesh his gleaming marble form.

"Steven," Niklaus screamed as he struggled against the shimmering wisps of darkness. "It's got me."

"Hold on, Nik," Steven shouted.

"I'll...try." As if in answer to Niklaus' silent cry, the asphalt and stone of the bridge deck again warped beneath Niklaus, melding in an instant with the white marble of his free foot and leg. Though the strain threatened to tear the White Rook in two, the stopgap anchor held.

"Don't know how long I can hold on," Niklaus grunted. "Help me."

Steven held tightly to the cool stone of Niklaus' massive finger and spun around to face the gathered forces of the Black, summoning the shield to his free arm. "Stop it," he shouted. "Let him go."

"As you wish." Dark energy crackled at the tip of the Queen's scepter. In response, the asphalt beneath Niklaus' foot erupted into a miniature volcano of black flame. The explosion sent them both hurtling into the waiting portal of shimmering darkness, the amused glint in Magdalene's gaze the last thing Steven saw before the hole in space took them.

Then, darkness.

🏵

"Well that certainly played out as planned." Magdalene examined the gaping hole her fireball had left in the asphalt. "As you said, my King, like sheep to the slaughter."

"In matters of the Game, it helps to know your opponent." Zed stood at the edge of the bridge, staring down into the waters that moments before claimed the white pouch known as the *Hvitr Kyll*. "Though I must admit the priest's message painted an unusually accurate picture of what occurred today. If we ever again cross paths, we must offer him our thanks."

At his own words, Zed's brow furrowed.

"What is it, sire?" Wahnahtah studied the King as if afraid to speak. "It's over, isn't it?"

"One would think, and yet, something about this seems...wrong." Zed stroked his dark beard. "Your assessment, my Queen?"

"They're gone. We're here." Magdalene strode over and brushed her ruby lips playfully across Zed's. "Simple as that."

"Perhaps," Zed answered, the disquiet in his eyes lingering. "Perhaps."

7

HOUSE & HOME

"How's your ankle?" Steven grabbed a grapefruit, plate, and spoon and sat opposite Niklaus at a small table in the work in progress otherwise known as Ron Springer's kitchen. "Any better?"

"Same as yesterday." Niklaus balled up a fist and knocked twice on the plaster cast that covered his left leg from the knee down. "Hurts like hell, but I can walk on it a little better."

"Still can't believe all they're giving you is aspirin." Steven shook his head. "Does that even cut the pain?"

Niklaus gave a bitter laugh. "About as good as you'd expect."

Steven's stomach rumbled. "Did you eat yet?"

"A couple hours ago." Niklaus motioned to the crumb-covered plate at the edge of the table. "Throbbing had me up around sunrise."

"It's been three weeks. I'd hoped it would feel better by now."

"Dr. Bolton said this should be the worst of it." Niklaus forced a smile. "And just like he predicted, the itching is almost worse than the pain."

"That's a good sign, I guess." Steven quirked his lips to one side. "You're stuck in a cast for what? Three more weeks?"

"If I'm lucky." Niklaus scratched under the edge of his cast. "Dr.

Bolton and one of his orthopedic buddies said I had one of the worst ankle fractures they'd ever seen. If the x-rays don't look good when they cut this one off tomorrow, it might be six." Niklaus chuckled. "Like you say every day, though: at least I've still got a foot."

"Ah." Steven raised his spoon in salute. "There's the optimist we all know and love."

"Morning, boys." Ron strode into the room and took a seat at the head of the oval table. "You two want the usual eggs and flapjacks?"

"Sounds good." Steven took a bite of grapefruit. "I'll take mine scrambled with cheese."

"Over easy." Niklaus peered around the kitchen. "We have syrup, right?"

"Picked up the groceries yesterday while you boys were finishing up the storm door." Ron grabbed a cast iron frying pan down from its hook on the wall. "Grabbed some pork chops for dinner. Is that all right?"

"Only if you never want us to leave." Niklaus shifted in his seat. "Thanks, Ron."

"In fact…" Steven joined Ron in the kitchen "Let me give you a hand."

He handed Steven an old apron. "Much obliged."

An Army cook in his younger days, Ron showed his appreciation for Steven and Niklaus' efforts daily by feeding them like kings. Steven wasn't sure how much weight he'd put on since coming to stay with former Staff Sergeant Springer, but his well-worn jeans were certainly fitting tighter than he remembered.

"We'll need to take care of this again later today." Steven leaned across the puddle forming around Ron's old Frigidaire and retrieved a carton of eggs. "How many more days?"

Ron groaned. "God only knows."

Around Homestead, linemen were restoring power block by block, but progress remained slow. Three weeks in, Ron, Steven, and Niklaus were still working by candlelight and gas lamp after sunset and cramming as much as possible into each rapidly shrinking mid-October day. They'd converted Ron's refrigerator into an actual icebox and obtained a block of ice from town every day or two to keep the food cool. The power company had promised to get the electricity on Ron's street back up by the end of the week, but they had said the same the week before.

And the week before that.

The puddle, at least for the moment, remained a necessary evil.

"Thank God for gas." Ron lit the stove and set the cast iron pan atop the flame. "So, what are you boys up for today?"

"We were thinking about taking the day off and checking out the rest of town." Steven handed Ron the carton of eggs. "Might end up at that coral castle place you've been talking about. The house is finally back in reasonable shape, and it looks like the weather might cooperate for a change." Steven rested a hand on Ron's shoulder. "Care to get out of the house, maybe shuttle us around for a couple of hours? That is if Dorota isn't planning to drop by today."

Ron cleared his throat. "You know as well as I do she's coming by tomorrow morning for a big Sunday breakfast with the three of us."

Steven smiled at the knowledge even Ron Springer's leathered cheeks could still blush a bit. The kind woman from the hospital waiting room had come calling once or twice weekly and always arrived with a picnic basket filled with one or more Polish treats: *pierogi* dumplings filled with cabbage for lunch, *gołąbki* cabbage rolls stuffed with minced meat for dinner, *pączki* pastries filled with sweet fruit for dessert. For Niklaus, her visits always brought a smile as the food and company reminded him of home and Dorota so much of his grandmother. Steven appreciated the visits as well, as they took his mind off the disaster in New York, the impossible situation in which they were trapped, and the crippling panic that filled his heart every time Audrey's face flitted through his mind.

No one, however, enjoyed the visits more than Ron.

"Anyway, you want to go meet Old Ed, eh?" The older man picked up an egg and studied it as he worked to change the subject. "I'd be happy to take you. Been meaning to go check in on the old codger anyway and see how he's getting along." With an efficiency borne from decades of practice, he cracked the brown egg and half a dozen more into the well-worn cast iron pan and mixed the yolks and whites with a wire whisk. "Can't imagine he's had a ton of visitors the last few weeks, what with the storm and everything."

"Sounds good. What say we head out after breakfast, maybe beat the heat?"

A flutter at Steven's chest drew his attention. He reached into his front shirt pocket and withdrew Amaryllis from her customary refuge.

Days had passed since Steven had given the dragonfly pendant so much as a passing thought and over three weeks since the first mention of Edward Leedskalnin had prompted the still-healing bruise just below Steven's left collarbone. He had hoped to wait until Niklaus' ankle fully recovered before pursuing the potential lead, but the insistent beating of the dragonfly's wings let him know the time for waiting was over.

"All right, Amaryllis." Steven kept his voice low as he returned the bejeweled dragonfly to her cotton cave. "Let's go see what this Leedskalnin guy has to say."

"**W**e're closed." A dour-faced Edward Leedskalnin stood before the enormous revolving door that served as the main entrance to his castle of grey stone. No more than five feet in height, the man's presence far exceeded his size. His accent reminded Steven a little of Niklaus'. "In case you haven't noticed, a hurricane just tore this town apart."

"Come on, Ed." Ron's lips spread wide in a toothy smile. "You can't tell me a couple of guests wouldn't do your disposition some good."

Leedskalnin's frown held for just a moment longer before his face broke into a half grin. "Do I smell biscuits?"

"Fresh out of the oven." Ron held up a wicker basket in one hand and a red thermos in the other. "Brought coffee too."

"In that case, come inside." Leedskalnin turned and rested his palm against the eight-foot high slab of coral. "Anyone bringing breakfast is worth a moment or two of my time." At his touch, the door spun on its axis as if it were made of paper mâché.

"How is that possible?" Steven whispered to Niklaus as they approached the door. "That door's got to weigh—"

"Around three tons," Leedskalnin interrupted, a sparkle in his eye. "You should see the back door." The diminutive man held open the perfectly balanced monolith and offered a slight bow, allowing Ron, Steven, and Niklaus room to pass. "Welcome to Rock Gate Park."

Niklaus and Steven passed beneath the eight-foot arch and into the castle proper and shared an awestruck glance. Impressive from the outside, the engineering required for the interior exceeded anything either of them had ever seen. According to Ron, Leedskalnin claimed to have quarried, carved, and placed every stone in the park alone without the aid of anything more than his truck and some very basic tools, a feat that seemed impossible.

"You built all of this yourself?" Steven's gaze flicked from one enormous hunk of coral to the next. "By hand?"

"It's not hard," Leedskalnin answered with smile, "if you know how." He led them toward a grotto comprised of a circle of coral chairs and benches surrounding a rectangular table.

"Now." Leedskalnin sat in one of the coral chairs and motioned to one of the benches. "Sit. Let's have those biscuits."

Ron set the basket down on the stone table and peeled open the red and white-checkered cloth within as Steven and Niklaus took seats around the enormous stone table. The twin smells of fresh baked bread and melted butter filled the air.

Leedskalnin grabbed a biscuit and a small knife from the basket. "Jam?"

"Just some strawberry preserves." Ron produced a small jar from the basket and handed it to Leedskalnin. "Marjorie's recipe."

The man licked his lips greedily. "That will do nicely."

As the four of them gorged themselves on the products of Ron's morning labor, Steven took in the sights. Straight ahead, a forty-foot-high obelisk at least twenty tons in weight pointed skyward, an homage to agent Egypt. The far corner wall supported a miniature solar system complete with a pair of crescent moons resembling a mismatched pair of lobster claws. In the opposite corner, Leedskalnin's dwelling place dominated the area just inside the revolving door, though its narrow entrance and single slit window connoted a prison cell more than a home.

"So, you…live here?" Steven asked.

"Many men have built their own homes from scratch," Leedskalnin answered. "I simply prefer to work with sturdier materials." He studied Steven's features. "I'm curious. What brings you three out today? Visitors have been pretty scarce since the storm."

"We're from out of town and stuck in Homestead for the foreseeable future." Niklaus poured himself a cup of coffee. "We've been helping Ron get his house back in order for the last few weeks."

"He's been telling us this place is a must see." *And the magical dragonfly in my pocket told us to check it out.* "I must say, this place is pretty impressive. How did you manage to—"

"Don't even bother." Ron shook his head. "Ed would sooner give up one of his legs than reveal how he put this place together."

Leedskalnin's lips turned up in a mischievous grin. "Let's just say I understand the laws of weight and leverage better than most people." He looked on Niklaus with a discerning eye. "I get the impression your friend here knows what I'm talking about." Steven's eyes shot to Niklaus who looked just as surprised at the strange comment.

"You're German, I'm guessing?" their odd host asked Niklaus.

"My mother," Niklaus answered, "thus the name." A wistful sigh passed his lips. "My father, though, is all Polish. I spent my childhood in Krakow and came to the US for university a decade ago. These days, I claim Atlanta as my home."

"As I have found my place here in Homestead." Leedskalnin narrowed his eyes at Niklaus. "And your family? Did they survive the Nazi invasion?"

Niklaus considered for a moment before answering. "They fled the country and are safe."

He patted Niklaus' hand. "That is good to hear, my friend."

"So, Mr. Leedskalnin," Niklaus asked. "Why a castle in the middle of Florida?"

"Please, call me Edward." He took a deep breath in through his nose. "My doctors advised me to move here many years ago, and they were wise to do so. Seems my lungs prefer the warmer climes these days." He gestured to the coral walls surrounding them. "As for the castle, allow me to ask you a simple question, young man. Have you ever been in love?"

"Once." Niklaus flushed. "It didn't work out so well."

"I thought I sensed a kindred spirit." Leedskalnin's eyes glazed over. "My love's name was Agnes. We were to be married many years ago, but she left me on the eve of our wedding. She thought me too old for her and, though she never admitted it out loud, too poor. After that, nothing remained for me in Latvia...so I came to America."

"So, this castle," Steven asked, "it's all for her?"

"Initially." Leedskalnin swept his arms wide. "I began this project to commemorate what I'd lost, but as the structure began to grow in size and scope, it became my masterpiece, a fitting tribute to lost love and a fortress where I could never be hurt again." He shot an earnest glance at Niklaus. "Sound familiar, my friend?"

Niklaus lowered his head but didn't say a word.

"You feeling well, Ed?" Ron's expression had grown progressively more puzzled as the conversation progressed. "All this talk of lost loves and the like doesn't seem quite like you."

"These men aren't the usual visitors." Leedskalnin turned back to Niklaus. "I felt the need to build something. Something that would last, you know? Exist long after I was gone. Stretch across time. You understand exactly of what I speak, don't you, young man?"

Niklaus raised his head from his chest, his eyes expressing without a word he knew all too well what Leedskalnin was trying to impart.

More importantly, the words triggered a memory in Steven that set his heart racing.

Something that would last. That would stretch across time.

Like...a photograph.

Steven excused himself and motioned for Niklaus to join him, leaving Ron and Edward alone at the coral table.

"What is it?" Niklaus asked. "I think I was getting somewhere with the old man."

"Don't worry. I think I know why we're here, and though it's a long shot, I think I know how to get us home." Steven let out an incredulous laugh. "He knew. Dammit, he knew all along." His eyes narrowed. "And he didn't tell me."

"What are you talking about, Steven?" Niklaus raised an eyebrow. "Who knew what?"

"Grey. He knew this was going to happen. Knew we'd be sent back in time. That's why..." Steven's stroked his chin, his grin growing bigger by the moment. "Okay. We'll need to pack a few things. Get a couple bus passes. We can do this."

"What?" Niklaus asked. "Where are we going?"

Steven's strange grin blossomed into a full-on smile, growing all the wider at the buzz of fluttering metallic wings in his shirt pocket. "I may be dead wrong about this, but it looks like we're heading back to New York."

Steven and Niklaus took a couple of days helping Ron Springer get his house and life back in order before heading north. Winter drew closer every day, and they wanted to be established in New York long before the weather turned cold. Plus, with Dorota's visits growing more frequent, they were clearly leaving the man in good hands. On their last day, they allowed him to cook them one last cholesterol-laden breakfast before driving them to the bus station.

"Now, you boys be careful, you hear?" he called from the window of his truck. "And don't go getting in any more trouble. I won't be there to bail you out in the big city."

Steven smiled and shook his head. If a better person than Ron Springer walked the earth, he hadn't met them. At times, he reminded Steven a lot of his father. A trusting man, he'd never once questioned their dubious story about the circumstances leading to them being in Florida, a benefit of the doubt they'd never be able to repay.

"Two boys of good character," he'd always said. *"That's all I need to know."*

"We'll be careful, Mr. Springer," Niklaus said. "Thanks for everything."

"And tell Dorota we're sorry we didn't get to say goodbye," Steven added with a wink.

Ron shook his head and smiled. "Will do."

Ron's two sons had both signed up for the Navy and neither had returned from the Pacific as yet, though telegraphs confirmed they were both alive and well. His daughter, Janey, had driven in from Louisiana a few days after the hurricane, and though she had at first balked at two strangers living with her dad, watching Steven and Niklaus work to put back together the house where she'd grown up had quickly won her over to their side. Still, she lived several states away and could only stay for a few days. This left Ron with only Steven and Niklaus to keep an eye on him. Though they'd only known each other a few weeks, Steven had grown quite fond of the "old codger" and took great pleasure in knowing that he'd found a friend in Dorota.

A friend, and maybe more.

"There's someone for everyone," Steven's father had always said. *"Believe it, son."*

The memory of his father's kind words punctuated the thousandth return of Audrey's freckled face to his mind's eye, sending Steven's intestines into knots.

God, let them both be all right.

"If you two are ever back in Homestead, you have a place to stay, understand?"

"Yes, sir." Niklaus nodded.

Steven waved goodbye. "Take care, Ron."

As the blue Ford pickup pulled away, Steven considered Ron Springer's offer and recalled similar words from a pair of friends with even more years in their rearview mirror. As an image of Arthur Pedone's face floated through his memory, Steven's heart filled with conviction they were on the right path, though the old man he met the first night of his induction into the Game would be anything but old in 1945.

I just hope I recognize him. Steven chuckled. *God knows he won't recognize me.*

"What are you grinning about?" Niklaus studied Steven from beneath a quizzically raised eyebrow.

"Oh, nothing." Steven checked his watch. "Sign says the bus is pulling out in five. We'd better move." He picked up his duffel bag and slung it over his shoulder. "Here goes everything."

8

LOVE & WAR

T he post-war mood in Manhattan was infectious. The war had catapulted New York City into the role of capital of the world and since the historic moment at 7:03 p.m., August 14, 1945, when the Times Tower zipper sign announced the Japanese surrender to Truman, all rules had been off. Fiorello La Guardia, in the middle of his twelfth and final year as mayor of the Big Apple, extended the national curfew of midnight by an hour. Clubs across the city were filled nightly with the soon-to-be parents of the baby boom generation as they jitterbugged and lindy hopped till the wee hours. The sidewalks of Broadway were filled every night as hits like *Oklahoma* and *Carousel* graced the stage. Leonard Bernstein commanded the New York City Symphony to greater and greater heights, securing his place in musical history. Not even the jubilant mood of the day, however, could save the Yankees from finishing their season at 81-71 and well behind the Detroit Tigers who went on to take the Series from the Chicago Cubs in a blowout Game 7.

With just over two months till Christmas, the city approached the holiday season for the first time in six years without the specter of world war. Soldiers had begun to trickle back to the U.S., though the majority of New York City's 850,000 servicemen remained in Europe and the Pacific. Wives, daughters, and mothers, conversely, still held their positions in the factories, mills, and offices back home. Though a time of celebration for most, many would never see their husbands, fathers, and sons again, their lives sacrificed in a brutal war against a madman. Still, optimism seemed the rule of the day and change was in the air.

❁

No more than a day had passed since Steven and Niklaus' arrival to New York, yet Steven felt as if he'd fallen into one of those History Channel documentaries Archie always watched. Different people, different accents, different slang. Cars he'd only ever seen in movies. Times Square, devoid of the technological trappings that would define it in the next century. Broadway back in the day before every third musical represented a retread of a Disney movie. The thousand little things that defined a generation, all at odds with everything Steven ever knew.

It was terrifying.

It was wonderful.

He had no idea where or when the priest and the others had ended up, but he prayed they had landed in as fortunate a situation as he and Niklaus had.

That is, if having a room the size of a large walk-in closet could be considered fortunate.

Though the clerk at the hotel desk had referred to the space as a double, Steven slept so close to Niklaus that he felt more than heard the man's deep snoring. Between the constant drone three feet from his ears and his own lumpy mattress, a decent night's sleep had proven an impossibility. He'd finally nodded off for the hundredth time when a sliver of sunlight peeked through the lone window of their room and hit him square in the face. His back ached as if he'd taken a few punches to the kidneys, and his arm tingled as if covered in ants.

"Rise and shine, I guess." He sat up in bed and noticed the soothing sound of running water from beneath the closed bathroom door.

"Nik's already up and at it." He checked his watch. "Well, it *is* ten in the morning."

That left the last bit of morning and the afternoon to look for work. The scant cash Ron had been able to spare was only going to last a few days. Though the fall in New York had proven relatively temperate, winter would be upon them long before their business in the Big Apple was complete, and finding a way to pay for more permanent lodging, not to mention food, remained at the top of the list.

Niklaus stepped out of the bathroom draped in nothing but a threadbare towel. After rummaging through the faded green duffel bag Ron had provided for their trip, he drew out a pair of boxers and some trousers he'd purchased the day before.

"Morning, Nik." Steven rose from his bed and walked to the tiny window, flinging his forearm back and forth in an attempt to shake the feeling back into his hand. "How'd you sleep?" he asked, though he already knew the answer.

After two and a half months of almost constant contact, he knew Niklaus' habits almost as well as he knew his own. The man slept like a stone—and a particularly loud stone at that—which struck Steven as fitting, considering his rocky alter ego.

"About average." Niklaus slid into his trousers. "And you?"

"Not nearly as painful as our last trip to New York, so there's that." Steven stretched upward, his back popping with a sound like falling dominoes. "Ahh. That's better."

"So." Niklaus crossed his arms. "We've made it to Manhattan almost three months before Grey and your friend are due to arrive. What would you suggest we do now?"

"We wait." Steven pulled out the old wallet Ron had let him use and flipped through the few bills left inside. "In the meantime, we're going to have to get out there and find jobs. Even in 1945, I'm guessing New York isn't a cheap place to live, and it'll be a long several weeks if we don't eat."

"Agreed." Though Niklaus put up a good front, the doubt in his voice came through loud and clear. He'd scoffed initially at the thought of leaving sunny Florida for a New York winter and had only been convinced after Steven explained the plan a good dozen times.

A plan even Steven recognized as, at best, a long shot.

Still, it remained the only plan they had.

"You need the bathroom?" Niklaus thumbed in the direction of the closet-sized space that somehow held a sink, shower, and toilet.

"No, you finish getting cleaned up." Steven slid by on his way to the door. "I'll go scrounge us up some breakfast."

As Steven headed up the sidewalk looking for whatever passed for an IHOP at the end of the Second World War, he reviewed the convoluted logic that brought him and Niklaus to New York in the first place. The epiphany had struck him weeks before as they stood at the center of Ed Leedskalnin's Rock Gate Park.

The clipping. He meant for me to see it.

Long before Niklaus, Archie, Audrey, or even Emilio and Lena, the first individuals Steven had met after his induction into Grey's insane Game were Arthur and Ruth Pedone, an elderly couple who lived on the coast of Maine almost sixty years in the future. His evening in the Pedone home remained as fresh in his memory as if it had occurred yesterday: Ruth's warm smile, Arthur's hearty laugh, their cozy little house in Old Port just a few blocks inland from the Atlantic, the couple's kind hospitality.

Most importantly, he remembered an old newspaper clipping that hung in a prominent position on the wall of their living room. The clipping showed Arthur, barely out of his teens and a returning war hero, walking off a boat arm in arm with a slightly younger appearing version of Grey, Steven's mysterious mentor.

The date on the paper? January 4, 1946. *Two months and change in the future.*

At the time, Steven thought Grey had shown him the clipping solely to prove his unbelievable claim of longevity. Now, he wasn't so sure.

He must have known all of this was going to happen. Steven shook his head from side to side, trying to clear the cobwebs. *And the only way he could possibly have known was if I told him. Or will tell him, if and when we find him.*

The possibilities made Steven's head throb. Working out the real-world practicalities of teleportation had been hard enough. Trying to wrap his brain around honest-to-God time travel stretched his mind even further. In the weeks since their fateful trip to Rock Gate Park, Steven had combed his memories for any hint about what he should do next, culling ideas from H.G. Wells' *Time Machine* to *The Terminator* movies and everything in-between.

In his mind, he replayed the scene from *Back to the Future* where Marty McFly first confronts Doc Brown in 1955. The mental image of Grey sporting Christopher Lloyd's shock of white hair all askew brought a smile to Steven's face, though he hoped convincing Grey of his claims would prove easier than it did for Michael J. Fox's squeaky-voiced time traveler.

One thing Steven marked as relatively certain: the Grey of 1945 would have neither a flux capacitor nor a silver DeLorean.

But he does have the pouch. Or at least knows where it is.

Steven's entire plan banked on the supposition that the Grey of this era would somehow be able to use the *Hvitr Kyll* to send them back to the present just as its dark counterpart had forced them into the past. The logic seemed sound, though Steven, like Niklaus, had his doubts.

The smell of sizzling hash browns sent Steven's stomach rumbling and brought him back to the situation at hand. A sign that stated simply "Breakfast" pointed to the door of a small diner just off the sidewalk. Steven fell in at the rear of the line and counted the money left in his wallet. Though he and Niklaus carried only the few dollars Ron Springer had forced them to accept as a thank you for all their help, the shockingly low prices on the menu posted by the door gave Steven hope they wouldn't starve.

At least not today.

We have enough to last us a week or so. Steven laughed. *These people would freak if they saw the prices at a Starbucks.*

The sound of screeching tires rent the air. Steven leaped from the sidewalk's edge and dropped into a low crouch, yanking the pawn icon from his pocket like a gunslinger of old drawing his weapon. Before he could take another breath, a pale green Studebaker ran up onto the curb where he'd been standing and crashed into a light pole just a few feet away. A quick scan of the road revealed the cause of the accident: a screaming toddler in a little blue sailor suit had somehow made his way out into the street. Steven was moving before he even fully registered the entire situation, but even his well-honed reflexes were no match for the child's mother's as she dove into the street and snatched her child to safety.

Kid's safe. Steven turned his attention to the wrecked car. *Better check on the driver.*

Built of sterner stuff than the cars from Steven's youth, the Studebaker remained for the most part intact other than the chrome front bumper and grill that wrapped around the crumpled light pole like a gripping fist. A thick plume of white steam spewed from beneath the rippled hood, obscuring Steven's view of the driver.

"Are you all right in there?" Steven shouted as he drew close.

At first, no one answered, and then the driver's side window rolled down and a long willowy arm reached out from within the vehicle.

"I'm okay." A woman's voice, colored with as New York an accent as Steven had ever heard. "At least, I think so." The woman wrapped her lithe fingers around the door's outside handle, but no matter how hard she tried to work the latch, the door refused to open. "Hey, mister, can you give me hand here?"

Steven rushed over, took the woman's hand, and helped her climb out of the car's open window. Despite the awkwardness of the situation, her egress hit him as strangely graceful. As Steven wrapped his arms around the young woman's narrow waist and lowered her to the well-worn sidewalk, heat rose in his cheeks.

Holy. She's a knockout.

Since their arrival in 1945, Steven couldn't shake the feeling he'd been transported into one of those old black-and-white movies his mother had always loved so much. The style of clothing, the diction, even the way people walked brought a surreal sense of the passage of time. He'd considered how strange it would be to run into one of those old-school movie stars decades before the relentless march of time turned them into the senior citizens he knew almost exclusively from supermarket rags. Could this be his chance?

The woman standing before him would have given Lauren Bacall a run for her money in the looks department. Dressed conservatively in a white cardigan and a long black skirt, her shoulder-length blond hair curled inward to frame her face in the style of the day. Her full lips painted ruby red and her dark eyes the stuff of which poems were written, something about the sparkle in her gaze seemed undeniably, almost hauntingly, familiar.

"Are you all right, Miss…?"

"Matheson. And yeah, I'm okay. Ten fingers, ten toes, and all that." Her smile sent Steven's already speeding heart into the next gear. The image of Audrey's face that played across his mind's eye a moment later did nothing but stoke the guilty fire at his core.

"You're sure?"

"Neck's a little sore, but otherwise, I'm fine." She stepped to the front of the car. "More than I can say for this thing." Her eyes grew wide. "What happened to the kid that ran out in front of me? Is he—"

"He's fine." Steven pointed down the street. "His mother grabbed him up. None the worse for wear, as far as I could tell." He smiled. "Kid's lucky you have such good reflexes."

"Thank God. I don't know what I would've done if…" Emotion caught up with the woman and she fell into Steven, sobbing. After a few awkward seconds, he put an arm around her shoulder.

"Hey, don't cry. Nobody got hurt and cars can be fixed." He pulled her chin up to his and felt another pang of guilt as her doe-eyed gaze met his. "Everything's going to be okay."

Before either could speak again, a black-and-white police car pulled up, followed shortly by another. Steven stood by for a few minutes as the pair of officers took their time interviewing the beguiling Miss Matheson and arranging for her car to be towed. Amused and, strangely, a little jealous, he watched the beautiful young woman flirt her way out of anything resembling a ticket or charge.

And all the while, the nagging familiarity continued.

I know her. He racked his brain for answers. *But how?*

A few minutes passed before a tow-truck arrived to take the car away. One of the officers, an older man with a receding hairline and prodigious belly, took off while the younger of the two stayed behind to chat up the damsel in distress. The likely rookie policeman did his best to make the whole encounter seem official, but the dance was one Steven had seen a thousand times before. He was, as Walt Disney had coined, twitterpated, not that Steven blamed the young cop. After all, it wasn't every day Venus came down from Olympus to chat with mere mortals.

Despite his best efforts, the officer seemed unable to convince the young woman to let him drive her home, and so, with a tip of his hat Steven had only seen in Westerns and on the occasional episode of *The Andy Griffith Show*, he bid her a good day.

As the cop pulled away, Miss Matheson picked up the large tote bag she had retrieved from her trunk and headed in his direction. The brightly colored tote appeared for all the world like an extra-large birthday present from six decades hence, though instead of crumpled tissue paper, pink tulle and scarlet muslin billowed from the top.

Tutu, maybe? As she drew close, Steven noted her size, poise, and grace. *Yep. Definitely a dancer.*

"I'm sorry." She shot Steven a wink as she joined him back by the door to the diner. "I didn't even ask your name."

"It's Steven. Steven Bauer."

"Well, *Steven Bauer*, I hope you'll at least let me buy you a cup of coffee. It's the least I can do for my knight in shining armor."

In the half hour since the accident, the remaining breakfast crowd had moved on as noon approached, allowing Steven and the lovely young woman he'd pulled from the wrecked car to walk right in and sit down at an empty booth at the back of the diner. No sooner had Steven slid into his seat than a middle-aged woman in a gingham dress appeared with two coffees and took their order.

"Who's the other muffin for?" Miss Matheson asked as their waitress scurried away.

"My buddy, Nik." Steven picked up the steaming mug of coffee before him. "He's waiting back at the hotel."

"No cream?" She dumped two teaspoons of sugar and a splash of milk into her own cup. "You must have a stomach of iron."

"It goes in faster that way." Steven downed half his cup. "For me, it's more about the caffeine than anything else."

"Hmm." She shot Steven a quizzical look as she took a sip from her own cup. "Good coffee is meant to be savored, not gulped."

"Noted." Steven smiled and mirrored her more measured approach. "This *is* a pretty strong brew."

"You should try the coffee at my father's restaurant. That'll wake you up in the morning." She held her cup below her nose and inhaled, taking in the rich aroma before bringing the cup to her lips again.

"Family business?" Steven asked.

"A deli on the Upper West Side. I've been helping out there the last eighteen months since my brother got called away to fight the Germans." She glanced at her watch and her eyes grew wide. "And I have totally lost track of time. My shift starts in just a few minutes and I'm going to be late. Papa's going to kill me." Her face went a shade paler. "Especially when I tell him about the car."

Steven shrugged. "I'm sure he'll just be glad you're all right."

Her lips spread in a knowing smile. "You don't know my father."

"True enough." Steven reached for the check, but his fingers didn't prove fast enough. "So, what do you do at the restaurant?"

"Oh, whatever Papa needs." She pulled a few coins from a velvet change purse and stacked them on top of the check. "Greeter, cashier, bussing tables—"

"*You* bus tables." Steven had guessed the young woman might be a Broadway starlet or a nightclub showgirl, not a minimum wage worker at a family restaurant.

"And what's wrong with bussing tables?" A hint of righteous anger flashed across her gaze. "It needs to be done, doesn't it?" She puffed up her chest. "Don't think just because I'm petite that I can't do as much work as a man."

"Whoa, whoa, whoa." Steven held his hands before him, palms out. "That's not what I meant at all. I guess I just pegged you for a... different line of work."

She raised an eyebrow. "Such as?" Her angry pout blossomed into a mischievous grin.

"I don't know. Nightclub singer? Broadway starlet?" He remembered the eruption of tulle and muslin exploding out the top of her bag. "Maybe...professional dancer?"

The woman lowered her eyes and blushed, then glanced up at Steven with the same innocent stare as before. A look he recognized all too well, Audrey's face again flashed across his memory bringing with it a fresh surge of guilt.

"That was sweet. As far from the truth as it could be, but sweet. Thank you, Steven." She took his hand. "For everything."

The waitress cleared her throat. "Two blueberry muffins."

"Can you put them in a bag?" Steven asked. "We both have to get going."

As the waitress walked away, Steven caught a hint of disappointment in the pair of Audrey Hepburn eyes that stared from across the table.

"It's a shame we have to cut this short," she said. "We barely got a chance to talk at all."

"The city's not that big." Steven gave her fingers a gentle squeeze and pulled his hand away. "Maybe we'll run into each other again."

"That would be great." Her voice held no small amount of enthusiasm. "And thanks again for coming to my rescue." A half-smile returned to her features. "Hey, if you're ever passing through the Upper West Side and are hungry for the best Reuben in the city, you should stop by. We're Dante's Deli."

Steven laughed. "Sounds pretty ominous."

"Oh, nothing like that. Dante was my grandfather's name. He started the deli some forty years ago. We're up on the Upper West Side."

Steven raised an eyebrow. "You said that."

"I did, didn't I?" A touch of color blossomed on her cheeks.

"Well, it was a pleasure meeting you, Miss Matheson." Steven's cheeks grew warm as well. "Hope they're able to get your car fixed and that your dad doesn't blow a gasket."

"Thanks." Her eyes turned up into the same mischievous smile. "And by the way, as my own personal knight in shining armor, I think you can get away with just calling me Ruth."

9

ROOM & BOARD

S teven and Niklaus faced little trouble securing employment at
a certain dining establishment on the Upper West Side of
Manhattan. Their offer to work mainly for lodging and food
garnered them an enthusiastic handshake from Mr. Matheson and a
quiet squeal from his daughter. The extra help would clearly free Ruth
up to pursue other interests, but her furtive glances throughout the
short but obligatory interview process left Steven wondering whether
her excitement had more to do with the possibility of the two of them
sharing a roof.

"The main things I need help with are keeping the place straight
and the dishes clean." Matheson's words, flavored with even more
New Yorker accent than Ruth's, came across as stern but kind. "I've
been doing it all since my son went off to fight in Europe—"

Ruth coughed under her breath as she walked by with a tray piled
high with glasses, plates, and silverware.

"With Ruthie's help, of course." Matheson shot his daughter an
amused smile. "Just the two of us for over a year and a half now. You'd
think, times being what they are, that people would be chomping at
the bit to have any sort of job, but keeping this place afloat through
the war has been nothing short of a miracle. Everything else in our

lives got pushed to the back burner. We barely even make it to church anymore, and it's been months since Ruth brushed the dust off her ballet shoes."

Steven shot Ruth a quizzical glance, and at her wide-eyed stare, quickly changed the subject. "One thing we haven't covered yet is where you'd be putting us up." He glanced around the relatively cramped deli. "We don't want to be in the way."

Matheson stroked his chin. "We can clear some space in the back storage area, I guess. Nothing too glamorous, but it's heated. There should be just enough room for a couple of industrious young men to make a temporary home." His eyes went up and to the right, as if he were performing some complex calculation. "Let's see. There's an old couch and a decent size cot we can bring down from upstairs. That should work for beds until we can do better."

"One of them could stay in Tommy's room." Ruth bit her lip coyly and avoided Steven's gaze. "That way, they could both have a bit of privacy."

Her father cocked his head to one side in consideration.

"That won't be necessary, sir." Steven took a step in the direction of the storage room. "I'm sure there's plenty of room in the back, and we'd hate to intrude on your family space."

"Very well, Mr. Bauer. You've sold me. You and Mr. Zamek can stay and work, though why you won't accept even a small wage is beyond me."

Niklaus stepped in. "If we're still here after a month, we may wish to renegotiate, but for now, a roof over our heads and food in our bellies will be more than enough."

"All right, fellas. Sounds like a done deal. Some basics. We're open seven days a week, six-thirty to seven except Sundays when we close at three. I need at least one of you boys on the floor before six every morning for set up. Clean up after each meal usually takes half an hour or so, a little more if we're busy at lunch, so don't expect to be freed up before a quarter to eight most nights. If we're slow in the afternoon, I can probably cut one or both of you loose for a while if you have errands to run." Matheson fumbled in his pockets and produced a collection of keys that looked like a prop from a movie set. He pulled off a ring of four and handed them to Steven. "This is an extra set of keys the two of you can share for now. Any questions?"

"No, sir." Steven slipped the keys into his pocket. "We'll get started this afternoon."

"Spectacular." Matheson peered around the deli. "The lunch crowd seems to be thinning out. I think I'll head to the market and stock up on some staples." As he returned the remainder of the keys to his pocket, he turned to Ruth. "Honey, do you still have the keys to the car?"

"Umm, about that." Ruth stared at her shoes for a moment, then looked up into her father's eyes. "Come upstairs for a minute, Papa. I need to tell you something." She turned to Steven and rested a hand on his arm. "Steven, can you and Nik keep an eye on the place for a few minutes?"

Nik grabbed a damp rag and started wiping down the nearest table. "We're on it. Anybody else comes in, we'll have them wait at the front till you get back."

"Thanks." Ruth escorted her father to the door leading to their apartment upstairs, leaving Steven and Niklaus alone with the last three afternoon patrons of Dante's Deli.

Niklaus raised an eyebrow. "Looks like she hasn't told him yet."

Steven shook his head and let out a mournful chuckle. "I don't think that discussion is going to go too well. Ruth's dad seems like a pretty no-nonsense kind of guy."

"To be honest, though?" Nik moved on to the next table. "I don't get the impression she's all too worried about what her dad thinks."

Steven raised an eyebrow. "What do you mean?"

"Come on, man. The girl hasn't been able to keep her eyes off you since we got here. If you think for a minute she's going to pay attention to a word coming out of 'Papa's' mouth, you're delusional."

Niklaus was right, and Steven knew it all too well. Since their arrival earlier, the lovely Miss Matheson had done little to hide her attentions. Mr. Matheson either hadn't noticed it or, more likely, had been too polite to say anything.

"It's funny." Steven chuckled as he collected plates and silverware from a table by the window. "I kind of figured she'd take a shine to you once she got a look at the two of us side by side."

Niklaus scoffed. "You're the one who pulled her out of a wrecked car. Do you honestly think I'd have a snowball's chance in hell?"

"But between the two of us, you're the one that looks like he leaped off the cover of *Men's Health*." His eyes dropped to Niklaus' ankle. "Current injuries notwithstanding, of course."

Niklaus shook his head. "Steven, one of these days you're going to figure out exactly where you fit into the scheme of things."

"What do you mean?"

"Our little team of junior league superheroes are the best friends I've ever had. Before I got pulled into this stupid Game, I didn't know a group of people could care for each other the way we do. I'd take a bullet for any of them, and they for me. Still, there's no doubt about who the linchpin of our group is. I may tower over all of you, pardon the pun, but you're the one everyone looks up to."

"Doesn't feel that way." Steven lowered his head. "I mean, the last time we were all together, Lena and Audrey could barely look at me, and Emilio only went along with me out of concern for Lena's safety."

"You just don't get it." Niklaus sighed. "Look. Even when you're arguing like cats and dogs, Lena hangs on every word you say. Emilio respects you a hell of a lot more than he lets on. And Audrey, well, you know."

Hearing and saying their names aloud, especially Audrey's, ripped Steven's heart open anew. "God, I hope she—everybody is okay."

"You and me both." Niklaus jammed his hands in his pockets. "Sorry. Didn't mean to bring up a sore subject."

"It's okay." Steven waved goodbye as the last three customers all headed out for the afternoon. "It's not like Audrey isn't on the tip of my brain the moment I wake up every day."

"I can only imagine." Niklaus' gaze trailed over to the door where Ruth and her father had disappeared. "Back to my original point, though. You shouldn't act so shocked that little Miss Matheson finds herself all smitten with you. As far as I'm concerned, it's right in line with the rest of reality." He grinned. "The Tao of Steven Bauer, maybe?"

"Regardless of how infatuated she may or may not be with me, it's not like I'm going to do anything about it."

Niklaus downshifted into his best impersonation of Spock. "Because you might upset the space-time continuum?"

"Something like that." Arthur and Ruth Pedone's faces from six decades hence flitted across his memory. "Not to mention, as you pointed out, things with me and Audrey are a bit complicated."

Niklaus shook his head. "Doesn't seem too complicated from where I'm standing."

"I don't know. We're fighting for our lives in a Game where any or all of us might die any second unless, of course, we choose not to play, at which point the world apparently tears itself apart and we all die anyway. And that's assuming you and I can find a way to rescue the others and get all of us back to the present before everything goes down." Steven massaged his temple to keep the newly forming headache at bay. "That's about as complicated as it gets, my friend, and not a place for romance."

"I don't know. Can you imagine a better place to fall in love than fighting together to save the world?"

"I—" Steven stumbled on the words, unsure of even his own answer.

Niklaus sat at one of the tables and took a sip from an untouched glass of water. "You know, I never told any of you what I was doing on top of the King tower that night."

Steven perked up while doing his best to maintain a façade of cool. Niklaus had made it all too clear from the very beginning that any discussion about finding him drunk atop a skyscraper in the middle of the worst storm to hit Atlanta in a century was off limits. Steven had avoided the gossip among the team as best he could, but he'd be lying if he said his curiosity hadn't been piqued. He had no doubt Niklaus had shared at least part of the story with Archie, albeit in a bit more professional capacity, but otherwise, Niklaus had kept mum about that night.

"Nik, we found you at your absolute bottom. The man we met that night isn't you." Steven sat opposite his friend, who was clearly upset. "We can talk about it if you think it'll help, but you don't have to."

"Actually, I do." Niklaus took another sip of water, though the weariness in his voice suggested he would have preferred something stronger. The mirth and ever-present sparkle gone from his eye, his somber gaze spoke volumes. "Believe it or not, that day was a perfect storm before the first drop of rain ever fell."

Steven rested his elbows on the table and leaned in. "Tell me."

Niklaus sucked in a deep breath. "So, the building where you found me? I'd been working there for just over six years. Investment banking."

Steven nodded. "I knew that part."

"The bank does a lot of business in eastern Europe. As you can imagine, being fluent in Polish and German and serviceable in a few other languages proved a good skill set to have. I rose through the ranks quickly, promotion after promotion, every bit the American Dream."

"Until?"

"One stupid error. Fat thumbed a major transaction that influenced several hundred accounts." Niklaus' trademark grin made a brief appearance. "Funny how one decimal place can really bring out the bad side of most investors."

"They couldn't fix it?"

"Took them the better part of a week. Lots of money had to unchange hands. A bazillion transactions had to be reversed. I worked two weeks of sixteen-hour days trying to set everything straight. And then, on the day of the storm…"

"They fired you."

"I showed up that morning and they had security standing on either side of my office door. I had five minutes to pack up the few things in my office and get out. After everything I'd done for them." Niklaus lowered his head. "And that was just the first half of the proverbial one-two punch."

"God," Steven said, "what else?"

Niklaus sucked in a breath. "Her name is Victoria."

"Victoria." Steven took a sip of water to clear his throat. "Who's she?"

"The day you found me, that whole week, in fact." Niklaus' chin hit his chest. "None of that was how it was supposed to go down." His hands balled into fists. "I had it all planned."

"Had what all planned?"

"Just suffice to say that somewhere among the rubble we left between the King and Queen towers in Atlanta sits roughly ten thousand dollars of compressed carbon and platinum."

"A diamond?"

Niklaus nodded. "Despite the shit show at work, I'd planned for that to be the night. Fancy dinner, candlelight, violins, the real deal. When I called her that morning to tell her I'd been fired, she sounded a bit cagey right off the bat. When I pressed her about what was going on, she didn't waste any time telling me about the other guy." He gulped down the rest of his water. "Almost cliché, right? Fired and dumped in the space of fifteen minutes?"

"Wow." Steven shook his head. "That's a lot to take."

"And the biggest irony of the whole thing? The only reason I made the mistake at work in the first place?" Niklaus grunted. "I was late getting back from lunch after picking up the stupid ring at the jewelry store." He massaged his temples. "She never even saw the damn thing."

"What did you do?" Steven kicked himself, the answer obvious.

"I got drunk." Niklaus let out a long sigh. "At the nearest bar by the fastest means possible. Three sheets to the wind before the lunch hour was done." He let out a sad laugh. "By mid-afternoon, I'd charted a course back to the King tower and found my way up to the roof."

"Oh, Nik." Steven squeezed his friend's shoulder. "I'm sorry."

"When the heavens opened up, it was like the final insult." Niklaus rested his face in his hands. "And the state I was in? I was pretty much..." His voice went quiet. "...teetering on the edge."

"I'd wondered." Steven pulled back his hand and rested it on the table. "You were up there in the middle of a thunderstorm. Were you trying to—"

"I don't know exactly what I planned to do up there." Niklaus pulled in a deep breath. "What I do know is that you, this Game—hell —even the Black Pawn using me for target practice. All of that, somehow, saved me." His smile returned. "If that's not irony, I don't know what is."

"You know, you're smiling about getting drilled with half a dozen arrows and getting pitched off a skyscraper."

"True." Niklaus straightened up in his chair and absently massaged a spot at the center of his chest. "Hurt like hell, but I'm still here."

"In 1945." Steven didn't even try to keep the bitterness from his voice.

"Still, even this, being trapped in the past, might be part of a bigger picture we just can't see yet."

"Wow, you're Captain Optimism today." Steven crossed his arms. "I mean, we are talking about the worst day of your life."

"Yes." Niklaus' smile quirked to one side. "And no." He rose from his seat and collected plates, glasses, and silverware from the next table and placed them in a bin. "What I'm trying to say is there's a point to all this."

"A point?" Steven grabbed a rag and wiped down the table that Niklaus was clearing. "Do tell."

Niklaus pulled a shoulder up in a subtle shrug. "This Game of Grey's, for all its insanity, hit me at my absolute lowest. And I'm not alone in that. From what you've said, you were in the midst of a long spiral after losing…"

"Katherine."

"That's right. Katherine." Niklaus finished clearing the other table and returned to his seat. "You'd lost someone. Emilio had just lost his brother. You found Archie locked up on a psych ward. Hell, Audrey was literally sitting on death's door."

Steven leaned forward on his elbows. "What are you trying to say?"

"Don't you see? The Game needs each of us, but in a strange way, each of us needs the Game as well." Niklaus pushed back from the table. "If you and the others hadn't shown up that night, God knows if I'd still be alive. Audrey would still be in Oregon, lying in a bed waiting to die. Archie would be stuck behind a locked door with a bunch of smug assholes in white coats diagnosing him with paranoid delusions. Our favorite hothead teenager would probably be six feet under, likely having taken Lena with him. And you'd still be fighting to reclaim your life from the shitstorm you've been through the last couple of years. Instead, we've all found each other, and in each other, hope." Niklaus poured himself another glass of water and raised it in a joking toast. "Here's to the man who literally leaped off a skyscraper to save my ass."

"Cheers." Steven raised his own glass and let out a quiet laugh. "You know good and well you'd do the same for me."

"Precisely." Niklaus raised an eyebrow. "We've all got each other's backs."

"All of us…" Unbidden, Archie's cool stare washed across Steven's mind's eye.

"Somehow," Niklaus continued, "in the midst of all this madness, we've found our tribe."

Steven shook his head, smiling. "A nice sentiment. Doesn't get us or the others any closer to home."

"Actually, it does." Niklaus steepled his fingers beneath his chin. "Consider this. If this Game of Grey's can pluck each and every one of us from the worst days of our lives and put us on a better path, do you believe for a second it will leave us scattered to the four corners of space and time to die years before we're even born?"

"I suppose not." Hope swelled anew in Steven's heart. "In fact, there's something I should probably tell you."

Niklaus chuckled. "That you've met Ruth somewhere before?"

Steven raised an eyebrow in surprise. "How did you know?"

"I'm not blind, Steven. The only thing clearer than the fact that this girl has the hots for you is that you are way more familiar with her than you should be with someone walking the Earth three decades before you were born."

"You're way more perceptive than you let on, Nik."

"Nah." Niklaus shook his head. "It's just you have the worst poker face I've ever seen."

Steven laughed, remembering an older Ruth's similar observation from what seemed a lifetime ago. "Fair enough." He stared off into space. "Guess that's why the pouch chose me to be the front-line fodder in this stupid Game."

"Front-line fodder." Incredulous, Niklaus peered across the table at Steven. "Is that how you see yourself?"

"All of us have our role in this thing, Nik. You, Emilio, Audrey,

Archie, even Grey." He whipped the marble icon out of his pocket and held it between them. "And my role is Pawn. Plain and simple. If and when this Game goes down, I have no delusions about what that means."

"You're serious, aren't you?" Niklaus finished off his water and placed the glass with the rest of the dirty dishes. "It's what I was saying before. Grey may be King, but everyone knows who the leader of our little pack is." He shook his head in disbelief. "Everyone, apparently, but the leader himself."

"Look." Steven raised both hands before him. "My job was to find all of you and gather you together. That doesn't make me your leader."

"Like hell it doesn't." Niklaus let out an exasperated sigh. "Think about it. When Grey is off doing whatever it is he does when he's not with us, who does he trust to keep us all safe?"

Steven let out a bitter laugh. "A fat lot of good that's done."

"Stop it. Grey trusts you explicitly. Both Emilio and Lena worship the ground you walk on, even when they don't necessarily agree with what's coming out of your mouth. Archie may be a tough nut to crack, but nine times out of ten, even he follows your lead. And even a blind man could see the way Audrey looks at you." Niklaus crossed his arms and grinned. "I hate to break it to you, but I didn't follow you all the way to New York because I think you're an idiot."

Steven allowed himself a smile. "Good to know, Nik. Good to know."

The door leading to the upstairs apartment opened, and Mr. Matheson strode over to their table. His face a couple shades redder than before and a newly engorged vein marking the north-south corridor of his forehead, his words somehow came out quiet and reserved.

"Mr. Bauer, I apparently owe you a debt of gratitude."

Steven rose and shook Matheson's offered hand. "I'm guessing Ruth told you about the car."

Matheson ran his coarse fingers through his thinning red hair. "I'm just glad no one was hurt." A quiet groan escaped his lips. "Wish I could say the same about my bank account." He studied Steven, his crooked lips forming an afraid-to-ask grimace. "How bad is it?"

"The front end was pretty banged up, and you're probably going to need a new radiator, but that's about it. The fine folks at Studebaker built you a pretty solid car there."

"I'm not sure what I'm going to do." He pulled a handkerchief from his back pocket and wiped the sweat from his flushed brow. "The car will be in the shop for days, and I need it to run the business. Groceries? Supplies? How will I keep this place running?"

"Don't worry, sir." Steven shot Niklaus a quick glance. "Nik and I can run errands and keep everything going till you get your car back."

Niklaus smiled. "It's the least we can do since you're giving us a place to stay."

Matheson laughed. "You boys are a godsend, and there's no 'giving' about it. You two are already earning your keep." He glanced around at all the cleared tables, the redness in his cheeks diminishing a shade. "The place looks great."

"Thank you, Mr. Matheson." Steven glanced around for a closet. "If you'll show us where the mops and brooms are, we'll finish cleaning up the place for the dinner crowd."

"Please, Steven, call me Stuart." He pointed to a small door behind the far end of the counter. "And everything you need is in there."

"Got it." Steven slid behind the counter and opened the closet door on an assortment of cleaning supplies. "We'll have this place spic and span in no time."

Matheson headed for the door. "In that case, I'm going to run check on the car. When I get back, we'll work on putting together sleeping arrangements for you two." He chuckled as he rested his fingers on the handle. "Both of you gents need to be up bright and early tomorrow. Saturday mornings are crazy, and if we're not ready for the breakfast crowd when they descend, God help us all."

"Understood."

Matheson donned a fedora hanging on the coat rack by the door and stepped outside. "Ruth will be down in a bit. While we were talking, she went and got herself all worked up. If I know my daughter, she won't come down again till she's presentable."

"We'll take care of everything, Mr. Matheson." At the man's raised eyebrow, Steven added, "I mean...Stuart."

89

"I'll be back in an hour."

No sooner had Mr. Matheson pulled the door to than Niklaus elbowed Steven in the ribs. "Wow. Already on a first name basis with her father."

"Ha." Steven walked to the door, peered out onto the busy city street, and turned the door sign from Open to Closed. "Just till Ruth comes back down. I can make a mean ham on rye, but I don't know anything about running a restaurant."

They set to work picking up the few remaining dishes, wiping down each of the tables, and sweeping and mopping the floor. As they worked, Steven did his best to explain his connection to Ruth, her connection to Arthur Pedone, and Arthur's to Grey.

"This is exactly what I was talking about." Niklaus leaned on his mop. "The two of us may not be able to turn to stone or summon weapons from midair, but this is still the Game."

"How so?"

Niklaus motioned around the place. "What are the odds of going back in time sixty years, heading for the most populated city in the country, and running into somebody you know on the first day? Especially when that someone is supposed to end up married to the guy you're there looking for in the first place?"

"What are you boys talking about?" Ruth stood in the doorway, her eyes still a bit puffy from crying. Her cardigan and full-length skirt replaced by a pretty day dress with a floral print, she was breathtaking. "Sounds pretty serious."

A stray lock of hair hung across Ruth's left eye, and Steven shuddered as he imagined brushing it to one side, his fingers brushing her cheek...

To say he didn't feel some attraction to their lovely new friend would be a bold-faced lie.

Still, his feelings for Audrey notwithstanding, this was Ruth.

Arthur's Ruth.

Somehow, the elderly woman who had taken him in, fed him, and kept him safe on the worst night of his life now stood before him young, vibrant, and, strangest of all, interested. Though the warmhearted grandmother who lived in Portland, Maine may have been well into her eighties, the woman he pulled from the smoking car this morning in Manhattan looked like she just stepped off the set of *Casablanca*. Steven understood all too well that this Ruth was destined to spend the next fifty to sixty years with one of the two men they had come to New York to find. For now, though, she seemed to only have eyes for him, and a part of him liked it.

"Umm, we were just discussing one of the old movie serials from the thirties." Steven pulled a title from the recesses of memory. "*Flash Gordon Saves the Universe*, I think."

"I saw that one with Tommy when we were kids." Ruth smiled and ran her fingers through her blond curls. "That Buster Crabbe is one well put together man."

"We talked to your dad." Steven took a step in her direction. "Are you all right?"

"I'm fine. Papa's pretty upset, but he'll get over it. He loves that car, but I'm pretty sure he loves me more." Ruth smiled. "He bought it for Mama back before she got sick. Lot of memories riding around on those whitewalls."

"Your mother. She's…?"

"Mama died a couple years back, not long before Tommy left for the war. I was just a junior in high school when we lost her. Papa took it pretty hard. We all did." A solitary tear made its way down Ruth's cheek. "I miss her, you know? Papa did a great job and everything, but sometimes a girl wants her mother."

"I lost my mother early, too." Steven rested a hand on her shoulder. "I know how it feels."

"Just so you know," Niklaus interjected, "we locked up till you came back down. Didn't want the place to burn down or anything."

Ruth laughed. "Probably smart." She stepped gracefully to the front of the deli, unlocked the door, and spun around on one foot in a fluid pirouette. "Nik, would you mind if I talked to Steven alone for a minute?"

"Of course not." Niklaus shot Steven a knowing glance. "I'll be in the kitchen."

Ruth waited for Niklaus to disappear into the back before drawing close to Steven. "Thanks for not spilling the beans about me still dancing." Her gaze dropped to the floor. "Having to tell Papa about the car was rough enough."

"He doesn't know?"

"Papa thinks I've been out running errands for the deli every week. 'No time for silly dreams when the world is at war,' he always says."

"So, you're lying to your father?" The back of Steven's neck grew hot.

"I'm not lying." Ruth took another step toward Steven. "I'm just... not telling him everything. It's complicated." She raised her lithe arms above her head in a graceful ballet pose. "I don't want to be disobedient, but does that mean I have to give up on going after the things I want in life?"

"But he sounded so sad before." Steven did his best to ignore the frenzied bass drummer that had taken up residence in his chest. "You know, about you having to give up your dancing. Which you apparently haven't." His brow furrowed. "Why can't you just tell him?"

"Papa has enough on his plate right now. If he knew I'd started dancing again, he'd bend over backwards to make sure I made every practice, every performance, get me anything I needed, no matter the cost. Also, without me, he'd have to hire more help we simply can't afford. It's a mess." She took a deep breath and let it out. "So, I go early in the morning or late at night and give him one excuse or another. He trusts me, and regardless, I'm not doing anything wrong. It's just ballet."

"Well, now that we're here, he's finally got some help. That should free you up, don't you think? Maybe it's time to spill the beans."

"Maybe." Her lips broke into a subtle smile. "In fact, I was giving that very idea some thought before I came back down. For now, though, we'll keep it our little secret." Ruth took one last step into Steven's space and brought her lips next to his ear. "You can keep a secret," she whispered, her breath warm on his skin, "can't you?"

10

KISS & TELL

Steven lay on his back beneath white silken sheets, his stomach tied in knots as he stared at the full head of blond hair spilled across his chest like a river of finely spun gold.

How could he have let this happen? A double betrayal, he wasn't sure whose gaze he feared more, the woman he professed to love or the man destined to marry the woman in his bed.

Just this once, he justified, *and I won't let it happen again.* Even as the words crossed his thoughts, he wondered if they represented an empty promise. One arm trapped beneath the warm form curled next to him, he brought up the opposite hand and ran his fingers through the silky locks that tickled his chest with his every breath.

"You awake?" he asked.

"Mm-hmm." The affirmative was followed by a quick kiss at Steven's collarbone that sent a shiver all the way to his toes.

"We need to talk about this."

Another kiss at his neck was followed by a quick nod of assent.

"Tonight was..." Steven paused, at a loss for words. "Tonight was incredible. No. More than that. Unforgettable. But it cannot happen again."

The delicate fingers meandering their way down his chest stopped in their tracks.

"I know everything seems perfect," Steven continued, "but this is wrong. Wrong in ways you can't begin to understand." He waited for a response but was met with only silence.

"Don't hate me for saying this, but there's someone else." At his words, her body stiffened against his. "There's always been someone else. I'm sorry I haven't had the guts to tell you till now, but there it is." Met again with silence, Steven grew impatient.

"Won't you please say something? Anything? I know all of this must be difficult to hear, but it's the truth. I don't want to lead you on, at least not any more than I already have. Tell me you understand."

"Oh, I understand." The woman's form shifted beneath the silk sheet until she came face to face with Steven. Framed by Ruth's blond curls, Audrey's hazel eyes gazed at Steven with a mixture of sadness, anger, and disappointment, all awash with tears of regret. "Nice to know you haven't completely forgotten me."

Steven bolted awake, his heart working like a jackhammer. He extricated himself from the twisted flannel sheets and sat on the edge of the cot, the metal frame and concrete floor cool against his calves and feet. In the darkness of the deli's storage room, the only sounds other than Niklaus' quiet snoring were the gentle hum of the refrigerator and the occasional drip from the sink's leaky faucet. He buried his face in his hands and groaned in frustration. Nothing he did, however, erased the nightmare image of Audrey's accusing stare from his mind's eye.

"Dammit," he whispered to no one. "I haven't done anything wrong."

But the situation wasn't that simple.

That night wasn't the first he'd dreamed of Ruth in the near month and a half since he and Niklaus took up residence in the storage room of Dante's Deli, but it was by far the most vivid, and the first time Audrey had made an appearance.

Steven hadn't slept well in days as the temptation to give in to Ruth's frequent and not-so-innocent advances grew stronger. Every day, she found some new way to insinuate herself into his space: sometimes subtle, sometimes overt, always persistent. The close quarters of the deli made conversation all but unavoidable, leaving Steven navigating a never-ending maze of nuanced questions and double entendre. And there were times, more than Steven would care to admit, when he asked himself why he was pushing her away her in the first place.

A flash of movement across the room caught Steven's attention. He and Niklaus usually left the door to their quarters ajar a good foot or two to allow the air to circulate. Otherwise, the moist heat from the radiator left the room a sauna by morning.

There, in the space between door and jamb, a female figure stood silhouetted in the dim light coming from the kitchen. Though over three months had passed since his icon had served as anything more than a marble paperweight, Steven instinctively grabbed for the pawn resting on the floor beneath his makeshift bed.

"Who's there?"

"Sorry," came a whispered voice. "I didn't mean to scare you." The form retreated into the kitchen a step, Ruth's curls reflecting the scant light of the space like strands of solid gold.

"Is everything all right?" Acutely aware he wore nothing but a torn pair of gym shorts, Steven pulled a sheet across his lap. "What time is it?"

"A little after one," Ruth said, her voice quiet and more than a little sad. "Can we talk?"

"Well, we're both up, it seems." Steven reached for his pants. "Let me get on some clothes, and I'll come out. We can put on some cocoa. All right?"

"Okay." Ruth stepped out of the doorway, leaving Steven confused in the near darkness. Had the dream been a prophetic vision? Considering the images still circulating in his mind's eye, he banished the thought.

Steven slipped on one of his two pairs of jeans, a flannel shirt, and socks and stepped out of the storage room, leaving Niklaus to saw logs in relative peace. Ruth stood on her tip-toes with her back to him, reaching for a large brown tin from the top shelf. She wore pink-and-white-striped pajamas that, despite their loose fit, showed off her dancer's form. Steven crept up behind her silently, trying at some level to put off the inevitable, if even for another few seconds.

"Here, let me help." Steven reached past her and grasped the can of powdered cocoa, the tin much lighter than the first time he'd pulled it down weeks ago. "Hmm. Looks like we're running a little low."

Since their arrival, the evening beverage of choice at Dante's Deli had been hot chocolate. Sometimes the four of them and sometimes just Steven and Ruth, the warm sweetness had become an all but expected part of most evenings, though the post-midnight rendezvous made for quite a different experience.

As Steven brought the industrial-sized can down and set it on the counter, his elbow brushed Ruth's shoulder. Her body stiffened at his touch, causing scenes from his dream to again flash unbidden across his thoughts.

Along with a fresh wave of guilt.

Ruth grabbed a couple of mugs and prepared each with three heaping spoonfuls of cocoa as Steven set some milk on the gas stove to boil. After a tense minute or so, he broke the silence.

"So, what's got you up at this hour?"

"Couldn't sleep." Ruth raised both arms above her head and stretched as she valiantly fought back a yawn. "I'd been lying in bed and staring at the ceiling for an hour or two. Thought I'd come down and see if you were up."

"Bad dreams?"

"Oh, nothing like that." She brought her hands before her in a dancer's pose. "I just have a lot on my mind."

"Like what?" Even Steven debated whether he was playing dumb or, in fact, fishing for a response.

"A million different things." Ruth sighed. "Tommy's last letter said he's due back in a month but he's going to miss Christmas. Papa's still hobbling around from twisting his ankle last Tuesday, so I've barely set foot out of the deli in nine days. I'm doing my best to stay in shape

—even practiced in the alley out back this week—but there are only so many hours in the day."

"Sorry to hear that." Steven shot a glance back in the direction of their quarters. "You know...unlike your dad's, Nik's leg is almost back at a hundred percent. He and I both could step up and help out a little more around here. Your dad's been letting us work alternating shifts since he hired that new kid last week, but we're both available every day if you need us."

"Oh, sure, that would fix *everything*." Ruth did little to hide the sarcasm in her tone.

"What's that supposed to mean?"

"Don't you know?" Ruth asked, her gaze incredulous. "Are you completely oblivious?"

"Just spill it, Ruth." Steven crossed his arms. "What are you trying to say?"

"You want to know what's on my mind?" Her eyes narrowed. "What's got Ruth all in a dither? Well, I'll tell you, Steven. It's *you*. Or, more specifically, *us*." Before Steven could respond, Ruth's hands shot up in exasperation.

"Look, I've been throwing myself at you for weeks, staying late after the dinner shift, skipping practice to be here in the morning for set up, and nothing. It's like you're ignoring me, and sometimes, it seems on purpose. The whole thing is getting a bit embarrassing." Ruth's gaze fell to the floor. "I really thought you liked me."

"I do like you, but—"

"What's wrong, then? Don't you find me attractive?" She looked up at him with those brown movie star eyes, and it took everything Steven had to look away.

"Of course I do." He clawed through his hair. "It's just...there are things you don't know. Things I wish I could tell you but can't."

Her hands went to her hips. "We've stood side by side eight to twelve hours a day for over a month, Steven Bauer. What kind of secrets could you be keeping? You've got to sleep sometime."

"It's nothing like that, and everything with us is fine. It's something from before I met you." Steven met her gaze. "Actually...*someone*."

"Oh." The color rose in Ruth's cheeks bringing a remembrance of

Ruth's own comment about his poker face, or lack thereof, a remark that wouldn't be made for another sixty years. A grin broke across his face.

"This isn't funny." Ruth rose from the table and stalked to the sink. "I didn't come down here in the middle of the night to be laughed at."

Steven stifled a reflexive chuckle. "Oh, come on, Ruth. I'm not laughing at you." He checked on the not-yet-boiling milk and joined her at the counter. "I was just remembering something an old friend said to me once."

"You must love this." Ruth buried her face in her hands. "Having a woman sneak into your room in the middle of the night gushing like Scarlett O'Hara in *Gone with the Wind.*"

"You think I love this?" Steven's eyebrows shot up in exasperation. "You think this is easy? Take a look around, Ruth. The two of us? Here? The middle of the night? Alone? Do you know how easy it would be to just—"

The color in Ruth's cheeks rose another notch, her expression shifting decidedly more wistful. "So, you do feel it." She turned to face Steven, her trademark mischievous grin spreading across her face. "Whatever would this 'someone' of yours think?"

Steven immediately regretted his words. "Now look who's making fun."

"Sorry. Just glad to know I'm not the only one flapping in the breeze here." Ruth pulled a little closer. "What's her name?"

"Audrey." Just speaking her name made his pulse race faster. "Her name is Audrey."

"Audrey, huh?" Ruth's piercing gaze fixed Steven to the spot. "And where exactly is this mysterious woman who hasn't come up in conversation in almost two months?"

"I wish I knew." Steven's shoulders dropped. "Believe me."

"She left you?"

"We're...separated at the moment."

"You're married?" Ruth swatted Steven's arm. "And you didn't tell me?"

"No, Ruth. I'm not married. That's not it at all." Steven peered up at the ceiling as if searching for some sort of answer. "Audrey and I?

We're *physically* separated. I haven't seen her in months and have no idea where she might be." He let out a long sigh. "To be honest, I'm not even sure she's alive."

"Not sure she's...alive?" For the first time in his memory, Ruth's voice took on a tone of alarm. "Steven, what in the world have you gotten yourself into?"

"You wouldn't believe me if I told you." His eyes slid closed. "Most days, I can barely believe it myself."

"But you are in some kind of trouble, aren't you?"

"Not at the moment." Steven shot another sidelong glance in the direction of their bunks. "But if everything goes according to plan, I'll be right back in the thick of it before you know it."

Ruth touched Steven's arm. "You say that like it's a good thing."

In the weeks since arriving in 1945, Steven had spent most of his waking moments trying to figure out how to get back to their own time, to the Game, to Audrey. The addition of Ruth to the picture had, at times, muddied the waters a bit, but no. Their plan was set, their path clear.

"It's what I've got to do." Steven rubbed his brow. "I don't have any choice."

"Before she died, Mama used to say, 'There's always a choice.' Maybe this crazy plan you and Niklaus have to get back to this Audrey person will work. Maybe it won't. Only time will tell. Right now, though? I'm the one standing here." Ruth's eyes and lips melted into an innocent yet knowing smile. "So, I guess what I'm asking is, here and now at one-thirty in the morning in my father's kitchen, what are you going to do, Steven Bauer?"

Steven's stomach churned like he'd swallowed a brick with a side of mortar. "You know, you don't have to make this so damn difficult."

"But that's just it, Steven." Ruth edged closer. "It's not difficult. It's not difficult at all." She brushed the back of her fingers across Steven's cheek. "We're just two lonesome people who managed to find each other right here in the middle of the greatest city in the world." Her head tilted to one side as she pulled in tight to Steven's body, her eyes drifting closed. "Miracles like that don't happen every day."

Steven pulled away. "But this isn't the way it's supposed to happen,

Ruth. I can't explain it any better than that. Just understand that I know without a shred of doubt I'm not the man for you." He avoided her gaze. "Even if I wanted to be."

"You *know*?" Ruth's nostrils flared, her eyes wide with frustration. "What the hell kind of thing is that to say?"

"Listen, it's just—"

"No. You listen." Ruth put her finger in Steven's chest. "Do you think I'm stupid? Can't figure things out for myself? You and Niklaus show up in New York City, no identification, no job, no money, somehow avoided the draft." She eyed him warily. "You're on the run."

"That's a part of it." Steven shook his head. "Mostly, we're just out of our element."

"Are you with the mob?" Ruth crossed her arms and studied Steven, curiosity cutting the anger in her gaze. "Or maybe...spies?" She inclined her head toward the back room. "Niklaus is a great guy, but it's pretty clear every time he opens his mouth that he's not from around here."

"No, no. It's nothing like that." Steven searched for a way to explain the situation in a way that wouldn't have Ruth calling for the men in white to take him away. "Still, Nik and I *are* in a bit of a jam. We came to New York to find the only person we know of that can help us."

"Wait," she asked, a hint of fear coloring her words. "Are we in danger? Papa?"

"Honestly, the less you know, the better off you'll be." Steven rested a gentle hand on Ruth's shoulder. "Once we catch up with the man we're looking for, everything should sort itself out, at least I hope so. God knows I haven't a clue what we'll do if he can't help us."

"You talk in circles, Steven Bauer." Despite her exasperation, Ruth smiled. "You know that?"

Steven laughed, Grey's face flashing across his mind's eye. "I was taught by the best."

"Well, looks like you're going to be sticking around for a while." Ruth motioned to the space between them. "We still need to figure out what we're going to do about this."

"I told you, Ruth. I can't. No matter what either of us feels, there's—"

Ruth put her finger across Steven's lips. "I don't want to hear any more about your crazy plans, and I definitely don't want to hear any more about *her*." She wrapped a lithe arm around Steven's waist and pulled him close. "There are only two people in this room right now, and I'd like to keep it that way."

"But—"

Ruth quieted Steven's protest with a kiss. The first was soft, like a rose petal falling onto still water. The second, however, was passionate. Desperate.

"Ruth," Steven muttered as she pulled away to take a breath. "Stop." Even as he spoke the words, he felt his resolve begin to crumble. "Please."

A quiet cough from across the room interrupted the moment. Steven looked past Ruth and found the girl's father standing in the doorway that led to the Mathesons' upstairs apartment. Ruth spun out of Steven's arms and gasped as she met her father's strangely calm stare.

The scarlet in Stuart Matheson's cheeks matched the thinning red hair atop his head, the vein that divided his forehead bulging as if it were fit to burst. He opened his mouth to speak, but rather than the shouting Steven expected, the man's voice came out quiet and exact.

"Mr. Bauer, would you mind explaining exactly what you're doing standing in the kitchen of my restaurant at one-thirty in the morning kissing my only daughter?"

"It's not what it looks like, Mr. Matheson." As the words exited his mouth, Steven wondered if the first few decades of motion pictures had already left them as cliché as they hit his ears. "I swear."

"Don't worry, Papa," Ruth grumbled. "Steven has made it abundantly clear he's not interested in pursuing this matter any further." And with that, she stormed out of the kitchen and up the stairs, leaving Steven alone with her father.

"Well," Mr. Matheson said after what seemed an hour of painful silence, "let's hear it."

"Ruth came down earlier. Said she couldn't sleep and wanted to talk." New heat rose in Steven's cheeks. "I think she—we—got caught up in the moment."

"So, what you're telling me," Matheson muttered, crossing his arms, "is that Ruth, my Ruthie, is responsible for all this?"

"No, sir." Steven suspected his first name basis with Stuart Matheson had taken a hit. "My father always said it takes two to tango." Ugh. Another platitude. "But I didn't plan this. Not after everything you and your family have done for Nik and me."

Matheson took a limping step into the room, his ankle still clearly causing him some difficulty, and motioned to the table where Steven and Ruth had been sitting moments before. "So, how long has this been going on? Surely you don't expect me to believe I just happened to walk in on your first little liaison."

"Oh, tonight was definitely a first." Steven let out a nervous chuckle. "Believe me." He sat at the table and Matheson joined him. "You've got to know I never meant for this to happen."

"Bullshit." Matheson stared earnestly across the table, the redness in his face fading with each passing second. "I may be getting older, but my eyes work just fine. I see how Ruth looks at you." He chanced a careful grin. "And how you look at her."

Steven raised an eyebrow. "What are you saying?"

"What I'm saying is…well…I suppose…" Matheson's expression shifted from scarcely controlled anger to something akin to acceptance. "Ruth could do a hell of a lot worse."

"I don't understand." Truth be told, Steven understood perfectly. The realization filled him with an entirely different sort of trepidation.

"You're clean cut, a hard worker, dependable, and get along with pretty much everyone you meet." Matheson studied Steven with an appraiser's eye. "Things have certainly been a lot easier around here since you showed up."

"Thanks." Steven rested his elbows on the table. "Just doing our part to earn our keep."

"So," Matheson said through a half-smile. "I suppose this is the part where I ask you your intentions."

"Intentions?"

"You're sleeping under my roof, eating from my table, and apparently spending more time with my daughter than even I'd realized. I'd just like to know where your head is." He waited in vain for an answer. "You know. Plans for the future. Where you see yourself a decade from now. That sort of thing."

Steven searched for anything that might stem the tide of this conversation. Grey was due back from Europe in just over a month, at which point the topic of Steven and Ruth's future would hopefully become moot. Still, a lot could happen in a month.

"Mr. Matheson, I mean you and your family no disrespect, but I wasn't blowing smoke before when I told you I never meant for anything to occur between Ruth and me."

"Oh." The smile melted from Matheson's face. "I see."

"It's just that...Niklaus and I are only going to be around for another few weeks. After that, you won't be seeing us anymore." Steven cleared his throat. "You have to know I'd never hurt your daughter. What you saw tonight won't happen again. It can't."

Steven and Ruth's father stared across the table at each other for what seemed an eternity. Then, just when Steven couldn't take another second, Matheson reached out a hand and slapped his shoulder.

"I've got to tell you, Steven. My daughter has had boys swarming around her since she hit twelve, but you're the first I'd even consider letting near her. I don't understand everything you've got going on, but I appreciate your candor. That being said, though, I don't envy you having to tell Ruth—"

"You're leaving?" Ruth stepped from behind the door leading upstairs and rushed toward them, tears coursing down both her cheeks.

"Yes." Steven rose from the table just before Ruth all but tackled him with a frantic embrace. "And soon. That's what I was trying to tell you before."

"But what about me?" She cocked her head to one side, her voice strained. "What about...us?"

Matheson rose from the table. "Perhaps I should give you two a moment." He turned toward the door through which Ruth had entered, glancing back across his shoulder at his daughter. "I'll be upstairs if you need me."

As Matheson disappeared through the door, Ruth squeezed Steven even tighter, her arms far stronger than they appeared. She held him for what seemed an eternity before finally letting go. Taking a breath, she stepped away from him, though she refused to meet his gaze.

"So," she murmured, "I get to spend the next few weeks saying goodbye to you."

"If it's too hard, Nik and I can leave." Steven lowered his head. "Just say the word."

"Oh, like Papa and I are going to kick you two to the curb three days before Christmas. No, you and Niklaus stay as long as you need. Just don't be surprised if I don't stick around to watch." Ruth pinched the bridge of her nose. "I'm pretty tough, but spending twelve hours a day around you knowing you're about to vanish back to wherever it is you came from is a little much to ask." She raised a shoulder in a quick shrug. "You two and Papa can pretty much run the place, anyway. Not to mention, since business has been picking up, he can probably afford to keep the new kid, at least till Tommy gets back from Germany."

"And you can get back to dancing." Steven shot her a friendly wink. "Or at least let on that you never stopped."

Ruth smiled through her tears. "It would be nice not having to lie anymore." Her gaze dropped to the floor. "So, this Audrey person must be pretty special."

"She is, but it's more than that." Steven shook his head. "Nik and I, we just don't belong here. I know it sounds strange, but someday you'll understand. I promise you that."

"How did I get this so wrong?" Tears ran anew down Ruth's face. "Everything felt so right, just like the fairy tales Mama used to read to me and Tommy when we were kids."

"Let me tell you something, Ruth. Sometimes the fairy tale does come true, and if anyone deserves to find her prince, it's you."

Ruth wrapped her arms around Steven's chest again, but this time her desperation was tempered with acceptance. "If...*when* you find her again, you tell this Audrey she's one lucky woman."

"Will do." Steven returned the embrace, his chin resting atop Ruth's head. "You going to be able to sleep?"

"I'll manage. I always do." Ruth broke away and turned for the stairs. "Sweet dreams, Steven."

Steven lingered a few minutes getting the kitchen back into shape for the morning rush before slipping back into their back room quarters. As he sat down on his cot, Niklaus snorted and sat up on his own makeshift couch-bed.

"Steven?" He sounded like he had just come out of a coma. "Is that you?"

"Yeah." Steven chuckled. "It's me."

Niklaus checked his watch in the dim light. "Damn. What are you doing up? It's almost two o'clock in the morning." He stretched his muscular arms above his head and let out a long yawn. "Did I miss something?"

11

ARRIVALS & DEPARTURES

The two weeks leading up to the fourth of January were bittersweet at best. Steven and Niklaus spent both Christmas and New Year's Eve with the gathered Matheson clan, though neither felt much like celebrating. The first four days of 1946, a year neither were ever meant to experience, had to go off exactly as planned, or they would never see their own time again. The stress and the waiting weighed on both of them. But for Steven, the pain went a bit deeper. The holidays had never been remotely the same since losing his mother years before, and with Katherine's death on Christmas Eve two years back still an open wound, the "most wonderful time of the year" had become anything but wonderful.

Despite the season, the Matheson family were going through the motions as well, the perfunctory dinners and gift exchanges feeling almost staged as all involved remained focused on the imminent return of Ruth's brother from Europe. The letters from France and Germany Ruth had shown Steven painted an impressive picture of one Thomas Matheson: young, passionate, patriotic. As he read the brave and insightful words of a man six years his junior, he wondered if such a person wasn't far better suited for Grey's great Game. Audrey's courage, Emilio's audacity, Lena's steadfastness, Archie's indomitable will, Niklaus' humor, even a bit of Grey's wisdom: aspects of all his friends echoed through the scrawled messages from another continent, another time.

"Your brother is quite the hero." Steven folded the last of the battle-stained letters and slid it back into its ragged envelope. "You must be proud."

"You don't know the half of it." Ruth appeared as bright as Steven had seen her in days. "I can't wait for him to get home." Her lip trembled. "Do you know what it's like to spend every waking minute knowing someone you love is in harm's way?" Color rose in Ruth's cheeks. "Stupid. Of course, you do. Sorry."

"It's all right." Steven brushed her chin and smiled. "My situation is…unique."

"What about you isn't?" Ruth let out a throaty chuckle and headed upstairs, leaving Steven and Niklaus alone behind the counter.

I'm going to miss that laugh. Steven's mouth turned up in a rough semblance of a smile. Ruth had backed off considerably since their twilight rendezvous before Christmas. Though a part of him missed the attention, right was right, and he kept his cards close to his chest. *Don't want to break the girl's heart any more than I already have.*

As the time leading up to Grey's impending arrival to New York continued to tick by, an undeniable sense of ending grew in Steven's mind. Goodbyes had never been easy for him, and with each passing day, he disengaged more and more from the Matheson family, spending most of his time with Niklaus and discussing the next steps in their bid to return to their own time.

Ruth's return to the world of dance had clearly made it all a bit easier. Steven and Niklaus both had indeed stepped up their efforts around the deli to fill in for her frequent absences as they'd discussed. Not having her around as much had helped assuage both Steven's sadness and guilt over the coming parting of ways, though her occasional entreaty of "you can always visit" always brought the emotions roaring back.

Steven and Niklaus, on the other hand, had grown closer by the day. Brothers of a sort in their shared loss, they kept each other sane as the days passed and deftly avoided the topic of what they would do if a certain immortal wizard didn't show up as expected.

"Tomorrow is going to be an odd day." Steven peered around the deserted deli, empty even for mid-afternoon. Mr. Matheson had gone upstairs to get some rest in preparation for the dinner crowd, and Ruth had retired to her room to primp for a late afternoon audition. "For all his mystical know-it-allness, at this point in history, Grey doesn't know either of us from Adam." He laughed. "Unless, of course, there's something else he hasn't told us." Steven raked his fingers through the brown mop of hair atop his head. "What if he won't help us? God, what if he thinks we're the enemy?"

"I have no doubt that someone as smart as Grey will be able to figure it out." Niklaus let out a quiet chuckle. "And won't it be nice to be the one in the know for a change?"

"Here's one. What if he believes us and can't do anything about it? Just because Zed zapped us into the past doesn't mean Grey has the ability to send us back. The black pouch is what sent us here, but from what Grey said, the corrections are what power the pouches. The next one of those isn't happening for another sixty-six years."

"Don't start second guessing yourself now, man. Win or lose, tomorrow is it." Niklaus slapped Steven on the back. "Time to put on your game face."

That night, Steven and Niklaus worked well into the evening helping Ruth and Mr. Matheson put the kitchen in order after a particularly busy dinner shift. Once they were done, Steven put on a pot of coffee and heated some milk for Ruth's cocoa while she and her father put together a few left-over pieces of lemon meringue pie from the refrigerator. As they gathered around their usual table at the back and enjoyed their customary after-hours dessert, a pit opened in Steven's stomach. What if this meal was the last the four of them would ever share?

"We're leaving in the morning," Steven revealed at a lull in conversation. "Early."

Both Ruth and her father took the news in stride, though a slight twitch at the corner of Ruth's mouth revealed far more than Steven suspected she would have liked about her true feelings on the matter.

Steven rested his elbows on the table, trying to keep his focus on Matheson. "I hope you two will manage all right without us."

"Of course, we will." Mr. Matheson let out a quick sigh. "I had a feeling you boys were leaving soon. Fortunately, we've got young Andrew helping during the day, and one of Ruth's cousins is looking for some part-time work till spring hits. We're going to be just fine." He squinted at Steven. "Is there anything *you* need?"

"No." Steven's gaze shot to the back room that had been their home for weeks. "We're mostly packed already. I suspect we're going to be traveling light."

"We might want to grab a bite on our way out." Niklaus peered around the deli. "If that's all right."

"You wound me, Niklaus." Matheson's palm went to his chest in faux shock. "At this point, you two are practically family." He eyed Steven knowingly. "And both of you, please understand. If for any reason things don't work out, you have a place here."

Steven smiled, remembering Ron Springer's similar offer. "Thank you, Mr. Matheson."

"It's Stuart, Steven. I don't know how many times I have to tell you that."

"So, Steven Bauer," Ruth asked with no small amount of trepidation in her voice, "the big day has finally arrived."

"Looks that way." Steven checked his watch, a paranoid tic that had manifested in the last few days. "The man we've been awaiting is supposed to arrive in New York tomorrow. If everything works out, this will all be over soon."

"Well, don't be in too much of a hurry." Ruth crossed her arms and looked away.

"Honey." Matheson rested a hand on Ruth's shoulder. "Steven and Niklaus have their own lives to lead and, from what I can gather, important things to take care of." He took his daughter's hand. "You've known this day was coming for weeks."

"I know." Ruth's bottom lip shot out in a subtle pout. "I just wish he didn't sound so damn happy about it." She locked gazes with Steven. "Will we even see you in the morning?"

"Probably not." Steven rose from the table, unable to face the sadness in Ruth's eyes. "We're planning on taking off well before sunrise, and unless things really go sideways, we're not coming back."

"So, this is goodbye." Tears gathered at the corners of Ruth's eyes leaving Steven wondering how many times in the preceding nine weeks he had made the young woman cry.

"Can you two excuse us?" Steven's gaze shot from Matheson to Niklaus and back.

"Of course." Matheson rose and shook Steven's hand. "Godspeed, son. Whatever it is you two are facing, I wish you all the best." He headed for the stairs to their apartment, pausing before he stepped through the door. "Like I said, if you ever need a place to stay…"

"Thank you, Mr. Matheson." Niklaus rose from the table. "Good to know we've got options." He shot Steven a quick glance. "I'll be in the back." Both Niklaus and Ruth's father shut their respective doors, leaving Steven and Ruth alone for what felt like the last time.

"You're really going?" She rose from the table and stood before Steven. "Nothing I can do or say to keep you here with us?" Her eyes dropped. "With me?"

"I'm sorry, Ruth." Steven went to the front window of the deli. "Like it or not, our time here is up."

"I know." Ruth joined him at the window. "Believe me." She held back the tears as the two of them stared out at the lamplit street, her heaving shoulders revealing a different truth.

Steven wrapped an arm around her. "I don't know if it helps, but I'm going to miss you."

"Don't go getting all sentimental on me now." Ruth punched him in the arm. "You're the one who's choosing to leave."

"I didn't choose this." Steven's hands shot up in exasperation. "I didn't choose any of this. I'm just a…just a…"

I'm just a pawn in all of this.

In his shirt pocket, Amaryllis pinched Steven's chest for the first time since Florida.

"Look," he said, wincing at the sudden pain. "Like I've told you a dozen times, I'd explain everything to you if I could, but I can't. You wouldn't understand."

Ruth turned away, her body visibly trembling. "Then, by all means, just go. All that's coming out of your mouth are just empty words anyway."

Steven took a step toward her. "I wish things were different."

"Don't you dare say that." Ruth's hands balled into fists. "It's cruel." She spun around and locked gazes with Steven. "No matter what nice little platitudes come out of your mouth, you're still leaving, regardless of what I say or feel, right?"

"This is how we're going to leave it, then?" The knot in Steven's stomach rivaled the pain brought on by the presence of the Black. "With hard feelings between us?"

"I'm sorry, but this is all I've got. I'd tell you to take it or leave it, but you've already made that call." Ruth stormed for the door through which her father exited moments before. "Goodbye, Steven."

She paused for a moment in the open doorway, not looking back, then bolted up the stairs and out of sight.

"This is miserable." Niklaus pulled his hands out of his pockets and rubbed them together with vigor. "You know, I left Poland for a reason."

"Miserable, but necessary." Steven stood with Niklaus in the early morning drizzle, both bundled against the cold coming off the bay. "Just keep your eyes open, all right?"

The truth? There were about a thousand places Steven would rather be on a frigid January morning. More, he couldn't dismiss the image of Ruth staring down from her second-story window as he and Niklaus left out not two hours before. Still, their one shot at returning home would be walking by any moment, and they had to be ready.

A crowd had gathered on the dock: wives, parents, children, reporters, photographers. All waited in the pre-dawn twilight for the soldiers aboard the moored naval frigate to disembark. As Steven overheard one story or another from the dozens surrounding him and Nik, he understood why Tom Brokaw had dubbed this "The Greatest Generation." The palpable joy evident in every face, in every description of a loved one, in every barely visible photograph, stirred in Steven a pride that normally remained dormant. Only in the weeks and months after September 11th had he ever experienced such single-minded unity and surety in the mission of the U.S. Military. Despite being the very definition of a fish out of water in 1946, he had never felt prouder to be an American.

"How much longer do you think it'll be?" Niklaus checked his watch. "We've been here for over an hour."

"As long as it takes." Steven blew warm air into balled fists. "We screw this up, we're stuck—"

A tap at Steven's shoulder interrupted his thought.

"Excuse me." The words bore an accent from somewhere near the Great Lakes. "Either of you gents have a cigarette?"

Steven and Niklaus turned to find a well-dressed man in his mid-forties wearing a buttoned-up tweed trench coat standing behind them. Beneath his bowler hat, the man's waxed mustache reminded Steven of an airplane propeller.

"Sorry." Steven slid into a practiced smile. "I don't smoke."

"Gave it up." Niklaus stroked the whiskers at his chin. "Bad for the complexion."

"Too bad." The man sucked frigid air through his teeth. "I could really use a drag."

"Wish I could help." Steven extended a hand. "I'm guessing you're waiting for your...son?"

The man took Steven's hand and gave it a vigorous shake. "My oldest. Supposed to be on board this ship, or at least that's what the telegram said."

"How long has he been gone?" Steven asked.

"A year and a half, most of it in France." The man puffed up his chest a bit. "Two Purple Hearts, I'll have you know."

"Two?" Steven studied the man's features. "Is he—"

"He's fine." A smile broke beneath the waxed mustache. "He is a Buchanan, after all."

"Dad!" A young boy, no more than ten, ran up and pulled at the older man's coattails. "I see him! I see him! Roy's home!" The boy sprinted away toward a group of soldiers making their way down the gangplank.

The man shrugged at Steven and smiled. "Ah, to be young again." He headed off after his son at just shy of a jog, shouting, "Wait up, Woody! I'm coming!"

Niklaus and Steven eyed each other. Though Audrey's grandfather had never mentioned his surname when they'd met, Buchanan was Audrey's mother's maiden name, a fact made more than clear in the dozens of stories of her mother's youth and her all-too-short marriage to the love of her life, one John Richards.

"Do you think it's possible?" Steven asked. "I mean, there could be dozens, even a hundred Woody Buchanans, right?"

"He's about the right age to be Audrey's grandfather." Niklaus smiled as the boy and his father reunited with a strapping young man in uniform with a chest full of ribbons just visible in the dim light. "And Audrey never ceases to remind us that she comes from a military family."

"We'll probably never know." Steven headed for the front of the crowd. "Come on. We've got bigger fish to fry."

Two years. Arthur Pedone's nose ran like a river in the morning chill. *Two years and it comes down to these last two steps.*

The flash of dozens of cameras blinded the young man as he stepped off the gangplank and onto the dock. He offered the various photographers his most convincing smile, though truth be told, the last thing he wanted to deal with after months in a war zone was yet another barrage of flashing lights. He glanced back across his shoulder at the naval frigate that had been his home for the last several days and slapped the back of the man walking next to him.

"Looks like we're finally home, Rex." Arthur's breath came out like thick smoke in the frigid morning air.

"It would appear that way." Sergeant Rex Caesius clasped Arthur's shoulder. "If all goes well, you should be a free man again in a matter of days."

"Right. Free. Speaking of which, you never did answer my question."

Caesius shot Arthur an amused glance. "And what question would that be, Arthur?"

"What in the blue blazes am I going to do now?" Arthur pulled the collar of his coat up around his neck. "It's not like colleges were beating down my door before I left and 'expert with an M-1' won't get me too many interviews on this side of the Atlantic."

A quiet chuckle passed Caesius' lips. "Robert Frost said that 'Home is the place where, when you have to go there, they have to take you in,' if I am not mistaken."

"I'm not going back there, Rex." Arthur's expression grew stony. "Maine has seen the last of me, I promise you that." He squinted through the morning haze at the city before them, the lights from the windows of the various buildings like thousands of eyes staring down at them. "Who knows? Maybe I'll stay here. Try out the Big Apple for a while."

"That sounds like a fine idea, my friend, though I would not be so quick to dismiss your home, your roots, your family." Caesius stared off into the distance. "Some things that are lost can never be regained."

Arthur pondered the words for a moment. "Hey, it's not like I'm not going to visit. I just want to try something new. Something exciting. Something—"

A pulse of sound erupted from the duffel bag slung across Caesius' shoulder. His expression shifted from casual nonchalance to acute awareness.

"This cannot be." Caesius dropped the bag and worked at the lock that held it closed. "At least not now. The time has not yet come."

"What are you talking about?" Arthur watched as Caesius fumbled in his pocket for the large ring of keys he kept there. "What's going on, Rex?"

Caesius ignored the questions as he labored to get the duffel bag open. From within, he pulled out a small pouch, its white leather old and weathered. Embossed around the top of the bag were strange symbols the likes of which Arthur had never seen while a silver cord tied around the pouch's neck held it closed. Freed from its olive drab prison, the pouch began to drone in earnest.

"What is that thing?" Arthur stared at the pouch. "And why is it making such a racket?"

"That 'racket' is exactly what I was counting on." The voice came from behind Arthur and Caesius. "Though I'm kind of surprised you can hear it."

Arthur turned and squinted through the dim light of early morning to find two figures heading in their direction. Bundled in a heavy overcoat, the man in the lead appeared to be in his late twenties and, in the parlance of Arthur's infantry brethren, moving with a purpose. Behind him rushed a man who towered over most of the soldiers milling about on the dock, his broad shoulders and close-cut blond hair not unlike that of many German soldiers he'd encountered in the preceding months. Both faces were turned up in earnest half-smiles touched with an undercurrent of worry.

And strangest of all, a look of recognition.

"Sergeant Caesius?" The man in the lead spoke in hushed, harried tones. "May I have a word with you?"

"Certainly," Caesius asked with a hint of trepidation. "And who, may I ask, might I have the pleasure of speaking with?"

"My name is Steven Bauer." He offered a slight bow. "This is my associate, Niklaus Zamek."

"Who?" Arthur shot Caesius a puzzled glance. "What do you two want?"

"Bauer, eh? And Zamek?" Caesius' mouth turned up into a crooked grin. "Fate, it seems, has lost all sense of subtlety."

"You know who we are then?" Steven crossed his arms.

Caesius raised a curious eyebrow. "Not precisely, Mr. Bauer, nor can I fathom how you possibly could have found me without the very artifact I hold in my hand, but I suspect I know why you are here, at least in part."

"I certainly hope so." Steven let out a relieved sigh that exited his mouth in a plume of steam. "We've come a long way."

12

BOYS & GIRLS

"Let me get this straight." Arthur Pedone put up a hand to block the wind whistling through the dark alley, lit a cigarette, and took a long drag. "Up until four months ago, you gents were alive and well some sixty years in the future and now you're stuck here in 'the past.'" He let out a chuckle. "What, did your jetpacks run out of fuel or something?"

The curiosity and wonder in the visage of the man who decades hence would call himself Grey negated Arthur's incredulous stare. "All sarcasm aside, my friend does pose an interesting question." He studied Steven for a moment, his grey eyes fixing him with their steely intensity. "Assuming, of course, that the pair of you are still in possession of your faculties, tell me: how is it that you came to be displaced in time?"

Steven shot him a sardonic grin. "I'll give you one guess."

Caesius whispered a single word. A name. "Zed."

Steven lowered his head in a grim nod. "As I understand it, killing us wasn't an option."

"So he did the next best thing." Niklaus spread his arms wide. "And here we are."

"You've all been reading too much H. G. Wells, I'd say." Arthur took another drag off his cigarette. "I like a good science fiction story as much as the next guy, but if you start spouting off about time machines and Morlocks, I'm leaving."

"Now, Arthur." Caesius shifted his gaze to his friend. "Let us hear them out. I suspect their story is far more interesting than any fiction you have read."

"Going by Caesius these days, huh?" Niklaus stroked his chin and smiled. "I took Latin for a couple years in university. Clever."

"I have always felt that what we call ourselves becomes part and parcel of who we are, would you not agree, Mr. Zamek?" Caesius studied Niklaus. "Your appellation, for instance, speaks of strength, power, invincibility, and yet you hide behind walls of your own design and hurl barbs at the world below." He turned to Steven. "And you, Steven Bauer. A conundrum, indeed. A leader, yet still a follower. Always at the forefront, yet ever a step behind. You seek answers to questions you can barely voice."

Niklaus and Steven shared a disquieted glance.

"Do not be dismayed." Caesius offered both men a warm smile. "Though we have yet to discuss the specifics of your banishment to the past, it is clear the two of you are among the Chosen for the coming iteration of the Game. Trust that in many ways I understand each of you better than you understand yourselves."

"Chosen?" Arthur's hands went to his hips, his brow bunching together in consternation. "What in blue blazes are you three talking about? Rex?"

Caesius rested a hand on Arthur's shoulder. "I am sorry, my friend, but there are things about me you do not know nor could ever understand." At his friend's insistent stare, he added, "It would take considerable time to even begin to explain."

"Well, from where I'm standing, it looks like we've got nothing *but* time." Arthur dropped the cigarette to the wet ground and stamped it out with his foot. "Let's hear it."

"You trusted him before." Steven took a breath. "I mean, you trust him sixty years from now. Whatever. God, this is confusing."

Caesius let out a resigned sigh. "Very well, though might I suggest we seek somewhere less exposed to continue our discussion?"

"Agreed." A connection that had sputtered in Steven's mind for days suddenly flared to life. "In fact, I think I know just the place."

※

The quartet waited outside Dante's Deli for better than half an hour in the frigid January air. Arthur, his slight build providing little protection from the cold, shivered despite being bundled up in his government-issue trench coat. Still, not a single complaint or grumble left his lips. Even Niklaus kept his tongue for the most part, though Steven guessed a sarcastic remark or two swam just below the surface. Only Caesius seemed unaffected by the bone-chilling cold. His patient demeanor bordered on stoic, and as always, Steven wondered what thoughts danced behind those tired, grey eyes.

"You're sure they won't miss us?" The anxiety in Arthur's voice came through loud and clear. "I mean we're pretty much AWOL, Rex."

"Everything will be fine, Arthur." Caesius crossed his arms, a smug half-grin on his face. "I have made certain arrangements to ensure neither of us will be missed today."

Steven knew all about such "arrangements" and wondered briefly if anyone in Chicago had given his existence so much as a second thought since the man standing across the circle had first come into his life. Even now, better than half a century before they were fated to meet, the man he knew as Grey seemed possessed of a confidence and surety Steven not only admired, but envied.

The sky had just begun to pink when the lights inside the deli came on. Stuart Matheson stepped into the dining area from the kitchen, his russet hair still wet from his morning shower. Moving slowly as if he hadn't slept well, he grabbed a damp rag to wipe down the wood countertop. Steven tapped at the window, giving the man a start. With a quizzical expression plastered across his face, Stuart let the four men in and, after a few brief introductions, showed them to a table at the rear.

"So," Steven asked, "where should I begin?"

"At the beginning." Caesius steepled his fingers below his chin. "Where else?"

For the better part of the morning, the four men discussed the series of events that led Steven and Niklaus to their current predicament. Stuart provided the quartet an impressive spread of bagels and pastries and kept their coffee cups full but otherwise left them to their business. The new kid, Andrew, despite having followed Niklaus around like a baby duckling since his first day on the job, also gave their table a respectful distance. The third member of the deli's staff and the one Steven had counted on seeing, however, was nowhere to be found.

As Steven told his tale, he made a conscious effort to leave out any mention of Arthur or Ruth's involvement. Learning too much about the future, particularly that his wife of better than sixty years most likely waited under that very roof, likely represented more than the already-baffled nineteen-year-old veteran across the table could take.

Caesius took in all Steven said with little reaction, his usual hawk-like expression as impassive and inscrutable as ever, though one aspect early on in Steven's tale seemed to captivate his attention more than any other.

"You claim I charged *you* with collecting the remaining Pieces." A rare look of surprise crossed the man's features. "Of this you are certain?"

"You made it pretty plain. 'This task is yours and yours alone,' I believe were your exact words. Not much wiggle room on that one."

Caesius' eyes slid shut, a long sigh escaping his lips.

"What is it?" Steven had seen that look before. "Does that mean something?"

"It is nothing." Caesius looked again at Steven, his eyes even more tired than they had been a moment before, and sipped at his coffee. "So, you drew your icon from the pouch and adopted your role as the Pawn. What then?"

Steven debated whether to push the issue. Caesius was avoiding telling him something, and he had a sneaking suspicion this particular something was quite important. He could read in the man's weary gaze, however, that it was a discussion best left for another day.

As the man he knew as Grey continued to hang on his every word, Steven marveled at how their roles had reversed, he the one with all the answers and Caesius the one asking the hard questions. Still, regardless of the impossibility of the situation, the grey-eyed mystery man who claimed to have been alive for centuries maintained a certain calm, and Steven guessed that even in that moment, the man knew more than he let on.

An hour into his tale, Steven finally came to the events of the Brooklyn Bridge and their fateful encounter with the Black. He recounted the last words Grey had said before disappearing into darkness.

"So, it is to be today."

"On the bridge that day." Steven stroked his chin. "You seemed to know what was about to happen. What Zed intended to do. I can only assume that knowledge came as a result of this conversation."

"And your point would be?"

"My point?" The exasperation in Steven's voice came through loud and clear. "Why in the hell don't you warn us of what's coming?" His eyes narrowed. "You could've at least saved yourself, right?"

Grey sighed, a placating smile spreading across his face. "The answer to your question is quite complex, but at its root, quite elementary as well."

Steven's cheeks went red hot. "For God's sake, just this once, can't you just answer a damn question?"

Caesius paused, weathering the tsunami of Steven's frustration, though his smile did dim a bit. Strangers and yet not strangers, the pair studied each other without a word for a moment that seemed to last hours. Stuart brought a fresh pot of coffee but wisely held his tongue as the conversational stalemate continued. Arthur didn't say a word, and even Niklaus managed to keep quiet for once.

"Very well," Caesius said eventually. "Simply put, the way things happened is the way things happened."

"But, you know what's coming." Steven's hands shot up in exasperation. "I'm sitting here telling you Zed is going to con us all into a trap and, barring a miracle, win the Game. Can't you change that? Don't you care?"

Caesius let out a weary sigh. "I know it seems counterintuitive, Steven, but these events are written and cannot be changed. You and

Niklaus sit here in a deli in New York City decades before either of you were born because the events of one day unfolded the way they did. Any attempt by me or anyone else to change the events of that day would ultimately fail, as the impetus to do so would be predicated on this very conversation. What you have described is what *did* happen to you and what *will* happen to me."

"But..."

"I appreciate your concern, Steven, but it is ill-placed." Caesius' smile returned. "As I see it, I now know that I will live to see the next iteration of the Game, that all of the White Pieces will be safely gathered together, and that they will have a true leader to guide them."

Steven let out a sarcastic chuckle. "Some leader I am. In case you missed it, Nik and I are stuck in 1946 while the rest of the White, including you, have ended up God knows where or when."

"If you truly believed that," Caesius washed down a bit of bagel with a gulp of coffee, "you would not be here."

"He's right on that one, Steven." Niklaus broke his uncharacteristic quiet, his gaze filled with admiration. "Things may look impossible, but we're going to make it out of here."

Steven raised an eyebrow. "That's pretty optimistic, don't you think?"

"Don't you get it?" Niklaus asked. "This little side trip back in time is all part of a bigger picture. It's like I was saying before. We haven't been removed from the Game. This, all of this, *is* the Game."

"The Game." Steven rested his forehead in his hand. "And what makes you so sure?"

"Look." Niklaus leaned in. "Our grey-eyed friend here rescues you from a blind date from hell, and then, in the space of three days, you pluck the rest of us from the wreckage of each of our lives and set us on a path to greatness. Not one of us looks back, and in days, it's like we've all known each other forever." His face lit up with hope. "It's fate, Steven."

"Fate."

"Yes. Fate." Niklaus motioned around the restaurant. "Here we are, sitting in a deli in the Manhattan of 1946 having bagels and coffee with a man you won't meet for decades. We were sent here by a man who is his opposite in an eternal contest that decides the direction of the world, all in an effort to win said competition by default." He swept his hands wide. "Move and countermove. Attack and defense. All of it, nothing but parts of one giant, convoluted, incredible Game."

"Your friend speaks wisdom." Caesius smiled. "I could not have said it better myself."

Steven groaned. "You two are making my brain hurt."

"That makes two of us." Arthur let out a sarcastic laugh. "Do any of you have any idea how crazy all of this sounds? It's like you... Wait. Who in the world is that?" Through the course of the conversation, Arthur's expression had shifted from incredulous to confused to attentive and back again, but in that moment, he appeared nothing short of enthralled, his gaze suddenly fastened on a point across Steven's shoulder. A familiar gasp followed by the sound of shattering glass made perfectly clear the object of Arthur's attention.

Ruth stood by the counter, her cheeks already rose-red with embarrassment, amid a pile of broken glass that had recently been a tray of juice glasses. She stooped for a moment in an attempt to clean up the glass before abandoning the chore and rushing to the back.

Arthur rose from the table. "Someone should help her."

Caesius stopped Arthur with a glance. "Steven?"

"This mess is my fault." Steven motioned for Arthur to sit back down. "Let me take care of it."

He stepped through the door to the kitchen and found Ruth fuming by the broom closet. He stood there for a moment, not knowing what to say.

"I thought you left." Ruth's glare struck him, her anger all but palpable.

Steven raised his hands before him in surrender. "We did, but the four of us needed a place to get out of the cold and talk."

"So you came here. Fantastic." The bitterness in her words seemed foreign. "Any port in a storm, I guess."

"It's not like that, Ruth. It never was. You know that."

"What I know, Steven Bauer, is that you seem intent on finding a new way every day to rip my heart out and step on it. I didn't sleep a wink last night after you told us you were leaving. I finally dozed off around five-thirty this morning, completely overslept, and missed helping Papa open the deli. And then, when I finally get downstairs, look who's still here." Her eyes grew narrow and cool. "Dammit, is this all some kind of game to you?"

A flash of heat hit Steven's cheeks. *You have no idea.*

"Look, Ruth. I know this is hard for you, but I don't know how many times you want me to say I'm sorry."

"I don't want you to say you're sorry, Steven. I just want you to go." Her gaze dropped to the floor. "Please."

Niklaus popped his head into the kitchen. "Don't worry about the mess, you two. Andrew said he'd help me clean it up." He sidestepped Ruth and grabbed a broom and dustpan from the closet and headed back into the dining area. "You two take your time."

Ruth cleared her throat. "Thank you, Niklaus."

"No problem." As Niklaus returned to the front, Ruth fixed Steven with an exhausted glare that seemed out of place on such a beautiful face.

"Listen and listen well. I'm going back upstairs to start this day over." She pressed a finger into Steven's chest. "When I come back down, I'd really appreciate it if you were gone."

A hundred retorts sprang to Steven's lips, but, in the end, all that came out was a simple "Okay."

Without another word, Ruth headed back into the deli proper with Steven close behind. Every attempt to restart the conversation stopped with a raised hand. Ruth's fingers had just brushed the door-knob leading upstairs when an unexpected voice stopped her in her tracks.

"Excuse me, miss." From a spot on the floor by the counter, Arthur rose, a soiled envelope in his hands. "I believe you dropped this." He held it out to her. "It looks important."

Ruth checked the front pocket of her apron and met Arthur's gaze.

"It's a letter from my brother." She strode over, gave Arthur's chest full of ribbons a quick once-over, and took the envelope from him. "He'll be home soon as well." She turned back for the stairs to continue her grand exit, but Arthur caught her shoulder.

"He was stationed near Paris, wasn't he?" The young man's voice dropped a few decibels. "I recognize the post."

"Yes." Ruth turned back to again face Arthur. "His name's Thomas. Thomas Matheson. He's infantry. Been over there a year and a half."

"Thomas Matheson?" Arthur's face lit up with recognition. "Do you mean Tommy?"

Ruth's eyes grew wide, a wide smile blossoming on her face. "You know Tommy?"

"Wouldn't recognize him if he walked up to me on the street, but yeah. I know Tommy."

"How's that?" Ruth studied Arthur with a quizzical eye. "Either you know him or you don't."

Ruth's shoulders unhunched, the anger and hurt and frustration all melting into her usual earnest posture as the curiosity returned to her gaze. Forgotten for the moment, Steven couldn't decide if he felt slighted or relieved.

"I've been stationed in northern France for the last six months working with the quartermaster for our unit." Arthur beamed at the attention from the lovely young woman. "Tommy was the supply NCO for a company south of us. We must've talked at least twice a day since August, but always over coms." A flash of recognition crossed Arthur's features. "Wait. Tommy's sister. You must be... Ruthie. You're a dancer, right?"

"Ruth." Her already pink cheeks grew red hot. "Just Ruth. And yes, I practice when I can, though life is pretty busy these days." She bit her lip. "You have quite the memory."

"On important things. Mostly, though, Tommy just likes to talk about his family." Arthur peered around the main dining area, the tables slowly filling with customers. "So, this is the famous deli on the Upper West Side. I told Tommy I'd drop by someday. Never dreamed it'd be so soon."

"Would you like to see some of his letters? I've kept all of them." Ruth's eyes dropped to the floor. "We could see if he mentioned you in any of them."

"That would be great, unless..." Arthur glanced at Steven.

"We'll be fine." Steven smiled. "You two have at it. We'll finish up out here, and I'll make sure Sergeant Caesius doesn't leave without you, all right?"

Arthur gave Steven an eager nod. Ruth gazed at him as well, her face a potent mix of anger, longing, confusion, and perhaps even a hint of apology.

"Thanks," Ruth said after a pregnant pause. "I won't keep him too long. Promise." She turned to Arthur. "Funny. I don't think I caught your name."

"You never asked." His face broke into a smile, his cheeks flashing a bright pink. "It's Arthur. Arthur Pedone."

"Then wait here, Arthur Pedone." Ruth rushed upstairs to her family's apartment and returned thirty seconds later with a box full of letters. "Let's sit over here. Grab your coffee."

The pair took over a table in the far corner of the deli and soon were laughing like old friends. Steven rejoined Caesius and Niklaus at their table, a wide smile plastered across his face.

Niklaus laughed. "Why the big grin, Steven? You kind of just got dumped."

"That's one way of looking at it." Steven's gaze trailed over to the table where Ruth and Arthur gazed at each other in exactly the same way they would six decades hence. "But the way I see it, those two just proved both your points."

"How so?" Niklaus asked.

Caesius leaned across the table. "Unless I miss my guess, Steven is finally accepting that some things are simply meant to be."

13

TOUCH & GO

With Ruth and Arthur busy at the far corner of the deli swapping stories about her brother and getting better acquainted, Steven, Niklaus, and the man calling himself Caesius were finally free to get down to business.

"Young love." Caesius grinned, his eyes flashing as he caught Steven's gaze. "There is more to their story, I assume."

"Perceptive as always." Steven sighed. "They haven't seen the last of me—that's for sure—though it's going to be a while."

Strangely stung by the sudden reversal in Ruth's attentions, Steven took a deep breath and accepted that a train that had been moving in the wrong direction now rocketed down the correct track. Ruth belonged with Arthur. He'd seen it. And *he* belonged with Audrey.

None of that stilled the subtle pang of envy at his core.

The human heart. Still the biggest mystery of all.

Caesius' face grew solemn. "So, to the matter at hand."

"Yeah." Niklaus rapped his knuckles on the table. "How the hell do we get back to where and when we belong?"

"The non-cryptic version." Steven raised an eyebrow. "If you please."

"I promise to be as forthcoming as I can." Caesius let out an amused chuckle. "Now, once again from the beginning, if you will."

Steven reviewed step by step the events that led up to his and Niklaus' banishment to the 1940s. The earthquake leading to the destruction of the Brooklyn Bridge. The discovery of the severed cables bathed in black fire. The dark doorways in space that took each of their friends, including Grey himself. The loss of the pouch to the Black Pawn's arrow. Their final stand as the Black King sent them spiraling into the past.

The past that had become their present.

As Steven finished, Caesius narrowed his eyes in concentration. "It would seem Zed used the flux of energies left in the wake of the bridge's destruction to open doors that led not only to other places, but to other times as well." He pulled in a deep breath through his nose and shook his head slowly from side to side. "My old friend is nothing if not inventive."

"So, that's how we got here." Steven traced a drop of condensation on the table, forming a circle on the checkered tablecloth. "What we need to know is how to get back."

Caesius nodded. "A conundrum, indeed."

"And there's something we haven't discussed." Steven crossed his arms. "The last time we spoke before Zed sent you to God knows where or when, you said the Game was almost upon us. We've been here in the 1940s over three months. Without us to bring 'balance to the Force,' who's to say Florida isn't under water or that California hasn't fallen into the Pacific?"

"Or worse, what if Zed has already won and everything we're doing is pointless?" Niklaus set down his coffee. "Steven doesn't like to think that way, but the fact remains that we know nothing about what's happening there. Nothing."

"And you have come to me for answers." Caesius looked on them with a measure of sympathy and no small amount of pride. "Your loyalty and faith in me is truly humbling. Regardless, though I wish I could reassure you regarding the events to come, I'm afraid the intricacies of traveling through time are beyond even my centuries of experience." Steven's heart raced at the statement, but before he could say another word, Caesius' frown broke into a smile. "That being said, one flaw exists in Zed's plan that he has perhaps overlooked."

Steven perked up. "And that would be?"

"As we constructed the rules governing our shared endeavor, no aspect held more importance than ensuring the Game would reliably be played at the correct time and place throughout history to prevent the disasters caused by another unchecked correction. In the event that either Zed or I or even both were to die between iterations, we instituted fail-safes to ensure the Game's inevitability."

Niklaus let out a solitary laugh. "So, we can add your Game to death and taxes?"

"Indeed." Caesius' eyes slid out of focus. "In fact, each of you have already experienced this phenomenon, albeit to different degrees." He studied Steven for a moment. "Consider. A lone Pawn with no experience and minimal preparation faces the gathered Black pantheon, defeats them on every front, and manages to collect all the Pieces to his side without a single fatality. You are clearly both brave and resourceful, Steven, but I suspect the magicks of the Game may also have been at play."

Steven's cheeks grew hot. "Good to know, I suppose."

"And you, Mr. Zamek. Last second rescues and split-second decisions aside, you survived a fall that would have killed any man alive."

"But I pulled the rook from the pouch." Niklaus' shoulders bunched in frustration. "You're saying that wasn't me acting of my own free will?"

Caesius tilted his head to one side. "What I am saying is that your decisions on some level were likely guided by a higher power."

"So, our actions, our choices, our very wills." Steven's hands balled into fists. "They mean nothing?"

"The contrary, in fact. Each of you was chosen by the Game based specifically upon the kind of person you are and the decisions such a person would likely make. Still, up until the first moment of actual play, the Game has a vested interest in keeping all of you very much alive." Caesius swirled his coffee and sucked down the last dregs from his cup. "From a universal perspective, all that matters in the end is that the Game is played. Everything else is mere pomp and ceremony."

"Including our lives?" Niklaus eyes narrowed.

"That's cold, Grey." Steven looked away, unable to meet his someday mentor's grey gaze. "Even for you."

Caesius leaned back in his chair, seeming unaffected. "Nevertheless, it remains the truth."

"Pomp and ceremony." Steven didn't even try to keep the frustration from his voice. "Zed said the same thing once."

Caesius laughed. "Even our opponent speaks the truth from time to time, though he usually twists it to serve his own agenda."

"So, the Game wants to be played." Niklaus leaned in, resting his elbows on the table. "We've got that part. What does that have to do with us being stuck in 1946?"

"The two of you, along with the others, no longer walk this planet as mere individuals, but as a part of something greater than yourselves. Until such time as you surrender your icons at the conclusion of the coming iteration, a tether exists between each of you as well as the Game itself that cannot be severed by any measure of distance or, I hope, years. Were the six of you not displaced from your native time, the Arbiters would simply pull you from your various locations across the globe to the Board at the appointed time of play regardless of your circumstances. Though temporal shifting of the various Pieces was never a consideration, the fail-safe magicks of the Game should be more than enough to draw you back to where and when you belong."

"You *hope*?" Steven asked. "*Should* be more than enough?"

Caesius held up his hands in surrender. "I considered a myriad of eventualities in the building of this Game, Steven, but banishment of the various Pieces from their own time falls beyond even my wildest dreams."

"All of us are linked together." A memory of his lone psychic conversation with Audrey as she fought to escape the Black Knight flitted through Steven's mind. "And all of us are linked to the Game." He massaged his temple as a twinge of familiar pain erupted above his eye. "And now, we just wait until the Game begins some sixty years in the future and hope it yanks us all back to the present in time for the Black to descend on us like a pack of wolves?"

"I never said that you should sit and wait idly, Steven. Only that your efforts to return to your own time should be rewarded…if I did my job correctly all those many years ago."

"So, I get to go gather everyone together again, and this time without the aid of the pouch."

"I never said that either." Caesius rummaged in the duffel at his feet and produced the white pouch Steven would first hold in his hands six decades hence. "The *Svartr Kyll* sent you here. It will take the *Hvitr Kyll* to send you back." He held the crumpled bag out to Steven, the silver cord at its neck wound tight. A barely audible hum emanated from its worn leather surface.

"Whoa." Steven raised his hands. "I can't take that. That'll mess up everything."

"Take it." Caesius pressed the pouch into Steven's hand. "It is the only way."

"But if you give me the pouch now, how will you have it in the future to give to me in the first place?"

Caesius smiled. "When that day comes, Steven, rest assured the *Hvitr Kyll* will have long since returned to my possession. As I explained before, those events have already occurred, and things that have been written cannot be unwritten."

"Funny." Niklaus cracked his knuckles. "You sound pretty confident for someone who just told us he wasn't that well versed in the ins and outs of time travel."

"Yeah." Steven shook his head. "A bit daunting knowing we're betting our lives and the fate of the world on your best guess."

"A guess indeed, but an educated guess." A playful smirk played across Caesius' lips. "If there is one thing I have learned in my centuries on this planet, it is the fine art of extrapolation."

Steven held the pouch before him. "So, we have a car, but the car has no gas. As you explained it, the pouch and all the icons only fully function during a time of correction, and the next one of those isn't for another sixty years."

Caesius dropped his chin in a grim nod. "I was pondering that very question. Without the energies of a correction to empower the pouch, what you hold in your hand is scarcely more than a bag of aged leather. Only at a crossing might you find enough ambient energy to serve your purposes, and it would have to be a significant crossing at that." He eyed Steven. "I assume I taught you about such things."

Steven let out a quiet laugh. "Yeah, you covered that on day one."

"Excellent." Caesius thought for a moment. "I suppose we could arrange travel for the both of you to the British Isles and take advantage of the nexus at Stonehenge. If any place has the requisite power to satisfy your needs, it would be there. Unfortunately, I am less familiar with similar locations on this continent."

"Stonehenge, huh?"

A sharp pinch at Steven's chest brought to his mind an image of a castle.

A coral castle.

"Strangely enough…" He stroked Amaryllis' metal wings. "We may have a lead on just such a place."

Ruth and Arthur rose from the table in the corner, Ruth gathering together the various letters from her brother and Arthur studying her every move. Seeing them together, Steven couldn't help but smile. The electricity between the two, the furtive glances, the flushed cheeks. His eyes slid closed as he imagined the doting elderly couple that still danced around the kitchen in their eighties, the pang in his chest evaporating with final recognition that their trip to the 1940s had accomplished at least one thing of importance.

"We should be heading back, Rex." Arthur's downcast eyes flicked in Ruth's direction. "We've already missed the entire morning. Probably shouldn't push our luck."

"Very well." Caesius rose from the table. "Gentlemen?"

"We should be heading on as well." Steven stood, and though he avoided her gaze, Ruth's eyes burned into him. "We have quite a few miles ahead of us." He caught Niklaus' eye and inclined his head toward the door. "Ready?"

The four men gathered at the door, joined by Ruth and her father. Stuart Matheson gave each his usual firm handshake, taking care to lock gazes with one Corporal Arthur Pedone before returning to the counter to serve the gathering lunch crowd. That left Ruth, her shifting gaze and shuffling feet breaking Steven's heart all over again.

Caesius took the young woman's hand. "Miss Matheson, my

deepest thanks to you and your father for your warm hospitality this morning." He stepped out into the crisp afternoon air. "Two lost souls recently returned from war could not have asked for a better reception."

"Yeah," Arthur chimed in. "Thanks for everything. I'd love to—"

"Come, Arthur." Caesius took the young man by the elbow and pulled him toward the door. "These three need a moment to say their goodbyes."

"But—" Arthur said.

"Fear not." Caesius raised an eyebrow. "I have little doubt you will be seeing Miss Matheson again."

Arthur's already pink cheeks blossomed like a pair of red roses. Without another word, he shook hands with both Steven and Niklaus, offered Ruth a quick nod, and followed the man he knew as Sergeant Rex Caesius out onto the sidewalk.

Silence filled the space between the trio that had become not quite family over the preceding weeks. Steven searched Ruth's eyes and found there a resigned sadness that left a hole in his heart.

"Sorry for the surprise reappearance this morning. We had nowhere else to go."

"You're always welcome here." Her voice cracked with emotion. "You know that."

"This is goodbye, Ruth. For real this time." He placed a kiss just above her brow. "If everything goes the way it's supposed to, we won't be coming back."

"I know that." She nodded subtly, her lips trembling with emotion. "Take care of yourself out there."

"I will." Steven offered her his best smile. "You know, with me and Niklaus gone, you and your dad might need a little more help around here, especially if you plan to continue with your dancing." He inclined his head in the direction of the door. "A nice regular job might be just what a certain soldier fresh off the boat from Europe is looking for."

Ruth laughed through her tears, her cheeks pink. "I'll keep that in mind." She turned to Niklaus, her gaze flicking momentarily in Steven's direction. "Keep an eye on him, will you?"

Niklaus smiled. "For you, Ruth, I'll use both eyes."

Ruth wrapped her arms around his chest and squeezed. "I'm going to miss you around here, you big lug."

"Ditto." Niklaus pulled her off her feet and spun her around, bringing a quiet giggle. "One last pirouette with my favorite dancer."

As Niklaus returned her to the floor, she dropped into a low curtsy and swept her arms wide. "Take care, Nik."

"Right back at you." Niklaus gave Ruth a quick salute and headed for the door. "See you outside, Steven."

Steven inhaled to break the awkward silence, and Ruth countered by placing a slender finger on his lips. Leaning in, she gave him a quick peck on the cheek and excused herself to the kitchen. Dazed, Steven peered around the deli and found Mr. Matheson at the counter doing his level best to avoid his gaze, his head shaking in clear disappointment.

"Well," Steven muttered. "I guess that's that."

Steven exited the deli and found Caesius, Arthur, and Niklaus waiting at the corner. The air had warmed a bit since the early morning, but the falling drizzle still left him chilled to the bone. He pulled his coat close about his body and rejoined the others.

"I suppose this is goodbye for us as well," Steven said.

"I must return with Arthur to our unit." Caesius offered Steven a hand. "Even the series of carefully crafted 'suggestions' I left among our leadership will only cover our absence for so long."

"These aren't the droids you're looking for." Niklaus spread his arms wide and took a slight bow. "Am I right?"

Steven ignored Niklaus and took Caesius' hand. "You can't come with us, can you?"

A memory of another time and place. His mentor's voice.

I can advise you as you walk this path, but this task is yours and yours alone.

Caesius shook his head. "Alas, I cannot. Though from your perspective, all of this happened long before you were born and as anything we say or do is already a matter of history, it is prudent that we now part ways. I already know far more about my future than I should, and I now need to contemplate carefully what to do with that information." He gestured to the pouch already hung at its customary position at Steven's hip. "Your wit and judgment have guided you well thus far. Continue to trust your instincts and may the *Hvitr Kyll* deliver you to your friends and return all of you safely home."

Niklaus groaned. "And, God willing, the right decade."

Caesius nodded. "Indeed."

"And what about me?" Arthur leaned against a lamppost, eyes wide. "What am I supposed to do now?"

"I don't know." Steven glanced back in the direction of the diner. "You mind sticking around the area for the next few weeks and checking in on Ruth and her dad for me from time to time? You know, to make sure they don't need any help after Nik and I head out?"

Arthur grinned, every bit the lovesick schoolboy. "You don't think she'd mind?"

Steven shot Niklaus a wink. "I can all but guarantee she won't."

"Watch out, though." Niklaus slapped Arthur on the back. "She's a real firecracker."

The four of them exchanged farewells and then Caesius raised a hand above his head and snapped his fingers. Two seconds later, a yellow Packard Clipper pulled up and the cabbie ran around to open the rear door. Niklaus attempted to climb in the back, but his six-foot-four frame didn't fit, prompting a move to the front.

As he settled in, Steven met Caesius' gaze one last time. "See you in six decades."

Caesius smiled. "Until our paths again cross, Steven."

Steven climbed into the cab's back seat, rolled down the window, and saluted the youngest among them. His simple goodbye would echo in the young soldier's mind for the next six decades, all but forgotten until a fateful night a few years into the next century when that same voice would signify it was his turn to help a weary traveler.

"See you around, Arthur."

"Here it is." Ron Springer pulled into the small parking area adjacent to Rock Gate Park. The sun was setting and the shadows cast by the monolithic planets at the back of the Coral Castle stretched like clawed fingers onto the two-lane road. Only one other car sat parked in the lot, and Steven could just make out the flicker of a lamp in the window of Edward Leedskalnin's tower apartment.

"Still not sure why you boys wanted to come back here." Ron peered through the windshield at the darkening sky. "Especially this late in the evening."

"We lost something, something important." Steven rested his fingers on the door handle. "We're hoping to find it here."

"Must be pretty important." Ron quirked his mouth to one side. "I hope Ed found whatever it was and saved it for you."

Niklaus surveyed the walls of the massive stone edifice. "If anyone has what we need, it's him."

"You know, I was a mite surprised when you boys showed up on my doorstep earlier. Not much here in Homestead to attract a couple of young bucks like yourselves in the first place, much less bring you back for a second look."

"More than you might think." Steven opened the door and climbed out of the truck. "And I couldn't help but notice a woman's touch here and there around your house."

"Things with Dorota going well, I'm guessing?" Niklaus shot Ron a conspiratorial wink.

A hint of color darkened the man's leathered cheeks. "She keeps coming around. Wouldn't be very gentlemanly to turn her away." Ron's face screwed up in a quizzical grimace. "You boys sure you don't want me to wait for you? It's going to be dark in half an hour."

"We appreciate the offer," Steven said, "but if this all goes down as intended, we'll be moving on tonight."

"But you came back to Homestead the way you left," Ron said. "On a bus."

"Don't worry," Niklaus said. "We've got it covered and appreciate all you've done."

"All right, then." Ron shifted the truck into reverse. "Good to see you boys again. Send Old Ed my best, and if you're ever back in this neck of the woods, don't be strangers."

As Ron pulled onto the road and accelerated away, Niklaus turned to Steven. "You know, if this doesn't work, we're stuck at 'Old Ed's' place without a ride, and last time I checked, all of the guest furniture was made out of rock."

"It has to work." Steven strode toward the enormous stone revolving door that led into Rock Gate Park. "Grey said it's the only way." He pressed his hand against the gigantic hunk of coral, amazed again at how the three-ton stone spun as easily as the revolving glass door at the front of Macy's. He and Niklaus stepped through the colossal stone doorway and found Edward Leedskalnin directing a family of five toward the exit.

"I hope you enjoyed yourselves and do come again if you're ever…" Leedskalnin stopped midsentence when he spotted Steven and Niklaus. "…back in the area."

The family's trio of children ranged in age from toddler to teen. The youngest sprinted from stone to stone with the unbridled enthusiasm of the three-year-old set, her dark hair in beaded braids clacking in the near dark. The oldest, a girl Lena's age, trudged along with her head down and her hands in her pockets. The middle child, a boy likely two to three years into elementary school, watched everything in silence, a fascinated sheen in his gaze. Their mother and father herded them toward the door like trained border collies, the man walking close enough that Steven caught a whiff of his pungent aftershave.

"Hey, Nik." Steven nodded in the father's direction. "That man look familiar to you?"

"Maybe." Niklaus shot the man a sidelong glance. "Sort of a dead ringer for Richard Pryor, with maybe a touch of…Morgan Freeman?"

"Yeah. Maybe that's it." Steven tried not to stare as the man followed his family out the massive stone door. "Still, I'd swear we've met him somewhere before."

"So, you two gentlemen came back." Leedskalnin eyed them both, his body tense with apprehension. "A little late for another tour of the park, don't you think?"

"We're not here for a tour," Steven said. "But you know that, don't you?"

Leedskalnin took a step back, his eyes shifting left and right. "Listen, I don't have much money."

Niklaus laughed. "Come on, Mr. Leedskalnin. You can't seriously think we came back after three months to rob you here in your own home."

Leedskalnin furrowed his brow. "Then, what is it you want?"

"The truth?" Steven crossed his arms. "We need your help."

"Why do I get the impression I'd be better off if you two were just simple robbers?" Leedskalnin shook a finger at Niklaus. "Something told me I'd be seeing the two of you again. A...feeling I got when you were here before."

Niklaus studied the tiny man standing before him. "What kind of feeling?"

"That you, of all people, understand." Leedskalnin peered up into Niklaus' dumbfounded face and stretched out his arms to the walls surrounding them. "This castle didn't build itself, you know." The old man giggled with glee. "Not a day goes by that someone doesn't ask old Ed, 'How'd you do it?' or 'What's your secret?' or the like." He snorted. "As if I'd ever tell." With a theatrical spin, Leedskalnin sat on one of the stone benches by a nearby grotto and motioned for Steven and Niklaus to join him. "Even if I did, I imagine few, if any, would have the mental framework to comprehend the truth. But I don't need to tell you that, do I, Mr. Zamek?"

Niklaus shook his head, comprehension dawning on his face. "Either you feel it or you don't."

Leedskalnin smiled. "Precisely."

Steven's heart raced. "Do you believe in destiny, Mr. Leedskalnin?"

"I did, once." He motioned again to the surrounding walls. "Now I create my own." A half-crazed laugh escaped his lips. "Did you two truly come all this way to discuss philosophy?"

"You could say that." Steven sat by Leedskalnin. "Strange though it may seem, I believe we were brought here for a reason."

"And what reason might that be, my young friends?" The gleam in the man's eyes suggested he already knew at least part of the answer. "What is it you hope to find here?"

"An answer." Steven rose and rested a hand against one of the grotto's upright stones. "When Ron Springer brought us here before, he told us you'd spent almost a quarter century building this place the first time and that a decade ago, you spent another three years moving the whole thing to where we stand now."

"Is there a question in there somewhere?" Leedskalnin's face twisted, the look of a criminal wishing to be caught.

"Only the obvious one." Steven gestured to the ground at their feet. "Why here? Why this place? Ron Springer told us he thought you moved to a more private location..."

"But people who really want privacy don't sell tickets to the public for daily tours of their home, do they?" Niklaus closed his eyes and sniffed the air. "There's something special about this place, isn't there?"

Leedskalnin rose and walked toward the rear of the park. "Come. I want to show the two of you something."

He led Steven and Niklaus to another revolving stone door at the rear of the park that made the hunk of coral guarding the front entrance look like a paperweight.

"In 1936, I discovered that my calculations regarding the park's original location were off a bit. Like you said, I spent three years moving this entire structure the ten miles from Florida City to the ground on which we now stand. The first thing I erected: this door." He pressed upon the rough surface of the door with one finger, and the entire stone turned as if it were made of Styrofoam. "Ah... perfectly balanced, as always."

"But why here?" Steven peered around in the failing light. "What is it about this place?"

Leedskalnin's grin grew wider. "Your friend knows."

Steven followed Leedskalnin's gaze to find Niklaus standing with his arms held wide, fingers outstretched, eyes closed, and his lips hanging slightly open as if in rapture.

"This is it, Steven." Niklaus opened his eyes, his gaze that of someone who just awakened from a pleasant dream. "The energies that helped build this place. I can feel them."

"You're sure?" Steven asked, hope and doubt warring in his tone. He glanced down into his shirt pocket at the green dragonfly pendant that rested there. Despite Steven's hope for some kind of confirmation they were on the right track, Amaryllis hadn't so much as fluttered a metallic wing since they'd left New York.

"As sure as I've been about any of this." Niklaus stroked the door's stone surface and a shiver passed through his body. "Try the pouch."

Steven reached into his knapsack and pulled out the sack of bleached white leather with its frayed silver cord. The pouch hummed in answer, and Leedskalnin took a step back as if he feared a swarm of bees might erupt from its tightly drawn mouth.

"What is that?"

"It's a key, so to speak." Steven approached the monolithic doorway. With each step, the pouch's humming crescendoed, almost as if Steven were nearing another of the Pieces. He touched the pouch to the nine-ton slab of rock, and something akin to electricity ran up the length of his arm. He gently pressed on the gate and set the immense stone spinning. A faint glow shimmered off its rocky surface, and as the three men looked on, the door's slow revolution began to accelerate.

"What in the..." Steven's words were lost in the twin cacophony of the pouch's escalating drone and the grinding gyrations of the enormous stone. Faster and faster, the door revolved on its axis until its very substance appeared ephemeral and ghostlike.

"What now?" Niklaus' eyes filled with trepidation. "I didn't come all this way just to walk into a solid stone food processor."

Steven stood staring at the whirling door, his fist clenched around the pouch, knuckles white. Then, in a calm even voice, he stated simply, "Take us to the others."

The glow of the whirling stone doubled in intensity. Steven readied himself to test his theory, but before he could take another breath, Niklaus stepped into the shimmering cylinder of light and disappeared.

"Wait. Where did he go?" Whatever smug air of understanding

Edward Leedskalnin had seemed to possess moments before vanished along with Niklaus. "What is happening here?"

"No time to explain." Steven stepped to the door. "Unless I miss my guess, I'm betting this train won't be in the station for long."

And with that, Steven took one last fateful step and a moment later was somewhere far from Florida and hurricanes and a heartbroken genius within his hall of stone.

Alone in the dark, Edward Leedskalnin watched, mouth agape, as the door he'd hewn out of quarried coral some twenty years earlier slowly decelerated, the silver scintillation of its exterior fading quickly to darkness. After a few seconds, the stone came to rest slightly ajar within the doorway. Edward ran a finger along its rough surface and jerked his hand away, the stone as hot as a live coal. He rubbed at his eyes and laughed aloud, his excitement interrupted a moment later by the sound of shouting voices.

"He's got to be here somewhere." A man's voice, like rumbling thunder.

"Sweetie?" A female, her words pinched and filled with anxiety. "Are you here?"

Edward spun around and found the couple that had left minutes before storming toward him. The mother's face was screwed up in panic while the man appeared more angry than afraid.

"Mr. Leedskalnin." The man crossed his arms. "Our son is missing. Have you seen him?"

Edward shrank away from the man's smoldering anger. "Your son?"

"Our middle child." The man pulled a red handkerchief from his back pocket and wiped the sweat from his brow. "We stopped to get gas on the way out of town and realized he wasn't in the car. Is he here? Have you seen him?"

"There's no one here but me, as far as I know. The last two guests just…left. I'm—"

"Mama?" The voice, little more than a whimper, came from just a few feet away, behind an enormous bathtub carved from stone. Edward rushed over with the frantic couple close on his heels and found a dark-skinned boy shivering on the cold earth. The mother dropped to the ground at the boy's side and swept him up in her arms while the father spun Edward around and grabbed him by the shoulders.

"What have you done to my son?" he rumbled.

"Nothing." Edward's knees went weak with fright. "I didn't know he was there. I swear."

"Papa." The whispered word ended in a choked sob. "I'm sorry. I'm so sorry."

"Son." The man pushed Edward aside and knelt by his wife and son. "Did this man hurt you?" When the boy didn't answer, the father grabbed his arms and shook him. "Did he?"

"No, sir. But—"

"Why didn't you get in the car?" The mother's even tone carried a gravity no amount of shouting could match. "It's not safe being on your own, honey, especially when we're so far from home. You're only seven years old. What were you thinking?"

"I...I didn't want to sit in the back with Henrietta." The boy's face twisted into a scowl. "She was being mean."

"She was mean? That's all you've got to say about this?" The father stood and put his hands on his hips. "Your mother almost had a heart attack." The father trembled with anger, his jowls flapping like a bulldog's. "Now, get up off that ground and go get in the car."

"But Papa! You won't believe what I saw. Those men—"

"Archibald Ignatius Lacan, I do not want to hear another word." The father's words echoed in the Coral Castle like an angry god's. "Do you understand me?"

"Yes, sir." The boy's voice was barely a whisper.

"What was that?"

The boy refused to meet his father's gaze. "Yes. Sir."

The man turned to his wife. "Take Archie on to the car, honey. I'll be along in a minute."

As Mr. Lacan and Edward exchanged awkward apologies, Mrs.

Lacan took her son by the hand and led him to the three-ton gate at the front of the park.

"I don't know what you were thinking." She rested a hand against the enormous stone. "Don't you ever try anything like this again, Archie. You hear?"

"Yes, ma'am."

Mrs. Lacan let out a sigh. "If you know what's good for you, I'd suggest you keep quiet the rest of the evening. Your backside is already going to hurt enough when we get to the hotel. You say anything more to your father about this, you're just going to make him madder."

"Okay, Mama. I'll keep quiet." A mischievous grin crossed the young man's face, the devious glint in his eye driving away all other emotion. "I can keep quiet for a long, long time."

14

COWBOYS & INDIANS

One second, Steven stood in an eccentric genius' castle forged of coral; the next, on a tree-lined ridge covered in snow and ice. To his right, Niklaus stared out across the winter landscape with an expression just shy of disgust.

"Great. Another forest." Niklaus dropped his duffel bag into the six inches of snow at his feet. "Ugh. And still winter to boot."

Steven pointed toward multiple plumes of smoke rising into the sky in the distance. "Looks like there's a town a mile or two southwest. I think we can get there before sunset." The late afternoon sun rested two handbreadths above the top of the trees. "Assuming, of course, that I've correctly guessed the time of day."

"At least we know which direction to go this time." Niklaus rummaged in his bag and produced the black trench coat the Matheson family had helped him purchase for the New York winter. "Though I'd take sunny Florida over this frozen ridge any day."

"Agreed." Steven scooped up a handful of snow and took a palate-freezing bite. "Great," he said, wincing. "Brain freeze."

"Look on the bright side." Niklaus slid into the trench and buttoned it all the way to the top. "At least I won't be hopping over tree roots on a broken ankle this time."

For the next hour, they hiked across a rugged pine stand that had yet to feel a logger's axe. Snow blanketed the ground and dampened all sound but the rhythmic crunch of Niklaus and Steven's footfalls. Half a mile into their snowy trek, they startled a family of jackrabbits beneath a fallen tree.

Scattered, Steven considered, *just like us.*

"So," Niklaus asked. "Who do you think we're here for?"

"Not a clue." Steven held the pouch before him, the white leather bag silent in his hand. "Even when the pouch was leading me to you guys the first time, I was making it up as I went along."

"Hm." Niklaus raised an eyebrow. "I figured you'd have developed an intuition about that kind of thing by now."

Steven laughed at that, his breath steaming in the cold. "At the moment, my intuition has us cross country skiing without the benefit of skis."

"It's not so bad." Niklaus slapped Steven's back. "We've made it this far, haven't we?"

"I suppose." Steven slung his duffel bag farther up on his shoulder. "Call me selfish, but I hope it's Audrey. Not knowing if she's all right is killing me."

"I get that." Niklaus grew silent for a moment. "Something just occurred to me. The pouch led you to each of us before, but as I understand it, that only worked because of the Game. Do we have any way of knowing if it's going to help us wherever or whenever we are now?"

"I have no idea. When we caught up with Grey in New York, it certainly responded, and I've got to believe it didn't bring us to this place without a reason."

Steven and Niklaus continued their slow progress through the dense forest for another hour, the conversation sparse other than occasional flurries of speculation about the others and who might await them in the town ahead. Twice they passed clusters of men whose dress appeared Native American. Their features obscured, bundled as they were against the cold and snow, they offered only somber nods as they passed, a gesture that Steven and Niklaus echoed.

"At least there are people here," Steven muttered.

As the sun began to sink behind the trees, a clearing opened up before them, the snow-covered cut in the trees divided by two parallel ruts in the snow.

"These look too narrow to be tire tracks." Between the twin furrows were hoofprints, at least four sets. "What do you think?" Steven knelt to examine the tracks. "Wagon? Carriage?"

Niklaus stooped to take a closer look. "Our luck, it's probably a chariot."

Steven glanced up and down what was most likely a dirt road covered in ice. "In any case, I'm guessing we're even further back than last time."

"Looks that way." Niklaus started down the road in the direction of the plumes of smoke rising into the sky. "I guess we'll find out soon enough."

Steven and Niklaus followed the tracks into the edge of a small town that resembled a set from *Lonesome Dove*. The few homes and barns scattered around the periphery ramshackle at best, the main section of town appeared to be in reasonably good shape, some might even say quaint. The streets were quiet, and other than a trio of horses tied up outside the local saloon, the town seemed deserted. Only a smattering of boot prints in the snow revealed otherwise.

Steven peered up and down the town's main thoroughfare. "Where is everybody?"

"In case you forgot, it's cold out here." Niklaus wiped his runny nose on the sleeve of his coat. "I imagine they're cooped up for the winter. Either that, or Rod Serling beat us here."

The sound of hoofbeats heralded a lone rider entering town from the opposite direction. He hitched his horse in front of a building marked "General Store" and plodded through the snow in their direction. His brown Stetson pulled down tight about his ears, his pace was that of a man with a mission.

Steven stepped into the street and flagged the man down. "Here goes nothing."

"You talk funny, boy." The man in the coffee-colored Stetson stroked his full mustache and eyed Steven and Niklaus with suspicion. His breath fumed like white smoke in the frigid air. "Where you from?"

"Back east." Steven's voice trembled, only half from the cold. The windswept town square could have served as the backdrop for any of a dozen Westerns he and his dad watched when he was a boy, and Steven knew how heated discussions on such streets were usually resolved. "My friend here is from Warsaw. Only been in the States a few years." At the man's confused stare, he added, "You know, Poland?"

Niklaus glanced left and right at the buildings on either side. "Well, technically—"

"I know where Warsaw is." The man's eyes narrowed at Steven. "What? You think 'cause I'm not dressed up like some east coast dandy, I'm stupid?" His gloved fingers brushed the revolver at his hip. "Anyway, I wasn't talking to him, boy. I was talking to you."

Steven took a step back and raised his bare hands in mock surrender. "Sorry. Didn't mean to offend. We're just trying to find a place to get out of the cold."

"Hmph. Try Dottie's. Down on the corner." The man bumped Steven's shoulder as he swept past, his boots leaving two parallel dotted lines in the snow behind his long duster. "Hope you've got cash."

"That went well," Niklaus said when the man left earshot. "Good thing you didn't ask him the time. He might've parted your hair with his trusty six-shooter."

"No joke. If everyone here's as hair-trigger as Wyatt Earp there, we'll have to really watch what we say."

Niklaus crossed his arms and donned his best Tonto impersonation. "What do you mean 'we,' *kemo sabe?* He said he wasn't talking to me."

"Looks like somebody besides me has watched a few Westerns." Steven headed for the center of town. "Remind me to laugh when my brain is done defrosting."

Steven and Niklaus passed the general store and a small building that doubled as a smithy/barbershop before arriving beneath a hanging wooden sign that said in simple script, "Dottie's Inn." The door, fashioned of ornately carved oak, seemed out of place surrounded by the dilapidated wooden boards that made up the building's outer wall. Nine small squares of beveled glass formed a diamond at the door's center and reflected the white brilliance coming off the snow-covered road.

Steven rested his hand on the brass knob. "You think there's any chance this Dottie person will let us work for room and board like Matheson did?"

Niklaus let out a quiet chuckle. "Not unless Dottie has a daughter who ends up with a crush on one of us."

"You know, Nik, if you get any funnier—"

A pair of rough-looking men stormed out of the inn and nearly knocked Steven to the ground.

"We should do it the way the old man said," said the first, the jagged scar running down his cheek appearing ready to split open as he hawked a gob of brown spit into the snow. "He hasn't steered us wrong yet."

"And I say we do it my way." The second looked out from beneath long black locks wet with pomade, his pair of predator's eyes flicking from Niklaus to Steven. "Pardon."

Steven couldn't have been more surprised by the simple word of courtesy. "Pardon us, umm…gentlemen."

"Nice coat." Slick jeered as he headed up the street with his associate in tow.

"What's your problem, anyway?" Scarface asked as the pair came to the general store. Though they kept their voices low, the quiet of the snow made even the faintest whisper travel. "Don't you want the money?"

"Of course I do," Slick answered. "Just remember that it's…" The pair rounded the corner at the smithy and disappeared from sight, leaving the town's main street again silent.

"Boy." Niklaus let out a lone chuckle. "We fit in great here."

"No kidding." Steven glanced up and down the street, then eased the door to the inn open a crack. "Shall we?"

Steven had spent many a lazy Sunday afternoon with his dad watching anything from *The Lone Ranger* to *The Cisco Kid* to Sergio Leone's spaghetti Westerns to *Young Guns*. From the moment he and Niklaus set foot in the small town, his father had been an almost palpable presence. A remembrance of the old man's countless sarcastic words of wisdom on how to survive the average "Sunday shoot 'em up" brought a smile to Steven's face, though he wondered ruefully if any of the advice would apply now that he found himself in the middle of an episode of *Deadwood*.

Steven and Niklaus stepped into the inn's deserted foyer, shook the snow from their coats, and moved toward the lone cast iron wood stove at the room's center. Both slipped out of their wet footwear and held their hands above the stove's roiling heat till they could again feel their fingers. As Niklaus thawed, he launched into a rant about how every place they ended up was more like the Arctic Circle than the one before and how he had left Poland for one reason and one reason only.

Steven laughed, though his mind was elsewhere, drowning in a sea of questions: Was his father still alive? Was Audrey? The others? Was everything back home going straight to hell in their absence? And above all, who were they here to find?

This Game is supposed to be chess. Steven groaned. *Not hide and seek.*

The front desk of Dottie's Inn remained vacant for a good quarter hour as Steven and Niklaus warmed themselves by the foyer stove. Red wallpaper featuring golden roosters covered the walls while a trio of oil lamps and a couple of upholstered chairs rounded out the room's décor. Steven was flipping through the inn's ledger when a door behind the desk opened and a young man barely out of his teens stepped out. Dressed in a black and white striped shirt and vermilion vest complete with a gold-chained pocket watch, his rumpled clothes and mussed hair suggested he had just awakened from an afternoon nap.

"Can I help you gentlemen?" His nasal voice sported a north-eastern accent.

Steven rose and walked to the desk. "We need a room. Two beds, if possible."

The man eyed Steven. "We're pretty full right now, but I might be able to find some space." He glanced down at his empty palm. "For the right, shall we say, incentive?"

"You're only the fourth person we've seen since we hit town." Steven eyed the nearly full rack of keys behind the man. "How packed can this place be?"

"Just wait till this evening." The man's head tilted to one side. "You'll see." He leaned in and lowered his voice. "And where might you gentlemen hail from? Those coats don't have any cut I've seen before."

Niklaus took the question this time. "We're from back east. Just hit town today."

"But the stage doesn't arrive till tomorrow morning." The man at the desk furrowed his brow and stared at their soaked pants. "How did you two get here? Horseback?"

Steven stepped in. "Look, do you have a room or not? We've been stuck out in the elements for hours and would really like to change out of our wet clothes and get a bite to eat."

"Of course, of course." The man's lips turned up in a strange grin. "Two beds, I believe you said?"

"Two beds." Steven had a good idea what the man was insinuating. Once again, one thing seemed clear: fitting in wherever and whenever they'd landed promised to be quite a challenge.

"And how exactly will you two gentlemen be paying?" An obsequious lilt colored the man's words.

Before Steven could formulate an answer, a blast of cold froze his backside even as the creak of the door leading outside hit his ears. The pouch pulsed on Steven's hip, and Amaryllis pinched Steven's collarbone hard enough to draw blood.

"Don't worry about payment from these two, Levi."

Though months had passed since Steven had last heard those wheezy tones, he had no doubt as to their owner. He and Niklaus spun around to find Archie standing in the open doorway. Beneath a thick mane of hair that had returned to its initial grey, the old priest's eyes surveyed the two of them, his gnarled hand resting on the brass door handle.

Whatever youth the Game had temporarily afforded the man had apparently fled.

"But, Mr. Lacan." Levi bit his lip. "You said that—"

"I know what I said, son, but don't worry. These two are with me." Archie flashed Steven a knowing grin. "I've been expecting them for some time."

15

STARS & STRIPES

An amalgam of every watering hole from the dozens of Westerns he'd watched as a child, the Wolf's Bend Saloon left Steven with the surreal sensation that he was merely dreaming and that any moment he'd wake up in the twenty-first century.

Or at least the back room of a 1946 deli.

Beneath a framed painting of a herd of horses charging across an open plain stretched a bar fully stocked with an impressive variety of whiskey along with a smattering of wine and a few other libations from somewhere across the Atlantic. In the far corner, a barrel of beer rested below a mounted bison head with glass eyes that followed Steven no matter where he went.

Five small tables with chairs and half a dozen barstools made room for twenty or so, though only a few seats remained empty. A man at the back wearing a threadbare suit and a brown bowler banged away at an out-of-tune piano, the tickled ivories producing a pleasant melody that registered as familiar, though Steven couldn't quite place the tune.

All present took note of Steven and Niklaus: a cluster of top hat-wearing gentlemen of wealth; a man covered with so much soot he could only be the local blacksmith; a trio of, no doubt, ladies of the evening. Between being new in town and the fact that their clothes and haircuts wouldn't come into style for half a century, they were hard to miss.

Archie stepped between Steven and Niklaus and moved behind the bar, prompting a trio of cowpokes to raise their glasses in unison.

"About time you got back, Archie." This man, the largest of the three, finished the last vestiges of his beer and wiped his mouth on a checkered sleeve. "We were about to come hunting for you."

"Yeah." Another, this one guilty of the worst comb-over in history —literally, Steven considered—crinkled up his nose. "Not good for business to leave your customers thirsty, Arch."

"Patience, gentlemen. The evening has just begun." Archie rested his elbows on the bar's dark wood. "So, what'll it be?"

"The usual," said the third, his words followed by a peal of coughing. "And make mine a double."

"Some whiskey to warm your feet, then." Archie poured a glass for each of the men and brought his attention back to Steven and Niklaus. "You two. Join me at the other end of the bar."

Steven and Niklaus moved to the corner and grabbed a couple barstools below the mounted bison head. Archie arrived seconds later with another trio of whiskeys.

"So, you're bartending these days?" Steven raised an eyebrow. "Does that fly with your other chosen vocation?"

Archie shrugged, a quiet laugh escaping his lips. "Way I see it, job's not that different. People come in, break some bread, drink some alcohol, confess their sins." He leaned in conspiratorially. "If you must know, the bartender took ill just a few days after Emilio and I hit ground. The job pays for a room at Dottie's and keeps food in my belly." He shook his head and smiled. "And I wasn't always a priest, you know." Archie ran his fingers through his kinky grey hair. "In any case, what else would I do in this state? Most jobs around here aren't exactly designed for senior citizens."

"You mentioned Emilio." Steven kept his voice low. "Where is he? Is he all right?"

"Last I saw him, he was doing just fine. Went to work at a ranch just outside of town a couple months back. He drops by the saloon every few days to check in."

"A couple months?" Niklaus asked. "How long have you two been here?'

Archie considered for a moment. "Going on four months, by my reckoning."

Niklaus shot Steven a questioning glance. "That's about as long as we were stuck in the forties."

"Where are we exactly?" Steven peered around the room. "And when?"

"Wyoming, winter of 1890." Archie turned up his glass. "Wolf's Bend sits just west of the Nebraska border."

"1890." Steven stroked his chin. "And what have you been up to besides serving whiskey to the local gentry?"

"Not much else to do. An old black man and a Latino kid stuck in the middle of the old west and—surprise, surprise—nobody's beating down their door to offer a hand up." The corner of Archie's mouth curled into a half-smile. "Truth be told, I'm pleasantly surprised the two of us are still alive and kicking."

"You got a Wyoming winter, while we got a Florida hurricane." Niklaus laughed. "Not sure who drew the short straw there." His brow furrowed. "Another thing. Before, you told that kid Levi you've been expecting us."

"It's true. That's why I insisted to Emilio that we not leave this town."

"But how could you have known?" Steven's gaze shot to Niklaus and back to Archie. "You said all your visions dried up after you drew your icon from the pouch."

"And now, it would appear, it's me that's all dried up." Archie downed his whiskey and poured himself another shot. "Three nights after we arrived here in Wolf's Bend, I had another vision. Not quite as clear as the old days, but I had a feeling it was more than just a wishful dream."

"A vision." Steven crossed his arms. "And what did you see exactly?"

"Our little meeting here, the three of us sitting at this very bar drinking a round and catching up." He pointed to the window behind Steven's head. "Snow halfway up the glass. Everybody bound up against the cold." He let out a chortle. "I just prayed it was this winter and not some time further down the pike."

"And that's it?" Steven took a sip of his whiskey, the liquid burning its way through his chest and warming his belly. "No other tidbits you'd care to share?"

"That's the only memory that stands out. Everything else has been nothing but normal dreams, at least as I recall." Archie raised his glass and downed his second shot. "So, your turn, Steven. From what Niklaus has said, the two of you ended up in Florida in the forties. How did you come to be here?" He glanced at the dragonfly pendant hooked to Steven's coat. "Was it—"

"Amaryllis has indeed been helpful of late, but Grey's the one who saved our bacon."

"Grey?"

"1946 vintage. We sought him out some sixty years before he first came looking for me." Steven debated exactly how much to tell Archie. "We used his pouch from 1946 to come here."

"Hmm." Archie considered for a moment. "Wait. I heard the pouch's pulse before. You brought the *Hvitr Kyll* from 1946 with you? Won't that screw up everything?"

"It was Grey's idea." Niklaus' mouth quirked to one side as he let go an exhausted chuckle. "He seemed to think everything would work itself out."

"But, it is here, right?" Archie asked, his words relaying something akin to hunger.

Steven pulled open his coat to reveal the white leather bag hanging at his hip. "I have it, though for all practical purposes, its batteries are dead." He shook his head in frustration. "Unless, of course, you know the location of a nearby crossing."

"Unfortunately, no." Archie steepled his fingers before his chin, the zeal from his voice already extinguished. "The maps around here barely have state lines, much less the location of mystical power nexuses." He shot Niklaus a quizzical look. "You two managed to find a crossing in 1946?"

"In Florida." Niklaus shrugged. "Somehow, we stumbled upon a place that would allow us to come here to 1890. Once we got close to the spot, the pouch did the rest." He downed his whiskey and placed the glass on the bar. "The rest is, literally, history."

"I doubt you stumbled upon anything." Archie pulled in a deep breath. "Not too many coincidences where the Game is involved." He refilled all their glasses. "So, the pouch brought you here? To Wolf's Bend?"

Steven chuckled. "By way of a snowy ridge about two miles northeast."

"A ridge we probably should've marked a little more carefully," Niklaus muttered.

"Even if we had, there's no guarantee that spot has enough oomph to send us away from here." Steven sighed. "We asked the pouch to find our friends, not a revolving door."

"Amazing." Archie shook his head. "Trapped out of your time, and you still manage to find Grey, Emilio, and me without breaking a sweat." He smiled, the unsettling twinkle Steven often found in Archie's gaze notably absent. "It would seem yet again that the pouch has chosen its Pawn wisely."

"I wouldn't go that far." Steven downed another shot of whiskey. "You see—"

"Hey, barkeep." One of the quartet playing poker in the corner walked over and laid a bill on the bar. His blue uniform marked him as U.S. Cavalry and the stripes on his sleeve indicated he was enlisted. "Another round of whiskey for me and my boys."

"Will do, Sergeant."

As Archie busied himself pulling glasses and pouring drinks, Steven leaned close to Niklaus. "All right. Archie's here and Emilio's apparently less than a day's ride away."

"That still leaves the matter of how we're going to get the pouch to take us to wherever Zed sent Audrey and Lena."

Steven's shoulders slumped. "One problem at a time, Nik. One problem at a time."

Niklaus raised a brow. "Do we try to get back to Florida?"

"I doubt we could find the spot." Steven shook his head. "The only person who knows where the Coral Castle is supposed to be built someday is an ocean away in Latvia and, unless I miss my guess, barely out of diapers."

"Stonehenge, then?" Niklaus cracked his neck. "Grey '46 said that Britain's favorite ring of stones would probably do the trick."

"Not sure how the four of us are getting back to the east coast and across the Atlantic with no money, not to mention the weeks to months that would take."

Archie sidled over and rejoined the conversation. "So, 1946, huh?" His face darkened. "That was the year my sister Henrietta died. My mother was never the same after that. Even her brother, my uncle Joe, coming home from the war couldn't bring her around."

"What happened to your sister?" Niklaus asked.

"We never quite figured that out. Our house sat only a couple blocks from the edge of one of New Orleans' major swamps. One afternoon Henrietta was playing down by the bayou. When dinner time came around, my mother called for her a hundred times, but she didn't come." Archie's voice grew quiet. "I'm the one who found her. Face down in the muck, her braids floating in the muddy water." His head dropped. "I can still see it like it was yesterday."

"God, I'm sorry." Steven clasped the old man's shoulder. "Didn't mean to drag up bad memories."

"Some wounds just don't heal, Steven." Archie's gaze grew hard and cold. "I think you'd agree with that sentiment, would you not?"

The hair on Steven's neck rose at the not-so-cryptic question, the dread coursing through him doubled by a lone flutter of Amaryllis' wings. Before he could respond, though, Niklaus offered his own opinion.

"The past is the past." Niklaus poured another round of whiskey. "What say we focus on the present? Maybe compare notes and start working on a way to get all of us out of here."

Over the next hour, Archie kept the saloon's clientele fed and watered with a bit of help from Steven and Niklaus, the trio trading stories of their months apart in between. Beyond tales of a truly wild west interspersed with a bit of local gossip, Archie had little to add. Steven and Niklaus, on the other hand, detailed for the priest their entire four months from beginning to end, hoping that in doing so, they'd find some clue as to what their next step should be. As they came to the end of their story, one detail in particular hit Archie like a ton of bricks.

"A castle?" he asked. "Made of coral?" His eyes slid shut. "Why does that sound so—"

"Barkeep!" The sergeant from before jammed his empty glass down on his table's scratched surface. "Another round for me and my boys here." His words slurred, he nearly fell out of his chair as he glanced across his shoulder at their end of the bar. "And make it quick."

Archie's mouth turned down in a practiced frown. "It appears you gentlemen have already had more than enough this evening."

The sergeant rose from his chair and walked to the bar. "Listen, old man. You come across pretty smart for a negro, but not smart enough to know when to shut your damn mouth. Now, pour another round for me and my boys or things might get ugly. Understand?"

"Perfectly." Archie lowered his eyes. "Another round of whiskey, then."

Steven stepped between them. "Excuse me, Sergeant, but we're talking here."

"Steven," Archie said. "Don't."

Steven searched Archie's eyes and found a look of defeat he'd never seen there before. "But Archie, he—"

"It's all right," Archie said. "I have the situation well in hand."

"You heard the man." The sergeant stroked his three-day stubble. "Maybe you and your friend should stay out of business that doesn't concern you."

Steven bristled. "I'm not sure who you think you are, but when a drunkard goes threatening a defenseless man well into his seventies, that definitely concerns me."

"You're asking for a beating, son." The sergeant cracked his knuckles. "And I'm more than happy to oblige."

Niklaus stepped between them. "Calm down. Both of you. This isn't—"

The sergeant swung at Niklaus' chin. Niklaus ducked to one side, just avoiding the wild haymaker, and landed an uppercut of his own, sending his attacker airborne. Cards and cash flew in every direction as the sergeant landed atop their gambling table, bringing the other three cavalry soldiers to their feet. This left Steven in the middle of a scene he'd enjoyed in a hundred different movies over the years: the barroom brawl.

Though he had to admit bar fights weren't nearly as much fun when the drunken brawlers were trained soldiers and the person they were swinging on was you.

Steven grabbed a barstool and brandished it before him like an amateur lion tamer as the two soldiers closest to him charged. The third helped the dazed sergeant up from the floor, and the two of them moved on Niklaus. Steven and Niklaus, in turn, pulled together, the bar to their rear, and waited for the circling jackals to pounce.

This is going to hurt, Steven thought. *A lot.*

Two clicks echoed in the space, and the business end of a double-barreled shotgun emerged from between Steven and Niklaus like a lethal flower blooming in stop motion.

"Now," came Archie's trembling voice, "why don't all of you gentlemen settle down. This may not be my place, but I'll not let you tear it apart."

"And what are you going to do about it, old man?" The sergeant took a step forward, his hands held before him in cautious surrender. "Shoot a United States Cavalryman right here in front of God and everybody?"

The door to the saloon slammed open and the resulting blast of cold air hit all involved like a bucket of ice water.

"He won't have to do anything." The unfamiliar baritone voice heralded the twin thuds of heavy boots on wood.

Steven glanced in the direction of the frigid blast of air and found two men standing in the saloon's open doorway. The first nearly as tall as Niklaus, his sharp blue eyes stared out from beneath a burgundy Stetson. A full salt-and-pepper beard of whiskers hid his face while his full-length duster almost concealed the shotgun at his side. The other, a stocky black man in his thirties, rested a hand on the six-shooter at his side, a silver five-point star girded within a circle of brass pinned to his vest.

"Everything all right in here, Mr. Lacan?" The darker-skinned man's accent hit Steven's ears as odd, reminding him of a college friend that hailed from Ghana with perhaps a touch of the Caribbean thrown into the mix.

"Right as rain, Deputy." Archie laid his shotgun on the bar. "Just working to clear up a little misunderstanding, isn't that right, gentlemen?"

The four soldiers, along with Steven and Niklaus, mumbled their agreement.

The man in the duster released the hammers on his shotgun and brought it across his shoulder. "That's funny. Looked to me like yet another brawl brewing in my favorite drinking establishment."

"Fear not, Sheriff. I have this under control." Archie brought out two fistfuls of glasses. "How about a round for everyone?"

"I sincerely doubt more whiskey is the solution to this problem." The sheriff stepped up to the sergeant and stared down at the shorter man's balding head. "Sergeant Percy. Do you remember what I told you two nights ago?"

The sergeant remained silent.

"While you and your men are in my town, I expect you to maintain a certain level of decorum."

"Yes, Sheriff."

"And if you and your men can't keep a rein on your behavior, I may have to insist you stay out in the pasture with the rest of your unit." His steely blue eyes narrowed beneath the rim of his Stetson. "I understand those tents aren't too warm this time of year."

"You understand right."

"This is the last time we'll be having this discussion, isn't that correct, Sergeant Percy?"

Percy shot Steven a glance filled with no small amount of ire. "Yes, Sheriff."

"Good. Now, why don't you and your men get back to your game while I introduce myself to these newcomers?" Percy and one of his men righted their table while the other two silently picked up the scattered cards and coins from the floor.

The sheriff offered Steven his hand. "I'm Tom Post. Sheriff around these parts."

"Steven Bauer." Steven did his best not to wince at the man's firm handshake.

"Niklaus Zamek." Niklaus fared a bit better with the sheriff's grip. "Pleasure."

"You two are new in town." Post studied them with a jeweler's eye. "What's your business here in Wolf's Bend?"

"Your bartender, actually." Steven inclined his head in Archie's direction. "We know the illustrious Mr. Lacan from back east."

"We're headed to California," Niklaus added, "but had to go the long way around to deliver a message to Archie here."

Post eyed them both with a hint of suspicion. "Is that right, Archie?"

"Indeed, it is." Archie's lips turned up in a half grin. "It seems a lifetime has passed since I last laid eyes on this pair."

Post grabbed a stool and sat down at the bar. "And how exactly do you know these gentlemen?"

Archie pulled a beer and set it down in front of the sheriff. "Now that's a long story."

"Good thing I like long stories." Post took a sip from his beer and glanced across his shoulder at his deputy. "Might as well pull up a stool, John. Temperature's starting to drop outside. I don't imagine too many people will be out after another half hour or so."

"I suppose I could kick up my boots for a few." The deputy took the stool to Post's left. "Afternoon, Archie."

"John." Archie pulled another beer and slid it across the bar. "Compliments."

"Thanks." The deputy gulped down a third of his glass and shot a sidelong glance at the disgruntled sergeant and his compatriots. "Those bluecoats giving you trouble?"

"No more than any other day." Archie glanced at the table full of U.S. Cavalry. "You know, they're no different from the horses they ride. Pen them up too long and they get restless."

The deputy shook his head. "You're more forgiving than most."

"In a previous life, forgiveness was just part of the job." Archie's mouth turned up in a rueful grin. "Old habits die hard, I guess."

Steven extended a hand to the deputy. "Hello, John. I'm Steven Bauer."

"John Ndure." Unlike the sheriff, Ndure didn't seem intent on breaking Steven's fingers. "I haven't seen you two around. When did you get into town?"

"They came in on yesterday's stagecoach," Archie interrupted. "I put them up last night until they could get a room of their own."

"Is that right?" Post peered down his nose at Archie and then returned his attention to Steven and Niklaus, the dubious cast to his gaze unchanged. "And how long can we expect to have you two around?"

"No more than a couple of days, I hope." Though on the surface, the conversation seemed friendly enough, Steven recognized the line of questioning for what it was: an interrogation. "Like Nik said, we have business out west that demands our attention."

Ndure reached out a hand and rubbed the wool lapel of Steven's coat between his fingers. "Where exactly did you and your friend come upon such fine coats? They look military, but they're of no issue I've ever seen, and plenty of soldiers pass this way."

Steven swallowed. "They're the latest style back in Virginia."

Ndure laughed. "They should serve you well, but if you're going to spend any time in Wolf's Bend, you're going to want to get some proper boots."

Steven glanced down at his waterlogged shoes and smiled. "Without a doubt."

"Shouldn't be too much of a problem, John." Post regarded Steven and Niklaus with a look devoid of so much as an ounce of friendliness. "Like Mr. Bauer said, they're going to be leaving in a couple days." He leaned in. "Isn't that right, boys?"

16

BLOOD & GUTS

"And I thought the back room of Mr. Matheson's deli was cramped." Niklaus' feet extended well past the end of the narrow mattress. "And who did they build these beds for, anyway? Hobbits?"

"At least it's warm." Steven peered out the tiny window by his head. "We could be out in the snow."

"True." Niklaus tossed a threadbare blanket across his naked feet and rolled onto his side. "So, what do we do now?"

"We track down Emilio as quick as we can, make sure nothing happens to Archie, and try not to get ourselves killed in the process. Beyond that, I just don't know."

"Sounds like a plan." Niklaus chuckled. "And hey, at least we made a good impression on local law enforcement."

Steven held back a laugh. "Right."

Their cordial inquisition at the saloon had gone on for another half hour. With Archie's subtle guidance, Steven and Niklaus had managed to avoid most of the more difficult questions about their sudden appearance in Wolf's Bend, though Steven had no doubt their every move would be scrutinized as long as they were in town. Post and Ndure's well-rehearsed "good cop, bad cop" routine was well ahead of its time, the careful back-and-forth coming across as if lifted from a prime time detective drama. In the end, Steven's earnestness and Niklaus' humor had won the pair over—at least a bit—but that didn't change the fact that neither of the two lawmen believed their story in the slightest.

And Steven didn't blame them.

"You think Post ever cracks a smile?" Niklaus asked.

"I'm guessing not. Especially when it comes to strangers who are clearly holding things back." Steven peeled the damp wool socks from his feet and slid between the sheets of an even smaller bed than Niklaus'. "I can't imagine trying to be the face of law and order in a world where every man walking down the street has a six-shooter at his hip."

"Not all that different from your America, Steven." Niklaus rolled over and picked up the candle from the stool that served as their shared nightstand. "At least here, you know everyone's packing heat." He blew out the candle, sending the room into a twilight state. "Back home, you never know who might be—"

A loud crack echoed from the hall, followed closely by another. Though muffled by the heavy oak of the door, the sound was unmistakable.

"What the hell?" Steven sat up straightaway and hit his head on the darkened gas lamp above his headboard. "Were those gunshots?"

"Sure sounded like it." Niklaus grabbed his clothes from the stool by his bed and headed for the door.

"What are you doing?" Steven peered at his friend through the dim light filtering in from the room's tiny window. "I thought we were trying *not* to get ourselves killed."

"I'm going to find out what the hell is happening." Niklaus slid into his faded jeans and buttoned up his shirt. "Though if I end up dead in 1890, I'll be wearing something besides a pair of long johns."

"All right." Steven rose and forced himself back into his still-damp clothes. "But you're not going out there alone."

Once dressed, Steven went to the door and peered out with Niklaus close behind. Two other doors across the way slammed shut as he poked his head out into the near darkness.

"No one out here." He stepped out into the hallway. "What do you think, Nik?"

"The gunshots sounded a little farther off." Niklaus pulled the door closed behind them and turned the key in the lock. "Maybe down by the desk?"

Together, they crept toward the stairs, Steven scanning the poorly lit hallway before them and Niklaus keeping an eye out for anyone behind. The spiral staircase at the front of the inn led back to the front desk where the young man named Levi had checked them in earlier that afternoon. Dark save for a single flickering lamp by the door leading outside and the dim glow coming from the stove in the front foyer, the desk remained conspicuously empty.

A groan from behind the large upholstered chair in the corner raised the hairs on Steven's neck. Despite his better judgment, he rushed toward the sound and discovered a man crumpled on the floor clutching his belly. The blood pumping between his fingers appeared black in the low light of the room, almost as dark as the man's familiar eyes.

"It's the man from the street." Niklaus knelt by the man's side, grabbed an old shawl from the back of the chair, and applied pressure to the man's belly. "He doesn't look good."

"No, he doesn't." Steven stepped around the growing pool of blood and dropped to one knee by the man's shoulder. Cradling his head in his hands, he stared into the panicked eyes of a man who knew he stood at death's door.

"Who did this to you?" Steven asked.

The man opened his mouth to speak, but all that came out was a string of blood-tinged coughs.

"This is bad, Steven." Niklaus grunted as he put his full weight into the task at hand. "I'm trying to hold back the bleeding, but I don't think I'm doing much good at all."

"Just keep holding pressure. Maybe there's a doctor in town who can—"

The man grabbed Steven by the front of his shirt and pulled him down to his face until their noses were nearly touching.

"*He—*"

The man's words cut off by another series of coughs, the last resolved into a gurgling sound that sent a shiver up Steven's spine. Memories of Katherine's last moments rushed through his mind, the awful rattle of blood filling her lungs a sound he'd never forgotten. He fought back the bile rising in his throat and brought his attention back to the matter at hand.

"He?" Steven asked. "Who?"

The man raised a crimson-soaked finger and pointed to the door leading to the street. "There." His arm fell to the floor and his eyes slid shut.

"Stay with him, Niklaus. I'll go for help." Steven rested the man's head on a cushion from the chair and moved for the door. "Maybe the sheriff can—"

The front door of the inn creaked open. There, silhouetted in the pale moonlight stood Sheriff Post, his shotgun leveled at Steven's midsection.

"Hold it right there, Bauer. Put your hands where I can see them."

"Sheriff Post. Thank God. Someone's been—"

"I said hands where I can see them." Post pulled back both hammers and raised the barrel of the shotgun level with Steven's chest. "I heard gunshots, and even in this light, I can see you're covered in blood."

"Wait." Steven put his hands in the air. "You don't understand. We found this man in the lobby. He's been shot."

Post lowered the shotgun all of an inch. "Show me."

Keeping his hands up, Steven motioned Post toward the corner of the lobby where Niklaus still held pressure on the dying man's midsection.

"We heard gunshots and came down to see what was going on." Steven lowered his hands and knelt with Niklaus by the man's side. "We found him like this."

"He was alone?" Post asked.

"By the time we got here." Steven shook his head. "We didn't see anyone else."

"Levi!" Never taking his eyes off Steven or Niklaus, Post lit a couple of lamps, stepped behind the desk, and rapped three times at the door there. "Get your chicken-shit ass out here."

A few seconds passed before the door opened a crack and the front desk clerk peered out.

"Sheriff Post?" came Levi's hesitant whisper. "Is everything all right?"

"Levi, are you aware there's a man bleeding to death in your front lobby not fifteen feet from where you sleep?"

"Bleeding to death?" Levi stepped out into the dim room, his eyes shooting to the corner where Niklaus hunched over the man's still form. "My God."

Post shook his head in disgust. "Looks like you didn't hear anything, which is funny since two of your patrons have already made it all the way from their beds to help the poor soul."

Levi's face went pale. "I…I must have slept through it all."

"Must have." Post studied Levi's attire, the exact same clothes he'd been wearing hours before. "In any case, why don't you make yourself useful and go track down Doc Jensen? It's a little late for house calls, but tell him I said it's important."

"Yes, sir." Levi ran from the inn, leaving Post alone with Steven and Niklaus.

"So." Post whipped the large chair around and sat his massive frame down. "Looks like you two boys are the only ones brave or stupid enough to come out of your room this fine evening." He chuckled under his breath. "Around here, you hear gunshots in the night, you stay put, lock the door, and hope whoever pulled the trigger doesn't come for you next."

"I'm getting that." Steven watched helplessly as the man grew paler by the minute. "You know, we actually ran into this man earlier today. He was the first person we met when we hit town."

"Funny." Post adjusted his hat. "Could've sworn Archie said you two pulled into town on yesterday's stagecoach."

"That's what Steven meant." Niklaus looked up from the wadded-up shawl gripped in his fists, the woven cloth saturated with the warm crimson oozing from the man's belly. "Today's been a long day, but we ran into him on the street yesterday."

Steven nodded. "He's the one who recommended we put up here for the night."

Niklaus shuddered. "Not sure he'd say the same tomorrow."

"I suppose not." Post's attention shifted to the floor beneath a table centered on the far wall. "And what do we have here?" He rose from the chair and sauntered over to the table, kneeling by the wall to keep Steven and Niklaus in his line of sight. With a blind swipe, he fished a revolver up from the floor and held it before his face. A puff of smoke wafted from the barrel. "Hm. Still warm."

Steven's guts tied themselves in knots beneath Post's suspicious stare. "Whoever did this must have dropped the gun there."

"Exactly what I was thinking. Unless…" Post stooped by the man opposite Niklaus and pulled open his coat. Each of his pair of holsters held a gun. "Nope. Didn't belong to this poor soul." He met Steven's gaze and raised a questioning eyebrow. "And where's your gun, Bauer?"

Steven's already knotted insides started performing full on somersaults. "Upstairs in the room." One lie led to the next. "Didn't strap it on before we came down."

"Is that right?" Post studied them both. "And you, Zamek?"

"Same." Niklaus shot Steven a harried glance. "Not too smart, I guess."

"Not smart at all." Post leaned forward and rested a finger at the man's neck, his other hand firmly gripping the stock of his shotgun. "Well, damn. Levi's going to wake up Doc Jensen for nothing."

"Sheriff Post." Steven raised his hands before his chest in surrender. "You have to believe me. Niklaus and I had nothing to do with this."

"I want to believe you, boys. I do." Post rose to his feet and rested the shotgun across his shoulder. "But first, you show up out of nowhere in my town with stories that don't add up. Then, less than twelve hours later, a man winds up dead at the place where you're staying, and the only people with blood on their hands are standing right in front of me." Post's eyes dropped to the dead man's waist. "Why don't one of you check this man's pockets? See if there's any clue as to who he might be."

Steven's brow furrowed. "You don't know him?"

"Haven't seen him around here before," Post mumbled, "though I know his type."

Niklaus produced a leather wallet with a folded-up piece of paper wedged inside.

"And there we have it." Post held out his hand. "Let me see that, Mr. Zamek, and let's shed some light on whatever malfeasance may have led to this man's untimely demise."

After a brief pause, Niklaus complied.

Post opened the wallet and pulled out the folded paper, his brow furrowing. "Hm. Just a photograph." He turned the grainy picture around so Steven and Niklaus could see it. "Anyone you boys know?"

"No, sir." Steven struggled to keep the shock from his face. "Can't say I've seen this man before."

"Same." Niklaus shook his head. "Never seen him before in my life."

Steven had played enough cards with Niklaus to recognize the man's poker face. He prayed Post didn't see right through their shared lie, as both of them knew good and well the identity of the man in the photograph.

Zed. The Black King. The architect of their banishment to the past and far closer than either of them had imagined.

"Hm." Steven kept his eyes focused on the dark gaze peering out of the photograph. "I'm guessing that whoever this poor soul is—or, I suppose, *was*—came to town looking for the man in the picture." He met Post's gaze. "Anything else in that wallet that might shed some light on who either of them might be?"

Post opened a flap in the folded leather and his eyes grew wide with not-quite-surprise.

"Well, boys, we may not know our dearly departed here's name, but one thing is certain." Post held up the open wallet to reveal a five-point star surrounded by a rippled shield pinned inside, the words "U.S. Marshal" etched into the metal. "Someone is going to be missing him."

"This is serious." Niklaus wiped a fine sheen of sweat from his brow. "Isn't it?"

Post studied Niklaus for a moment through his bushy eyebrows before returning his attention to Steven. "I know you two were hoping to move on in the next day or two, but I'd suggest rethinking those plans until this matter is settled. Leaving town right now might be looked upon...unfavorably."

17

TRACKS & TIMETABLES

"Y ou've got to admit," Archie slid a beer across the bar, "people sure have a way of ending up dead when you're around."

"Don't remind me." Steven took a swig from the glass. "And not just anyone, this time, but a federal marshal."

"Just another part of the Game, right?" Niklaus leaned against the bar and nodded to a table of ladies of the evening holed up in the corner. "I mean, if we could just show up, pick up Archie and Emilio, and head on to the next bus stop, we wouldn't know what to do with ourselves."

Steven shook his head. "You think ending up in the Wild West is part of Grey's Game?"

"There may be more to what Niklaus is saying than any of us understand." Archie's gaze flicked to the door and then back to Steven. "You two landed in 1945 and, against all odds, managed to track down Grey with the help of two individuals you won't even meet for another six decades. In doing so, you brought together those same two people, ensuring they'll be there sixty years in the future when it will be their turn to help you."

"Maybe." Steven hated to admit it, but the priest had a point.

"Now," Archie continued, "the four of us find ourselves in a tiny

Wyoming town none of us have ever heard of over a century before any of us ever met and a dead man is carrying a picture of the man who sent us here." Archie raised a finger as one of Steven's favorite college professors had always done when making a point. "Never forget that the visions that haunted me for months before we met have left me privy to the details of every iteration of the Game to date. The one thing each had in common? In the end, very little was left to chance."

Niklaus let out a quiet belch. "Still, I'm not sure why the Game would send all of us careening through time. From a strategic stand-point, it's the right move for Zed to make. If the opposing side never arrives, victory becomes theirs before the first Piece is even moved. From the Game's perspective, however, it's all wrong."

"Again, we're talking about the Game like it's a person." Steven groaned. "It's a construct, a set of rules, an obstacle to overcome."

"With Arbiters that may have personally saved our asses at least once or twice." Archie smiled. "From what I understand from the visions and what I learned subsequently from Grey, the Game must be played at the right time and place with both sides present or the great catastrophes of the past will begin anew."

"Hm. Maybe *that's* what Zed wants." Steven took another drink. "What's the saying? Some people just want to watch the world burn?"

"You keep bringing it back to Zed, but I'm not talking about his actions, or even Grey's." Archie cleared his throat. "I'm talking about the Game itself."

"Assuming the Game wants anything, or even *can* want anything," Steven raised an eyebrow, "you're suggesting it wants us to be here?"

"Look at everything that's happened to this point. Alone and unarmed, you survived your first encounter with the Black Queen."

Steven scoffed. "Don't forget about Grey saving my ass. Another few seconds, and I would've been Bauer flambé."

Archie continued as if he hadn't heard Steven. "Then, you rescued each of us from the circumstances of our own lives despite the constant interference of the Black."

"Interference." Niklaus absently raised his hand to his chest and rubbed the spot where months before he'd been skewered by the Black Pawn's arrows. "That's what we're calling it."

"When Lena was injured, the pouch could've taken you to any hospital in the world, but it brought her to me." Archie ran his hand along the bar's wooden surface. "The way I see it, Steven, it's exactly what Grey said. The Game wants to be played, plain and simple."

"So, nothing I do matters?"

"The opposite, actually." Archie smiled. "The Game may present opportunity…"

"But it's still up to us to run the gauntlet." Steven sighed. "That's just great."

"As I see it, there are no guarantees, as any of us could fall along the way. Still, just as Grey and Zed designed, for those of us who are mere Pieces, all roads lead to the Game."

"It's like I told you back in Manhattan," Niklaus said. "We weren't in New York a day before you ran into Ruth." He rested a hand on Steven's shoulder. "Archie's on point."

"That the Game itself has an agenda that involves us jumping through hoop after hoop to get back to our own century just in time to go up against a mob of super-powered assassins who plan to do their level best to end us?" Steven downed the remnants of his beer in three gulps. "Excuse me if I'm not jumping for joy."

"I'm sorry, Steven." Niklaus raised his hands in mock surrender. "Just trying to make sense of everything that's happening."

"Good luck with that." A blast of cold from the open door accompanied the familiar voice. "Archie and I have been working through this stuff for weeks and haven't been able to make heads or tails of any of it."

"Emilio?" Steven turned to find the White Knight framed by the saloon door, his torso wrapped in a woven poncho. An inch or two taller than Steven remembered—in part from the pair of scuffed boots that now covered his feet—he now sported a beard, his voice had dropped half an octave, and he stood tall with pride and confidence.

The boy Steven had met months before on the streets of Baltimore appeared well on his way to becoming a man.

"Emilio Cruz." Niklaus stood and extended a hand. "Get your ass over here."

His youthful exuberance tempered with a newfound maturity, Emilio strode over to Niklaus and gave the man a firm handshake that quickly shifted into a hug.

"You found us." Moisture brimmed at the corners of Emilio's eyes. "I can't believe you found us."

"Hey." Niklaus held Emilio at arm's length and shot him a mischievous wink. "You still owe me ten bucks from that last trip to Whataburger."

"I'll get right on that." Emilio's gaze cut to Steven, his brow furrowed. "What took you two so long?"

"Sorry," Steven said. "We caught all the red lights."

"Right." A hint of a smile peeked through Emilio's practiced frown. "And I'm the one who should be sorry." He clasped Steven's hand. "Thanks for coming for us."

"What else would we do?" Steven kept his voice low. "And you may want to hold your thanks till we're back in the correct century."

"Point taken."

"So." Niklaus tagged Emilio with a light punch to the shoulder. "Where'd all these muscles come from? You been working out with the cowhands down at the ranch?"

"Mr. Garringer keeps us all pretty busy and feeds us well. Between moving the cattle from pasture to pasture, keeping them fed and watered, catching any strays, cutting firewood every morning, and a hundred other things, there's not much down time. Hell, they've even let me birth a couple of calves this month." His face broke into a full-on smile. "Back home, I'd probably be Employee of the Month. Maybe even have my picture on the wall." Just as quickly as they'd broken, the clouds returned to his features. "Where's Lena?"

Steven shook his head. "I wish I knew. For a while, it's just been me and Nik. Now we've found you two."

Emilio raised an eyebrow. "Why did Zed zap us all to 1890 anyway?"

"If only it were that easy." Niklaus shook his head and laughed. "Steven and I have already spent half a year in the mid-1940s. Caught the tail end of World War II and nearly got taken out by a hurricane. Good times."

"The 1940s, eh?" Emilio shot Archie a quizzical look. "You've known they were coming all along, haven't you?"

Archie handed him a beer. "Didn't want to get your hopes up, kid."

Emilio turned back to Steven. "How'd you find us? Hell, how'd you get here?"

Steven eyed Niklaus. "You want to handle explanations this round?"

❀

As mid-afternoon stretched into evening, the saloon remained surprisingly empty with only the occasional cowhand dropping by for a quick drink before heading back out into the cold. The four men from another century took advantage of the long afternoon together, catching up on the various turns their lives had taken since being sent careening through time and space at the whim of the Black King.

Unlike Steven and Niklaus, Emilio's time in the past had been, for the most part, uneventful. Hired by a local cattle baron named Cyrus Garringer for his "strong back" and "phenomenal riding skills," he'd spent most of his time the preceding months working on the ranch and getting into the best shape of his life. The pay had been more than enough to keep him fed, clothed, and sheltered, and though he'd come into town every week or two to keep tabs on Archie, Garringer's ranch had become, for the time being, home.

When Emilio had finished, Steven and Niklaus took turns catching both him and Archie up on the events of their forced tour of the mid-1940s—the hurricane in Florida, their subsequent journey to New York City, "meeting" Ruth and Arthur for a second time, their reunion with Grey, the borrowing of the pouch, and their fortunate discovery of Ed Leedskalnin's Coral Castle. Above all, the discussion revolved around trying to parse the circumstances and forces that allowed Steven and Niklaus to travel across time and space to a tiny town at the corner of Wyoming decades before any of them were born.

At the end of Steven's tale, Emilio rubbed at his eyes as if waking from a bad dream. "And despite all of that, we still have no idea how to find Lena and Audrey or even the first clue how to get us back to where and when we came from."

"That about sums it up." Steven let out a long sigh. "I'm just as worried about them as you are, Emilio. Trust me. Unfortunately, till we figure out how to get the pouch to do its thing again and get us all out of here, Lena and Audrey's location is kind of a moot point."

"Dammit, Steven." Emilio slammed his fist down on the bar in a flash of anger more reminiscent of the young hothead Steven remembered. "You knew going to New York was a bad idea. I even agreed with you for once. Niklaus too. Why didn't you stick to your guns, man? We wouldn't be in this stupid mess."

"In case you've forgotten, the deciding vote wasn't his." Archie wiped down the bar with a damp rag, avoiding eye contact with Emilio. "We've already discussed this a hundred times, Emilio, as you well know."

Emilio's eyes drew down into slits. "You really want me to blame you for all of this, Archie?"

"I don't want you to blame anyone." Archie steepled his fingers before his nose and allowed his eyes to slide shut. "As hard as it may be for you to believe, *this* is what's supposed to be happening. Look at Steven and Niklaus' experience in the forties and the domino effect of their presence there. If not for their intervention, Ruth and Arthur Pedone might never have met, and therefore, wouldn't have been available to provide him shelter in our time. In fact, if Steven and Niklaus hadn't run into Grey some sixty years before Steven met him the first time, it's possible our mysterious mentor might not have had the first clue to seek out Steven in time, leaving him and the rest of us most likely dead at the hands of the Black." Archie opened his eyes and fixed Emilio with a dour stare. "I have no idea why the four of us currently find ourselves stranded at this particular juncture, but I believe if we remain patient that all will be made clear in due time."

"Patient?" Emilio finished off his beer and rested the glass back on the bar with a solid thunk. "You want me—us—to be patient while

Lena and Audrey are wherever or whenever they are facing God knows what?"

Archie slid into a smile Steven guessed hundreds of parishioners had likely seen over the decades of the priest's career. "What other choice do we have?"

"We found our way here." Niklaus puffed up his chest. "We'll find a way out."

"A way out, you say?" Sheriff Post strode in from the street with his deputy, John Ndure, close behind. Post shook the snow from his boots as Ndure shut the door firmly behind them. "I certainly hope the only two witnesses to the murder of a United States federal marshal aren't making plans to leave town."

"We're not going anywhere." Steven's eyes dropped. "Trust us."

"Understatement of the year," Niklaus muttered.

"What was that?" Post motioned for Archie to pull him a beer. "You certainly seem to like your jokes, Mr. Zamek. I hope that one wasn't at my expense."

Ndure pulled up beside Post. "I think he's just agreeing with that silly rhyme you always say. You've got to admit, 'Wolf's Bend is a dead end' has never been truer than the last few weeks. Though with the *train* arriving tomorrow—"

"Thank you for that, John." Post glared at Ndure, his eyes filled with vexation. "Thank you *so* much."

"What train? And why would there be a federal marshal in your town anyway?" Steven scrambled to come up with any hook in the conversation that might get the heat off him and Niklaus. "Is there something going on in Wolf's Bend we don't know about?"

"Just business as usual, Mr. Bauer." Post shot Ndure another withering gaze. "And about the marshal, I'm afraid I don't have the first idea. This may come as a surprise, but the United States government doesn't confer with me on such matters."

Steven studied Post. "And neither of you had ever met the man?"

"I'd seen him." Ndure furrowed his brow. "Just once. He perched at that table in the corner yesterday morning like a hawk inspecting the ground below for an errant squirrel. Looked like someone who might bear watching, though I clearly had him pegged all wrong."

"All wrong?" Niklaus asked.

"Strangers keeping to themselves in this establishment usually fall on the other end of the law." Ndure's gaze swept across Steven and Niklaus. "No offense intended."

"And you, Sheriff?" Steven asked.

Post shook his head and laughed. "Like I told you, Mr. Bauer, the first time I ever saw that man, you two were standing over his dead body."

"I'm curious." Steven managed to keep most of the fire from his tone. "Have you sent a telegraph back east to let the feds know about their guy?"

"The feds?" Post narrowed his gaze. "You know, Bauer, you sure ask a hell of a lot of questions for someone who just arrived in town."

"Just making conversation." Steven took a slug of his beer. "Figured the old adage about bad news not getting better with age would apply here."

With a harrumph, Post answered, "If you must know, I'm drafting the letter today."

"So it can go out on...tomorrow's train?" Emilio, silent for most of the conversation, asked this question a bit too quickly.

Post straightened his posture and fixed the boy with an accusatory stare. "And what is it you think you know about tomorrow's train, Mr. Cruz?"

"Trains come through every Wednesday." Emilio shrugged. "Today's Tuesday." He glanced down at the pocket watch dancing between his nimble fingers. "Not much else to talk about out on the ranch, Sheriff."

"All right. Seems there's more to this train arriving tomorrow than anyone is letting on." Steven's gaze danced between Post and Ndure. "Something we should know?"

"Nothing for any of you to concern yourselves with, Mr. Bauer." Post studied them all carefully. "Tomorrow is just another day."

"And the train?" Steven asked.

A flurry of hoofbeats from outside pulled Post's attention.

"C'mon, John," he ordered as he rose and headed for the street. "Let's go."

Once the sheriff and his deputy were long gone, Archie pulled Steven, Niklaus, and Emilio close, his voice dropping to a low whisper. "Post and Ndure are trying to keep everything quiet, but the murmuring around town is that tomorrow's train is carrying something special. Nobody knows exactly what this mysterious cargo might be, but there's a lot of conjecture." He cast a quick gaze around the saloon. "Whatever it is, though, they've moved up all the timetables and are rushing this particular train east."

"Wait." Emilio's eyebrows rose in anticipation. "Wasn't the California gold rush sometime in the 1800s? Could that be it? A carful of gold?"

"About forty years too late for that." Steven lowered his voice as the door to the saloon opened again allowing in a blast of frigid air as a collection of cowpokes filed in. "What could it be that's so important they're moving up all the stops?"

"Who knows?" Archie motioned the half dozen men entering toward a table at the back, among them the scar-faced man and his pomade-sporting associate from Steven and Niklaus' first moments along Wolf's Bend's main drag. "What I do know is that tomorrow seems like it's going to be one interesting day."

And look at us. Steven's fingernails dug into his palms. *Right on time.*

18

SONG & DANCE

"Do not mock the Ghost Dance." The Arapaho youth, his unwavering gaze electric with pride and unfaltering belief, leaned against the rail outside the general store and ran a shaking hand down the front of his shirt. Long-sleeved and fashioned of blue fabric, the ornate garment was decorated with dozens of stars and a quartet of birds the color of midnight. Green fringe hung from its sleeves and lower hem, the same color as the turtle embroidered above the man's belt buckle. "The sacred cloth protects us."

"Protects you?" Emilio asked. "From what?" His breath steamed in the morning chill. "That shirt's so thin, it's not even protecting you from the cold."

"Emilio." Steven shook his head almost imperceptibly. "This is neither the time nor the place."

The young man, barely out of his teens, narrowed his eyes at Emilio. "Do not dismiss the teachings of Wovoka." He raised his hands above his head with palms held outward, his face taking on the enraptured glow a young Steven had seen one too many times at his aunt's fundamentalist church. "When the earth shakes and the clouds fall and the sun goes dark in the sky, it is the invader who will finally face the truth."

"And by *invader*," Archie gestured to himself, Steven, and Emilio, "I'm guessing you mean us."

The youth turned to Steven. "Your people came and took everything, pushing the rightful keepers of this great land from the rivers and valleys that had been their home for generations, and all in the name of greed. With more than enough for all to share, your kind chose instead to rape, steal, and murder." His gaze leaped skyward. "Soon, the Ghost Dance will call the spirits of the countless slain to return and fight, and though the white man and their guns are powerful, both will fall before the justice brought by the risen dead."

With no idea what to say, Steven breathed a quiet sigh of relief as Archie took the young man's hand.

"I understand how you feel." Archie studied the young man with compassion. "How difficult it can be to see your people suffer. To see such oppression and feel powerless to do a thing about it."

The youth's lower lip trembled. "I watched my mother die because there wasn't enough food. For two months, she coughed up blood until the day she didn't cough again. I dance for her return." His gaze shifted to Steven. "And the return of many more."

Emilio shifted on his feet. "So, you truly believe this Ghost Dance will bring the dead back to life. I get that, as crazy as it sounds. Not that different from what my family heard at Mass every Sunday growing up. Still, I don't see what any of that has to do with thinking your shirt can stop bullets."

"Good luck talking sense to him." Sheriff Post approached from the Wolf's Bend Saloon, his characteristic swagger on full display. "Every tribe between here and California is buying into this 'Wovoka' person's crazy talk about the dead rising up and driving the white man back across the ocean."

"It's not crazy talk, Sheriff." The youth crossed his arms in defiance. "But merely a matter of time."

Post turned to Steven, Archie, and Emilio in a move clearly meant to snub the young man's enthusiasm. "Truth is, some Indian named Jack Wilson down in Nevada stared up at the sun too long during an eclipse, 'received a vision' that told him to start calling himself 'Wovoka,' and now spends every spare minute preaching about the end of the world as we know it." He inclined his head in the youth's direction. "Worst part is these Indian kids don't recognize the man for what he is and, as a result, have their collective tail feathers all in a bunch."

"And what do you consider this man who calls himself Wovoka to be, Sheriff Post?" Archie crossed his arms in a move that mirrored the youth's deliberate stance. "He sounds to me like a strong voice for a people oppressed, the kind who might someday have a federal holiday named after them." He shot Steven a sidelong glance. "What's so wrong with that?"

Post pointed at the youth's chest. "Some loony medicine man has convinced thousands of his faithful followers a cotton shirt will stop a six-shooter. I'm not sure where or when, but the time will come when a bunch of them get it in their heads they're invincible. On that day, a lot of this young man's people are going to die."

"You'll see, Sheriff Post." The youth stormed off. "You'll all see."

No sooner did the young man round the corner than Post's stern expression melted into an exhausted yet sarcastic grin. "So, what were you three doing talking to Billy?"

"Billy?" Steven asked.

"Billy Two Trees." Post gestured toward the door to the general store. "A year ago, he was one of the best workers we had in town. Dependable, friendly. Now, he's all swept up in this Ghost Dance business and has nothing but venom for people who used to be his friends."

"The beatings will continue until morale improves?" Emilio muttered.

"What was that, Mr. Cruz?" Post asked.

"Nothing." His gaze flicked to Archie. "Just know that some of us may understand a little better than you where this Billy Two Trees is coming from."

Post studied the two of them for a moment before letting out a noncommittal grunt. "Whatever. Daylight's wasting and some of us have places to be."

"Got to go check on that train?" Steven did his best to keep a smirk from his face.

Post gave Steven an appraising up and down glance. "We'll be talking later, Mr. Bauer. Unless I miss my guess, there'll likely be at least one or two men aboard more than eager to talk to the last man to see our friend, the U.S. marshal, alive."

"Don't worry." Steven glanced in the direction of the saloon. "I won't be venturing far in this cold."

"See that you don't." Post directed his attention to Archie. "And don't you go firing up Billy and his friends, Mr. Lacan. I actually like that kid. I'd hate to see anything happen to him."

"You got it, boss," Archie whispered, the sarcastic inflection so subtle Steven couldn't tell whether or not he imagined it. It wasn't the first time the priest had dropped into this particular voice, but it still hit Steven's ear as more bitter than anything else.

With a grunt, Post strode away, leaving Steven, Emilio, and Archie in the morning chill.

The general store had yet to open, as the shopkeep, Elmer Green, had been deputized the previous day to help Sheriff Post prepare the marshal's body for burial. With no physician or undertaker in town, the man who also acted as the local butcher had been the best the town had to offer. As Steven understood it, the forensic investigation had basically stopped at "he died of a gunshot wound," and, as a result, there was no good reason to hold off. The man surely had family back east that would want him to at least have a proper funeral even if justice at this point appeared quite the tall order.

"I figured Niklaus would be back by now." Emilio checked the pocket watch he now carried in the well-filled-out waistcoat that had become a trademark part of his style here in the nineteenth century. "You don't think he could be—"

"I'm fine." Niklaus' rolling baritone carried from half a football field away, the snow on the ground and low wind leaving the town all but silent. "But hip deep snowdrifts slow you down a little more when you're stuck as mere flesh and blood."

Steven laughed. "On the other hand, if you were a fifteen-foot tall walking tank made of marble, you might stand out a bit."

"Heh." Niklaus nodded. "There is that."

"So," Emilio asked, "did you see anything?"

"Nothing but the tracks, an empty depot station, and this town's poor excuse for a platform, all of it pretty much exactly as you described. I got there well before sunrise like Steven asked. As of twenty minutes ago, I remained one of the only few souls about."

"Hm." Steven stroked the stubble at his chin. "With all the hush-hush going on around here, I figured something was going down. I'm surprised you didn't run into our scar-faced friend and his buddy with the greased-down hair."

"And what if he had seen them? Better yet, what if they're the ones who killed the marshal? It doesn't change a thing." Emilio crossed his arms. "I know we're supposed to be the good guys and everything, but we're not here to solve a crime that happened decades before any of us were born. We should be focusing on getting out of here, not playing armchair detective." His gaze shot to Niklaus and then back to Steven. "Especially when the two of you are at the top of the list of suspects."

"I hear you, Emilio, and I'm open to suggestions." Steven's breath steamed in the cold. "Where would you like to start?"

"Someplace warmer than the middle of the street, perhaps?" Niklaus headed for the saloon. "I may be from Poland, but even I'm freezing my ass off."

"To be honest," Steven continued once they were inside and seated around a corner table, "neither Niklaus nor I have the first idea how to get us out of here. It took us months and some serious luck just to escape 1946 and make it here to you guys. Even the Grey we met there could only theorize about how we might move on from the next stop along our not-so-excellent adventure."

Archie sighed. "Find us. Find a crossing. Bring the pouch and hope for the best."

Steven nodded. "I agree we need to start looking for a way out of here as soon as possible, but as long as Post keeps showing up like a bad penny every time I turn around, we're pretty much stuck."

"I get that." Emilio pounded a fist on the table. "Doesn't change the fact that every passing day is another something could be happening to Lena and Audrey." He locked gazes with Steven. "Not to mention the rest of the world back home."

Steven raised an eyebrow and smiled. "No pressure, right?"

"One more thing, Steven," Archie added. "Be careful with Sheriff Post. He may come across as exactly the sort of person you'd expect to find as the head lawman of a backwater town in 1890s Wyoming, but he's smarter than you might think. Don't underestimate him or his curiosity about who you are and what you want."

"In that case, the feeling is mutual." Steven locked eyes with each of them, allowing his gaze to eventually settle on Emilio. "We'll find a way out of here, somehow. For now, though, all we have is today. What say we go check out what all the hubbub about this train is about?"

The train pulled to a halt beside the tiny depot station's platform in a cloud of smoke and steam made only the more impressive by the frigid morning air. Painted glossy deep green with bright red trim, the locomotive was yet another sight like something out of a movie. The cowcatcher at the front of the engine, the steel of its V-shaped grill glistening in the morning sun, had clearly served its purpose well. Atop the engine, the tall chimney spewed dark smoke into the grey Wyoming sky. The short cavalcade of cars behind the locomotive numbered six. The first five, each painted a uniform red with golden yellow trim and roofs, were filled with passengers who looked out on the town with curiosity and the relief of knowing they weren't going to have to go out into the cold.

The rear car, however, remained a mystery. Painted matte black with the occasional silver flourish, dark curtains obscured every window, and the lone entry appeared more like the door of a bank vault than that of a train car.

"Hmm." Niklaus folded his arms. "Private car, I'm guessing."

"And privately owned." Steven noted the morning sun glinting off the metal adornments along the car's front corner. "I'm guessing that's actual silver or maybe even platinum. Not your standard railroad fare."

"What always gets me when the train comes to town is how none of the cars are tagged with graffiti." Emilio pulled up beside Steven. "What now, fearless leader?"

"Yeah," Niklaus said. "Now that we're here, what should we do?"

"We're here to observe," Steven answered. "Unless I miss my guess, whatever has caused all the hubbub definitely has to do with that last car."

"I wish Archie could've come with us." Niklaus shoved his hands in his pockets to warm them. "He's got a sense for these things."

"Keeping everything in town business as usual is key for the moment. Post is already keeping an eye on all four of us, but for now, Nik and I are at the top of his list, and we should try to keep it that way. Leaving Archie at the saloon gives him at least a bit of plausible deniability."

"You sure you weren't a lawyer in a previous life?" Emilio laughed. "In any case, the train is only scheduled to be in town for a few minutes. If we're going to do anything other than watch it pull away, we'd better get started or—"

The coupled thunder of gunfire and hooves cut Emilio's thought short. Riding parallel to the tracks from the direction the train had just arrived came a pair of men on horseback, their heads wrapped in heavy cloth so that only their eyes were visible. One carried a six-shooter in each hand, but the blood-red cylinder clenched in the other's grip chilled Steven far more than any gun.

"Get down!" Steven leaped at Emilio and Niklaus, forcing them to the ground, and craned his neck around to watch as the unstoppable events unfolded before his eyes. Just as it had played out in his mind, the lead horseman fired round after round into the air, keeping every-one's attention on him, as his partner carried out the actual mission, flinging the lit stick of dynamite into the locomotive's chimney.

"Hands over your ears," Steven shouted. "Quick, before—"

The deafening roar hit Steven's ears even as the concussive blast from the explosion slammed his head into the ground. The wind knocked from him, he forced himself to roll over and check on the others, grumbling about how he'd known something was going to happen.

Yet again, for all the good it did them.

With ringing ears and his skull pounding like he'd gone a few rounds, Steven rose from the ground and wiped the blood from his nose. He helped Niklaus to his feet first and then bent to offer Emilio a hand, the latter clearly the more dazed of the two.

The locomotive, moments before a full-size version of one of Steven's childhood toy train engines, now lay sprawled open like an enormous metallic jellyfish with the front half blown open from top to bottom revealing dozens of steel rods bent in every direction.

"Wait a minute." Niklaus scanned the tracks in both directions for the pair of outlaws. "They blew the engine and…left?"

"Appears that way." Steven steadied a staggering Emilio at his side. "But why go to all this trouble if you're not going to stick around and reap the rewards?"

"If robbing the train isn't your actual goal." Emilio's eyes narrowed on the destroyed locomotive. "The real question is why else anyone would want to stop a train in the middle of Nowhere, Wyoming."

"Exactly what I want to know." Sheriff Tom Post strode up, one hand on the revolver at his side. "Not exactly surprised to see you three out here, though I can't imagine a better alibi than almost being blown up yourselves."

"Morning, Sheriff." Steven gave him a nod. "Any idea who did this?"

"Didn't see them." Post joined their circle. "I was busy checking out the depot when the engine blew. By the time I made it outside, the two men who did this were nothing but a pair of dust clouds down the tracks. You three, on the other hand, were right here. See anything that might give me a leg up?"

"Not much." Steven did his best not to shout, though his ears still rang from the explosion. "Two guys, heads both wrapped in dark scarves. The one in the lead kept everybody busy dodging bullets while his buddy chucked a stick of dynamite in the locomotive's chimney and blew the engine."

"Did you recognize either of them?" Post peered around the circle, taking his measure of each of them. "Anyone you've seen around town?"

"Nope," Steven answered with an emphatic glance in Emilio's direction. "With their heads all covered, they could've been anyone."

From the moment the two horsemen burst onto the scene, the pair Steven thought of as Scarface and Slick had held center stage in his mind's eye. Throwing a couple of complete strangers under the bus with no evidence other than a half-heard conversation and a gut feeling, however, didn't seem the best option. Especially where Sheriff Post was concerned.

"Anyone, huh?"

"We've only been in town a few days, Sheriff. Don't know too many folks around here." Steven jammed a finger into his ear to dull the pulsating ring. "That being said, if any of us comes up with anything, I'll let you know right away."

"See that you do." Post turned his head in the direction of the destroyed locomotive. "For now, though, time for me to start figuring out how to clean up this mess. Wish me luck, boys."

As Post strode across the wide platform in the direction of the ruined engine, the occupants of the train's first five cars piled out in a rush, the mob of panicked humanity quickly descending into chaos.

One thing was certain: Sheriff Post and the tiny town of Wolf's Bend, Wyoming both had some serious challenges coming in the next few days.

"How in the world are they going to fix this mess?" Niklaus asked.

"I don't have the first clue." Steven nodded to a shell-shocked woman trudging by carrying a screaming infant. "But one thing's for sure. There won't be any empty beds in town tonight."

"*Dios mío*, Look." Emilio let out an uncharacteristic gasp. "The engineer."

Steven followed Emilio's gaze to the rear of the destroyed locomotive where a bloodied man in a dark blue cap climbed from the wreckage and waved for someone to help him. In answer, a man in a conductor's uniform and hat and a trio of men in suits rushed to his side and quickly delivered him from what should have been an enormous metal coffin.

"Little miracles," Steven muttered.

"No kidding." Niklaus shifted his attention to the opposite end of the train, his eyes filling with a potent mix of hope and fear. "And speaking of miracles, I think I've figured out why we're here."

Closed moments before when Post had spoken with them, the fortified door of the jet-black car at the rear of the train now stood wide open.

Framed within the dark doorway stood a man they all knew far too well.

Squinting his eyes against the sunlight glinting off the snow, Zed stepped down onto the wooden platform. Both the dark duster covering his form as well as his lustrous black hair and beard stood in stark contrast to the white covering the ground just beyond the platform's edge. With keen eyes, he took in the situation for several long seconds before returning to his car. The door slammed shut behind him with an ominous peal that echoed like thunder.

"If that's truly Zed, then I have only one question." Steven glanced across his shoulder in the direction of town. "How in the world did Archie not see this one coming?"

19

PAWN & KING

"Zed is here?" Archie nearly dropped the half-washed glass in his hand. "Did he see you?"

"No, though even if he did, I don't think it'd be a problem." Steven's gaze shot to Niklaus and Emilio, then back to Archie. "This wasn't our Zed, or at least not the one from our time."

"The Zed of 1890." Archie's apprehensive stance melted a bit. "He'd have no idea who we are."

"Which means he's less likely to try to kill us." Niklaus let out a single laugh. "Right?"

"I would certainly hope so." Steven ran his nails across his scalp. "We'll see."

"But why is he here?" Emilio's brow furrowed, his volume growing with every word. "And why now? We've been here for months."

"Careful." Steven peered around the saloon. "Extra ears around."

Three tables sat occupied with the usual crowd, all far too involved in their own business to pay any mind to the ins and outs of their conversation. Post and Ndure, in particular, were clear across town and busy sorting out the chaos at the railroad depot, and the U.S. Cavalry, an almost constant presence in the saloon, hadn't made an appearance that day.

It was as much privacy as they were likely to get.

"All right." Steven pulled their circle tight. "As I see it, both Zed and Grey have been around for centuries. Just as we crossed paths with the Grey of 1946, it makes sense that we could run into his opposite here and now." He shook his head and sighed. "And assuming, as we discussed before, that the Game itself could be shifting certain events, it's even possible the four of us have been drawn to this particular place and time because Zed was fated to be here."

"But what happens if he sees us?" Emilio asked. "Won't that mess up everything that's already happened? I mean, he didn't know any of us when we first met." He considered for a moment. "Or at least didn't let on that he did."

"Neither did Grey." Steven stroked the stubble at his chin. "Though I'm starting to understand why he didn't." He let out a bitter laugh. "My status as Pawn in an eternal game of magical chess was a big enough pill to swallow. I doubt bringing up that he'd already met my time-traveling future self in 1946 would've helped his cause."

"So, we have no way of knowing if the guy gunning for us a century from now ran into all of us in Middle-of-Nowhere, Wyoming, almost a century before we were born. Got it." Niklaus took a breath. "The only question now is do we steer clear of him, or do we—"

Another blast of cold air hit Steven, this one accompanied by a pinch from Amaryllis, the first since Archie had walked through that same door to find them two days before.

"Barkeep!" The Black King burst through the door of the saloon. In his wake, a trio of Japanese women in traditional dress followed. "Your finest libations for me and my three companions, if you please."

"Well," Emilio muttered under his breath, "I guess that question has been answered."

Steven, Niklaus, and Emilio moved to one end of the bar, freeing up the space for Zed and his entourage to occupy the quartet of barstools at the other. With unparalleled manners, the Black King swept from lady to lady, helping each of them onto their seats before settling onto the stool at the far end.

"Is it possible," Zed said with a flourish, "that you serve wine in this establishment?"

"You're in luck, my friend." Archie reached behind the counter and produced an aged bottle, the lettering on the label rendered in Italian script. "We usually keep a bottle or two hidden away for the rare times we're graced with a more *discerning* clientele."

Zed took the bottle and regarded both it and Archie with an appraising smile. "You, sir, are quite well-spoken for a Negro slinging whiskey in this flyspeck of a town."

"Why...thank you, *sir*." Archie kept his cool, but Steven had been around the priest more than long enough to sense him bristling beneath his genteel facade. "We do try to keep things civilized, even here in the wilderness of the West."

Zed chuckled. "And what might the fine people of this town call you, barkeep?"

Steven's hand shot up subtly in an effort to keep Archie from answering, but the words had already passed the priest's lips.

"Lacan," he said. "My name is Archibald Lacan."

"Well, Mr. Lacan," Zed held up the bottle and motioned for Archie to draw closer, "I suggest we open this fine wine and drink to the twin fortunes of me finding the lone watering hole in Wyoming with a Sangiovese worth drinking and you crossing paths with a man who has both sufficient taste and funds to make such a find worthwhile for all involved." With another flourish, the Black King produced a small drawstring purse from within his black duster and withdrew a single gold coin. Placing it on the bar with a solid thunk, Zed's lips drew wide into a smug smile. "This should suffice, should it not, Mr. Lacan?"

Archie picked up the coin and deposited it in the pocket of his waistcoat. "More than generous, Mr...."

"Brenin." Zed offered a slight bow. "Victor Brenin."

"Thank you, Mr. Brenin." Archie pulled down a glass, inspected the rim for cleanliness, and placed it on the bar.

"And your lovely companions," Archie inquired. "Shall they be drinking as well?"

The oldest of the three said not a word but gestured toward the whiskey bottle across Archie's shoulder. Archie, in turn, poured her a finger of the amber liquid, followed by another and then another—each at her insistence—until the glass sat at over half full. With a smile, the woman grasped the glass and turned it up, downing the contents in one gulp before silently returning the glass to the bar. Unfazed, she cast a self-satisfied smirk at Archie and tapped the top of the glass, asking for another.

"One thing's for sure..." Emilio positioned himself behind Steven, just out of the Black King's field of vision. "We won't be drinking *her* under the table."

"No kidding." Steven crossed his arms. "And God only knows what other skills Zed's little harem brings to the table."

"I have a feeling we're going to find out all too soon," Niklaus murmured in Steven's ear. "What the hell do we do now?"

"The same thing we always do." Steven kept one eye on the Black King and the other on Emilio who, despite the brave face he wore, appeared very much like an animal with its leg caught in a bear trap. "Improvise."

"Mr. Brenin." Another blast of cold air hit them as Sheriff Post, backlit by the blinding sunlight reflecting off the snow, stepped across the threshold and kicked the sludge from his boots. "Good to know you made it through this unfortunate mishap unscathed."

Sheriff Post had barely halved the distance from door to bar before the three women in the Black King's company sprung from their chairs and adopted a defensive perimeter around the man. The few other patrons of the bar all went silent at the sudden standoff.

Post stepped back, hands raised before him in friendly surrender. "Whoa, whoa, whoa. Ladies, relax. I'm just the welcome wagon."

The women didn't budge an inch. The one in the lead cast a questioning glance in the direction of the man calling himself Victor Brenin while the other two stood motionless as if awaiting a command to attack.

"Definitely more than window dressing," Steven murmured to Niklaus. "Nice to know Zed's taste in women hasn't changed over the decades."

Niklaus shook his head. "Like we needed something else to worry about."

Like a serpent, Brenin slid from his barstool and stepped between the women to confront Post. "And who, sir, might you be?"

"Sheriff Tom Post." Post, who had been nothing but bluster and fire from their first meeting, shrank, at least a bit, at the Black King's cold stare. "The law in these parts." He brushed the fingers of his left hand across the sheriff's star hung next to his belt buckle, careful to keep his right far from the hilt of his six-shooter.

"That answers one question, Sheriff." Brenin looked Post up and down with a disparaging sneer. "Now, explain how you have the first idea as to my name."

Post pulled himself up to his full height. "I wouldn't be doing my job if I didn't keep tabs on the comings and goings in this town, now would I, Mr. Brenin?" He shot a cynical look in Steven's direction. "It's my business to know. Period."

"In that case, Sheriff Post, allow me to put your mind at ease." Brenin glanced back at the trio of women who appeared poised to kill anyone in the room that so much as breathed funny. "Ladies, stand down."

At his command, the trio of Asian women silently returned to their barstools as if nothing had happened. With a broad smile, Brenin again turned to face Post.

"Trust, Sheriff, that I will be residing in your quaint little town only for the time required to get another locomotive here to spirit me and my companions away." He let out a frustrated sigh. "Truth be told, were we not traveling in my favorite railcar, we'd be leaving on the first stagecoach." Brenin surveyed the saloon. "For the time being, however, we shall be taking advantage of your town's accommodations, such as they are." For the first time, the Black King met Steven's gaze. "What's the saying?" he asked with a dismissive snort. "Any port in a storm?"

A pop from behind the bar caught everyone's attention. Archie, the bottle of Sangiovese in one hand and a corkscrew in the other, offered a slight bow.

"Your wine, Mr. Brenin?"

"Thank you, Mr. Lacan." Brenin spun around and returned to his barstool. "A round of whiskey for the house." He shot a quick glance across his shoulder. "And make that a double for my new friend, Sheriff Post."

The saloon, quiet up to that point, erupted into cheers as Archie pulled down two fistfuls of glasses and poured a round, the last with an extra finger of alcohol. Post hesitated for all of half a second before stepping over to the bar and accepting the glass from Archie, downing his drink in a single gulp in an obvious effort to reestablish the pecking order.

"Thank you, Mr. Brenin," he intoned, sucking in a breath between his teeth.

"Of course, Sheriff." Brenin sipped at his wine. "My pleasure."

"Before I go, though, a quick question?" Post slid into a congenial smile, though Steven had little trouble seeing the gears working in the man's mind.

"But, of course." Brenin answered Post's smile with one of his own, each forced smirk disquieting in its own way. "My life is an open book."

Post produced a folded document from inside his coat and held up the grainy picture retrieved from a dead man's corpse days before. "Any idea why a federal marshal might've come to my town in the dead of winter carrying a photograph of you? A federal marshal who, I might add, happens to be quite dead."

"Dead?" Brenin asked, his expression unfazed. "And how might that have happened?"

"Murdered in cold blood." Post's gaze flicked in Steven's direction. "Bled to death in the front parlor of the local inn from a pair of gunshot wounds."

Despite his impressive poker face, even Brenin seemed a bit taken aback by the insinuation of guilt in Post's tone. "I haven't the foggiest idea about any of that, Sheriff. As you know, I and my associates have just arrived in your charming little hamlet." He leaned in. "I trust you have a theory you'd be willing to share, as the murder of a law enforcement officer carrying my photograph is, understandably, quite disturbing."

"Not yet." Post rose from his seat. "But I will." He moved to the door, but stopped short to turn and address the room. "Good day, all." He tipped his hat to Brenin's three companions. "Ladies."

As Post stepped out onto the snow-covered road, Steven's heart raced. The sheriff's entrance had provided a welcome distraction, but nothing now stood between the unarmed and powerless quartet of White and the man who would, without a doubt, gut them all without a second thought if he knew who they were.

"I think you three could use that drink." Brenin motioned to Archie who, in turn, slid a trio of whiskeys down the bar to Steven, Niklaus, and Emilio.

Steven raised his glass. "Thank you kindly, Mr. Brenin." He turned up his glass, the whiskey burning down his throat on its way to a stomach tied in knots. "A generous act indeed considering the circumstances that have led to your unplanned visit to Wolf's Bend."

"My, everyone has such good manners for such a backwater town." Brenin studied Steven for a moment, downed his whiskey, and strode over to offer a hand. "Mr.?"

"Bauer." Though Brenin's handshake threatened to break bones, Steven gave as good as he got. "Steven Bauer."

"Bauer, eh?" Brenin smiled, amused. "The pawn of the German chessboard." The Black King rested his glass on the bar. "There are lessons aplenty that can be gleaned from a study of the game of kings."

Steven forced a smile, though his teeth remained gritted. "Do tell."

Zed considered for a moment. "This…mishap with the train, for instance. Many would see only the inconvenience of being, at worst, briefly delayed." His slight grin widened into a full smile. "I, however, consider it an opportunity."

"An opportunity?" Steven asked. "In this 'backwater' of a town?"

"Anyone can win with the odds in their favor." Brenin stroked his dark beard. "But the play of a master is marked by how well they handle the inevitable setbacks."

"I couldn't agree more." Steven motioned in the direction of the door. "Due to circumstances beyond our control, my friends and I too find ourselves…temporarily displaced."

"Perhaps, then, fortune smiles upon us both."

"What do you mean?" Steven asked.

"Might you and your friends be seeking temporary employment?" Brenin's gaze wandered over Niklaus and Emilio. "You three certainly appear able-bodied young men. Perhaps we could come to some form of agreement."

"Perhaps," Steven said, "though, with all due respect, you're stuck here in Wolf's Bend just like us." He did his best to decipher Brenin's inscrutable gaze. "What sort of work might you have for us?"

"The West can be a dangerous place, Mr. Bauer, as you have clearly discovered. Three additional sets of eyes and ears in town would be more than welcome." He patted the drawstring purse at his belt. "And I assure you, I can make such an arrangement more than worth your while."

Steven shot Niklaus a quick look, hoping for some kind of answer in his friend's eyes, but found there only the same bafflement that ate at his own soul.

"Your offer, sir, is indeed generous." Steven forced a smile. "If you'll allow me time to discuss your offer with my associates, I can let you know our decision later this afternoon."

"Of course." The gleam in Brenin's gaze intensified. "Only a fool makes a move without considering all the potential repercussions."

Steven raised an eyebrow. "Another reference to your much vaunted 'game of kings,' Mr. Brenin?"

"Life is chess, Mr. Bauer." Brenin downed the last of his wine and turned for the door. The trio of women slid from their barstools and fell in behind him, their movements as synchronized as a ballet. "And each day, your next move, be it for good or ill."

"This afternoon, then."

"When you and your friends have made your decision, knock thrice at the door to my railcar." Brenin stepped out into the snowy street. "A warning, though. I don't like to be kept waiting."

Once Brenin and his entourage had left, Archie cocked his head to one side, eyes blazing at Steven. "I can't believe this. You're actually considering his offer."

"There's an old adage that says to keep your friends close and your enemies closer." Steven's eyes shot to the door, a part of him afraid the

Black King might return at any moment and kill them all. "Also, if anyone knows how to get us the hell out of here, it's the man who sent us here himself."

"Like he'd tell us anything." Emilio, who had remained uncharacteristically silent throughout the discussion, jammed his hands in his pockets, though he somehow kept his volume down despite the frustration in his tone. "Not to mention, if he finds out who we are, there's a good chance he'll kill us all on the spot."

"I don't know." Niklaus leaned against the bar. "He had all six of us dead to rights on the Brooklyn Bridge and chose to send us all packing instead of just ending us then and there."

"Bullshit." Emilio seethed. "He did this so time could do his dirty work for him."

"We're all still breathing," Niklaus answered, "aren't we?"

When Emilio didn't answer, Steven did his best to defuse the tension.

"Well, for the moment, all of us, Zed included, are stuck in the middle of nowhere in the winter of 1890. Like the man said, we can see it as a setback, or we can see it as an opportunity." Steven met each of their gazes. "Thoughts?"

No one said a word for several seconds with Archie eventually ending the verbal stalemate. "Any plan is better than no plan, I guess." He gathered their glasses and deposited them in a basin filled with dingy water behind the bar. "What's the play, Steven?"

"We find out what Zed is offering while steering clear of Post and Ndure as best we can till we figure out how to get the hell out of here." He studied Emilio's sullen expression and added. "We're all we've got, the four of us. No matter what, we can't forget that."

20

WHEELS & DEALS

"Mr. Brenin?" Steven knocked three times on the vault-like door. "It's Steven Bauer."

Half a minute passed before a hydraulic hiss hit Steven's ears. A flash of steam erupted around the door's edges, and a moment later, one of Victor Brenin's entourage of Asian beauties peered from the open door, her lithe form covered in a black silken robe embellished with embroidered pink flowers.

"Mr. Bauer." The Eastern accent coloring his name tickled Steven's ears. "Please, come inside." She gave him a frank up and down and a mischievous smile. "And watch your step."

"Don't worry." Steven stepped from the wooden platform onto the metal trio of stairs leading into Brenin's railcar. "That's pretty much the standard these days."

The woman led Steven inside, a subtle hiss hitting his ears as the door slid shut and resealed. She turned a dial on the wall, and a quartet of gas lamps at the corners of the space brought the dimly lit room to life. Steven worked to keep the surprise from his face, the sheer opulence of Brenin's mobile sanctuary beyond anything he had imagined.

The platinum flourishes that graced the body of the midnight-black box on wheels represented only the beginning of the car's extravagance. The corner lamps, along with every other piece of hardware in the space, ran the gamut of precious metals and gemstones, right down to the jade doorknobs adorning the doors at either end of the square room and the various rubies, emeralds, and sapphires dangling from the window curtains.

In every corner rested chairs carved from darkest ebony, their cushions fashioned from the furs and hides of creatures from every corner of the world, while the heads of many of those same creatures graced the various walls. Tiger and lion, caribou and wolverine, even a snarling polar bear all glared down at him as if ready to attack. The floor, covered with a thick Persian rug the color of dried blood, lay crowned with a low table decorated with an inlaid grid of sixty-four alternating squares of polished white marble and black onyx.

The chessboard rested, mid-game, with a white pawn positioned in the seventh rank directly before the black king and covered by a bishop from across the checkered battlefield. Had Brenin left the board that way for his benefit? Or could the position of the pieces be mere coincidence? Steven had no way to tell which was the truth, but the preceding few months had done little to bolster his belief in the latter.

"You and Mr. Brenin spoke earlier of his favorite game." The woman sat in a chair upholstered with zebra hide. "Do you play, Mr. Bauer?"

"You could say that." Again, Steven worked to keep his expression impassive. "My father taught me chess when I was young."

A cold pit opened at Steven's core, his imagination offering far too many potential options as to his father's circumstances back in the present. Taken by the Black, along with members of both Audrey's and Lena's families, Donald Bauer remained ever at the forefront of Steven's mind. Far bigger stakes were involved in this ancient Game that had taken over their lives—there was no doubt of that—but getting everyone's family members back safe and sound remained near the top of his list.

And the man responsible for taking them lounged behind one of the two doors leading from the room.

"Make yourself comfortable. Mr. Brenin asked me to keep you company until he was ready to meet with you."

A quiet moan from behind one of the doors brought heat to Steven's cheeks.

"I take it he wasn't expecting me quite so soon."

The woman leaned back in her chair and crossed her legs, a shapely knee emerging from beneath the hem of her sheer robe. "Mr. Brenin is, for the moment, indisposed, but I hope my company will suffice while you wait." Her eyes again trailed down Steven's form. "At your pleasure, of course."

Steven had walked this particular tightrope before.

Beautiful woman. Black dress slit up to there. Her every word all "come hither."

Right up to the moment she tried to burn him alive.

"What sort of business keeps Mr. Brenin in such posh accommodations?" Steven looked around the car, ignoring both her suggestive gaze and leading remarks. "If this railcar of his is any indication—"

"Mr. Brenin's affairs are his business and his business alone." Both her eyes and tone turned cold. "Your only concern should be his most generous offer to employ three men he has only just met."

"My apologies." Steven sat opposite the woman and interlaced his fingers. "I'm merely dazzled by the sheer opulence of what must be, no doubt, but a small example of Mr. Brenin's wealth."

She offered the barest of smiles. "Rest assured, Mr. Bauer, that Mr. Brenin has more than sufficient wherewithal to take excellent care of you and your friends."

"And what of you and your two associates?" Steven leaned in, resting his elbows on his knees. "How long have you three...worked for Mr. Brenin?"

"You certainly don't mince words, Mr. Bauer." The woman rose from the black-and-white upholstered chair and went to the window. "My sisters and I do not work *for* Mr. Brenin, *per se*. We merely provide him companionship, among other services. In return, he makes certain we want for nothing."

"Sisters, eh?" Steven raised an eyebrow. "That must be some arrangement."

"You haven't the first idea." Zed stepped into the room from the door to Steven's left. Dressed in an open shirt of white silk and loose black pantaloons, the man calling himself Victor Brenin appeared the very definition of a man of leisure. "Have you ever encountered a more exquisite woman, Mr. Bauer?" he asked, sitting in the chair opposite Steven. "Years ago, during one of my many excursions to the Orient, I first encountered Ume and her two sisters. Orphaned and hungry, I took them under my wing. And now, look how they've blossomed."

As if on cue, the remaining two sisters glided into the room, one from each doorway, dressed in floral robes similar to Ume's. One set of robes reminded Steven of the white cherry blossoms that filled the tree every spring in front of his childhood home and the other, the yellow mums his mother kept in clay pots on their porch every fall.

"Three sisters." Steven rose from his chair, memories of the town in Oregon where he first met Audrey flitting across his subconscious, every image surreal as if from a movie he'd seen in another lifetime. "Everything old really is new again."

"Their father was one of the last samurai who took part in the Satsuma Rebellion in southwestern Japan thirteen years ago. He and their mother both fell protecting their home from Meiji forces." Brenin gestured to the three sisters and bowed his head. "A tragedy, indeed."

"To lose one's family." Steven's intestines coiled. "Is there anything worse?"

Brenin's eyes narrowed subtly, the man clearly picking up on Steven's shift in tone. Barring the reading of minds, however, he couldn't possibly understand Steven knew all too well exactly the kind of man who hid behind his serpent's smile. Keeping his tongue, the Black King merely crossed his arms and waited for his opponent to make the next move.

"So, Ume." Steven glanced in the direction of the woman's two sisters. "Your two sisters? May I—"

"I am Sakura," said the one who had entered from the same door as the Black King. "The eldest." Her lips drew down to a tight moue. "And the least easily impressed."

"And I am Kiku." The third offered Steven what appeared to be a genuine smile. "A pleasure to make your acquaintance, Mr. Bauer."

"A pleasure, indeed." Clearly the youngest of the three, she must have still been in diapers when Brenin first took her in. In her innocent features, he found traces of Lena Cervantes, and in her beaming grin, the exuberance of Audrey Richards.

His heart ached, even as his resolve doubled. The man responsible for all of this misery sat before him—comfortable, happy, even smug.

Steven longed to wipe the self-satisfied smirk from his lips.

But justice would have to wait.

Steven didn't understand much about the mechanics of actual honest-to-god time travel, but one thing a childhood filled with science-fiction movies and television shows running the gamut from *Back to the Future* to *Planet of the Apes* or even *Bill and Ted's Excellent Adventure* left him with one simple understanding: Screw with the past at your own peril.

"So, Mr. Brenin." Steven retook his seat. "The offer you made earlier. What services do you believe my friends and I can provide?"

"Straight to business, then." The Black King shifted in his seat. "I respect that."

Sakura sat on the settee next to Steven's chair. "As Mr. Brenin stated before, it seems we are stuck in unfamiliar territory for the duration and merely would ask that you and your friends be our eyes and ears until such time as we are able to make our way east again."

Steven's brow furrowed. "And why do you believe anyone here would wish you ill?"

Besides the three men you seek to employ, of course.

"One does not rise to the top of society without making a few enemies, Mr. Bauer." Brenin steepled his fingers beneath his chin. "Look around you. There are many who covet the things I have." His eyes flicked in Sakura's direction. "The things I love." He stood and went to the window, peering between the curtains at the wilderness beyond. "I merely wish to remain undisturbed during my brief exile in this poor man's excuse for civilization."

"And why would you think anyone would come for you in Wolf's Bend? I doubt anyone even knows you're here."

"The small-minded exist everywhere, Mr. Bauer. Those who would take what isn't theirs. Those who would attack those who cannot defend themselves." His eyes narrowed. "Those who would destroy an entire locomotive just to make a particularly rich target a bit more—shall we say—easy to hit?"

"You think the two men who blew the engine did it to get to you?"

Brenin's gaze took on a patronizing slant. "Trains pass this way every week without event, Mr. Bauer, despite cars filled with bank notes and precious metals or dozens of people with wealth sufficient to travel cross country by rail. To my knowledge, there have been no railway robberies in this region to date, and yet, less than five minutes after a train pulling my car arrives in the Wolf's Bend station, its locomotive is left a pile of scrap metal by a pair of bandits no one has ever seen before or since." He took Sakura's hand. "Pontificate on coincidence all you like, but the implications of today's events are not hard to decipher."

Steven paused momentarily at the unexpected show of affection. "And what, may I ask, are you transporting that's so intoxicating it might bring out the criminal element?"

Brenin's eyes narrowed. "That is truly the question of the hour, is it not?"

And that, apparently, was all he had to say on the subject.

Steven opted not to push. "So, all you want us to do is keep you up on the various comings and goings here in Wolf's Bend?"

"For now." Ume rose from her chair. "You will report to me, a minimum of three times daily at ten, two, and eight, not to mention immediately, should you feel anything has occurred that might require Mr. Brenin's attention."

Steven crossed his arms. "All of that sounds quite doable, assuming we can come to an agreement on compensation."

"Name your price." Brenin rested his drawstring purse on the table at the room's center, just adjacent to the inlaid chessboard. "I suspect I can more than meet your expectations."

"A fair day's wages is all we require." Steven leaned back in his chair. "And, one small request."

"Interesting." Brenin leaned forward. "And what might this request be?"

"At a future date, time, and place of my choosing…" Steven crossed his arms. "The honest answer to a question."

Zed's eyebrow rose cautiously. "And what question might that be, Mr. Bauer?"

"I will ask when the time is right. Like you, Mr. Brenin, I like to keep my cards close to my chest." Steven forced a congenial smile. "Do we have a deal?"

Brenin pondered for a moment. "You think several moves ahead, Mr. Bauer. I respect that in a man." He extended a hand. "We have a deal."

Steven shook the Black King's hand for the second time that day, though this time the prodigious strength only parlayed into a firm show of respect rather than a concerted effort to break Steven's fingers.

"Before I go," Steven said, "I do have a suspicion as to identities of the men responsible for your current predicament."

"I thought you might." Brenin stepped back and held his hands before him, palms up. "Please, do feel free to share."

Steven cast his mind back a few days and detailed what he remembered of the pair he thought of as Scarface and Slick—their references to some plan that sounded anything but above board, the cryptic nod to a mysterious "old man," and the fact that neither Steven nor any of the others had seen the two men around town since.

"An 'old man,' you say?" Brenin said when Steven had finished, his brow knit together with worry. "Those were their exact words?"

"That's what they said." Steven studied the Black King's features, attempting to scry his adversary's thoughts.

"So, these brigands have a benefactor. Interesting." Brenin opened the railcar door and showed Steven out. "I wonder if even the two desperados in question have the first idea who it is they're dealing with."

"Wait. Do you know who they're—"

The dark steel door of the Black King's railcar closed in Steven's face with a quiet clunk, the sudden silence punctuated by the hiss of steam as the door again sealed itself shut.

21

BAD & WORSE

"Is it possible?" Steven gauged Archie's expression. "Could Grey be here?"

"I haven't had so much as a flash of him." Archie cast his eyes around the crowded saloon. "Now, keep your voice down. You've already got local law enforcement trying to pin a federal crime on you and accepted employment from a man who's tried to kill you half a dozen times. Maybe we *don't* try to get the rest of the town whispering about you anymore than they already are?"

"Who else could Zed be thinking of, then?" Steven brought his voice down a few decibels. "He was all calm and in control till I mentioned the 'old man' Slick and Scarface were talking about." Steven inclined his head to one side. "By the way, any word on them? You know either out here..." He motioned to the general hubbub of the saloon. "Or up here?" Steven pointed to his temple, an eyebrow raised in question.

"There are lots of 'old men,' Steven." Archie ran his fingers through his kinky grey locks. "Hell, I'm one of them." He laughed. "I know we were just discussing that all of this is happening for a reason and that everything pertains to the Game, but we should also consider the possibility that maybe these brigands really do just want to blow up a train."

"I suppose." Steven peered around the room. Most of the saloon's late afternoon clientele paid him no mind, but he found more than one furtive glance focused in his direction. Clearly, their arrival had become a matter of town gossip, and unless he missed his guess, the locals weren't organizing a welcome party.

Not that he could blame them. The whole "mysterious stranger found standing over a dying federal marshal" thing was anything but the stuff of good first impressions.

Niklaus strode into the saloon. "So, we're officially working for the 'man' now?"

"Apparently so." Steven sighed. "Just sealed the deal an hour ago."

Niklaus paused mid-step. "And our marching orders?"

"To keep our ears to the ground and report anything that might be counter to his agenda until he's long gone from Wolf's Bend."

"At least he doesn't want us to kill anyone."

"Not yet, anyway." Steven swirled the whiskey in his glass. "Any word on when the replacement engine will make it into town?"

"I spoke to the town telegrapher." Niklaus raised two fingers. "Train's a couple days out."

"And any whispers about how they're planning to get the other locomotive off the tracks?"

Niklaus pulled in a breath. "Yet another engine, this one coming from the east. From what I understand, one of the biggest in the fleet. Since the blown locomotive is still on the rails, they intend to have the big engine pull the wreckage a few miles east to the next town for scrap."

"Is that going to work?" Steven asked. "The locomotive is pretty much destroyed."

"One of the townsfolk used to work for the railroad. He said most of the force of the blast went either straight up or out to the sides, leaving the bottom of the locomotive for the most part intact. The internal steam engine may be so much scrap metal, but the wheels should turn."

"And if they don't?"

"Then all of us are stuck here for a hell of a lot longer than we hoped."

"Okay, then." Steven pounded a fist on the bar. "Assuming they can clear the tracks, that means we've probably got just over forty-eight hours to puzzle out the rest of all this."

"A little ambitious, don't you think?" Archie wiped down the bar, the motion all but robotic. "Trying to figure out the mysteries of the universe in two days?"

"I don't know." Steven's eyes slid shut. "But without Grey, we'd never have gotten out of 1946. If we let Zed head on down the tracks..."

"There's a possibility we'd be stuck here." Niklaus motioned for Archie to pull him a drink. "What if Zed is the only one that knows how to—"

A blast of cold hit as the door leading outside crashed open revealing a shivering Emilio, his eyes wide with fear.

"What's wrong, Emilio?" Steven turned on his barstool. "We weren't expecting you back for a couple more hours."

"I found them," Emilio got out between chattering teeth. "God help us, I found them."

"Scarface and Slick?" Steven rose and took a step toward the door. "Where?"

"Right here." The man Steven referred to as Scarface sauntered into the room with his pomade-coiffed associate close on his heels. "I hear you've been looking for us, Mr. Bauer, isn't it?"

An army of ants crawled up the back of Steven's neck.

"Been saying some not-so-nice things about a couple of gents you barely know, I hear." Slick slid out of a long leather duster and folded it over one arm, resting his opposite hand on the hilt of his revolver. "Not the smartest thing to do in a town this size, wouldn't you say?"

"You boys keep your guns in your holsters, you hear?" Archie pulled the shotgun up from behind the bar, the movement far more fluid than Steven would have anticipated considering Archie's return to septuagenarian status. "This is the only place in the whole damn town where everyone can get out of the cold. I won't have you or anyone else blowing holes in the walls. Understand?"

Slick raised both hands before him, the gesture mocking in its over-the-top congeniality. "Don't worry, Mr. Lacan. Nobody's shooting anybody today." His eyes went to Steven. "That is as long as Mr. Bauer here agrees to start keeping his unfounded opinions to himself."

"Let's talk about this." Stunned at the strange turn of events, Steven's mind worked frantically to put together a scenario where the two armed men before him could even know his name, much less his suspicions. He'd only shared his thoughts with his inner circle, and none of them had the first motive.

But that left only...

Zed.

Steven had left the Black King's side less than an hour before, but that was more than enough time to deliver a message to a pair of outlaws hiding on the outskirts of town.

Dammit.

He'd tipped his hand to the very person who controlled the opposite end of this particular chessboard.

Steven took a breath as he studied Scarface with as impassive an expression as he could manage. "First things first. May I ask what it is I'm supposed to have said?" With every eye in the saloon trained on him, he fought to keep even a hint of stammer from his voice. "Last I checked, the accused gets to hear the charges against him."

"An interesting turn of phrase, Mr. Bauer." Scarface strode over and rested an elbow atop the bar's wooden surface. "Seeing as how you're the one telling anyone who'll listen we were the ones who blew the train today."

"I'm not sure who's feeding you such misinformation." Steven crossed his arms, defiant. "But while we're on the subject of exploding locomotives, you don't happen to have a box or two of dynamite laying around wherever it is you happen to be staying, do you?"

Slick's hand flew to the hilt of his six-shooter, but Scarface kept his cool, his outstretched hand and Archie's shotgun all that kept his partner from gunning Steven down where he stood.

"Now, now, Clarence." Scarface allowed himself a smile and even a quiet laugh. "Mr. Lacan asked us not to shoot up his fine drinking establishment, and I aim to comply."

"Fine." Clarence's facile fingers slid from the grip of his revolver and into his pocket. "But you can't stay in here forever." He eyed Steven as a cobra might an injured rat.

"Okay, everybody. Cool down." Niklaus raised his hands before his chest. "Clearly, there's been a misunderstanding here. Nobody here wants to shoot anybody." His eyes cut to Archie. "Maybe a round for all involved so we can talk about this?"

As Archie rested the shotgun on the bar and assembled a round of firewater, Clarence moved closer, his every shifting step a serpent's advance. "Interesting accent," he said. "What is that? Russian?"

"Polish."

"Polish, huh? And what in the hell is a Polack doing this far west?" Clarence sneered. "You hop the wrong train or something?"

Niklaus' hands balled into fists at his sides. "Something like that."

"Never met a real-life Polack before. Tell me ab—"

"Clarence." The quiet word from Scarface shut down the mocking mid-syllable. "That's enough. We came here to settle things with Mr. Bauer and his friends, not to stir up more trouble." He offered Niklaus what seemed a genuine smile. "I courted a Polish girl once. Sweetest smile I ever saw."

"They don't come any sweeter." The White Rook's muscular form slackened a bit. "I'm Niklaus."

"My name is Earl." He gave Niklaus a subtle nod. "So, listen close, Niklaus from Poland. A word of advice for you and your friend?" His gaze flitted to Steven. "Stick to your own business if you know what's good for you." He studied Niklaus and the others through bushy eyebrows. "Are we clear?"

"We're clear," Niklaus answered, his voice quiet.

"Crystal," Steven added.

"That goes for all of you." Earl turned his attention on Emilio, who had remained silent throughout the conversation. "Particularly those of you who might find yourself asking the right questions of the wrong people around town, got it?"

"Got it," Emilio muttered, his gaze dropping to the floor.

Earl smiled. "No more nosing around, understand? Any more barking around about who might or might not be involved in this or that, and a dog might have to get put down."

"I said I got it, didn't I?" Emilio met Earl's cold gaze.

"Just making sure we're done with problems." Earl wrapped his callused fingers around the whiskey Archie had prepared and motioned for Clarence to join him. "Bottoms up."

"Barely watered down." Clarence rested his glass back atop the bar and shot Archie a sarcastic grin. "Will wonders never cease?"

Archie slid into a forced smile and rested a hand on the shotgun. "Do you gentlemen require anything else?"

"No, sir." Earl offered him an overly polite bow. "Though my partner and I have taken a liking to your little watering hole." He turned for the door and motioned for Clarence to follow. "I suspect we'll drop by again later, if that suits you, of course."

"That'll be just fine." Archie returned the shotgun to its home beneath the bar. "Just fine, indeed."

The pair were out the door before Archie dared say another word. The crowd, all of whom had watched as if ringside at a boxing match, immediately returned to their various conversations as if nothing had transpired.

Just another day in Wolf's Bend.

Steven, Niklaus, and Emilio gathered close in one corner while Archie worked to keep the saloon's clientele well lubricated with whiskey and beer.

"Well, that went well." Niklaus eyed the door. "Though I would argue your assessment of the most likely suspects appears to have been pretty much on point."

"I'm just glad no one got shot." Steven turned to Emilio. "Are you okay? What the hell happened out there?"

"I'm fine." Emilio shook his head. "I was just following up on a lead. Some of the cowhands had run across a pair of men holed up in one of Mr. Garringer's barns north of town. I grabbed a horse and headed in that direction, but when I got there, they were already on horseback and waiting for me."

"So, you hightailed it back here."

"Two on one, Steven, and they had guns. I didn't know what else to do."

"You did the right thing. They were all but ready to shoot us on the spot in front of a room full of spectators. Out on the open road, who knows what they might've done."

"But I led them right back here." Emilio's head dropped. "I'm so sorry."

"Hey, Emilio." He clasped the younger man's shoulder. "Don't beat yourself up. They made it pretty clear when they got here that they knew exactly who I was. I don't think you meeting them on the road —most likely on their way here—did much to change that."

"And like you said, they knew you were coming." Niklaus glanced again in the direction of the door. "None of this is good."

Emilio shuddered, from the cold or otherwise, Steven wasn't sure.

"Which leaves us with one question: How is that possible?" Steven searched the gazes of each of his friends. "Outside of the four of us, the only person we've discussed our suspicions with is Zed himself."

"Don't forget about his little harem." Niklaus raised an eyebrow. "Any one of them could have blabbed, right?"

"They work for Zed, though, and seem as loyal as they come." Steven's gaze wandered among the crowd occupying the saloon, half of them refugees from the destroyed train. "Why would Zed or any of his people want to help the very people who just blew up their ticket east?"

"Unless..." Emilio considered his words. "What if Zed himself is the 'old man'?"

"And all of this is just a way to get those two bandits to take us out." Niklaus shook his head. "Wouldn't be the first time Zed has tried to get rid of us without getting his hands dirty."

"All I know is that something foul is going on here. So far, we've got a dead U.S. marshal, a blown-up train, a couple of thugs who seem to be getting insider information, and the literal king of all badness in the world a few blocks away." Steven let out a sigh. "And somehow, yet again, we're stuck in the middle of it."

The remainder of the day passed, for the most part, without event. Steven and the rest of their quartet shared a meal at the back of the saloon as Archie worked the bar and kept the occasional disagreement among the patrons from spiraling out of control. They discussed everything under the sun, the firewater keeping the stories flowing deep into the evening. Well past sunset, however, they finally reached a point where there didn't seem much else to say. With a quick salute, Emilio left to ride back out to Mr. Garringer's ranch while Steven and Niklaus retired to Dottie's for the night.

They'd barely had a chance to get out of their boots when a knock came at the door to their room.

"Who is it?" Steven asked, the usual edge in his voice diminished a bit by the whiskey.

"It's me, Mr. Bauer," came a timid voice. "Levi."

Levi. The inn's clerk.

"What do you need, Levi?"

"May I come in?"

"Sure." Steven rebuckled his pants and stepped to the door. "Is something wrong?"

Steven had just turned the lock when a flurry of metallic wings sounded from the table where Amaryllis rested. Before Steven could take another breath, the door burst open and Sheriff Post and Deputy Ndure rushed into the room.

"I'm sorry, Mr. Bauer," came a squeaky voice from behind the two lawmen. "The sheriff said I had to—"

"Shut up, Levi." Post clamped a hand down on Steven's shoulder. "Hello, Mr. Bauer. Busy evening?"

"What are you talking about?" Steven knew better than to try to resist. "Has something else happened?"

Deputy Ndure moved on Niklaus, his gun trained on Nik's midsection. "Keep your hands where I can see them, Mr. Zamek. We need to ask you two a few questions."

"A few questions?" Post let out a gruff laugh. "That's one way of putting it."

"What's this all about?" Niklaus asked. "What is it you think we've done?"

"Like you don't know." Post raised a mocking eyebrow. "Fine. I've already found the pair of you standing over one dying man and let you walk. Now, the two gentlemen you had an argument with earlier today in front of the whole town has been found strung up in one of Cyrus Garringer's barns." Post yanked Steven toward him, bringing him so close, Steven could smell the moist tobacco tucked between his lip and gum. "I'm guessing you don't know anything about that either."

"We don't." Steven winced in Post's vice-like grip. "We've been at the saloon for hours. We left maybe half an hour ago and came straight here."

"You're quick." Post puffed out his chest. "I'll give you that." He cleared his throat. "Word on the street is you sent the Cruz boy out earlier today to scout out where these particular unfortunate souls were hanging their hats." He gave Steven a firm shake, and any doubt that Post wasn't a man to toy with evaporated on the spot. "Unless I'm misinformed."

No sense in lying.

"We did send Emilio to investigate claims that two strangers were holed up in a barn north of town." Steven sucked in a breath as the boring pain in his shoulder doubled under Post's fingers. "He didn't even make it there. The two men you're asking about were already on the way to confront us in the saloon."

"Which begs the question why two men you barely know were coming to find you, now doesn't it? Not to mention what you two were doing 'investigating' anything in the first place." Post's tobacco breath made Steven gag. "Anyway, I'm not sure why you brought Cruz in on all this. He always seemed like a pretty good kid."

"You have no idea." Steven made the next logical leap. "Still, leave him out of this. He's done nothing wrong."

"Maybe, though that's not exactly up to me, now is it?" Post's expression shifted to a subtle smile of victory. "So, you admit these two men who had their necks stretched in the last few hours already had some sort of problem with you. Now they're dead, and you two are talking out of both sides of your mouths." Post's grip relaxed slightly. "There's something you aren't telling me."

Steven's mind raced. Outside of their time-displaced quartet, the only people who knew anything about their suspicions of "Earl" and "Clarence" were Zed/Victor Brenin and his three traveling companions. He didn't know much, but he understood all too well naming them would only make matters worse.

Three people were already dead, and Steven couldn't risk that one of them might be next.

"What happens now?" Steven asked.

"Now? You two will be spending the evening in what passes for a jail in this town." Ndure motioned for Niklaus to sit. "Get your boots on."

Post pushed Steven down into a chair. "Something here smells rotten, boys, but lucky for you both, I still haven't quite decided it's the two of you." He stepped back and handed Steven on of his boots. "In any case, you're coming with us, and I'd advise you to comply." Post's voice dropped to a whisper. "There's been quite enough bloodshed in Wolf's Bend today already."

22

LOCK & KEY

"Freezing my ass off in an 1890 root cellar in Nowhere, Wyoming?" Niklaus let out a bitter laugh. "Before today, not even an honorable mention on the list of worst places I thought I might end up." He stood hunched between two rows of parallel log-constructed shelves, and munched on a turnip. The only illumination in the space came from a beam of pale moonlight eking its way through the crack between the double doors above his head. "I've got to say, though, it's moving to the top with a bullet."

"No pouch." Steven's chin dropped to his chest. "No dragonfly." He fished the marble pawn from his pocket. "We may still have our icons, but they're little more than paperweights unless we can find our way back to our own time." He sat on a makeshift seat cobbled together from a pile of sweet potatoes, swearing under his breath to never again complain about the lumpy old recliner in his apartment back in Chicago. "I hate to say it, Nik, but we're screwed."

"We haven't done anything." Niklaus knelt down to meet Steven's gaze. "Can't we just tell Post and Ndure the truth?"

"Three murders have been committed since we hit town, Nik. I don't know what we'd have to say to convince any lawman worth his salt that we're innocent."

"God only knows what happened to the Marshal," Niklaus said, "but you and I both know Zed is behind the other two deaths."

Steven sighed. "If we call out Zed and his squad of femme fatales, I'm pretty sure the body count will do nothing but climb."

Niklaus considered for a moment. "The least they could have done was stick us in a stone and mortar cell with a barred window in the back. If I'm going to be thrown into an honest-to-god jail in the Old West, I want the real deal." He took another bite from his turnip and threw it to Steven. "Instead, they've imprisoned us in the local produce section."

Steven took a bite from the other side of the purple and white root. "Good lord, Nik, did you watch anything but Westerns when you were a kid?"

"What can I say? I love the Duke, though I'm pretty sure that even on his worst day, he'd never stick someone in a hole like this." He peered around, his eyes squinted. "On the other hand, no sense complaining about the all-you-can-eat vegetarian buffet." He swept his hand around the tiny space, his mischievous smile just visible in the dim. "If you like beets and rutabagas, this must be heaven."

"Barred window or not, I guess we can rule out Emilio showing up with a team of horses and springing us." Steven fell back on the pile of tubers and groaned. "How would he ever find us in this hole, anyway?"

"I found you." The whispered feminine voice registered in Steven's mind as familiar. "You two are as loud as elephants and about as subtle. Now, stand away from the door lest you be injured."

"Audrey?" Steven's heart swelled with hope.

"No. Ume." The annoyance in her tone came through loud and clear. "Now, be quiet and let me concentrate."

"Ume." Steven stood, his legs tingling as if covered in ants, and huddled against the far wall with Niklaus.

"One of the sisters?" Niklaus asked.

"Yeah." Steven stared up at the cellar door. "The no-nonsense one."

"What do you think she's planning to—"

A loud crack echoed in the cellar. Niklaus and Steven covered their faces as splintered wood rained down on them. At first, Steven wondered if Ume had fired a gun or possibly employed a small explosive?

The truth was far more impressive.

Barely visible in the pale light, a diminutive hand retreated through the new gaping hole in the door.

Ume had literally punched straight through two inches of solid wood.

"Like I said before." Steven shook his head. "Zed has a type."

The door opened upward, allowing in the shine of the full moon above. Silhouetted against the starry night sky, Ume stood in a loose-fitting embroidered tunic over pants, the entire ensemble rendered in deep hues the color of Malbec.

"You came here?" Steven squinted, the full moon above blinding him momentarily after hours in the near total darkness. "For us?"

"Are you not in the employ of Mr. Brenin?" Ume stepped away from the edge of the door. "Did you think he would leave you here to rot?"

"I suppose not." Steven climbed out of the root cellar and helped Niklaus up. "Thanks."

"No, Mr. Bauer. Thank you." Ume gave Steven a subtle nod. "Your information proved not only accurate, but invaluable."

"Wait." Comprehension dawned on Steven. "It was you. You killed those men."

"Sakura and I, actually." Ume's eyes shifted left and right. "Kiku is still in training, and, regardless of her skills, the messier side of our work is…not to her taste."

"The sheriff thinks we did it," Niklaus said. "We're in big trouble because of you."

"Mr. Brenin does not take threats to his life lightly, nor does he appreciate being inconvenienced. We ensured those men paid for their deeds, though our method of correcting the problem has clearly led to unfortunate consequences for the two of you. Thus, my presence here and now." She smiled. "I would argue, however, that had you avoided a public confrontation with the two men in question, much of this unpleasantness might have been avoided."

Steven bit back the sharp retort at the tip of his tongue. "Thank you, Ume." He glanced up and down the snow-covered street. "So, what now?"

"Yeah." Niklaus closed the cellar doors behind them. "Post sees us around town, we're toast."

"Toast? What an odd statement." Ume stole to the side of a nearby building, her footfalls like autumn leaves falling to the ground, and motioned for Steven and Niklaus to follow. "Please understand. Those men left us no choice, and Mr. Brenin wanted us to leave a very clear message to anyone else in town who might assume a similar action would be tolerated. Unfortunately, our actions led to your banishment to that hole, and Mr. Brenin's instructions notwithstanding, it was my duty to set that right." Her eyes narrowed. "Consider our shared debt to you both expiated."

They continued through the town, Ume's silent tread made all the more impressive by both her ability to vanish into the shadows of the various buildings and even more so by the fact that she rarely left a discernible footprint in the snow. Steven and Niklaus did their best to match Ume in stealth, but compared to their rescuer, they might as well have been wearing cowbells.

"A question," Steven asked when they came to rest by the back corner of the town's general store. "Did you find out why they did it? Why they blew up the train?"

"They both kept their tongues, despite my best efforts." Ume crossed her arms. "Still, Mr. Brenin has his theories." She took a breath and grimaced. "As do I."

Niklaus stood. "And that's all you've got to say on the subject, I'm guessing." He'd barely taken a step in the direction of the street when Ume yanked him back.

"Stay down, both of you." Her voice took on a strange insistence. And the tone wasn't all that seemed strange. "I've risked much to free you. You will move when I say and not before."

"But—" Niklaus began.

Quiet.

Steven and Niklaus both froze in place, the emphatic tone of Ume's command made all the more jarring by the realization Steven wasn't altogether certain he'd heard the solitary word with his ears.

Not since he and Audrey had spoken mind-to-mind during her capture by the Black Knight months before had Steven experienced another person's thoughts directly entering his mind. He understood from Grey that only a rare combination of the Game's magic, the intervention of the Arbiters, and their own shared desperation had made such communication possible. With Ume, however, this form of thought-speech seemed as natural as talking.

You can do this? Steven asked, thinking the words rather than speaking them aloud. *When you're not, of course, punching through solid wood doors or running an inch above the ground?*

We all have our talents, Mr. Bauer. And since you have taken this particular talent of mine completely in stride, I'm guessing there is much about you that bears watching as well.

This is like that chick on Star Trek, *isn't it?* Niklaus' wide-eyed stare passed from Steven to Ume and back again. *The one who always hung out with the guy with the beard.*

Steven shook his head. *What didn't you learn by watching television, Niklaus?*

Quiet, you two. Ume paused. *However, I'm curious. What is this...television?*

Another time. Steven locked gazes with Ume. *A moment ago, you held us back. Is there danger?*

Not so long as you stay with me. Now, down. She motioned for them to huddle in the snow by the building's edge and stood over them in a low fighting stance. Her form still as a statue, even the rise and fall of her chest seemed to halt.

Seconds later, Sheriff Post, John Ndure, and a trio of men Steven didn't recognize wandered up the street. The nearest looked directly at them, and for a moment, Steven feared they'd spot Ume. He needn't have worried. Be it magic, skill, or some wondrous combination of both, one thing remained clear—people only saw Ume if and when she wished to be seen.

And if that ever became the case, six-shooters and shotguns notwithstanding, Post, Ndure, and the rest were in for quite a surprise.

Steven hoped it wouldn't come to that.

For all their sakes.

Once Post and his posse had passed, Ume unfroze and pulled Steven up from the snow. "Grab your friend. Let's go."

Across the road in less time than it took Steven to take a breath, Ume stood in the shadow of the eaves of a small woodshed and motioned for them to join her.

"You know," Niklaus whispered as Steven helped him to his feet, "her whole 'leave no tracks' thing doesn't do much good with you and me in tow."

"Just move."

Steven and Niklaus sprinted across the snow-covered gravel and joined Ume in the shadows. They rested there for all of two seconds before she led them away from the main road.

"Isn't this the way toward the depot station?" Steven asked.

"Indeed." Ume resumed her low whisper. "The town isn't safe. The only place we can keep you secure is in our railcar."

"Wait." Niklaus stopped in his tracks. "What about Archie and Emilio?"

"Sakura is gathering your friends. You four will remain with us until we reach the next state, at which point you will disembark and find your own way."

A flash of panic struck Steven center chest, and not just at the thought of being holed up in the Black King's railcar. "What about our things?"

Back at Dottie's Inn, stuffed inside a pillowcase and buried at the bottom of a duffel bag that wouldn't be stitched together for half a century rested the *Hvitr Kyll*, the white pouch of the Game and their only ticket out of 1890.

"If there is time, we will attempt to retrieve your belongings, but please understand that Mr. Brenin has already exercised significant generosity in sending us for you and your friends."

"Understood." Steven bit back the bile in his throat. "And again, thank you."

The three of them walked, one in total silence, the other two doing their best not to sound like a herd of rhinoceros. Snow-crusted trails that cut through forests that had never seen a logger's axe led to the wood line adjacent to the destroyed locomotive. The remainder of the train sat uncoupled from the pile of scrap metal on wheels, the last car all but invisible as a cloud swept across the bright full moon.

A flurry of questions that had bugged Steven since he'd first learned of the untimely deaths of Earl and Clarence resurfaced.

Who was the "old man" who hired the pair to blow the train in the first place? Why the hell arrange for such destruction if no follow up was planned, or at least none Steven and the others could appreciate? Above all, with the events in question occurring just after his and Niklaus' arrival in town and during the only time this century when four Pieces from the next iteration of the Game would come face-to-face with the opposing King, what were the odds any of it had occurred by chance?

Though the last question left him pondering everything he'd ever held true, he did know one thing beyond any shadow of a doubt.

In matters of the Game, coincidences were a rare thing indeed.

Ume rapped at the railcar's black door. Steven and Niklaus kept watch, fearful that at any moment, Post and his various deputies might spring from the shadows of the forest and end their mad dash for freedom.

A click, a rush of steam, and the door slid open. Within, Zed/Brenin stood in jet black robes, peering down at them with an imperious gaze.

"Mr. Bauer." His head tilted forward in a subtle nod.

"Mr. Brenin," Steven answered in kind. "Thank you for sending Ume."

His eyes flicked to Niklaus. "Mr. Zamek." Brenin stepped back from the doorway and motioned them forward. "Come inside. Quickly."

Steven and Niklaus climbed into the railcar with Ume close behind. Zed sealed the door and motioned for them to be seated.

"Sakura?" Ume asked. "Kiku?"

"Your older sister is gathering Mr. Lacan and the Cruz boy." Zed peered out between two slats of the nearest window. "As for Kiku, I sent her on an errand. She shouldn't be gone long."

"She is not yet ready." Ume fumed. "Sakura can more than care for herself, but Kiku…"

"Kiku could dismantle this entire town singlehandedly if she chose to do so." Zed slid into a beatific smile. "She may not possess your skills or your sister's raw talent, but she is more than able to mind her own back."

"We swore you our loyalty," Ume spat, not backing down an inch. "And Sakura a bit more. In the end, though, one thing has always been clear. Kiku is the youngest and therefore is to be protected at all costs."

"Dearest Ume, fear not." Zed's voice dropped into a practiced sing-song, almost hypnotic in its rise and fall. "No one save you and your sister care more for Kiku than I. Trust that I would not send her unnecessarily into harm's way." His gaze flicked to Steven. "And regardless, we have guests. Perhaps we can engage in this discussion at a later date?"

"Of course, Mr. Brenin." Ume's shoulders dropped, though the intensity in her gaze remained. "Though you'd best pray to whatever gods you worship that Kiku returns safely or our discussion may be one you do not enjoy."

Zed gave another nod, acquiescing the point. "Understood." He turned to Steven. "So, Mr. Bauer, I suspect you and I both remain troubled by the same question."

Steven let out a bitter chuckle. "Like what the hell is going on around here?"

"Cards on the table, I suppose." Zed produced a folded paper from his pocket. "I received this telegram a month or so ago requesting I head east from my winter home in San Francisco for a meeting of 'utmost importance' in the city of Chicago."

Where all of this began. Steven's cheeks grew warm. *And where your Black Queen nearly ended me.*

"Well, we're certainly hell and gone from Illinois." Steven studied the paper. "What did this person want?"

"I haven't the slightest idea." Brenin's fingers tensed, crinkling the yellowed paper in his hand. "Though I'm beginning to develop a few theories."

"Who sent the message?" Niklaus held out his hand, and Brenin, surprising Ume as much as Steven, handed him the paper. "Emanuel Lasker?" Niklaus asked. "Who is that?"

"A German mathematician and philosopher who also happens to be a rising talent in the world of chess." Brenin took a seat by the chessboard, the pieces all reset to their starting positions, and picked up the black king. "I've heard talk of him through certain channels. Seen analyses of his games. He doesn't play like anyone else in his sphere." He met Niklaus' gaze. "This game may be played here…" The Black King waved a hand across the board before holding the ebony chess piece to his temple. "But it lives here." His lips spread into a disquieting smile. "As surprised as I was to receive the correspondence, imagine learning that he wanted to meet with me in, of all places, the American Midwest."

"You confirmed the letter came from him?" Steven asked. "This Lasker?"

Zed lowered his head in frustration. "I was so flattered to receive such an invitation that I may not have exercised my usual due diligence." He returned the black king to its spot on the chessboard. "Even the best players may make an impulsive move from time to time, I suppose."

"What would he want with you anyway?"

"Let's just say my love for the game goes far beyond mere casual interest." Brenin stood and went to the window. "I've studied with many of the greats, and he appears destined to be a legend." He took a deep breath. "The things I could learn from him."

"But why chess?" Steven worked to keep from his gaze the fact that he already knew the answer all too well. "Why is this game so important to you?"

"Why, indeed?" Brenin turned to face them, his lips drawn tight across his teeth. "To understand chess, Mr. Bauer, is to understand life. Chess is more than a metaphor for war or strategy. Chess is everything."

Steven's intestines roiled at the words. "Everything?"

"Knowing what it is you want. Accepting what you have to do to achieve your goals. Understanding what you might have to sacrifice."

Brenin shivered with excitement. "This game, as you call it, represents every day of every life on this planet, every decision, every choice, every moment, all boiled down to its barest essence, a battle of black and white waged on sixty-four squares, the outcomes infinite." The Black King's eyes slid closed. "What else is there?"

A quick rap at the railcar door broke the momentary silence.

"Who is it?" Ume asked.

"Sakura." Though muffled by the door, the annoyance in the eldest sister's voice came through loud and clear. "I have the old man and the boy."

Again the door hissed as the steam-locked seal opened. Sakura stepped inside with Emilio close on her heels and Archie bringing up the rear.

"Quickly, now." Ume moved to one side and pushed Archie and Emilio toward a pair of matching chairs upholstered with zebra hide. "Eyes are everywhere."

Sakura secured the door. "I have brought them, Victor, as you asked." Her eyes searched the room. "Wait. Where is Kiku?"

"Sent on an errand," Ume responded, "against both of our express wishes."

Tempered anger flashed in Sakura's eyes. "Victor?"

"She is performing a minor task, one requiring neither your nor Ume's particular talents." Brenin smiled. "She will be fine."

"I'm certain she will." Sakura lowered her head, evincing submission, though the anger in her gaze mirrored Ume's. "Though we *will* be discussing this later."

"So, Mr. Brenin." Archie straightened himself in the plush chair. "You have all of us here. Do you mind telling us what it is you want with us?"

"Funny you should ask your question in that manner, Mr. Lacan, as I was similarly curious as to why one or more of the four of you fine gentlemen might be the one responsible for my being stranded in *your* presence."

Emilio rose from his chair, eyes narrowed and fists balled at his sides. "You think we had something to do with all of this?"

"Hold on, Emilio." Steven motioned for him to back down. "Mr.

Brenin just went to a lot of trouble to bring us all here. Perhaps we should hear him—"

"Victor Brenin!" The shouted voice, muffled by the steam-sealed door, brought all discussion in the room to a halt. "Open up that fancy can of sardines and come out here so we can talk."

"Excellent." Zed let out a measured breath. "Now we can finish this."

The Black King pulled down a metallic device from an ornately carved sconce, a thick wire connecting the silver cylinder to the wall, and spoke into it.

"Sheriff Post." Zed's voice, amplified by the old-timey microphone and whatever served as speakers outside the car, reverberated through the space and sent Steven's heart racing. "Right on time."

23

LAW & ORDER

"I thought you wanted to help us." Steven took a step back from Brenin, his knee hitting the chess table and knocking over several of the pieces. "What have you done?"

"What, indeed?" Ume flitted to the nearest window and peered out. "You sent us to collect these men from the constable's clutches, and now you've brought him and his rabble of coarse men to our doorstep?"

"I'm merely bringing all the pieces of this particular game together in one place so I can better ascertain the circumstances leading to our current predicament." Brenin pulled in a cleansing breath and let it out with no small measure of drama. "Clearly, someone has gone to a significant amount of trouble to ensure my presence here and now in this nowhere of a town, and as far as I can see, Mr. Bauer and his associates are the only ones who noted our arrival with anything more than passing interest." He locked gazes with Ume. "Not to mention, my dear, that your...discussion earlier with the two men who destroyed our train's locomotive provided little new information beyond the fact that they were more afraid of their mysterious bene-factor than me or, much to their detriment, you."

"But why break us out of Post's jail only to turn us right back over to him?" Though he tried to keep an even keel, Steven bristled before this man who, a century in the future, would send emissaries to kill rather than collect him. "In case you haven't noticed, Mr. Brenin, this isn't one of your games." His eyes narrowed. "Actual lives are on the line."

"Fear not, Mr. Bauer." Brenin flipped the switch that released the door's steam-lock and rested his fingers upon the handle. "As I was telling Ume, I merely wished to gather all involved at a location of my choosing so the necessary deliberation could occur in a relatively controlled environment."

"Controlled? We're trapped inside a stranded train car with no cover for a hundred yards in every direction, and Post has the manpower and guns of an entire town at his disposal."

"A little trust, Mr. Bauer." The Black King smiled. "Don't forget, had I so chosen, I could have left you and Mr. Zamek to rot in that root cellar this town calls a jail."

As Brenin directed Ume to open the door, Steven motioned for Archie and Emilio to stay out of sight. Outside, waiting in the cold a good thirty yards away, stood Sheriff Post, Deputy Ndure, and the three-man posse from before.

With one significant addition.

Amid the collection of unshaven men in their long coats and brimmed hats stood Kiku shivering in the cold, utter defiance pouring from her steely gaze.

Ume's voice dropped to a harsh whisper. "You sent our sister to bring those men?"

"Damn it, Victor." Sakura's hands balled into fists at her sides. "If any of them has laid so much as a finger on her..."

"My dears." Brenin motioned for the two sisters to remain calm. "Before she left, I gave Kiku full authority to answer any unseemly behavior in kind. The fact that those five men all stand there without a scratch would suggest nothing inappropriate has occurred." He cleared his throat. "As Kiku has told both of you on more than one occasion, she is a child no longer."

"Mr. Brenin." Post took a step forward, the snow at his feet coming to his ankles. "As requested, we've come to discuss the situation regarding two men who, up until an hour ago, were in my custody." He doffed his hat and held it at his side. "I must admit that I find this entire turn of events quite confusing."

Ndure gave Kiku a gentle push forward. "Message delivered, girl. Now, return to your sisters before they worry another moment." He offered Ume and Sakura a forced smile and raised his hands before him in a gesture of deference. "Your sister is unharmed, as anyone with eyes can see."

"Hmm." Niklaus pulled close to Steven's ear. "At least one of this town's lawmen was paying attention back at the saloon."

"The fact that Ndure recognizes they aren't dealing with three shrinking violets only helps our situation so much, though." Steven peered out at the sheriff and his posse. "Post thinks we're guilty as sin. All four of those men are packing at least a pistol or two, and I have no doubt 'Wyatt Earp' has his favorite shotgun under that coat of his." His eyes shifted left and right. "Even if we happen to have the Charlie's Angels of 1890 on our side..."

"Bullets are going to fly." Emilio let out a sigh. "Just like Baltimore."

Steven's mind skipped back through a cavalcade of memories: his pursuit of Emilio and Lena through the streets of Maryland's largest city, the gang war that claimed Emilio's brother, Carlos, and the four-way battle that nearly ended Steven's quest to gather the White before it had even begun.

Kiku stepped inside the railcar and into Sakura and Ume's waiting arms. Shifting into their native Japanese, her sisters took turns addressing her, their tone alternating between sweet relief and stern admonishment. Her features dark with appropriate contrition, she took the tongue-lashing in stride, though Steven caught more than one flash of mischief in the young woman's eyes.

"Enough stalling." Post holstered his six-shooter and pulled the shotgun from inside his duster. "Step outside, Brenin, so we can talk."

"I think not, Sheriff." Brenin held the microphone to his lips like a rock star. "I'm quite comfortable in my little home away from home, and it appears to be quite cold where you're standing." He shot Steven a knowing glance. "In fact, I suggest you and your men put away your weapons, as much for your own protection as for ours."

Post considered for a moment and then lowered his shotgun, motioning for Ndure and the three deputized townsfolk to holster their pistols as well. "Done." His breath steamed in the cold. "Lucky for you, I'm just curious enough to play along with whatever game it is you think you're playing. But know that, in the end, we're not leaving without Bauer and Zamek."

"And why would you wish to take them, Sheriff?" The surprise in Brenin's voice sounded almost authentic. "They've done nothing wrong."

"Nothing?" Post paced in the snow. "Two men are dead just hours after a very public argument with the men I have no doubt are standing just out of sight inside your car, men you claim as being in your employ. Believe me, Mr. Brenin, you'd be better served divorcing yourself from suspicion rather than breaking suspected murderers out of jail and harboring them from justice."

"While it is arguably regrettable that the two men in question shuffled off this mortal coil before their time, you have likely already deduced they are the pair responsible for destroying the fine locomotive that was transporting me and the rest of the refugees now residing in your town east in the midst of this bitter winter. Dozens could have perished if things had gone differently and all due to their malfeasance, not to mention the difficulties both your community and region now face with this rail line currently out of operation. Is the demise of two such reprobates truly such a tragedy?"

"Spoken like a true king," Archie muttered under his breath.

"Or politician," Niklaus added.

"Quiet," Ume whispered. "Regardless of your feelings about him or the current situation, Mr. Brenin is negotiating for both of your lives."

All of them remained quiet as Post responded to Brenin's eloquent oration.

"Very pretty words, and yet nowhere in there was a denial that Bauer and Zamek acted as judge, jury, and executioner for those two men, and all, it would seem, under your direction."

"Were they, in fact, guilty, I'd think they'd be met with reward and gratitude rather than the threat of imprisonment. Still, it doesn't matter, as, and let me make myself clear this time, Mr. Bauer and Mr.

Zamek had nothing whatsoever to do with the deaths of those two men."

"That's for a court to decide, Mr. Brenin." Post adjusted his hat. "And since you seem to know so much about what happened, perhaps you should come with us as well."

Brenin laughed. "A novel thought, Sheriff, but I won't be going anywhere with anyone."

"You can't stay in there forever." Post shook his head in mock sadness. "Your little black box on wheels may contain every amenity a man could desire, but I'm guessing food and water for eight is more than you were likely prepared for."

Brenin's smile evaporated. "You have no idea what I'm prepared for, little man."

"Enough." Post bristled visibly at the dig, bringing the shotgun back up and directing it at Brenin's midsection. "Come out of that car, or we start shooting."

Brenin sighed. "I'd hoped we could talk about this as men of logic, but your short-sightedness is making such discourse impossible. Please understand you will not be taking anyone from my railcar this day, nor will you threaten me or any of my associates again, lest you suffer the consequences."

"Consequences?" Post sneered. "Brave words from a man trapped in a box with two fugitives and a bunch of women." His hearty laugh steamed in the cold. "Next you'll be telling me it was one of your girls who strung up those two men."

"Sheriff Post." Ndure, who had remained silent for most of the conversation, narrowed his eyes at the crowd gathered in the railcar's doorway. "Something you may wish to consider." He whispered in Post's ear, and understanding blossomed on the sheriff's face.

"All of you." Post brought up his shotgun. "Out of that car. Now."

"Very well." Brenin cracked his knuckles. "When diplomacy fails..." He wrapped his fingers around a lever in the wall that Steven had dismissed as a simple lighting fixture and gave it a gentle pull. The resulting click led to a deafening grinding of gears that echoed in the space. Moments later, the business end of a multi-barreled gun blossomed above the open door, directed at the spot where Post and his posse stood. In answer, the sheriff dove to the snow-covered ground as the rest of his posse fled. John Ndure, alone, stood his ground without flinching.

"A Gatling gun," Archie whispered from his hiding place just inside the door. "Ensconced within the walls. Incredible."

"Not an inexpensive modification, I assure you." Brenin's finger stroked what appeared to be the gun's trigger at the upper limit of the ornately carved lamp/lever. "God willing, there will be no need to fire it." He let out a weary laugh. "Cleaning such a weapon is far from easy."

"Like you'd be doing the cleaning," Ume muttered.

Brenin gave the middle sister in his charge a sharp look and brought the microphone again to his lips. "Gentlemen, I brought you here to talk, but make no mistake, I can answer your gentle rain of bullets with a thunderstorm the likes of which you will not soon forget."

"Mr. Brenin." Ndure took a step forward. "No need for a standoff. We merely wish to—"

"This is no standoff." Brenin shouted directly into the microphone, the reverberation shaking the entire car. "This is a discussion between men."

Post pulled himself up from the ground and swept the snow from his battered duster. "Mr. Brenin, please stand down so we can talk about this."

"The time for talk is over." Brenin grasped the edge of the door and slid it half shut. "Strangely, I've changed my mind. About all of this." His voice dropped a few decibels. "A rare occurrence indeed."

"This is your last chance, Brenin." Post and Ndure sprinted for the railcar.

"Excellent speaking with you, Sheriff Post. Thank you for your kind visit." And with that, Brenin closed the door, the already familiar hiss of the steam seal locking them in.

A moment later, Post pounded at the door. "The new locomotive doesn't arrive for another day, Brenin. You're not going anywhere."

"Perhaps." Brenin spoke one last time into the microphone before returning it to its sconce. "Perhaps not." He glanced at the oldest sister. "Sakura?"

Her lips curled up into an obedient smile. "With pleasure."

And with that, the elegantly dressed woman stepped into the room she had previously shared with the Black King and closed the door behind her. At first, nothing happened, but as the entire car shook with a rhythmic pulse, Steven dropped into a low crouch.

"What's happening?" he asked. "What's that sound?"

"You will see." Brenin moved to the other side of the car and dropped into the most luxurious chair in the room. "Suffice to say that sound amplification and superior firepower aren't the only tricks my—what did he call it—'little black box on wheels' can perform."

A moment later, the entire railcar lurched in the direction opposite the destroyed locomotive. Archie nearly fell over, but Emilio caught him with a quick assist from Ume.

Niklaus' eyes grew wide. "Your railcar. It can move under its own power?"

"Welcome to the future, Mr. Zamek." Brenin smiled smugly. "Why depend on someone else's engine to provide your locomotion when you have the means to move all on your own?"

Steven rested his hand on the floor. "An internal steam engine?"

"You have an engineer's mind, Mr. Bauer."

Steven tilted his head to one side. "And you are years ahead of your time, Mr. Brenin."

"Fortune has shined on me for years, and I have chosen to invest my money wisely in pursuit of the American Dream. Life. Liberty." His eyes shot to Sakura as she reentered the room. "The pursuit of happiness."

Sakura gave Brenin a gentle bow. "The belly of the *Dragon* is hot, Victor."

"Excellent." He flipped open one of his armrests and pulled a lever hidden there. "Full steam ahead, then."

The car lurched again and with each passing second, accelerated all the more. A loud crash hit the door from outside followed by several loud reports.

"They're firing on the car." Ume groaned. "More maintenance."

"Maintenance?" Niklaus asked. "What if one of those bullets gets through?"

"You needn't worry," Brenin announced from his chair. "This car is designed to withstand a stray cannonball." The Black King reclined in his makeshift throne. "I think it can withstand the good sheriff's buckshot."

"I don't understand." Steven worked to keep the incredulity from his voice. "You're not going to return fire?"

"Mr. Bauer, I maintain that weapon mostly as a deterrent and revealed it simply to buy us time to negotiate our exit from the situation."

"But it works, right?" Steven grabbed one of the lamps to steady himself as the car accelerated again, careful to avoid the one with the ornately carved trigger. "The Gatling gun?"

Brenin's face darkened. "Of course it works. To threaten violence without both the capacity and willingness to follow through as needed would be the height of cowardice."

"But you've shown no issue with killing. Even today." Steven's gaze darted to Ume. "What's different now?"

"Mr. Bauer, I have no idea what you might think you know of me, but please understand. Above all, I am an honorable man. Sometimes in this grand game of existence, lives must be taken, some for the common good, and others, honestly, to advance whatever agenda I happen to be working toward at the time. The death of the two men who destroyed our locomotive fell well within both those parameters, and while I don't relish their shared demise, I believe fully that their deaths were necessary. Never think for a moment that killing is something I take lightly or enjoy." He leaned forward and grasped one of the white pieces from the chessboard.

"This pawn, for instance." Brenin placed the piece on the center of the board. "In any particular game, this lowly foot soldier can defend a square, protect another piece, provide a necessary barrier from enemy incursion, or even advance to the opposite end of the board and become far more than its humble origins would seem to allow." He then picked up the pawn and rested it on its side at the edge of the table. "Sacrificing such a piece is, at times, a necessary tactic to bring victory." Brenin peered down pitifully at the tiny hunk of white marble. "Once removed from the board, however, it is gone forever." He looked up at Steven through his dark eyebrows. "Do you understand?"

"I understand." Heat rose in Steven's cheeks, even as his heart threatened to pound out of his chest. "So, we're escaping for the moment, but there's one problem. Post and the rest of the world knows exactly where these tracks lead. What's to keep them from telegraphing ahead and having the next town block the tracks?"

"Very astute, Mr. Bauer, but there is no need to fear. As you might guess, I am prepared for even this contingency, though the nature of my plan is nothing any of you would believe."

Emilio, who'd been silent for some time, laughed. "Try us."

"Very well." Brenin cleared his throat. "All along the globe, there are places where certain energies exist that are beyond the ken of mankind as a whole. Much like the geysers in the American West or the hundreds of volcanoes that make up the Ring of Fire surrounding the Pacific Ocean, these nexuses of power may lie dormant for centuries, unseen, unheard, unfelt." His eyes closed in rapture. "But they are there. Ancient and arcane and filled with unmitigated power, all just waiting for someone who knows how to manipulate those energies to accomplish the impossible."

Archie cleared his throat. "You speak of crossings."

Brenin's gaze shot to Archie. "What do you know of crossings?"

"More than you might expect." Steven stepped in front of Archie. "Is there one nearby?"

Brenin paused, clearly flummoxed for the first time since they'd encountered him this century. "A few miles to the west." He peered out the window at the rushing trees. "This section of track is new to me, as even I haven't traveled every inch of this continent yet. I did, however, make a point of marking the locations of the various fonts of power along the way." His eyes narrowed at Steven. "One never knows when one might encounter something…unexpected."

"How much farther?" Archie asked.

Brenin turned to Sakura, whose eyes danced left and right in concentration.

"Just over four miles to the nearest one," she said, her eyes focusing on Kiku as if studying her, "but the spot thirty-seven miles farther down the track remains the strongest we've encountered in the last couple of days. For what you're proposing, I suggest we continue on."

"So be it." The Black King, still sitting upon his makeshift throne, crossed his arms and let out a haughty sigh. "Bring us to the crossing and pity anyone who attempts to get in our way."

The next half hour proceeded in near silence. Brenin sat at one end of the room atop the posh chair, his trio of associates surrounding him, begging the question of whether Brenin defended them or the three sisters, Brenin. Steven sat opposite the Black King with Niklaus, Archie, and Emilio as his opposite entourage. Between them, the table containing the sixty-four alternating squares of the chessboard rested, the pieces occasionally shifting with movement of the railcar, two barely restrained armies rattling their sabers in preparation for war.

Several minutes into their trip, Brenin broke the silence.

"It is no mere coincidence that brings us together, is it, Mr. Bauer?"

"I no longer believe in coincidence." Steven leaned forward in his chair. "I suspect you don't either."

"And yet," Brenin continued, "my gut tells me you are not the one responsible for the ruse that lured me to Wolf's Bend." He pulled the telegraph from his pocket. "Someone led me down quite a cherry path to get me to leave the warmth of my home in the dead of winter." He glanced around his posh sanctum on wheels. "Our current lack of want notwithstanding."

"Perhaps if you hadn't ordered the two men who destroyed the locomotive killed, we could've found out who hired them and put this mystery to rest." Steven interlaced his fingers. "Two pieces taken off the board too soon, Mr. Brenin?"

"They would not talk." Ume pursed her lips. "Whoever put them up to the task had instilled in them the fear of God."

"And we still don't know who shot that U.S. Marshal." Niklaus rested his chin in his palm and stared out the window. "Or why."

"Maybe it's unrelated?" Emilio raised an eyebrow.

"Your leader has already made it clear he doesn't believe in coincidence." Brenin locked gazes with Emilio. "I would suggest you follow his lead, young man."

"May God have mercy on all their souls," Archie interrupted, lowering his head in prayer. "And ours as well, for whatever part we played in their deaths."

Emilio crossed himself, an odd sentiment from the angry young man Steven met a year or so before. Niklaus didn't say a word, wisely opting to keep his trademark wit to himself for once. Even Steven allowed a moment of silence before continuing.

"I still don't understand why you brought Post to the train station," he asked. "If you intended to literally 'get the hell out of Dodge' with us in tow, why announce your plan?"

Brenin smiled. "My reasons are my own, Mr. Bauer, but suffice to say Sheriff Post and his collection of upstanding townsfolk and deputies are now looking for you and Mr. Zamek in a black railcar armed with a mysterious cannon and moving under its own power along a section of track that will soon be empty. A tall tale indeed, would you not say?"

"He knows what he saw." Emilio's grip went white on the arm of his chair. "Why wouldn't the world believe him?"

"The West is full of myth and folklore." Brenin set to straightening the chessboard, the various pieces displaced from their squares as the car lurched to one side. "Would you not prefer to be spoken of in the same breath with the likes of Paul Bunyan and John Henry rather than Billy the Kid or Jesse James?"

"Perhaps." Steven's eyes narrowed in concentration. "Wait. You said the track would be empty. What do you intend to do with your railcar when you reach the crossing?"

"Do with it?" Brenin laughed. "Why, I plan to take it with me." He gestured around the luxurious space. "Do you think I would leave this luxury-on-rails for someone else to enjoy?"

"You intend to transport this entire car?"

"With the eight of us inside," Brenin whispered, his voice all but jubilant. "Yes."

Kiku, who had stood silently with her eyes closed for so long that Steven had been curious if she remained conscious, opened her eyes and rested a hand on Brenin's shoulder.

"We're getting close, Mr. Brenin."

"Excellent." He turned to the eldest sister. "Sakura, slow the railcar." With a self-satisfied sigh, he rested a hand on the shoulder of the youngest. "Kiku, bring me the box."

"Yes, Mr. Brenin." Kiku slipped past the door leading to the end of the car Brenin and Sakura shared, returning a moment later with a square box of ebony with arcane sigils carved into the wood on each side.

"Do you want to do the honors, my dear?" Brenin asked.

"May I?" Youthful exuberance broke through Kiku's morose façade. "Really?"

"You've been practicing, haven't you?" He reached into the box and pulled out the *Svartr Kyll*, the pouch of black leather that held the various icons of Brenin's side of the Game and sister to the white pouch Steven was destined to receive over a century in the future.

The image of the *Hvitr Kyll* resting at the bottom of a duffel bag miles away in a town they'd likely never see again chilled him to the bone.

"What is that?" Steven asked as the Black King handed the bag of dark leather to Kiku, doing his best to keep any hint of recognition from his face.

"Our ticket home, Mr. Bauer." Brenin's lips turned up in a self-satisfied smile. "In honor of our previous arrangement, I will ensure your safe delivery from this place. After that, your fate and that of your friends is up to you, and any deal between us becomes null and void."

"What should we expect?" Niklaus asked, inclining his head in Kiku's direction. "When she does whatever it is she's going to do."

"Just wait, Mr. Zamek." Brenin stroked his full beard. "As you have, no doubt, ascertained by this point, my three charges each possess talents beyond that of the average person, a familial trait, if you will."

He gestured to the elder two. "Sakura's gift revolves around an innate understanding of how things work, and Ume's, her prodigious physical capabilities notwithstanding, a method of communication that goes beyond words." He stroked the youngest girl's hair. "Lastly, Kiku's gift is an inherent sensitivity to the many pins and folds that hold together the universe, a talent that far outstrips not only my own ability but that of anyone I've ever encountered."

"We're here." Kiku's voice shifted up an octave, her voice taking on a sing-song, otherworldly quality. "Stop the car and allow me to take us home."

And with that, the young girl, not quite a woman, began to dance. Jerky at first, but growing more graceful by the second, Kiku stepped in time with music only she could hear, the pouch held high above her head, her eyes half-closed as if in a trance. Three times around the room she went before falling exhausted to the floor.

Emilio rushed to her side. "Is she all right?"

Sakura went to her sister's side and pulled Kiku's head onto her lap. "She'll be fine. Performing the ritual simply takes a lot out of her."

With everyone else's attention focused on Kiku, Steven's gaze went to the window where the grey sky that had been their reality for weeks transitioned in a flash, replaced with blue skies decorated with wispy white clouds. A random sunbeam poured from between the drawn curtains and fell upon Kiku's face, illuminating the unconscious girl's features as if she were an angel glowing from within.

"It worked." Steven locked gazes with Brenin. "Where are we?"

Brenin rose from his chair and went to the door. The characteristic hiss of the steam-lock release was soon followed by the rumbling of tumblers as he pulled the door open onto a beautiful vista of crystal aqua-blue ocean and rugged coastline.

"Welcome, all of you," the Black King proudly proclaimed, "to California."

24

BLADES & BULLETS

"T his is your home?" Emilio spun around, agape at the sheer opulence of the walled compound with its own private stretch of railroad track, the place where the man fated to be their nemesis a century hence apparently hung his hat. "It's beautiful."

"You seem surprised." Brenin strode toward the three-story mansion painted in alternating tones of rich brown and pale yellow. "Did you expect that I lived in squalor?"

"No, it's just—"

"Take my advice, Mr. Cruz." Brenin clasped the young man's shoulder. "Each of us have only so many trips around the sun. Don't waste any of your time on anything but the best of what this life has to offer."

Emilio maintained his smile, but Steven had been around the boy long enough to know all too well what it took out of him not to recoil at the Black King's touch.

"Good advice." Emilio pulled away from Brenin, the move couched in an earnest appraisal of the man's home. "What business are you in that keeps you in this kind of place?"

Brenin laughed. "I'm a bit older than I might appear, Mr. Cruz, and have had the good fortune to have invested well over the years. This property represents far from the least of those investments." He spread his arms wide. "All of this? Mine."

"A truly enviable position, Mr. Brenin." Steven played to the man's pride. "I suspect we could all learn a thing or two about playing the long game from you."

"It's all simple math when time is on your side, Mr. Bauer. As far back as Archimedes, the concept of exponentiation has been a guiding principle for the most successful among us. In fact, the old story of the grains of rice and the chessboard comes to mind, now that I think of it."

As Brenin pontificated *ad nauseam* on exponential growth, Niklaus whispered in Steven's ear, his trademark grin in place. "So, Steven, what are the odds Zed and Archimedes were drinking buddies?"

"Not now, Nik." Steven tensed. "We're on the man's good side at the moment. Let's keep it that way."

Brenin led his makeshift entourage onto his home's generous porch. Bright white marble stairs inlaid with gold led up to a double door hand-carved top to bottom with scenes from the Far East, the steps guarded on either side by a pair of pawn sculptures two feet high fashioned from a dark stone that shimmered in the afternoon sun.

Steven hid his smirk. "You certainly have a defined style to your décor."

Brenin gave a humble bow. "Chess is life, and as Philidor said a hundred years ago, pawns are the soul of chess."

"What sort of stone is this?" Niklaus ran his fingers along the curves of the nearest statue. "Some form of black granite?"

"No one knows exactly. As legend has it, the original hunk of rock from which these two statues were carved fell from the sky and landed in a lake in the territory known as Tibet many generations ago. Once worshipped as a gift from the gods, I obtained their 'Fire from Heaven' during my travels and had a master sculptor prepare these for me."

Emilio bristled. "You stole their holy artifact?"

"You have quite the accusatory tongue, Mr. Cruz." Brenin let out a quiet sigh. "If you must know, I paid the village elders for the ugly hunk of black rock with a collection of precious stones that would be the envy of any country's royalty. Not one person in that village will have to be hungry or cold for generations." He fixed Emilio with an irate glare. "I may demand nothing but the best for myself and my home, but I am no thief."

"Take care, Mr. Cruz." Sakura wrapped an arm around her lover's waist. "Mr. Brenin is well known for his patience, but even *his* composure has its limits."

"Our apologies." Archie stepped in front of Emilio. "My young friend has spent the last several months living in a barn and is merely overwhelmed by the splendor of your home."

Ume's hands, clenched into fists at her sides, relaxed as she turned and unlocked the door leading into the house. "Please enter, all of you. Mr. Lacan, if you will, help me prepare us all a beverage. Perhaps a nice hot tea?"

"With pleasure, my dear." Archie followed Ume inside. "With pleasure."

Sakura stepped off the porch and headed back toward the dark railcar. "I will go and power down the *Dragon*, Victor."

"Excellent, my dear." Brenin kissed her hand. "Join us inside when you are done."

Steven couldn't help but note that despite the clear employer-employee relationship between Brenin and Sakura, a real affection shone in both their gazes, not to mention a clear mutual respect. He'd seen hints of similar interaction between the Black King and his Queen a hundred years hence, but the bond between Zed and Magdalene had nothing on this.

"So, Mr. Bauer." Brenin led Steven, Niklaus, and Emilio into an adjoining room. "Now that you no longer have to worry about the suspicions of a backwater sheriff and his toothless friends, what do you foresee as the next step for you and your friends?"

Steven stroked his chin. "I suppose we head back east."

He left the answer open-ended, fearing his eyes might betray an outright lie. They would, indeed, be heading back east at the earliest opportunity, but only to Wolf's Bend, and then, God knew where. Without a certain white leather bag that currently rested at the bottom of a duffel bag four states away, none of them would ever see their home again, and without their presence at the coming iteration of the Game, everyone and everything they'd ever loved remained in grave danger. He'd hoped that running into Zed might lead to a solution, but here they were, back to square one, a turn of phrase Steven suspected the man before him would find most appealing.

"In that case," Brenin said, "you are welcome to spend the evening here at my manor, but tomorrow, Ume will take you to the train station so you may resume your travels and get back to whoever or whatever awaits you on the opposite coast."

"That's very generous, Mr. Brenin, but I believe we'll—"

The crack of a gunshot from outside brought the conversation to a screeching halt. Steven's heart stopped for half a second and even Brenin, the very definition of grace under pressure, appeared shaken.

Ume returned to the room in an instant. "Mr. Brenin?"

Brenin's eyes narrowed at Ume. "Go."

Out the door before Brenin finished the word, Ume's steps remained as silent on the hardwood floor as they'd been on the snow-covered earth of Wolf's Bend. Steven followed, hot on her heels, with Emilio and Niklaus close behind. The sight that awaited outside Brenin's palatial home kicked them all in the gut.

Sakura writhed in agony at the feet of an angry Sheriff Post, a large chunk of her left thigh missing, no doubt a victim of the sheriff's smoking shotgun. Ume stood in the center of the large yard with no cover to speak of, frozen in place twenty yards from the business end of John Ndure's six-shooter.

"No!" Tears streamed down Ume's face, but she didn't move an inch as Ndure pulled back the hammer on his gun. "Sakura!"

"Don't move." Ndure drew his other gun and leveled it at Steven. "Any of you."

"They must have leaped onto the railcar before it got up to speed," Niklaus whispered. "What the hell do we do now?"

"She's bleeding to death." Emilio stared at Sakura's trembling form, his face drawn in terror. Before Steven's eyes, he reverted to the boy he met a year ago whose brother had been left in an alley to die, yet another victim of gang violence. "Somebody do something."

"Sakura!" Kiku cut between Steven and Niklaus and sprinted to her older sister's side, the only one courageous or foolhardy enough to brave the few yards of grass that separated them. "No!" Dropping to her knees, she threw her body across her sister's wounded leg. "Sakura..."

"This could've all been avoided." Post stepped around Sakura's bleeding form and marched slowly in the direction of the house, keeping Ume in his field of vision at all times. "The circuit judge was just two days out, Mr. Bauer. I'd planned to tell him that while the circumstances surrounding the recent events in Wolf's Bend all pointed to you and your friends, my gut told me you were innocent." Step after step, he drew closer. "How we got here to what appears to be the Pacific coast, I have no idea, but to know that you fled with Brenin and his trio of...associates makes me wonder if I was wrong."

"If you throw men you believe innocent in jail," Sakura spat between gritted teeth, "I'd hate to see what you do to those you think are guilty."

Post's eyes flicked in her direction. "You might want to put a bandage on that wound, my dear. And perhaps not be so eager to throw a kick at a man with a shotgun next time."

"Sheriff!" Ndure's word drew Post's attention. "Watch out—"

"I'll kill you." Kiku threw herself at Post, her long willowy arms beating him about the head and shoulders. "You hurt Sakura."

An impassive Post withstood the girl's blows like an ancient oak being pelted with hail. Right up to the moment, that is, when she drove the heel of her hand into the bottom of his nose. Cursing, he snaked a hand between Kiku's raised fists, wrapped his fingers around her neck, and hurled the girl to the ground.

"Careful, girl." Post wiped the twin streaks of blood from his lips and chin onto the shoulder of his duster. "Unless you want to suffer like your sister."

Kiku pulled herself up from the ground. "You're the one who is going to suffer."

"Don't make me kill you, girl." Post leveled his shotgun at Kiku's chest. "I don't relish the thought of a child's death on my soul."

"Kiku," Ume whispered, "don't."

"I have to." Kiku dropped into a low fighting stance. "She's our sister."

"Very well." Post braced for the recoil of his weapon. "But don't say I didn't—"

"Enough." Dressed in the full regalia of his position on the chessboard, the Black King stepped between Steven and Niklaus, nudging Emilio out of the way with the hilt of the black-hilted broadsword. "Kiku, Ume, behind me."

A wide-eyed Ndure fired his revolver at the man he knew as Victor Brenin, the resulting crack answered immediately with the clang of metal on metal as the King deflected the bullet with a lightning-fast swipe of his sword.

"Save your bullets, Deputy." The King brandished his weapon, extending the tip of the broadsword in Ndure's direction. "They will accomplish nothing but earning you the same fate as the good Sheriff Post."

Ndure holstered his pistol and stepped back, hands raised before him.

"Now." The King strode slowly in Post's direction, his black fur-lined cloak brushing the earth, with Ume and Kiku falling in behind him like soldiers following their general. "Lower your weapon, Sheriff, and I may show you more mercy than you showed Sakura."

"Stay back." Post backpedaled, the tip of his shotgun shaking as he struggled to maintain control of the situation. "Or I'll shoot."

"The time for empty threats is over." The King stepped up his pace, the three feet of gleaming razor-sharp steel held effortlessly before him. "Lower your weapon, Sheriff, and face your fate."

"Brenin, stand down!" Steven took a step forward. "No matter what he's done, this man is the law."

The King cast an unimpressed gaze across his shoulder. "My apologies, Mr. Bauer, but I recognize a higher authority. Pray that you never fall on the wrong side of my judgment."

Someday. Steven ground his teeth. *But not this day.*

"Run," he shouted to the two lawmen. "Both of you, if you value your lives."

In answer, Ndure took two quick steps backward before turning and sprinting away. Post took a couple seconds longer to process, but as the Black King broke into a dead run, sword held high above his head, even the stern sheriff turned tail and ran. The chase led to the tall wrought-iron gate that barred entrance into the compound. Ndure climbed up and over in a flash while Post remained stranded on this side of the spiked barrier.

"Mercy," Post cried, holding the shotgun across his chest in a defensive posture as his dark pursuer caught up to him. "Dear God, have mercy."

"Niklaus, Emilio, help Sakura. I've got this." Steven rushed to the Black King's side. "You don't have to kill him, Mr. Brenin. He's just a man doing his job."

"And I'm just a man defending my home." The King flicked his wrist, and his broadsword sent Post's weapon flying. "I suggest you pray to whatever deity you hold sacred, Sheriff, for it will be the last thing you—"

The crack of a revolver from beyond the gate shattered the air. The King's shoulder flew back from the impact, the broadsword dropping from his hand. Outside the gate stood John Ndure, his revolver still smoking.

"Now, Mr. Bauer. Step away from Sheriff Post, or I'll have to—"

A trio of gleaming silver objects whistled past Steven's ear and impacted Ndure's chest, shoulder, and gun hand, driving him back from the wrought iron bars and sending him sprawling to the ground. At each site bloomed a deadly flower of steel, the gleaming metal set off by the growing fields of red spreading at each wound. He glanced back and found Ume holding an additional set of razor-sharp stars in each hand, weapons he'd only ever seen before in the kung fu movies of his childhood.

Throwing stars. A silent tread that left no trace. Near invisibility.

The ability to punch through solid wood like a jackhammer.

Not to mention, the whole telepathy thing.

Steven wasn't sure about the other two sisters, but any doubt as to exactly who and what Ume represented left his mind.

Ninja.

And a particularly dangerous one at that.

Post took advantage of the moment and scooped up his shotgun, turning it on the gate and blowing off the lock. Beneath the metal arch in seconds, he pulled the gate shut behind him, the wrought iron bars deflecting two of the trio of stars Ume flung at him. The third found purchase in the back of his left shoulder, but the wound didn't slow him a bit. Scooping up John Ndure, Post dragged him sideways parallel to the compound wall and out of sight, leaving Steven standing over the wounded form of the man this century knew as Victor Brenin.

He knelt at the Black King's side, but instead of offering him his hand, he grasped the hilt of the broadsword and held it before his chest.

One fatal strike, and all of it would be over. No Zed, no gathered army of Black, no stupid Game to wreck all their lives. Just peace. And not just for Steven and his friends, but their families and loved ones as well. So many paths altered, so many lives endangered, and each person's fate bound to the wounded man who lay helpless at Steven's feet.

Checkmate in one move.

With little more than a flick of his wrist.

But, if he killed Zed now and the Game never occurred, what would happen to all of them?

Would Emilio survive the betrayal and gang violence that awaited him? Would Lena?

Niklaus, drunk and suicidal atop the King tower in Atlanta; what would happen to him if no one showed up to pull him back from the edge?

What would happen to Archie without the Game to give him purpose in the twilight years of his existence? Could Steven deprive the elderly priest the chance to taste the vigor of his youth one last time?

And that left the woman who had never left his thoughts despite the months since their banishment to the past: Audrey Richards, shriveled and dying from leukemia, would no longer have any reason for Steven to cross her path and bring her back from the brink, giving her a second chance at life.

Just as he would no longer have a reason to go to Oregon and rediscover joy within those beautiful hazel eyes.

Instead of a quick death, Steven offered the man destined to be his nemesis a hand.

"Let's get you inside, Mr. Brenin. Archie can tend to you while the rest of us try to help Sakura."

"Thank you." Brenin took Steven's hand, managing to maintain his composure despite the blood oozing from his shoulder. "It's funny, Mr. Bauer. For a moment, it seemed you were debating whether or not to strike me down with my own sword."

"I was merely arming myself." He pulled Brenin to his feet. "In case Ndure didn't exercise the better part of valor."

"It would appear, then, that our relationship has again reached an equilibrium." Brenin looked over at his lover. "May I speak to Sakura first?"

"Of course." Steven helped Brenin to the eldest sister's side.

Sakura's left thigh looked for all the world like an enormous predator had taken a bite. Just far enough down the leg that Niklaus' belt-and-stick tourniquet could staunch the bleeding, the wound still oozed the woman's lifeblood onto the California soil.

"My love." Brenin dropped to one knee. "I didn't know."

"You do hate being surprised." Despite her pallor, Sakura managed to find a kind smile for a man Steven would never have dreamed deserved kindness. "I've told you a thousand times, Victor. You can't plan for everything."

"I will find the man who did this, and I will end him." His gaze shot to Steven, a cold anger in his eyes. "I swear it."

"Swear only one thing to me." She took Brenin's hand and brought it to her heart. "That you will never leave my side, should I not see the end of this day or should I live another fifty years."

"You are not going to die."

Sakura voice cracked. "Swear that you will never leave me."

He squeezed her fingers gently. "I swear it."

Niklaus and Emilio carried Sakura inside, doing everything in their power to keep her leg still and minimize her pain. As Archie tended to her wound, Steven and Ume helped Brenin to his bed. The last thing Steven saw before passing the threshold again into his enemy's home was Ume as she headed for the gate to stand guard, a pair of matching short swords in her hands.

God help Post and Ndure if they come back.

Steven stood on the porch of Brenin's manor, hands gripping the bannister as he struggled to come up with their next move. As difficult as it would have been to return to Wolf's Bend before, going back now was all but impossible having just sent away the two top lawmen of the town wounded and angry.

"Mr. Bauer?" Kiku joined him on the porch. "Are you...well?"

"Better than Mr. Brenin or your sister." Steven turned to the girl. "What are you doing out here? Shouldn't you be with Sakura?"

"She's resting, as is Mr. Brenin." She pulled in a deep breath. "And, in any case, it's you I need to speak with."

"Me?" Steven stared quizzically at the girl. "What do you need?"

"It is not me that is in need, but you and your friends."

"What do you—" Steven shut up as the girl produced a familiar parcel from behind her back. "Wait. Is that—"

"Very early in our association, Mr. Brenin recognized in me a certain proclivity for manipulating the forces held within the dark leather of the *Svartr Kyll*. I have been trained since before I could speak with the power held therein." Her head dropped. "How could I not recognize the presence of his dark pouch's brighter sister?"

Steven reached into the pillowcase he'd borrowed from Dottie's Inn, his fingers tingling as they brushed the smooth leather of the *Hvitr Kyll*. He pulled the bag of supple white leather from its cotton shroud, and a low pulse filled the air, prompting Steven to clutch the artifact to his chest, fearful that Brenin might hear.

Kiku rested a hand on his wrist. "Fear not. I waited for Mr. Brenin to start snoring before I sought you out."

"But why are you helping me?" Steven's brow furrowed. "Is your loyalty not to Brenin?"

"You and I both know that isn't his name." Kiku smiled. "It's very simple, actually. From the moment we first met, you and you friends seemed out of place here." She ran her fingers along the silver cord that held the mouth of the pouch closed. "Or perhaps out of time."

"You know?"

She motioned to the pouch. "I thought that perhaps returning this to you would help you get back to wherever or...whenever you belong."

"More than you can possibly imagine."

"Oh." She reached into the pocket of her jacket. "And one other entity to help guide you on your way." She opened her hand and there, resting in her palm, Amaryllis shone green in the midday sun. "The workmanship of this dragonfly is exquisite. I've never seen its like."

"She's one of a kind, like the woman who gave her to me."

"There is truth in what you say." Kiku place Amaryllis in Steven's hand. "Unless I miss my guess, on both counts."

A sequence of faces echoed through Steven's mind's eye.

Young Ruth's exuberant gaze filled his memory, slowly fading into that of the kind old woman who had given Steven her most prized possession in an effort to keep him safe from harm. Arthur, as well, equally dapper as a young man in uniform or as an elderly man in a "Kiss the Cook" apron, flitted through his mind. And then, as always, the woman who had captured his heart from the first moment he'd seen her photograph hanging on the wall of an old house in Sisters, Oregon, what seemed a lifetime ago.

With Audrey's thoughtful gaze at the forefront of his thoughts, Steven pocketed Amaryllis and gripped the mouth of the pouch, its low drone doubling in intensity.

"I take it Mr. Brenin didn't pick the location of his home arbitrarily."

"Do you not hear the pouch?" Kiku closed her eyes and threw her head back, her expression akin to rapture. "It cries out to be used, to fulfill its purpose, its destiny."

Archie poked his head out, his grey hair spread about his face like the sun's corona. "Is that sound what I think it is?"

Steven nodded, pouch held before him, its low drone pulsing in time with his heartbeat. "Get Niklaus and Emilio. It's time to go."

B renin sprinted from the house, his black silk robe barely fastened. He held a solitary piece of crumpled paper in one hand and the *Svartr Kyll* in the other.

"Where are they?" His voice came out ragged, almost raving. "Lacan. Bauer. Where did they go?"

"I sent them on their way." Kiku sat lotus style in the center of the yard by a gnarled Japanese maple devoid of leaves. "They didn't belong here."

"What do you mean, 'on their way'? What have you done, Kiku?"

"Exactly what you've trained me to do since the moment you first placed the black pouch in my lap a lifetime ago." Her eyes turned skyward. "Brought order from chaos. Created forward movement from stagnation." She fished a chess piece from the pocket of her robe, a white pawn. "I moved the Pieces forward, toward their eventual endgame."

"You..." Brenin stopped mid-sentence. "Never mind. What's done is done." He held up the black pouch. "I'm guessing they were in possession of the *Hvitr Kyll?*"

"Strangely, both yes and no." Kiku's eyes slid shut, her mind going somewhere else. "The white pouch that spirited Mr. Bauer and his friends away no longer registers in my mind, and yet, the ever-present tether between your dark pouch and its white sister remains as strong as ever. What does that mean?"

"A word I rarely use..." Brenin stared down at the scrawled hand-writing that filled the yellow paper held tightly in his fingers. "The impossible."

"You've told me many stories over the years, Mr. Brenin, and no matter how incredible, you've assured me that each one was true." She reached up a hand to brush her fingers along the crumpled paper that shook in Brenin's trembling grasp. "What is that you're holding?"

Brenin's head dropped, as did his voice. "A message from one of our recently departed guests, Mr., or should I say, Father Archibald Lacan."

"The old man." Kiku rose from the ground and drew close. "What could he possibly have had to say to you?" She scanned the letter, her eyes growing wider with each line. "Can this be?"

Brenin sighed, folded the letter into quarters, and slid it into the pocket of his robe. "This letter represents the implausible solution to one mystery, and simultaneously opens the door on a hundred more." He took the girl's hand and turned to lead her inside. "But all of it is clearly a matter for another day." He smiled. "Would you care to join me for a game of chess?"

"Of course." She smiled. "I recently read of a new opening that I've been eager to try."

"Excellent."

Brenin led the girl to an upstairs parlor that boasted an uninterrupted view of the Pacific. At its center, yet another chessboard resided with all thirty-two pieces in place.

Brenin sat on one side, Kiku the other.

"The most difficult aspect of this game, Kiku." Brenin focused on the battlefield in miniature resting between him and his young charge. "What did I teach you?"

"The waiting, Mr. Brenin." She rested a finger atop her queen. "The waiting."

25

MISSIVES & MYSTERIES

One second, Steven, Niklaus, Emilio, and Archie huddled by the corner of Victor Brenin's *Black Dragon* railcar, hands interlocked around the mouth of the *Hvitr Kyll*. The next, they stood at the mouth of a darkened city alleyway, a frigid wind whipping through the narrow space between the brick buildings.

Steven trembled despite his World War II vintage trench coat as he took a quick survey of his friends. Quite the ragtag bunch, Niklaus stood in his long coat, denim trousers, and 1940s-style boots while Archie and Emilio appeared even more like a pair of random extras from a black-and-white Western now that they no longer had the back drop of Wolf's Bend for Steven to wrap his brain around.

"At least we didn't end up in the middle of the woods for once." Niklaus rubbed his upper arms, a shiver running through his muscular form. "Still, would it have been too much to ask for it not to still be the dead of winter?"

Steven glanced up and down the empty alley. "As long as Audrey and Lena are here, I don't care how cold it is."

"It was just a joke, Steven." Niklaus shook his head. "We can laugh or we can cry."

"Sorry." Steven shot his friend a stressed grin. "Still processing everything." His mind swam with so many loose threads and things unexplained.

Zed, the man destined to send his assassins for each of them a hundred years from the moment they'd just left, had seen each of them, learned their names and faces, but none of that explained how he would possibly know to look for them at the time of the Game. Zed struck Steven as shrewd and scarily perceptive, all traits of the chess grandmasters the man admired, but putting together that the four of them were, in fact, unwitting time travelers sent to the past by a future version of himself might be a stretch even for the Black King.

Not to mention all the mysteries that remained unanswered from 1890.

Who shot the U.S. Marshal at Dottie's Inn that night?

Who knew enough about Zed to successfully lure the Black King to Wolf's Bend in the first place?

Who was this "old man" who hired Scarface/Earl and Slick/Clarence to destroy the train engine and strand the man known as Victor Brenin in a backwater town in the dead of winter?

And above all, were all of those the same person?

In the distance a bell chimed, once, twice, three times.

"Guess that explains why there aren't too many people on the streets." Archie's breath steamed wispy white from his dark lips. "It's the middle of the night."

Emilio pulled up next to Steven. "So, fearless leader, any ideas?"

The boy's words, sarcastic and headstrong as always, were answered in kind by a more-than-welcome voice from the mouth of the alley.

"He's gotten you this far." Hope sprang anew in Steven's heart at the five words. "Maybe you should give him the benefit of the doubt."

Emilio spun around. "Lena?"

"In the flesh." The girl stood silhouetted in the yellow of a distant street light. "Well?"

Both froze for half a second and then rushed into each other's arms. Emilio swept Lena off her feet and spun her around, bringing a squeal of delight.

"Careful, *papi*." With a quiet giggle, she pulled away so she could look Emilio in the face. "You're going to leave us both dizzy and the sidewalk's coated with an inch of ice."

Emilio returned her to the ground. "Lena, thank God." He panted, out of breath. "I was so afraid I'd never see you again."

"Like I'd ever let that happen." Lena grabbed Emilio by his vest and pulled him in close, the resulting kiss cribbed from every teen movie ever made. Steven and Niklaus both looked away to give them whatever privacy they could. Archie, conversely, looked on with a gaping grin.

"Ah, to be that young again," he whispered just loud enough for Steven and Niklaus to hear. "For all its trials and tribulations, is there anything purer than first love?"

When Lena and Emilio were done getting "reacquainted," she took him by the hand and led him over to the others.

"Hiya, Nik." She beamed up at him. "Welcome to 1936."

"1936, eh?" Niklaus pulled her into a robust hug and glanced back at Archie. "At least we're only back *one* century this time."

"Praise God." Archie rested a hand on Lena's shoulder. "So good to see you, child. Please, know that I've prayed for you daily."

"Good to see you too, Archie." Lena whipped out an arm and pulled the priest into the hug. "Looks like your prayers have been answered."

When the three-way embrace ended, Lena turned to Steven, her head bowed in shame. "Hello, Steven."

"Lena." A thousand emotions swirled at his core. "I'm so glad to know you're okay. How have you—"

"You have to know…" she blurted out before Steven could get out another word, emotion choking every syllable. "I'm so sorry. It's all my fault. All of this. If I hadn't—"

"Stop." Steven took her chin and brought her gaze to meet his, offering the crying girl his most genuine smile. "First off, you aren't the one who sent us hurtling through time and space. All you did was stand by your guns when the shit hit the fan. Not everyone has that kind of guts."

"But, Steven—"

"Second, and far more important, you were right." He motioned for all of them to draw close. "All those people on the bridge that day. They would've died if it weren't for you. No matter what else has happened, those lives were worth it."

Emilio nodded in agreement, as did Archie. Lena looked to Niklaus, who studied her with his mouth held askew.

"You want to know the truth." His face broke into his trademark megawatt smile. "I always did want to see if I could bench press the Brooklyn Bridge."

"Oh, Nik, you big goof." She turned back to Steven. "So, I know there's a lot going on here, but I can't believe you haven't asked…"

From the first moment he'd seen Lena, the question had been on the tip of his tongue, but he'd held back in an effort to give the girl her moment.

"Audrey." Just saying the name made his heart jump. "Is she with you?"

"She's not far." Lena's brow furrowed. "I'll take you to her, but there's something you've got to know first."

A familiar ball of ice formed at Steven's core. "What is it? Is she okay?"

"Audrey's sick, Steven." Lena ran a fist across her tear-filled eyes and sucked in a breath. "*Dios mío*, she's so sick."

"Steven." The uttered word barely qualified as a croak. "Thank God."

"Audrey." Steven had waited months to hear that voice again, though he'd never dreamed that the next time he saw Audrey, she'd barely be able to speak. "It's back…isn't it?"

Long before Steven rescued Audrey from the Black Queen's assassination attempt and brought her into the fold of Grey's Game, she'd stood upon the threshold of death's door. The twin devils of leukemia and the chemotherapy that poisoned both cancer and victim alike had left Audrey bereft of hair, emaciated to the point of visible ribs and skeletal limbs, and so bedridden that her mother had to cut up her food and feed her by hand. The Audrey before him still possessed her long locks of auburn hair, but her sunken eyes, hollow cheeks, and weak voice told the real story.

"Grey told me something back in Roanoke." Audrey allowed her hazel eyes to drift closed. "Something I was either too ashamed or too afraid to admit."

"The Game." Something clicked in Steven's head, something that had crossed his mind more than once and been dismissed each time as too horrible to conceive. "It's all that's keeping you alive."

Archie rested a gnarled hand on Steven's shoulder. "Without the presence of the Game's near limitless power, her illness, much like the decades I have on each of you, is no longer held at bay."

"I couldn't bear to tell you, Steven." Lena traced a circle on the ground with the tip of her shoe. "You had to see it for yourself."

Steven met Lena's despondent gaze. "How long has she been like this?"

Audrey held up a shaking hand and inhaled to answer, but tears choked her voice and she flashed an imploring look in Lena's direction. "Tell him," she croaked.

Lena sucked in a breath. "We landed here in Chicago four months ago with nothing but the clothes on our backs." A quiet laugh fell from her lips. "Funny how having a debit card in your back pocket doesn't do you any good in the 1930s."

"We can relate." Emilio encircled Lena with his muscular arm and pulled her close.

Visibly bolstered by his nearness, Lena kissed Emilio's cheek before continuing. "We had to come up with some money and a place to stay. Fortunately, this hotel was down a couple housekeepers, and when we told them we'd work for room and board, we discovered we were more than qualified for the job."

"That was late October," Audrey croaked. "Back when I still felt okay."

Lena patted Audrey's leg. "We made it through Thanksgiving, Christmas, New Years. Made some friends. Even got invited to an occasional home-cooked meal with the family of one of the other cleaning ladies."

Audrey smiled. "Esmeralda." The single word sent her coughing.

"Don't talk, *chica*." Lena shot Steven a concerned glance. "So, everything was going fine till we hit February. One day, Audrey just didn't want to get out of bed. She hurt all over, the nodes in her neck got all swollen and tender, and the next day, she was burning up with fever." She shook her head. "I thought she might be coming down with strep throat or something, but Audrey knew what it was right away."

"The leukemia." Audrey spoke the word as if naming her executioner.

"It wasn't long before the nosebleeds started," Lena continued. "Then she lost her appetite, started losing weight." She lowered her head. "I can't bear to see her this way."

Archie knelt by the bed and took Audrey's hand. "Are you in any pain, child?"

"Pretty much everywhere." Audrey reached up a trembling hand, her fingers brushing Archie's silver mane of kinky hair. "It's funny. I've never seen you like this."

"You mean my natural state?" Archie offered her a kind smile. "It would seem the Game is good for both our constitutions."

Audrey got out a single laugh before a coughing fit sent her into spasm.

Niklaus pulled close to Steven. "I don't know much about medicine, but I'm guessing there's nothing in this decade that's going to help her."

Steven sat on the bed and squeezed Audrey's knee gently, afraid he might hurt her. "Did you two try to go to a hospital?"

"A week ago." Lena shook her head. "With a little nudge, the doctors actually came to the correct diagnosis pretty darn quickly. The treatment options, on the other hand, weren't anything Audrey wanted to try."

"Audrey?" Steven asked.

"No." She cut him off with a harsh whisper. "I've been failed by the most cutting-edge medical technology the twenty-first century can provide." Her weak hands balled into fists at her sides. "Call me crazy if the thought of burying a couple dozen 'radium needles' in my skin or taking a blood transfusion from a complete stranger didn't exactly fill me with hope."

Steven buried his face in his hands. "I'm sorry. I just don't know what else to do."

"It's simple, isn't it?" Emilio stepped up. "We get her and the rest of us back to where and when we belong."

"We've already done it twice, you know." Niklaus shot Audrey a beaming smile. "We can do it again."

"We've got the bus." Steven patted the pouch at his hip. "We just need the gas."

"Hell, we were barely in 1936 five minutes before Lena found us. Things are looking up." Niklaus narrowed his eyes in the girl's direction. "And while we're on the subject, you said you'd tell us once we got to the hotel how you knew to come find us in that alleyway."

"Something else you're going to have to see to believe." Lena burrowed in the top drawer of the table by her bed and produced a yellowed envelope with her name written in ornate script across the front.

"*Lena Cervantes.*" Steven took the envelope. "Whoever wrote this knew exactly who they were looking for."

"And where to find you," Niklaus added.

"Not to mention when." Lena motioned to the envelope. "Look inside."

Steven pulled a similarly yellowed piece of stationery from the aged sleeve.

"*Dear Miss Cervantes.*" He read aloud, shaking his head in disbelief. "*Early on the morning of February 24, 1936, a quartet you've been awaiting for some time will be passing through Chicago. Arrive at the address below before the clock strikes three or your paths will not likely cross. If that occurs, I won't be able to help you further. May fortune shine upon you all.*"

He handed the letter to Emilio who read the last line.

"*A Friend.*"

Archie took the letter next and inspected the fine calligraphy. "Who could this be?"

Lena shrugged. "I don't have the first clue."

Steven stared down at the envelope. "When did you receive the letter?"

"Someone slid it under our door a couple weeks after we arrived in Chicago." Lena gestured in the direction of the hall. "One morning it was just lying there on the floor."

"And you waited." Steven took the letter back and held it up to the light. "With nothing more than this, you waited for us."

"I, or rather, *we* have waited for months for you to arrive." Lena laughed. "As for tonight, I've been up for a while."

"Don't let her downplay any of it." Audrey's voice came out a rough whisper. "She's been out there every night for a week on the off chance the letter writer got the day wrong."

"Like I said." Lena shrugged. "A while."

"Well, we're here now." Steven handed the letter back to Lena. "And now that we're all back together—"

"Not all of us." Emilio went to the room's tiny window. "We still don't know what happened to Grey."

"I found you and Archie." Steven's gaze shot to Lena. "And together, we four made it here to 1936 and Lena and Audrey." His hand went to the pouch at his side, the leather warm to the touch. "We'll find Grey too."

"Agreed," Lena said, "but first, we've got to take care of Audrey."

Steven sighed. "Which begs the question, where do we go to find another crossing?"

Niklaus straightened up. "We could always look up Ed Leedskalnin in Florida or try to find the site of Zed's California compound. We know both of those work."

Archie shook his head. "Audrey is in no shape to travel." His eyes cut to Steven. "Whatever we do, it's going to have to be close by."

"The first time we ran into Grey, and the second time, Zed. If only we knew someone here in 1936 we could ask for help."

"About that…" Lena let out a sarcastic laugh and shook her head. "Not sure if this qualifies as 'help,' but there's one more thing I haven't told you yet."

"You're serious?" Steven asked from his perch on the hard city bench. "She's...here?"

"Live and in color." Lena motioned across the busy street to the ground floor entrance of Pioneer Trust and Savings Bank, the doorway flanked by a pair of three-story Grecian columns and shielded from the sun by an ornate marquee. "I doubted my senses when I saw her the first time, but I've come back more than once, and there's no denying it's her." She checked her watch. "Ten past five. All the bank clerks head out around now every day, and she's usually at the back of the pack."

"And you're sure it's not just someone who looks like her?" Steven squinted as the sun came out from behind a cloud and beamed down upon the city street from the west. "What if this woman is simply her great grandmother?"

"I've heard people call her by name as they walked past, heard her speak." Lena shivered, and Steven guessed it wasn't just from the cold. "It's *her.*"

Steven shook his head. "She did mention our initial meeting wasn't her first trip to the Windy City, but this?"

Together, they sat in silence, Steven holding an open newspaper before his face like he'd seen in any of a dozen spy movies while Lena rooted purposefully through a purse she had borrowed from one of the other cleaning ladies. Five o'clock came and went, then fifteen past. Half a dozen women in conservative attire flooded out en masse followed a few minutes later by a collection of men in dark business suits.

As the bottom of the hour approached, Steven glanced in Lena's direction.

"Maybe she didn't come to work today." He checked his watch for the hundredth time and started to get up. "We can try again tomorrow, I guess."

"Won't be necessary." Lena caught Steven's wrist and inclined her head in the direction of the door. "There she is."

A familiar icy sensation welled up from Steven's core as he caught sight of the woman who had haunted his nightmares for months.

Her jet-black hair, curled into a wavy bob, just kissed her chin on one side.

Her dress, a long green satin number with fur at the sleeves and neck, stretched down her body to mid-calf, a far cry from the revealing black dress she wore at their first meeting.

Her heels, as black as her heart, remained firmly planted on the sidewalk as she turned to walk up the street away from Lena and Steven.

A pinch at his left collarbone from Amaryllis confirmed beyond a doubt the woman's identity, a confirmation punctuated by the chill in his heart when he met her gaze for all of half a second, those unmistakable emerald eyes burning into him like both fire and ice.

"I wasn't sure till this moment whether or not I truly believed you, but you're right." Steven folded the newspaper and left it on the bench as he headed up the sidewalk, Lena close on his heels. "God help us all, that's Magdalene." His hand instinctively went to the pawn in his pocket despite the fact that the forces necessary to empower the icon of the Game would not exist for another eighty years. "Somehow, that's the Black Queen."

26

HUNTER & HUNTED

"How is this possible?" Steven whispered to Lena as they followed Magdalene up the sidewalk half a block back. "Assuming she's somewhere in her twenties here in 1936, that would put her over ninety back home."

"Not that different from Archie, I guess." Lena pulled her coat tight about her. "Who's to say our team is the only side with a member who's been pulling social security for a few years?"

"Good point." Steven shuddered, only half from the cold. "Still, you're not the one that was nearly seduced and then burned to a crisp by a someone who's possibly a nonagenarian."

"You couldn't possibly have—" Lena began to answer, but as the woman they were following rounded the next corner, Steven grabbed her arm and pulled her behind a newsstand to avoid a quick cross-shoulder glance from their quarry.

"Sorry. Didn't want her to spot us."

"Calm down, Steven." Lena sighed. "No matter who or what she may become seventy years from now, here she's just a bank clerk, nine to five like clockwork." Lena stepped from behind the newsstand and continued up the sidewalk. "Not to mention, she has no idea who we are or that we even exist."

"Seriously?" Steven followed close behind, scanning the sidewalk to no avail, the woman in green nowhere to be seen. "You know as well as I do what kind of person Magdalene is. In 1936, she may not yet have become the woman we know, but that doesn't mean she isn't dangerous." He motioned to the empty sidewalk before them. "What do we do next? Your call."

"We follow her. She can't have gone far."

Lena shot up the sidewalk as fast as she could without drawing unwanted stares. Steven worked to keep up, narrowly avoiding collisions with an elderly woman carrying a bag of groceries and a man in a dark suit big enough to play defensive line for the Bears.

"Best watch yourself, pal," the man muttered under his breath.

Steven offered him an apologetic grunt and continued his pursuit of Lena. Another block, and the girl finally slowed enough for him to catch up to her. Pulling in a deep breath, Steven stepped into the alleyway where Lena awaited.

"Funny," she said. "I could've sworn I saw her duck in here."

Steven poked his head out of the alley, scanning both directions for the elusive woman in green. "We lost her."

"But how?" Lena crossed her arms and shivered in the cold. "She can't possibly run in those shoes."

"It's a big city, Lena." Steven leaned against the brick of the building to his left. "She could be anywhere." He jammed his hands in his pockets. "Guess we try again tomorrow."

"I don't like being followed." The voice from above their heads carried a not-so-faint Irish lilt, icy in its delivery. "You may think you're quite the clever lass, girlie, but the two of you are about as subtle as a herd of buffalo."

As one, Steven and Lena's gazes leaped skyward to find Magdalene staring down at them from a second-story fire escape, her dismissive stare identical to that of the woman who would try to kill each of them more than once eight decades hence. Steven braced to bolt from the alley but froze in place when he noticed the snub-nosed pistol in the woman's hand.

"Why are you two tailing me?" Magdalene gripped the rusted iron of the rail with one hand while maintaining a bead on Steven's head with the other. "You've got ten seconds to answer and I'd better like what you have to say."

"Or what?" Lena's hands went to her hips, her gaze shifting into a defiant glare Steven had seen on more than one occasion. "You going to call the cops?"

"Funny."

Magdalene's curt answer hung in the air for all of two seconds before a firm grip descended upon Steven's shoulder. Simultaneously, a gruff hand caught Lena by her upper arm, yanking the two of them together. Steven turned his head to one side and met gazes with the linebacker he'd almost collided with a block back.

"This the girl who's been spying on you, Miss Byrne?" Uttered in as thick a Chicago accent as he had ever heard, the words sent Steven's heart racing.

"Yes, Milo." Magdalene descended from her perch, a predator drawing closer to her prey. "She's the one."

"And this mook?" Milo shoved Steven forward. "Who's he?"

"No idea." She trailed a finger down Steven's chest, a faint smile of amusement on her lips. "Never seen him before."

Milo's grip on Steven's shoulder doubled in intensity. "You want I should take care of this situation?"

"Not quite yet." Magdalene studied them both. "First, a question or two for my new pair of shadows."

Just a bank clerk.

The words echoed mockingly through Steven's psyche as he waited for Magdalene to speak again.

Nothing in this Game is ever what it seems.

"What's your name, boyo?" she asked Steven. "And don't be telling me any fibs or I'll know. You understand me?"

"My name is Steven. Steven Bauer." He pulled his shoulder free from Milo's grip and shot the man a hard look. "Now, let go of Lena's arm. You're hurting her."

Milo shot Magdalene an inquisitive look and at her quick nod released his grip on Lena's arm. Lena, in turn, ran her fingers down the sleeve of her coat, smoothing out the wrinkles left by Milo's gorilla-like hand.

"And you," Magdalene asked. "I believe 'Steven' here called you 'Lena'?"

"Lena Cervantes." Two words, uttered with no emotion save cool disdain.

"By the way," Milo uttered, "they know your name too." He cracked his knuckles. "Heard them mention it when they were following you up the street."

"Of course they do," the woman fated to become the Black Queen hissed.

"Look," Lena whispered, "all we want is—"

"Just a child." Magdalene cupped Lena's chin in her taloned fingers, the movement as sudden as a serpent's strike. "At first, I thought it coincidence, me picking your face out of the crowd again and again, but three times in one week? Surely you don't take me for a fool, or worse, unobservant." She squeezed Lena's jaw until the girl squinted in pain. "If you know enough about me to have reason to follow me through the streets of Chicago day after day, then you should know full well I am neither of those things."

"Please, don't hurt her." Steven stepped forward to help Lena, but froze at the sight of Milo's massive hands balling into fists. "Look, we're not here to hurt you or whatever it is you think we're doing."

"Then what *do* you want?" Magdalene released Lena with a shove and turned to face Steven. "You have piqued my interest, Mr. Bauer. Please, tell me, what it is you and your young lady-friend want with me."

Steven sucked in a breath, the next words out of his mouth somehow the truth. "Strange though it may sound, we need your help."

"My help?" Magdalene's lips parted in a mischievous smile, a lone eyebrow raised in question. "And what precisely is it you think I have to offer?"

"That's," Steven stammered, "a bit hard to define."

Grey and Zed had each, directly or indirectly, helped them along their way by simple virtue of their knowledge of crossings and the intricate workings of their respective mystical artifacts. Whatever this

"Magdalene Byrne" of 1936 might be, immortal wizard and purveyor of an eternal Game of good versus evil, she was not.

"Miss Byrne." Milo's dull gaze shifted from Steven to Lena and back. "Sorry to interrupt, but shouldn't we be having this conversation in a bit more secluded location?"

Magdalene retreated a step, taking a moment to glance up at the darkening sky. "Ever the careful one, Milo. I suppose that's why I keep you around." She spun on one heel and proceeded down the alley. "Bring them."

Shoved forward perhaps a bit harder than Milo intended, Steven and Lena shared a conflicted glance before following the woman in green. Milo shuffled along behind them, the potent mix of cologne and cigar wafting off him all but pushing them down the pebble sidewalk. Another block passed beneath their feet before Magdalene stopped at a set of stairs leading down into darkness.

"Be it ever so humble, eh, Milo?"

"You know it, Miss Byrne."

Magdalene disappeared down the shadowy subterranean stairwell. Steven's every instinct screamed for him to run, but the return of Milo's vice-like grip to his shoulder drove all such foolishness from his mind.

"Down the steps. Both of you."

Steven obeyed the grunted command without question and crept down the dimly lit stairs with Lena at his side.

"Don't worry, Lena," he whispered. "Just follow my lead. I'll get us out of this."

The girl nodded bravely, but a flash of fear in her eyes reminded Steven yet again that no matter how much of a fighter the girl next to him had proven to be, she was still just that: a sixteen-year-old girl.

At the bottom of the stairs, Magdalene stood before a black door. She rapped twice and then twice again. A few seconds passed before a small window at eye height slid open.

"It's us, Jimmy." Magdalene shot a dithering glance back at Steven and Lena. "And we have guests."

The eyes behind the window flicked in Steven's direction and then the window slid shut. The trio of deadbolt locks clacked in sequence, and the door opened on a dazzling vision, far from the dismal dungeon Steven expected to lie across the threshold.

Low tables lit by candlelight stretched in every direction, all surrounding a half-moon-shaped raised platform at the far end of the room. Atop the stage, a grand piano shone beneath a lone spotlight beside a metal stand holding one of those bottle microphones from all the old black-and-white movies. Three chairs on the opposite end of the stage sat paired with trumpet, trombone, and clarinet. Empty except for the four of them and the man Magdalene had called Jimmy, the space appeared ready for an evening of revelry.

Unlike Milo, who looked very much like a shaved gorilla in a rumpled suit, Jimmy appeared very much a gentleman's gentleman. A muscular chest and arms filled out a short black tuxedo complete with spats atop highly shined shoes. A pencil-thin mustache decorated a scarred upper lip, the scar made all the more prominent by the man's pursed lips.

"And who exactly are these two ragamuffins?" he asked.

Magdalene sighed. "The girl is the one I told you about who's been tailing me after work every couple of days." She gave Steven an appraising look. "Tall, dark, and almost handsome here, however, is new to me." The hint of flirtation in her gaze went cold. "He was with the girl, though, so he's fair game."

And...right back where I started. Steven worked to keep any emotion, fear or otherwise, from his face. *Being chatted up by the Black Queen at a night club in Chicago.* A quiet groan escaped his lips. *Where this Game is concerned, history does tend to repeat itself a bit.*

"Fair game, huh?" Lena crossed her arms, sheer defiance driving the fear from her gaze. "And what exactly do you plan to do with us?"

"Lena." Steven grasped her arm just above the elbow. "Let's don't—"

"Listen, girlie," Magdalene spat, cutting Steven off mid-sentence. "I'm not sure what you think is happening here, but I recommend you watch your mouth."

"And if I don't?'"

"Lena." Steven squeezed, gently. His young friend was clearly scared, but, unfortunately, not quite scared enough. "Stop."

"On the contrary, Steven." Magdalene laughed. "Let the girl dig her own grave."

Jimmy checked his watch. "This joint opens in a couple hours, Mags. You think we can wrap this up?"

She bristled at the diminutive of her name. "How many times must I remind you, Jimmy? My name is Magdalene."

"Yeah, yeah, yeah." Jimmy let out a solitary chuckle. "Star of the show in every way that counts, right?"

Her eyes drew down to slits. "And don't you forget it."

Another set of double knocks at the door drew all their attention and, for some reason, elicited a flurry of metallic wings at Steven's chest.

"Expecting someone, Jimmy?" Magdalene asked.

Jimmy inclined his head in the direction of the door. "Milo, go see who it is."

Milo peered out through the sliding door window. "Huh. It's a bunch of old dames."

"Ah. The cleaning ladies." Jimmy again checked his watch. "They were due hours ago. Had to do most of the heavy lifting myself."

"Should I let them in?" Milo asked.

Jimmy strode over and peeked out himself. "Looks like the usual crew. Let them in."

Milo unlocked the trio of deadbolts and ushered in the quartet of women, all well into their seventh decade. A plump Latino woman led the way, followed by a slender black matron with hair the color of a snowy sky, an Asian woman whose unwrinkled face didn't match the wisdom in her gaze, and a freckled Irish lady whose hair still retained the red of her youth.

That's going to be Audrey someday. Steven's fingernails dug into his palms. *But not if Magdalene ends us right here in 1936.* His eyes slid shut. *How could I have underestimated, of all people, the Black Queen of this stupid Game?*

Jimmy pulled the four women aside to discuss what remained to be done to get the club ready for the evening, leaving Steven and Lena with Magdalene and the hairless ape who served as her bodyguard.

"So," Magdalene whispered, "whatever shall we do with the two of you?" She pursed her lips in concentration. "It's clear you know more about me than the fine people down at Pioneer Trust & Savings." Her gaze flicked back and forth between Steven and Lena, her green eyes as cold as the Arctic. "I have no idea what it is you believe about me or how you may have come to be in possession of such knowledge, but I really don't like having people nosing around in my life." Her voice dropped a few decibels. "Not now."

Steven stepped in front of Lena. "Look, clearly we made a mistake seeking you out. Let us go in peace and you'll never see either of our faces again."

At least...not for another few decades.

"Please." Lena's gaze dropped to the floor. "I'm...so sorry I bothered you."

"Yes." Steven couldn't guess how much the feigned apology cost Lena. "We're sorry."

"You're sorry?" Magdalene chuckled. "That and a nickel will buy you exactly nothing in this town." She pulled in a full breath, straightening up and drawing her shoulders back proudly. "You mess with Franco Abbadelli's girl, you don't just walk away scot-free."

"Someone say my name?" The voice, colored with more than its fair share of Italian overtones, echoed from the far end of the room. There, framed by an open doorway, stood a man with tawny skin and chestnut hair slicked back and glistening in the low light of the room. His white tuxedo shirt lay unbuttoned halfway down his chest while his black pants, impeccably pressed, just brushed the tops of his highly shined black wingtips.

Magdalene's face broke into a beaming smile. She made a beeline straight across the room for the strikingly handsome man who in turn swept her into a passionate kiss. Steven and Lena both looked away, and even Jimmy and Milo found other places to focus their attention during the half-minute spectacle.

When they were done, Abbadelli cast an appraising look in Steven and Lena's direction.

"And who, my darling, might our new friends be?"

Magdalene squeezed Abbadelli's hand. "This 'Lena Cervantes' is the girl I've been telling you about who's been tacking herself on to the end of my shadows the last few weeks after work." Her dismissive stare fell upon Steven. "And her friend, Mr. 'Bauer' here, chose a particularly unfortunate day to tag along."

"Truly unfortunate, indeed." Abbadelli shifted his gaze to a point across Steven's shoulder. "Milo, take them out back." He turned and disappeared back through the door with Magdalene a step behind. "You know what to do."

"You got it, boss."

A second later, Abbadelli poked his head back into the room. "Know what? I'm feeling merciful. Let the girl stay." He ogled Lena from across the room. "I'm sure we can find a use for someone with her obvious talents."

"But, Franco—" Magdalene began, her words cut off by a squeeze of her fingers that nearly took her to her knees.

"My club, sweetheart." Abbadelli released her hand. "My rules."

"Yes, Franco." The two words, barely a whisper, represented the most vulnerable Steven had ever seen the woman standing before him. "Of course."

"And what about him?" Milo directed a fat thumb in Steven's direction. "The usual?"

"He looks pretty resilient." Abbadelli steepled his fingers below his chin and smiled. "Use your imagination."

27

MOBSTERS & MOLOTOV COCKTAILS

The alleyway behind Franco Abbadelli's night club sat empty save for a small dumpster, a pair of rickety metal chairs, and a half-starved cat that regarded Steven as if he might be on the menu for later. Milo threw Steven to the cold cobblestone wet with melted ice.

"You know, Mr. Abbadelli said to be creative, but if you want to know the truth, I don't enjoy this part of the job all that much." He cracked his knuckles. "If it's all the same to you, I'm all about quick and painless."

Boy, are you in the wrong field. "You could always let me go."

Milo laughed. "I said I didn't enjoy my job at times, not that I wasn't good at it."

Steven pulled himself up, his confidence swelling with his feet again firmly planted on the ground. Studying Milo's massive form, he guessed the man outweighed him by a good hundred pounds. No way he was winning that fight. Trying to outrun him was an option, but he had a nasty feeling the mob enforcer was quicker than he looked.

"Maybe we can make a deal. You tell Abbadelli I'm finished, and you'll never see me again. I can pay—"

"Stop." Milo groaned in exasperation. "Look. Even if you had the money to pay me better than Mr. Abbadelli, you're crazy if you think I'd betray the boss. He's one of the most powerful men in Chicago, period. He wants you dead, you die." Milo pulled a snub-nosed handgun from inside his coat and directed the business end at Steven's chest. "Case in point."

"Wait." Steven raised both hands before him. "There's something you don't know." Audrey's face filled his mind's eye. "There's a girl."

Milo shook his head, never taking his eyes or the gun off Steven. "Isn't there always?"

"She's sick." Steven took a breath. "I mean, *real* sick. If you don't let me out of here, she's going to die."

"So, you're keeping two little chickadees. One sick at home as well as the girl in the club." Milo's lips spread in a knowing grin. "A man after my own heart."

Heat rose in Steven's cheeks, even as his hands balled into fists at his sides. "You don't have the first idea what you're talking about."

"You know what? You're right." Milo dropped another iron grip on Steven's shoulder and forced him to his knees. "We didn't come out here to talk." He stepped around Steven and pressed the barrel of his pistol into the back of his head. "Any last words before I—"

A loud thunk echoed in the space, cutting short the mobster's question. The cool metal at the back of Steven's head fell away, and a moment later, the ground all but shook as Milo's massive form crumpled to the ground. The man's skull remained mercifully spared from the cruel cobblestone at their feet, his shoulder taking the brunt of the fall.

Steven craned his head around, unsure of who or what he might see. A friendly face brought a wave of relief.

"Emilio." He allowed himself to breathe again. "Thank God."

"You don't know the half of it." Emilio's hand, still holding the section of now-bent pipe that took Milo down, shook like a leaf in a hurricane. "We barely made it here in time."

Niklaus stepped from behind the dumpster where Emilio must have hidden moments before. "You didn't think we'd let you get taken out by a gorilla in a cheap suit, did you?"

"But how the hell did you two even know where to look for us?"

Steven glanced in the direction of the door leading back into the club. "We only just made it here ourselves."

"Another letter, just like the one Lena received weeks ago. Same handwriting and everything."

Before Steven could spare the revelation another thought, Emilio reminded them all they had a more pressing concern.

"Lena." Emilio let the pipe drop to the ground and headed for the door. "Let's go."

"Wait a second, Emilio." Steven caught him by the arm. "You go in there half-cocked, you're going to get yourself killed."

"And Lena, too," Niklaus added.

Emilio resisted for a couple of seconds and then stopped in his tracks and turned around. "Fine." He shook Steven's grip from the sleeve of his coat. "What's the play, fearless leader?"

Steven considered for a moment. "The guy who owns this place, not to mention sent me and Milo there out here to have our little talk, decided five minutes ago to spare Lena's life. Considering the man's line of work, it isn't likely his reason for doing so is anything any of us would like to consider. For the moment, though, Lena is alive, and we can work with that."

"And Magdalene?" Niklaus asked.

"She's in there. The big guy's moll, it would appear."

Niklaus strode over to the door. "So all that stands between us and Lena is this poor man's Al Capone and his little woman?"

Steven gestured to Emilio's discarded weapon. "And however many gangsters he has in his employ, each of them most likely armed with more than a lead pipe."

"We've faced worse odds." Emilio retrieved Milo's pistol. "Come on, Steven. Time's wasting."

Steven cast his mind back a few minutes, recreating a map of his forced exodus from the dining room of Abbadelli's club to the frigid alleyway behind the building: The kitchen, filled with white-hatted cooks, sous-chefs, and wait staff. The dark hallway that connected to the stairs leading up to street level. The sign on the small door they passed just before Milo had dragged him up those very stairs and out into the cold.

"Hold on." Steven narrowed his eyes at the door leading back into the club. "Unless I'm way off base here, I have an idea."

❀

"You're going to get us all killed." Emilio stood watch at the corner of the hall while Steven worked to pick the lock on a small door marked with an admonition against smoking in the next room. "You know that?"

"What do you think they have in there?" Niklaus asked.

"Something too flammable to let anyone light up." The lock turned with a triple click and Steven opened the door. "I suppose we'll find out."

"How'd you learn to do that?" Niklaus asked as he followed Steven into the dim hallway beyond the door.

"When I was a kid, there was a year or two where I became obsessed with escape artists. Read everything the library had on Houdini and the like. Wanted to prove I could do everything those guys could. I even saved up and bought myself a set of lockpicks along with some handcuffs, padlocks, and the like. I practiced till I could get myself out of pretty much any room in the house." Steven shook his head. "Never dreamed I'd be calling on those skills again."

"None of us dreamed any of this would happen." Emilio pushed past Steven and into the darkened storage room. "Let's get to work."

The three of them split up, each taking one of the three narrow aisles beyond the door. Shelf after shelf of canned tomato paste, olive oil, and other ingredients were all that Steven found. Niklaus similarly reported bins of fresh vegetables and various spices. It wasn't until Emilio's whispered "jackpot" that Steven allowed himself a moment of hope.

"What did you find?" He joined Emilio at the room's back corner.

"Something we can use?" Niklaus asked, joining them a moment later.

"Just this." Emilio held up a pair of bottles of liquor labeled *Rhum Caïman*. "Highest alcohol content this side of Everclear."

Steven cocked his head to one side. "And what do you know about Everclear?"

"Don't worry." Emilio worked at the foil at the top of the bottle. "I didn't start drinking till I hit 1890 with my favorite whiskey-slinging priest, but trust me..." A sad smile spread across Emilio's features. "With a brother like Carlos Cruz, I inherited more than a passing knowledge of the wonderful world of alcohol."

"How many are there?" Niklaus asked.

Emilio handed him the first two bottles and reached into the darkness of the bottom shelf. "If all of these are rum, then eight."

"More than enough," Steven whispered. "And I found these." He held up a stack of folded white napkins. "Let's get to work."

"**I**s she ready?" Abbadelli paced the strip of dance floor in front of the stage. "I want to see what our new *piccolina* looks like all dolled up."

"These things take a little time. A little makeup, a few finger curls in her hair, a few spritzes of perfume." Magdalene strode between the tables toward Abbadelli. "By the way, in case you were wondering, the dress you had just laying around happens to fit her perfectly." Her eyes narrowed. "Funny how it wasn't in my size."

"You're not our only performer, my dear." He pulled Magdalene into his arms and nuzzled her just below her ear. "And, as you know, I'm always prepared."

"Oh, you are that." Magdalene turned her head to one side, leaving the kiss Abbadelli intended for her lips exiled to her high cheekbone.

"I put on the dress." From the women's washroom across the way, Lena stood framed by the doorway, hands on her hips and mouth pulled to one side. Her simple street clothes exchanged for a slinky white dress with accents the color of ripe cherries, she clearly had Abbadelli's undivided attention. "What do you want me to do now?"

"Ah, I knew something special hid buried underneath those tomboy togs." He motioned for her to join him by the piano. "Come over here. Let's see if our newest cigarette girl knows how to sashay across a crowded room."

Fuming, Lena stalked toward Abbadelli, fists at her sides.

"Stop." Abbadelli shook his head. "I said sashay, not stomp." He swirled his finger in the air. "Now, give me a spin."

Lena raised a finger of her own before spinning around and grabbing a chair from a nearby table. With as little grace as possible, she sat backward on the cloth seat and rested her elbows on the back of the chair. "You don't know it yet, Mr. Abbadelli, but you're going to regret this."

"Regret?" He laughed once, his lips pursed in a contemptuous smirk. "I don't know the meaning of the word."

"You will." Lena raised an eyebrow and returned Abbadelli's disdainful stare in kind.

"Your friend is dead and no one else on the planet knows where you are." Magdalene glided over to Lena's table, showing her, no doubt, how a "sashay" was done. "We could chop you up and feed you to the dogs and no one would be the wiser."

"Overconfidence always was your Achilles' heel, Maggie," Lena said, granting the someday Black Queen half a second before returning her attention to Abbadelli. "And now—"

Magdalene pounded her fist on the table. "Do not presume to speak as if you know the first thing about me, child. You don't know anything about who I am or what I'm capable of."

"Don't I?" Lena rose from her seat. "You talk a big game, Mags, but that's pretty easy when you have your mobster boyfriend here with all his men and guns to back you up. Not to mention, of course, that you still let him touch you even as he's flirting with a sixteen-year-old girl right in your face." Lena's eyes went up and to the side, as if deep in thought. "Cockiness mixed with low self-esteem. Must suck to be you."

"Shut your insolent mouth." She rushed forward and slapped Lena across her face. "I've had people filleted for less." She grabbed one of the champagne flutes from the table and smacked it against the back of a chair, leaving a crystal dagger in her trembling hand. "And, most importantly, you stupid cow…" Her green eyes went glacier cold. "My name…is Magdalene."

"Now, now, my dear," Abbadelli intoned. "No need for such dramatics." He calmly strode up behind Magdalene and took her by the shoulders. "The cleaning ladies only come once a week." He motioned to the far corner of the room where the quartet of woman continued to dust, sweep, and otherwise refine the room's decor, all the while doing their best to ignore the scene taking place at the room's center. "Let's not make them even more of a mess to clean up." He cast an angry glance in Lena's direction. "Would be a real shame if we got blood all over the place, don't you think?"

Jimmy stepped in from the kitchen. "Everything all right out here?"

"Nothing we can't handle." Abbadelli returned his attention to Lena. "A little less attitude from you and I think you might actually fit in quite well here."

"What makes you think I'd stay here a second longer than I had to?" Lena glowered in Abbadelli's direction. "Much less work for you?"

"Oh, people have a way of coming around to my way of thinking." Abbadelli pulled Magdalene into him. "Isn't that right, my dear?"

Ignoring Abbadelli, Magdalene grasped Lena's chin in her taloned hand. "Just try and escape. The last person who did met the same end as your friend. You want to bleed out in a back alley like him?"

Abbadelli shot a concerned look toward the rear of the club. "Where is Milo, anyway? I know I gave him permission to work out a little of his frustration on Mr. Bauer's face, but he's usually a bit more efficient than this." His eyes flicked to Jimmy. "Can you go check on—"

"*Fuego!*" The heart-stopping scream came from the Latina cleaning woman, her ample face pale with terror as she pointed toward the front of the club and the thick black smoke pouring under the door.

"What the hell?" Jimmy sprinted to the door, stripping a tablecloth from a bare table and snagging a pitcher of water from another as he ran. The quartet of cleaning women nearly bowled over the club's owner as they bolted as one for the kitchen.

"What have you brought upon my place of business?" Abbadelli pushed Magdalene out of the way, grabbed Lena's shoulders, and shook her. "Who's doing this?"

Magdalene's face fell, even as the color rose in her cheeks and the anger in her eyes. "Bauer."

"Give that lady a prize." The door to the kitchen flew open as Steven stepped out into the club. In one hand, he held a bottle of Abbadelli's best rum, its mouth stuffed with an alcohol-soaked rag; in the other, a lit Zippo lighter.

Magdalene drew back even as Abbadelli stepped forward. "You are far more resourceful than I imagined, Mr. Bauer. What a shame that fate has set us on opposite sides." Any joviality left the man's features as he crossed his arms, a cool detachment oozing from his every pore. "I suppose the only thing left to ask is, what now?"

"Now, Mr. Abbadelli." He held the makeshift torch high above his head and brought the lighter dangerously close to the cloth. "We talk."

28

THREATEN & DEFEND

"All right, Mr. Bauer." Abbadelli released Lena and took a step in Steven's direction. "You are understandably upset, but let's not do anything rash."

"You mean like kidnapping and attempted murder?" Steven moved to a table covered with folded cloth napkins and allowed the lighter's flame to flirt with the rag hanging from his makeshift bomb. "Just making sure I'm clear on what we're discussing here."

Abbadelli froze in his steps. "Fine." He raised his hands before him, palms out. "You have my undivided attention."

"Hey, boss." Jimmy worked to stuff the wet tablecloth beneath the club's main door. "I've got the smoke stopped, but the door is hot as an oven." His voice dropped a few decibels. "We're not getting out that way."

"Only one way out of here, then, and that's through me." Steven held the bottle-made-bomb before him. "Let me leave with Lena unless you want to see this place go up in flames."

"You strike me as a moral man, Mr. Bauer. What of the cooks in the back? And the waitstaff?" Abbadelli crossed his arms, defiant. "Would you endanger their lives as well?"

Steven tilted his head to one side and slid into a snide grin. "I talked all your employees into taking the rest of the evening off." He brandished the bottle of rum before him and threatened again to set the cloth alight. "Strangely enough, they didn't need much convincing."

Jimmy pulled up alongside Abbadelli, the trained placidity of his expression at odds with the beads of sweat coursing down his forehead. "What now, boss?"

"Simple." Magdalene stepped in front of both men, grabbed Lena by the hair, and brought her champagne glass shiv to the girl's jugular.

Lena jerked away instinctively, leaving a small line of blood beneath the angle of her jaw.

"You want the girl to live, right?" Magdalene's lips parted in an all too familiar smile. "Then put down that bottle before you blow yourself to smithereens."

Steven set his jaw. "Do you really want to see this place burn to the ground?"

"Not especially." Magdalene's eyes narrowed. "Do you really want to see this beautiful girl bleed like a stuck pig?"

"Lena!" Emilio charged from the kitchen. "Get away from her, *bruja*."

Dammit. Steven ground his teeth in frustration. *He was supposed to stay out of sight.*

"Emilio," he whispered. "Stand down. I've got this."

Magdalene's gaze flicked to Emilio and then back to Steven. "Ah, so *this* is Miss Cervantes' little lover boy. Excellent. I must admit, Mr. Bauer, handsome though you are, the thought of you with such a young thing frankly turned my stomach a bit."

Emilio's fists went white at his sides. "Says the woman who's screwing a man old enough to be her father."

"Careful, boy." Abbadelli raised a conciliatory hand in Magdalene's direction, his voice shifting into a quiet sing-song. "My lady love has quite the sharp sliver of crystal less than an inch from your girl's neck. Magdalene Byrne may be known for many things, but an even temper isn't one of them."

Emilio shook with anger, but one look into Lena's terrified eyes convinced him to keep his tongue.

"So, Mr. Bauer. It would appear we have reached an impasse." Abbadelli studied him like a pool shark lining up a shot. "A stalemate if you will."

Stalemate. Steven tasted bile. *As if there were any question all of this was still somehow part of the Game.*

"Mr. Abbadelli." Steven worked to keep any hint of emotion from his voice. "It's clear that you're a man who understands the fine art of negotiation. All we want is Lena. Give her to us, and we'll leave this place without another word, never to be seen or heard from again." He clicked the Zippo lighter closed. "I have no desire to leave this place a smoking cinder." He reopened the lighter, and with a flick of his thumb, the flame returned to its previous glory. "But make no mistake, hand her over, *right now*, or this place goes up like the Fourth of July."

Abbadelli glared, a war playing out on his face.

"Let her go," he said after what seemed a century.

"B-but—" Magdalene sputtered. "We can't let him win."

"Do you want to see everything we've built go up in smoke?" Abbadelli's voice grew as sharp as a barber's razor. "Let. The girl. Go."

Magdalene considered for a moment, a battle raging in her own furious gaze, the crystal edge drawing blood anew from the skin beneath Lena's ear.

"Emilio," Lena whispered. "I love you."

"Mr. Abbadelli." Steven lit the cloth hanging from the mouth of the rum bottle. "Last chance."

"Enough." Abbadelli grabbed his lover's hand and pulled the shattered champagne flute from Lena's neck, a single drop of blood flying from the crystal's razor edge and staining the pristine white cloth atop the nearest table.

"Lena!" Emilio shouted, not moving an inch.

Abbadelli knelt by Lena's side. "Get up, Miss Cervantes, and go to your man." When Lena hesitated, his voice dropped to a low growl, his gaze locking with Steven's. "Now, before I change my mind."

Lena ran to Emilio's arms. "Thank God, *papi*. I never thought I'd see you again."

"You're safe now, *mami*." Emilio held Lena tight in one arm and leveled an accusatory finger at Magdalene with the other. "As for you, if we ever cross paths again..."

"Don't you worry, boyo." Magdalene stepped forward, a snake drawing close to strike. "If we do indeed cross paths again someday, only one of us will walk away."

"Come on, you two." Steven stepped backward toward the kitchen, holding the lit bottle of rum like the grenade it had become. "Let's get out of—" His words cut off by a pinch at his left chest, he cast his gaze left and right looking for the cause of Amaryllis' warning.

"Steven," Emilio shouted. "Look out!"

"Milo, no!"

Abbadelli's bellowed command barely registered in Steven's mind as a force like a flying cinderblock impacted the back of his head, sending him to his knees. His vision went black and his ears roared as the flaming bottle flew from his hand. Somewhere in the distance, a cacophony of shattering glass ended in a blood-chilling scream.

Seconds to centuries later, Steven's senses returned, and everything had changed.

Milo lay on the floor as unconscious as they'd left him in the alley half an hour before, the scattered pieces of one of the dining room's chairs lying about his fallen form in disarray.

Emilio and Lena had an arm beneath each of Steven's shoulders and were dragging him backward toward the kitchen.

And not ten feet away, Jimmy and Franco Abbadelli worked frantically to put out a fire that had engulfed one of the club's tables.

No.

Not the table.

The person atop the table.

Magdalene, her satin dress rendered into so much ash, lay atop the charred tablecloth as naked as the day she was born. Her skin blistered and red, her face had taken the brunt of the flame, no doubt from the fur collar that had caressed her neck and cheeks moments before. Her hair as well, perfectly coiffed with whatever product was the rage in 1936, had gone up in flames, leaving her scalp barren and charred. Her breathing ragged, every inhalation came coupled with a whistling sound that raised the hairs on Steven's neck.

He wasn't sure which unnerved him more, the stridor in her every inhalation or the screams that fell between.

"Good God," Steven whispered, finally able to form words. "I didn't mean to—"

"Get the hell out of my club," Abbadelli shouted as he threw pitcher after pitcher of ice water onto Magdalene's exposed body. "And God himself have mercy if I ever lay eyes on any of you again."

Emilio and Lena pulled Steven into the kitchen, the door swinging shut on the terrible sight of Magdalene's immolated form. They were halfway to the stairs leading to the alley when the strength finally returned to Steven's legs.

"Hold on a second, you two." He got his feet beneath him and stood. "I think I've got this."

The room spun for a few seconds before stabilizing just a couple degrees askew. Steven took a few careful steps before leading Emilio and Lena for the exit leading to the club's back alley. Only the subtle hiss of the gas burners and the sputtering of the various abandoned pots and pans filled with food no one would ever eat broke the kitchen's strange silence.

As he rounded the corner and hit the club's back hallway, the answer as to where Niklaus had gone became apparent.

"Nik!" Finding his friend's massive form crumpled at the bottom of the stairs leading out, Steven rushed to kneel at the man's side. "Are you okay?"

"I think so." Niklaus looked up at Steven, his eyes glazed over in a bemused stare. "Did you save Lena?"

"She's fine." Steven stepped aside, revealing Lena's flustered half-smile. "But there's no time for reunions. We've got to get out of here."

Emilio knelt with Steven at Niklaus' side. "What happened to you, Nik?"

"I set the fire at the front door like we talked about and then sprinted back to the alley to join you guys. Halfway down the stairs there, I ran into a group of old women rushing for the exit. I dodged to one side to let them pass when out of nowhere, one of them tagged me with a punch to the chest that dropped me like a rag doll."

"A single punch?" Lena asked.

Niklaus nodded. "She hit me, square in the breastbone. A second later, I got really hot and my legs went out from under me." A few blinks allowed his bleary eyes to focus on Steven's. "She followed the other women out, leaving me in a pile at the bottom of the stairs. A minute later, that big lug from the alley came back inside looking ready to rip someone's head off. Stepped right across me like I wasn't even there." Niklaus' disjointed gaze dropped to his chest in defeat. "I tried to stop him, but I couldn't move."

"That must have been some punch." Steven rubbed at the back of his head. "I can relate." He offered Niklaus a hand. "Think you can get up? Not sure how much of a head start we have."

Niklaus offered Steven a weak smile. "I'll give it my best shot."

Steven helped Niklaus to his feet and, with Emilio's assistance, they made it up the stairs to the door leading to the alley.

"None of this makes any sense," Emilio said as Steven opened the door. "Why would a random cleaning woman in 1936 even know who Nik is, much less hit him?"

"And what did she do to you?" Lena waited until everyone made it out and closed the door behind them. "I mean, you're a pretty big guy. Did she—I don't know—drug you?"

"No," Niklaus groaned, "but that was one hell of a punch." He shook his head in disbelief. "Dropped me like a puppet with its strings cut." He leaned against the brick and turned to Emilio. "And her appearance here today was anything but random."

"What do you mean?" Steven asked.

Niklaus pulled an envelope from his coat pocket. "After gorilla boy came through, she returned just long enough to leave this with me."

"Another letter." Steven took the envelope and peered inside. "Did you read it?"

Niklaus laughed. "I'm still seeing two of you, so…no."

Steven opened the envelope and inspected the contents—another folded missive, the paper yellowed and crumpled like the letter that Lena had showed them earlier.

Niklaus squinted in the dim light. "What does it say?"

"Yeah." Lena drew close. "And is it the same handwriting from my note?"

"Looks like it." Steven could barely read even the first sentence, the fine script difficult to make out with only a lone sputtering streetlamp providing illumination. "Same fancy calligraphy. We'll study this along with the other two letters when we're safe back at the hotel." He returned the letter to the envelope and shoved it into his coat pocket. "You okay to travel, Nik?"

"Is the other option staying here and freezing my ass off behind the nightclub where I got taken down by a freaking senior citizen?" Niklaus took a few hesitant steps, and then headed for the mouth of the alley. "Come on, everyone. Coast is clear."

Lena and Emilio followed, leaving Steven alone for a moment. He peered up and down the dimly lit space between the buildings, hoping that somehow, the mysterious woman helping them might reappear and explain what the hell was going on.

Meow.

Directly above his head, crouched on a low fire escape, a jet-black cat peered down at Steven, its green feline eyes iridescent in the low light of the space. The all-but-invisible creature sent his mind flitting back to another Chicago club and a night that wouldn't occur for another seventy years, leaving his chest heavy with anxiety, anticipation, and no small amount to guilt.

The woman who would become the Black Queen of this strange Game that had taken over all their lives lay burned and screaming on a table a few dozen steps away. Flashes of her hairless scalp, ruined face, and burned body, all flavored by a potent combination of agonized screams and the stench of burned flesh set his every hair on end.

Steven had wondered for months what could fill a human being with such fire, such rage, such burning hatred.

The answer, ironically, left him cold.

29

QUESTIONS & ANSWERS

Dearest Steven Bauer,

You and your five friends now stand reunited. Each of the events necessary to ensure that all will be as it should upon your return to your own time are now complete. Though the iteration of the Hvitr Kyll in your possession does not hail from your own era, this version of your mentor's artifact will serve more than well enough as both conveyance and guide. One last crossing and all that has gone awry should be set right.

This letter is the third and final assistance you will receive from me. I have no doubt that you are curious as to my identity, but the time for that revelation has not yet come. Simply know that I owed you a great debt and that debt is now fulfilled.

May good fortune travel with you on your journey home. Do not tarry, for the Game awaits.

-A Friend

Back at the hotel that had been Audrey and Lena's home for the last few months, Steven sat on the bed next to Audrey's sleeping form, the mysterious message resting on his lap.

"You've read that thing a hundred times, Steven." Niklaus eyed the letter, his dubious gaze that of a man unsure if his foot rested on a landmine. "You think it's going to start sprouting new words?"

"There's got to be a clue here somewhere." Steven rested his hand on the letter, crumpling the paper. "The woman who wrote this and the other letters went to a lot of trouble both to help us and to make sure we knew we were being helped."

Lena cleared her throat. "Again, you're assuming the woman from the club is the one who wrote the letter in the first place."

Steven groaned. "If *whoever* wrote this is such a 'friend,' then why does it feel like we're all being led down the cherry path?" He folded the letter together with the other two missives from their mysterious benefactor and shoved all three back in his pocket.

"I'm just glad you've all returned safely." Archie breathed a sigh of relief. "When the second letter appeared under our door, I feared the worse."

Steven rubbed at the bruise below his eye, one of many that had blossomed since his back-alley chat with Milo. "We're fine." He brushed Audrey's hand gently with his fingertips. "But we're back to square one on getting ourselves home."

"Not to mention we just created a monster." Niklaus cracked his neck. "The Black Queen…"

"Is all our fault." Steven buried his face in his hands. He didn't know which struck him as stranger, the fact that the woman who had attempted to first seduce and then kill him at the beginning of all this was apparently a nonagenarian or that the flames which had nearly ended all of their lives had likely been kindled by his own hand. "No wonder she hates us all so much."

"And yet, she never let on that she knew us." Emilio held Lena tight, the two of them standing over Audrey like a pair of guardian angels.

"None of them did." Steven's eyes narrowed. "Not Magdalene, not Zed, not even Grey."

"Think it's one of those space-time continuum things like Doc Brown is always going on about in the *Back to the Future* movies?" Niklaus did his best to catch everyone's eye and brighten the moment with his trademark smile. "Like, one of them says the wrong thing, time rewrites itself, and all of a sudden we're the bad guys and sporting goatees?"

Steven chuckled at that last bit. "Yeah, Nik, I'm sure it's something like that." He looked up into Archie's concerned eyes. "You're sure nothing changed with Audrey while we were gone?"

"No change." Archie took a seat opposite Steven on the bed and rested a hand on Audrey's forehead. "It's strange, you know? My time in the Game may represent only a few months of my life, but the ability to heal with just a touch like Jesus and his Apostles was a dream come true—an answer to years of prayer." His head dropped. "To sit here and watch Audrey wither away, knowing that in another time and place I could help her, is a nightmare."

"We're all powerless for the moment." Steven patted the pocket that contained the trio of letters. "But if what this third letter says is true, we may be closer to home than any of us understand."

"Good." Audrey's eyes flickered open. "Because the last time I felt this bad, it almost killed me."

Audrey's feeble response to her own joke came out more cough than laugh. Steven maintained his concerned smile, refusing to let the fear show on his face.

An old fear Steven knew all too well.

A rapid fire of images hit him like a freight train going full tilt through a lifetime of memories.

His mother's beautiful smile juxtaposed with the straight set of her lips as she lay in the coffin.

Katherine's sparkling eyes the night he asked her to marry him followed an instant later by the moment those eyes closed forever.

The terror in Audrey's gaze as the Black Queen summoned black flame from the pits of Hell itself to burn her alive in her bed.

"No." Steven turned his head away. "Not this time."

Audrey reached weakly for Steven's face. "I take it from all these bruises the talk with Magdalene didn't go as well as you'd hoped."

"Believe it or not," Steven said despite the lump in his throat, "she got the worse end of the deal by a solid mile."

"Really? That's—" Audrey's reply descended into a peal of hacking coughs.

"It's okay, Audrey." Steven patted her back, feeling more and more helpless by the second. "Everything's okay." He met Lena's gaze and raised an eyebrow, the unspoken question answered with a resigned nod that sent a fist of ice straight through his chest.

It can't end this way. Steven rested his hand on the small of Audrey's back, wishing he could pour his strength, his very vitality into her wasting body. *It can't.*

"Don't try to talk." Archie took Audrey's hand. "A lot has happened since Lena and Steven left earlier to track down our friend with the fiery disposition. Listen for a minute and let them catch you up."

Steven and the others pulled no punches reviewing the events of the preceding hours: the providence of the second letter; Steven's near death at the hands of a gorilla in a suit named Milo; their mad plan to save Lena.

And last, the Black Queen's fiery fate.

With every twist of the tale, Audrey gasped or winced or laughed or applauded, but as Lena and Emilio described in excruciating detail the immolation of Magdalene Byrne, she didn't bat an eye or show an ounce of emotion.

When they were done, Audrey raised a trembling hand. "May I see the last letter?"

Steven pulled the envelope from his pocket and extricated the third of the collection of yellowed pieces of paper folded within.

"Hm." Audrey squinted at the fine script. "The letter says that the pouch will serve as both our way home and our guide to get there."

"That's it." Steven craned his neck around to read the letter again, as if afraid Niklaus' joke about new words appearing on the page had come true. "Right?"

"And that we need to find 'one last crossing' to get us home."

Steven leaned in close. "I feel like you're picking up on something I missed."

"It may be nothing." Audrey folded the letter and rested it on her lap. "But when you were traveling at the beginning, you'd always end up pretty wasted when the pouch would take you to a specific location to find one of us, right?"

"Yes."

"I was thinking about what you told me about arriving in Florida, then Wyoming, and most recently here in Chicago." Audrey's tired eyes filled with hope. "Not once did you mention feeling tired on any of those jaunts. Is it possible there's a reason for that?"

"Crossings." Steven's eyes grew wide in wonder. "It's not just about finding the right place from which to take off…"

Audrey squeezed his knee. "But finding the right place to land."

"The woods in Florida. The ridge in Wyoming. The alleyway here in Chicago. None of those places are random." Steven rose from the bed. "Without the energies of the Game to empower the pouch, it's been taking us where and when we need to go each time via the path of least resistance. How did I not see it?"

Niklaus stepped up. "Not like it would've done any good. You think we could've found our way back to the exact spot in the woods in Florida?"

"I suppose not."

"Or back to where we appeared in Wyoming?"

Steven shrugged. "We could've followed our own tracks back, maybe."

"Not in that blizzard." Archie steepled his fingers before his face. "I'm guessing to travel from crossing to crossing, the spot has to be exact." The priest smiled. "And now, we have that."

"How so?" Steven asked.

"Our mysterious helper." Archie eyed the girl with a warm smile. "Her first letter took Lena right to the place where we arrived from Wyoming. I'm betting the crossing there can function as both an entrance…"

"And an exit." Steven sucked in a breath. "The way out."

"If that's the case," Audrey sat up in the bed, "then let's not wait another—" Yet another peal of coughing cut her words mid-sentence.

"Audrey's right." Steven rubbed her back and offered a silent prayer that they would somehow get back in time to save her. "Pack your bags, everyone." Worry and hope and pain and relief all warred for supremacy in Steven's soul. "We're getting out of here."

"This is the place?" Steven asked. "You're sure?"

"Yes, Steven." Lena pointed to the ground at Steven's feet. "You were here, Niklaus here, and Archie and Emilio stood right there."

"This is the spot." Audrey sat in a chair they'd "borrowed" from the hotel, wrapped head to toe in blankets to protect her from the elements. She still shivered, but from the cold or the excitement, Steven wasn't sure. "I can feel it."

"The pouch would seem to agree." Niklaus motioned to the *Hvitr Kyll* hanging at Steven's side, its quiet drone a welcome return after days of rarely broken silence. "Shall we give it a shot?"

"Gather round, everyone." Steven assumed his position behind Audrey's chair. "Unless I miss my guess, we'll only have one shot at this."

"Home, then?" Archie asked. "You're sure that's the best play?"

"As we agreed." Steven shuddered in the cold. "Audrey's life comes first."

Their reunion was complete, save one. The most important piece. Their King.

But if they lost their Queen in the process...

"We'll find Grey—I swear it—but first we've got to get everyone well." Steven surveyed all of them, and in their steadfast gaze, found the vote unanimous. "I found all of you. We'll find him too."

At Steven's beckoning, Lena and Emilio came up on one side, Archie and Niklaus the other, and with Steven, the five formed a tight circle around the White Queen upon her humble throne. Steven grasped the *Hvitr Kyll* in one hand and held out the other, palm down. Each of the others placed their hand atop his with Audrey going last. The struggle of simply raising her arm clearly took its toll on her fragile form.

"Here." Steven broke from the huddle and reached for her forearm. "Let me help you."

"No." She brushed away his hand with sudden strength. "You focus on the pouch. I've got this." With Herculean effort, she brought her hand atop Archie's, the effort leaving her visibly winded. "There," she panted, "see?"

Hold on just a little longer, Audrey. Steven looked skyward. *And God, if you're listening, please help us. This has to work.*

His gaze cut to Archie whose knowing glance suggested he had somehow heard Steven's silent prayer. Though everyone else stared expectantly at the pouch Steven held above Audrey's head, Archie's eyes were, as always, fixed on him. The hairs on Steven's neck, already on end, tingled in warning, but as usual, nothing in Archie's words or actions crossed enough of a line to warrant telling the others.

And yet, the feeling remained.

Could he be wrong? Could everything he'd been noticing for months all just be a bizarre misunderstanding?

Yet again, questions for another day.

Without warning, the pouch emitted a skull-shaking drone and pulsed in Steven's hand like a beating heart.

"Just like old times," Emilio whispered under his breath.

"Do it, Steven," Niklaus said. "Take us home."

"You heard the man," Steven voiced to the pouch as he held its warm leather high. "Return us to our time." He focused, as he had at Victor Brenin's ranch in California and Ed Leedskalnin's Coral Castle and every other time he'd brought the pouch to bear.

This time, however, nothing happened.

"What's wrong, Steven?" Lena's voice trembled. "Why are we still here?"

Frustrated, Steven gripped the pouch even tighter. "*Hvitr Kyll,* ancient pouch of the Game, I command you to take us home."

Again, the pouch answered with nothing but a continued drone.

"I don't understand." Despite all his misgivings, Steven turned to Archie. "Why isn't the pouch responding?"

Archie considered for a moment. "In all things, the pouch serves the Game. I would argue that in every other instance, your desires and the Game's have been the same."

"The Game doesn't want us to go home?"

"We must go home," Archie answered. "That much is clear. But, perhaps, not quite yet."

Steven's eyes flicked in Audrey's direction. "She might not have much time left," he whispered to Archie. "If we go off on another jaunt right now, she might not make it."

"I may be sick," Audrey croaked, "but my ears work just fine." She removed her hand from the huddle and gripped Steven's wrist. "Take us where the pouch needs us to go. I'll be fine."

"But, Audrey..."

Her grip doubled in strength. "Pouch, hear your Queen. Take us from this place so that we may continue our path home." Her weak voice grew in volume with each word. "Now."

The pouch screamed in answer, the pulse shaking Steven's teeth.

"Where is it taking us?" Emilio shouted over the cacophony.

"I have no idea," Steven bellowed as the pouch's drone doubled in volume, "but I think we're about to find out."

In an instant, the dark Chicago alleyway faded into nothingness, replaced by desert sands and a landscape that belonged on a 70s album cover.

"The pyramids." Lena gasped. "I never thought I'd see them in my lifetime."

"And you haven't." Steven stood opposite the rest, his gaze focused on a completely different wonder. "This is fourteen centuries before any of us were born."

Lena spun around. "And how could you possibly know—" Her gaze followed Steven's into a shallow valley to the west. There, two sides of light and dark formed up on a checkered battlefield of blinding marble and glistening obsidian, the squares each better than twenty feet across. A line of foot soldiers armed with spears fashioned either from white poplar or dark ebony formed the vanguard of both forces while the back row of each side broke down into four pairs of warriors. Each corner boasted an armored chariot driver holding the reins of an equally armored stallion in one hand and an implement of war in the other. Mounted warriors occupied each of the next squares, one side armed with spiked maces, the other with cruel flails. Where the bishops should have been waited a sight that Steven still couldn't believe, though he'd seen all of this before.

Archie looked on agog at the bronze-plated behemoths. "My, how things have changed."

"Archers atop elephants." Lena looked on in disbelief. "Instead of archbishops."

"And at the center, two men." Audrey's voice cracked. "Where are the Queens?"

Steven smiled, remembering the moment he asked Grey the exact same question. "As I understand it, the Game always reflects the rules and mechanics of chess at the particular time of that iteration. The queen didn't become a part of the game for a few more centuries."

"Lucky me." Audrey peeled away one of the blankets of her cocoon. "I must have come along right on time."

"Why do you think the pouch brought us here, Steven?" Niklaus asked. "You told us about this already."

"No clue. Shocking as it is, I saw all of this in a vision when I first met Grey months ago." A brisk wind sent a spray of sand into Steven's eyes. "Make no mistake, though. This time, we're actually here."

"Is the Game going to make us watch?" Lena's brow furrowed.

"I suppose that's a possibility, though from what I remember Grey saying, this one ended as he'd planned." Steven's eyes narrowed. "With no fatalities."

Zed held the King's position among the Black while Grey occupied the same square along the back row of the White. None of the other faces were familiar, though their features ran the gamut—African, Arabic, Asian, Slavic—a cross section of the world populace that might have passed through Egypt when the northeast corner of Africa was the de facto center of the world.

As they drew close, the first iteration of the Game began to play out before them. One Pawn advanced, then his opposite. A mounted soldier among the White leaped from the back rank and took up a defensive position near the center of the board. In answer, one of Black's elephant-mounted fighters thundered out from the back row. Archer drew bow. Horseman raised mace. Tension mounted with each bloodless move leaving the time-displaced White breathless as each awaited the first blow.

And then, in the blink of an eye, they were all somewhere else.

The stench hit Steven before his eyes registered where they were. Previously filtered through memory, the unmistakable smell of death now assaulted his senses directly. He fought not to retch, a battle neither Lena nor Niklaus won that day.

"Where are we?" Emilio asked.

Stonehenge, a stone's throw away, had borne witness to the slaughter of the fifteen figures in blood-stained white that lay around the checkered battlefield.

"Why is the pouch showing us this crap?" Niklaus wiped his mouth on the sleeve of his coat. "We are all more than aware of what awaits us."

"I suppose," Steven said, "but you haven't seen or experienced it." Bile filled the back of his throat. "None of us truly have."

Beneath the sunless sky, the aftermath of Grey's first defeat to Zed's machinations stretched before them all. A feast for flies and vultures alike, the remains of the ancient wizard's second army served as a potent reminder of exactly how far yet they all had to go.

"Zed did this." Audrey rose from her chair and knelt by the crumpled form of that iteration's White Queen, her head turned at an impossible angle. "And he'd do it again, if it served his purposes."

Reality warped around them again, and in an instant, they were in another place altogether. A blizzard raged around them, obscuring everything but the six of them within a swirling mass of blinding white.

"Where?" Niklaus asked.

Even blinded by the snow, Steven had no doubt as to exactly where they were. "Antarctica." A bitter wind whipped through their circle with icy teeth that clawed at their eyes, their hands, their faces.

"But why?" Lena asked.

"The third iteration of the Game happened here." Steven grabbed Audrey by the shoulders and pulled her close before another frigid gust could send her frail form to the ground. "The one Grey would never speak of."

"Why wouldn't he?" Emilio asked between chattering teeth. "The third round of the Game ended in a stalemate with Zed denied a second victory, right?"

"From what Zed said, yes." A shiver shook Steven's entire body. "But, apparently at a great cost."

At Steven's words, the storm abated as if one of the ancient gods of myth had willed it so. With the snow gone and the wind stilled, he and the others found themselves atop a craggy glacier looking down upon a valley of ice.

There, a battle raged, the likes of which Steven used to believe only happened in summer blockbusters.

Two lines, one dark and one light, charged across the alternating squares of black and white, the Pawns of this previous iteration of Grey's great Game.

At one edge of the checkered battlefield, a pair of armored warriors in jet, their black steeds clad with a mix of chain and plate mail, battled silver-clad knights mounted atop polar bears covered in armor of gold and alabaster.

Several stories above them, two giants of ice traded blows with a pair of onyx titans, each impact sending tremors through the entire glacier.

The center of the board held two women, one wrapped in glistening ivory, the other in darkest sable. The two Queens circled each other like mongoose and cobra, silver lightning crackling around the White Queen's hands and orbs of darkness around her opposite's.

Surrounding the pair of Queens, the four bishops held aloft ornately carved staves as if performing an ancient ritual lost to history.

And there, at the back of each army, the Kings waited. At one end of the board stood a much younger version of the man they knew as Grey in the glowing raiment of the White King, platinum crown at his brow and broadsword, held aloft, gleaming with a blinding silver sheen. At the other stood Zed, his black cloak extending to the snowy ground and his silver crown glowing a deep purple as he rested his hands atop the pommel of his broadsword, his weapon's point buried in the ice at his feet.

"This isn't a Game." Lena covered her mouth with her hands. "This is carnage."

"The ceremonial bringing together of Black and White to stave off the destruction of the world has been Game only in name since Zed abandoned all sense of decorum and fairness after the first iteration." Archie's breath steamed in the cold. "The only question that remains is exactly how this ends."

"You don't know?" Niklaus asked. "In all your visions, you never saw what happened here?"

Archie recoiled, as if struck. "I have." His eyes grew wild. "But what I saw won't remain in my head. It's as if—"

And with that, the words left him, as if the very breath had been taken from his lungs.

"It's as if what, Archie?" Steven looked into the priest's eyes and found only a blank stare. "What were you going to say?"

Archie blinked once, twice, and shook his head. "Steven?"

"Archie, this is important. What was it you were going to—"

A deafening explosion echoed up from the canyon below. The pair of giants formed from black stone stood triumphant as one icy colossus stumbled backward from the board while the other, reduced to fragments of ice the size of school buses, rained down upon the checkered battlefield like judgment from the gods. In seconds, nearly all the Pawns and half the Knights, Black and White alike, lay crushed beneath the White Rook's fragmented corpse. Only one of the White Bishops survived, the other a victim to the falling ice that moments before had likely been a friend. The remaining Knights, atop horse and bear respectively, each leaped to safety before charging at each other anew from opposite corners of the board. At the battle's center, protected by a dome of scintillating ebony and silver, the Queens continued to circle, neither taking their focus off the other for even half a second.

And the Kings, neither of whom had budged an inch from their initial position, both looked on dispassionately as the battle waged on.

"What now?" Niklaus shivered from head to toe, not just from the biting wind but also from the shock of witnessing his fellow Rook's absolute destruction.

"What always happens when one side gets the numerical advantage." Steven narrowed his gaze at the battlefield below. "The endgame."

Their opposites on the checkered battlefield eliminated from play, the pair of onyx behemoths turned their attention on their remaining adversaries. The lone White Bishop still standing was the first to fall, her robed form hurled into an outcropping of rock by a single kick from the nearer of the two Black Rooks. The lone White Pawn that had escaped the rain of icy death went down a second later beneath an avalanche of black stone summoned by the second. The remaining Black Knight took advantage of his opposite's momentary distraction and struck the White Knight's breast plate with a spiked flail, crushing his foe's armored ribcage with an ear-splitting clang and sending him flying from his ursine steed. The pair of Black Bishops converged on the remaining White Bishop, driving him from the board.

"That leaves the White Queen." Audrey looked on, the tremor in her weak voice breaking Steven's heart. "She's all alone."

"Not quite." Steven pointed to the far end of the board where a lone White Pawn struggled to pulled himself free from the icy debris. "There's still hope."

As the gathered Black descended upon the White Queen, Steven took Audrey's hand and squeezed it tight. The woman in white below held her own for a while, but the outcome was never in doubt.

"Come on, Grey," Steven whispered, holding on to hope. "Don't let her down."

The pair of Black Rooks converged behind the White Queen, blocking any retreat, while the Black Knight leaped from square to square, hindering any attempted advance on the Black King. The two Black Bishops maneuvered themselves into position around their master, leaving the Black Queen to hammer away at her opposite's defenses. Just as all seemed lost, the White King stepped forward and faith surged in Steven's heart.

"Here it comes." A slight smile found its way onto Steven's face. "The moment of truth."

The White Queen chanced a single glance back in hope of finding refuge in her King's eyes. After a moment that seemed to last a year, the man they knew as Grey shook his head slowly from side to side and raised his arms to the glaciers on either side of the great board, the pouch in his hand glowing like a miniature star. Energy crackled around the White King and a sonic shudder went through the glacier at their feet followed a moment later by an ear-splitting cracking as tons of ice that had been present since Jesus walked the earth began to break apart.

"My God..." Steven held aloft the pouch and grasped Audrey's shoulder. "Everyone, with me." As the other four all fell in on Steven, he murmured, "Anywhere but here. Anywhere but here. Anywhere..."

The pouch emitted a deafening pulse, and the universe swirled around them again. One by one they disappeared from Steven's sight until only he remained, the magic of the pouch holding him aloft as the glacier disintegrated beneath his feet and an avalanche to end all avalanches descended upon the checkered battlefield below. The Queens, Black and White alike, screamed at the impending icy doom, their voice drowned out in the cacophony of fracturing ice. Zed slipped off the crown of the Black King and stared up in disbelief at the nullification of his well-laid plans. The White King hesitated but a moment before holding aloft the *Hvitr Kyll* of this time, and vanished in a flash of silver.

"It can't have ended that way." Steven looked on as Zed as well disappeared from the chessboard in a ripple of darkness, leaving his Pieces to face their icy fate. "Grey wouldn't have let that happen." As the falling ice swallowed up the checkered battlefield, Steven's head dropped. "And yet, he did."

Floating there in a cocoon of silver energy, Steven readied himself to send himself after the others, his heart racing as he pondered what he'd just seen.

No, not his heart, but the iridescent dragonfly of metal that resided there and had guided his steps for so many weeks. He brought his hand to his chest to pull Amaryllis out into the light, hoping she might provide some sort of insight into what he should do next, but she had already worked herself to the top of his pocket and teetered there precariously. His trembling fingers reached to grasp her just behind her wings when, for the first time Steven could recall, she took flight as if truly alive.

"No!" Steven's hand shot out to pluck Ruth's magical gift from the air before she could escape, his instinctive flail pulling his gaze to a section of pristine ice along the opposite ridge.

There, nestled among the blinding white, his eye caught a flash of grey.

Or, perhaps, a flash of...Grey?

REUNIONS & REGRETS

"Could it be?" As wisps of silver energy played around Steven's form ready to transport him home, he shifted his attention to the crevice in the ice across the valley. "No. Take me there."

Another pulse of bone-shaking sound, and Steven vanished from one side of the glacier only to reappear in the narrow fissure of snow and ice he'd spied a second before.

"Grey," he shouted. "Are you here?"

"Steven." The single word, colored with his mentor's unique accent, echoed from across his shoulder. "You shouldn't be here."

Steven turned and found Grey standing before a floating doorway of darkness. "Grey." The man appeared emaciated, as if he hadn't eaten in weeks. Or longer. "What's wrong?" He gestured to the shimmering hole in space. "And where does that lead?"

"Go from here." Weakly, Grey motioned to the pouch. "Do not follow me."

And with that, he retreated into the darkness, leaving Steven alone in the icy crevasse. A moment later, the ice at Steven's feet shook even as the dark doorway to God knows where began to ripple like a flag in a high wind.

"The hell with that." Steven rushed the doorway and dived through even as the hole in space collapsed about him. Half a second later, he landed facedown, his elbows and knees taking the brunt of an icy landing.

Grey stood before him, hungrily devouring a small bowl of what could only be described as gruel. As Steven rose from the ice, his grey-clad mentor hid the stone bowl behind his back and scowled in exasperation.

"I told you not to follow me."

"Last I checked, you were the White King of this Game." Steven set his jaw. "I can't imagine a scenario where I *wouldn't* follow."

"I cannot bear for you to see me this way." Grey brought the bowl back around and resumed his ravenous consumption of its contents. "King, indeed."

"What happened?" Steven asked. "Where are we?"

"Zed, it would seem, truly has a talent for torture." The corner of Grey's mouth turned up in an ironic half-grin. "He could have simply left me to die, but instead, he has provided the barest of subsistence so that I can relive my worst moment again and again for all perpetuity."

"Your worst moment?" Understanding blossomed in Steven's mind, revealing not only where they were, but when. He turned just in time to watch the valley below transform into the enormous black and white checkered pattern that had all but come to define his life. "He's making you watch," Steven swallowed, "as they all die."

"As I kill them, you mean." The bowl dropped from Grey's fingers, the spilled gruel staining the ice like a spatter of blood. "I stopped counting how many times I've relived these few hours after the first thousand or so. I tried for weeks to simply avert my gaze, close my ears, not to see it, hear it, smell it. But it draws me back every time."

"The doorway," Steven asked, "it sends you back each time to the exact same spot a few hours earlier?" Understanding blossomed in his mind. "To just...before..."

"More or less." Grey hung his head in shame and exhaustion. "Sometimes there is food, albeit the poorest fare Zed can put together. Most times, there isn't. I refused it at first..."

"But hunger is hunger." Steven took a step toward his mentor. "I get it."

"Every time, it's the same." Grey peered across the edge. "The board appears, the opposite sides take their positions, the Black achieves the upper hand quickly and never gives it back, and the massacre of Stonehenge threatens to repeat itself, leaving Zed on the precipice of victory." He turned to Steven, sadness, rage, and defeat all warring on his face. "Please understand. He couldn't be allowed to win again. That much power in his hands..."

"That's why you never told me—us—about Antarctica."

"You never asked." Grey looked away. "Even after Zed's taunt all those months ago."

"I don't think I wanted to know." Steven gave Grey a rueful smile. "And somehow, I already did."

"I know my words must ring false, Steven, but this is the reality. The Game that Zed and I created is forever. It cannot be undone, no matter how much I might wish it otherwise."

"You could always go back and warn yourself, maybe change the rules set in place to keep Zed from capitalizing on all the loopholes." Steven held the pouch before him. "The two of us standing here is living proof it's possible."

"Possible to go back, perhaps." Grey let out a steamy breath. "To change the past, however, is impossible."

"You're saying that nothing we've done has changed a thing." Steven's hands flew up in frustration. "What about when we found you and Arthur in 1946? I'm assuming you held that back from me, how we'd already met decades before I was born."

"Everything that happened in your various forced sojourns to the past only led to the eventuality of this iteration of the Game you and I still play even at this very moment."

Steven considered Grey's words. Without their interference, Ruth and Arthur would never have met. Zed wouldn't have such insight into their identities.

The Black Queen would not exist.

As much as it pained him to admit, their interference in the past had only solidified the future they'd already lived.

"So, Zed provides you just enough sustenance to keep you alive so you can bear witness to your darkest moment again and again for all eternity."

"If I go through the door, I reappear at this moment." Grey gestured to the ground at his feet. "If I choose not to go through the door, the glacier collapses, I fall to my death, and then reappear here at the same moment regardless." He gestured to the high walls of ice surrounding them and the impossible climb down to the battlefield below. "No way to escape. No way to intervene. My fate, to watch again and again as those I called friend fall, some at the feet of our shared enemy and some by my own hand."

"But this time, it's different." Steven held aloft the pouch. "Time to break the cycle."

Grey laughed bitterly. "I saw you all across the way. Watched as you all took in my greatest failure." He let out an anguished sigh. "Do you honestly believe any of them would follow me again after seeing that?"

"Any broken trust will take time to heal, of course, but that's beside the point." Steven rested a hand on Grey's shoulder, grateful his mentor didn't brush away the small gesture of kindness. "As you've told me a thousand times, like it or not, the Game is happening. When it does, we will either emerge victorious or be found wanting, but we don't have the first hope of even beginning if we don't have our King to lead us."

Grey peered into Steven's face with a sad smile. "Truer words were never spoken."

Steven held the pouch between them. "Then, shall we?"

Below them, the board filled with Pieces, sixteen on each side: Zed and his dark forces on one side, this century's Grey and the gathered White on the other. Those standing with the White King appeared hopeful and ready to fight, all unaware of the carnage about to occur. Grey looked down upon them all and allowed a single tear to roll down his cheek before turning to Steven.

"Now that you are here, I cannot bear to watch another moment." He lowered his head. "Take us from this place." His voice dropped to a whisper as Steven grasped his wrist. "Far away from this...tragedy."

"One ticket out of here, coming up." Steven held aloft the pouch, his voice dropping to a whisper. "*Hvitr Kyll*, take us to the others."

❀

S teven closed his eyes on the frozen wasteland of sixteenth-century Antarctica and opened them again upon a beautiful sunset, the last rays of sunlight disappearing behind the flat top of a mesa in the distance. The characteristic alternating white and red layers of rock meant they could only be in one place.

"The American Badlands." Grey pulled away from Steven and took a single step forward. "But when?"

"Not sure." Steven glanced skyward at a vapor trail that split the heavens, the plane that left the white scar across the otherwise clear blue firmament long gone. "But it's a pretty safe bet we're a little closer to home than 1537."

"Steven?" The familiar voice, stronger than he'd heard it for some time, came accompanied by a rush of footsteps from behind. "Oh my God...Grey?"

Steven turned just in time to catch Audrey in his arms as she nearly tackled him with excitement.

"Whoa, whoa." Steven chuckled. "I'm fine." His gaze shot to Grey. "We're both fine."

He returned his attention to Audrey and renewed hope swelled in his heart. A far cry from the woman he'd parted with minutes before, her eyes held a renewed strength, her cheeks their usual ruddy complexion, her hair its ambient shine.

"And you?" Steven asked. "You're..."

"Fine as well, apparently." Audrey stepped back so Steven could take a look at her. "I'm guessing that we're all finally back where we belong." She ran her hands down her body. "I feel as good as new."

"Are you sure?" Steven studied her eyes. "You're...okay?"

"I'm better than okay." She spun her index finger around, and, in answer, a tongue of mist danced at her fingertip like a snake charmer's pet. "I'm back."

"As are we all."

Archie's voice. Young and strong again.

A fact Steven found simultaneously comforting and disconcerting.

The priest he'd met in a hospital half a continent away at the beginning of all this had been an old man and not in the best of health. That had all changed, however, with the advent of the Game, and for the majority of their time together, the Archie he'd known had been the vibrant young man who strode toward him on a mesa at sunset. Flanked by Emilio and Lena on one side and Niklaus on the other, he and the others all appeared back at a hundred percent.

In any other circumstance, the moment would have been perfect, the homecoming for which they'd all been fighting for months and risked everything to attain.

But there, at the back of his mind, remained the same old fly in the ointment that had worried Steven for months.

Archie's gaze, rejuvenated by the energies of the Game, retained the same cryptic gleam that had unnerved Steven since the moment they met.

Not a doubt remained in Steven's mind.

A reckoning was coming.

But not this day.

The priest and his escort descended on Steven and Audrey in a rush of hugs and tears. Both Niklaus and Lena beamed with jubilant grins in the moment, and even Emilio had emerged from his usual funk into something resembling a good mood.

"I was so scared." Audrey pulled close to Steven's ear. "When you didn't reappear with the rest of us…"

Steven gave her shoulders a gentle squeeze and slid into his most reassuring smile. "As you can see, I had some business to attend to."

"Clearly." Emilio waggled a thumb in Grey's direction. "Where'd you dig him up?"

"He was there, in Antarctica." Steven shot Grey a questioning glance and at his nod, continued. "Across the valley from us. Zed had left him stranded in a crack in the glacier."

"He made you watch." Lena's eyes dropped. "How cruel."

"Must have been rough." Emilio's eyes narrowed in anger. "Not exactly your finest moment, Mr. Immortal Wizard."

"Emilio." Lena grabbed him by the hand and pulled him into her. "Quiet."

"Why?" Emilio shook off Lena's grip and stalked in Grey's direction. "We all just saw what he did. How he fixes problems when things aren't going his way." He put his finger in Grey's chest. "Why would you think any of us would believe a word you say now? You've proven beyond a shadow of a doubt that you'd sacrifice this whole group if it accomplished whatever agenda you have rolling around inside that centuries-old skull of yours."

"Emilio!" Lena pulled up beside the boy, her mercurial features flitting between anger, embarrassment, and concern. "Show some respect."

"Respect?" Emilio all but spat.

"Yes, Emilio." Steven echoed Lena's plea. "Please. Let him explain."

Emilio sucked in a breath to continue his tirade, but one look into Lena's determined eyes and he deflated.

"Fine." He crossed his arms and set his jaw. "Tell us, Grey. Tell us the grand reason why you basically rage-quit your own Game the minute it wasn't going your way."

"You've answered your own question, Emilio." Grey shook his head sadly. "Despite my every precaution, months of training each of the Pieces in the use of their various abilities, countless hours discussing strategy and tactics, Zed's savagery remained the deciding factor. Where I taught the White how to win, he taught the Black how to kill. Even more so than at Stonehenge, what we designed to be a simple contest of wills descended into a massacre."

"We saw." Niklaus stood at the edge of the gathered White, his face pale. Steven had little doubt the image of the White Rooks' fate from the Antarctic battle was replaying in his mind. "I still don't understand why you quit on them, though. Why not let the Game merely play to its conclusion? What were you afraid of?"

"I do not wish to sound melodramatic, Mr. Zamek, but the fate of the world depended on that moment." Grey paced the rocky mesa, his tattered sharkskin boots barely holding together. "I saw what happened after the second iteration, what Zed did with the energies he subsumed after the slaughter at Stonehenge." He let out a bitter laugh. "Suffice to say that the period historians refer to as The Dark Ages were far darker than they might otherwise have been."

"What happened after you wiped the board in Antarctica, then?" Steven's brow furrowed with concern. "Where did those energies go?"

"With no clear victor, most of the residual forces left by the correction dissipated back into the ether from whence they originated. Both the *Hvitr Kyll* and its dark sister absorbed a fair amount of the power, some of which you and the others employ when using your various abilities. A fraction of the energies, however, remained for the intervening centuries, at times magnifying what should have been minor meteorological or geologic events to disastrous proportions." Grey offered Steven a weak smile. "Much like the catastrophes you and the others responded to over the last several months. Most were inevitable, as the coming correction seems fated to be the strongest yet, but the leftover energies from Antarctica certainly made most if not all the events you railed against far worse than they would otherwise have been."

"So," Emilio bristled, "you started a Game you can't control, had to wipe out friend and enemy alike last time to keep your former bestie from creating hell on earth for five centuries, and the result of that decision has put countless lives at risk, resulting in all of us running around like chickens with our heads cut off putting out fires that you started. And now, we're supposed to line up with you as our commander-in-chief and simply hope things are going to be okay?"

"In short," Grey lowered his head, "yes."

Emilio's gazed dropped to the ground, his fists trembling at his sides. "Are you all listening to this?"

"Emilio." Lena's eyes grew wide as she focused on a point past his shoulder. "Wait."

"Wait?" he continued, barely taking a breath. "Come on. What sane person would so much as consider following this man another second?"

"*Papi.*"

Lena's intent gaze pulled Steven's attention to the edge of the mesa.

Hope, it seemed, had sprung in the east.

"Emilio," Steven whispered. "Look."

"What?" Emilio shouted in exasperation.

Steven pointed. "There's something you ought to see."

Emilio spun on one heel, and every ounce of venom drained from his expression when he locked gazes with the last set of eyes he'd ever dreamed he'd see again.

"Rocinante!" He rushed to the horse's side. "But how?"

Grey appeared at the boy's side, a smile on his face for the first time since their pained reunion began. "Horses, surprisingly, are quite good swimmers."

Lena came up alongside Rocinante's other flank. "But how did he get here?"

Steven joined the circle. "I'm guessing he walked."

"But how would he know to come here?" Emilio asked.

"Animals know many things that humans aren't privy to." Grey held out his hand, and Rocinante nuzzled his palm. "Even humans who have walked the earth for over a millennium."

The tender moment between horse and wizard took the remainder of the wind out of Emilio's sails.

"You know?" Emilio shoved his hands in his pockets. "I'm still not happy about any of this, but for the moment, we're truly *all* back together, and that deserves some kind of celebration." He gave Grey's emaciated form a quick up and down. "I don't know about the rest of you, but I'm starving." His eyes dropped to the pouch at Steven's side. "Think that thing can find us a pizza place with a table for seven?" At Rocinante's whinny, he added, "Horse friendly, of course."

"Dinner it is." Steven held aloft the *Hvitr Kyll* and, without a moment's hesitation, took Audrey's hand. "Pouch, you know what to do."

BLACK & WHITE

"Let me get this straight." Steven sat with Grey in a coffee shop a few blocks from Times Square. "All of us have been gone almost half a year. Six months of our life passed by."

"You lived each of the days." Grey sipped from his rich mocha, the swirling brown and white in the foam like the wings of some giant bird of prey. "Did you not?"

"But only a week has passed here in the present." Steven did a quick calculation. "Are we all simply going to live the rest of our lives five months older than we're supposed to be?"

"First, the Game is nigh." Grey passed his hand through the air, indicating the here and now. "You and the others are precisely where and when you are supposed to be."

"And second?" Steven asked.

"You have barely missed anything, and what you've gained…" Grey pulled in a breath. "All of you have visited other times and seen sights that no one else will ever see. Many would consider such an experience a blessing."

Steven let out a bitter chuckle. "Didn't feel like a blessing when we were fighting for our lives."

"It never does." Grey took another sip from his mug. "Remember with whom you are speaking, Steven. How many friends and family I've had to watch wither and die while I carried on for the supposed good of the world."

"It's just strange." Steven gulped down his black coffee. "That's all."

"I would argue that the experience has left you all with a greater appreciation of what you do have."

Steven raised a brow. "Is this the part where you tell me I've lived more in the last six months than most people do in their entire lives?"

Grey laughed. "I have had centuries to observe the human condition. If there is one commonality in souls the globe over, it is that people as a rule wish their life away on a daily basis." His smile diminished. "And no more so than in the 'developed' world." He mused for a moment, lost in his thoughts. "Television. Books. Sporting events. Even sleep. All nothing but momentary escapes from what can seem a life sentence of alternating pain and boredom."

"Wow." Steven shook his head. "Your future career as a motivational speaker is a lock."

"I merely speak the truth, Steven." Grey held up his mug as if toasting. "You and the others have had the experience of truly being removed from your own time. I doubt any of you will ever take another moment for granted."

"That's a safe bet." Steven's smile grew wide.

Grey turned in his chair to follow Steven's gaze. There in the doorway stood Audrey wearing a sundress with a bright floral print and her hair pulled back in a ponytail. Her smile and knowing gaze banished any of the remaining cobwebs from Steven's still waking mind.

"Sorry I'm late." She pulled up a chair to the low table. "Had a couple of errands to run this morning."

"Errands." Steven chuckled. "Wow. We really *are* home."

"Where is everyone else?" Audrey asked.

"Here."

Niklaus strode into the shop with Emilio and Lena close behind. Archie, taking up the rear, hesitated just inside the doorway before heading to the counter to get his customary triple-shot espresso.

"Morning, Nik." Steven raised his mug. "Emilio. Lena."

He shot a quick wave to Archie, who had fallen in line behind a pair of women wearing tank tops and yoga pants, the de facto uniform for the establishment per Steven's assessment from the preceding couple of days.

"Everyone okay?" Steven asked. "Anything out of the ordinary?"

"Everything's fine with us." Lena sat at the table and pushed out a chair for Emilio. "Nothing to report."

"Same." Niklaus pulled over a chair and rested an elbow on the table. "Other than the fact that I didn't sleep last night."

"Again?" Audrey rested a hand on his wrist. "The same nightmare?"

"Every time I close my eyes. I can't unsee it." Niklaus let out a mighty yawn, followed by a full body shudder. "The pair of White Rooks shattered to their core, their fractured bodies raining down on the rest of the board, killing friend and foe alike." He stared at Steven with bleary eyes. "That can't be how it ends for me."

"It won't be." Steven clasped his friend's shoulder. "Right, Grey?"

"The time of battle is coming," Grey answered, "and on that day, all I can promise is that I will prepare you, teach you, stand with you, fight with you, and, if necessary, die with you."

"So glad am I to hear that you are resigned to your fate, old friend." Zed stepped from a swirling hole of darkness onto the well-worn wooden floor of the cafe. "Not that it matters. I may not have been prepared for your unique method of preventing my last victory, but rest assured that I will not be caught unawares again."

Steven and the others all leapt up from the table, icons in hand, ready to fight.

"Now, now." Zed steepled his fingers below his chin. "All of you may relax and continue to enjoy your morning repast. I have come alone and unarmed and bear you no ill will." His lips spread in a vicious smile. "At least not this day."

"Why are you here, then?" Steven asked as Archie rushed to the table. "What do you want?"

"Merely to let you know that your return has not gone unnoticed." He motioned to the bustling coffee shop. "Your attempt at losing yourselves at the center of the busiest city on the continent is admirable, but my eyes are everywhere." His gaze meandered over to

Grey. "Did you truly believe I would not know that you, of all people, had returned?"

Grey rose from his seat and stood nose to nose with his opposite. "How dare you?"

"How dare *I*?" Zed crossed his arms. "This should be interesting."

"How many months—no, years—did we spend crafting this Game, all in an effort to correct the mad hubris of our ancestors?" Grey seethed, the righteous anger pouring from him unlike anything Steven had ever seen. "How many of our friends sacrificed their very lives to bring our insane solution to fruition? How many?" He put his finger in Zed's chest. "And now, not only have you perverted the very thing you helped create to the point that it is all but unrecognizable, but you have abandoned whatever honor remained in your soul."

Zed's perverse smile faded into an expression of barely veiled annoyance. "All those centuries ago, in your zeal to be the savior of an undeserving world, you forgot one simple fact." He brushed Grey's finger away. "That every contest has but one winner. All others are simply...well..." He cast his gaze around the room, his eyes lighting on each of the White in turn before meeting Steven's gaze in the end. "You may curse my name, hate my methods, even raise my offenses to the highest of high, but in the end, I will prevail. The mighty Arbiters of Old, the spirits of old friends, both yours and mine, have not seen fit to sanction or even censure my actions thus far."

Grey's eyes narrowed down to slits. "How they cannot see the depravation in your every word and action is beyond me."

"As this most recent iteration of the Game began, I feared just that." Zed's smile returned. "But then I realized something." The wizard in black drew uncomfortably close to his opposite. "After witnessing you, the supposed paragon of all that's good and right in this world, destroy in Antarctica the very construct you now seem hellbent on preserving, leaving friend and foe dead in the wake of your decision, it would seem the two sides of this little Game we play are no longer so black and white. Would that be fair to say...*Grey*?"

In a move that seemed more from Emilio's playbook, Grey's hand balled into a fist and was well on its way to impact Zed's face when Steven caught his arm.

"Whoa, Grey," he said. "Don't let him push your buttons."

"Trust me, Steven. They are all well and truly pushed." Grey sucked in a deep breath in a vain attempt to brush off Zed's taunts. "As well he knows."

"So," Zed said to the group at large, "it seems that neither removing you from the board nor shifting you to a time and place where you are no longer a nuisance has proven effective at keeping the lot of you from being a collective thorn in my side." He returned his attention to Grey. "Therefore, as distasteful as I may find it, you have left me no choice. If it is a third slaughter you want…" His eyes cut to Niklaus, who jerked back as if struck. "It is a slaughter you will get." He offered the slightest of bows. "Until we meet again."

Before any of them could so much as inhale to make a response, Zed disappeared through another dark doorway in space, as if he were never there. No one said a word. The hair rose on Steven's neck, both in response to the barrage of threats as well as the oddness at seeing not one person in the crowded coffee shop so much as blink an eye at the bizarre turn of events.

Zed's cloak of anonymity had clearly been working overtime.

"So this is how it is to be." Grey sat back at the table and rested his forehead on his palms. "What I intended as an act of supreme kindness for the world has instead descended into an exercise in abject cruelty."

"That wasn't your intent." Lena rested a comforting hand on Grey's shoulder. "All of us know that."

"It doesn't change the reality." Grey met each of their gazes in turn. "This boulder I've sent hurtling down the mountain of time cannot be stopped, and each one of you rests in its path." He pounded the table. "Gods. I swore that this time I would keep myself from getting close. Friendship clouds judgment."

"I don't know." Steven glanced across the table at Audrey. "Sometimes when you care, things become surprisingly clear."

"We'll kick his ass." Emilio sent a punch into his own palm. "Isn't that what you were saying on the way here, Archie?"

The priest lowered his head and ran his fingers along his newly cropped scalp. "With our return to the time of this most recent iteration of the Game, the visions have again retreated. But one thing is clear from what I've already seen: this particular gathering of the White embraces an aspect none of the others ever has."

They all waited expectantly for Archie to complete his thought, and in practiced pulpit style he held out the moment for as long as he could.

"A sense of...family," he proclaimed eventually, the proud smile on his face sending Steven's self-doubt into overdrive.

"Pardon?" This new voice came from behind Niklaus' massive form. He shifted out of the way, revealing a young Asian woman of college age standing with a yellowed envelope in her hands. "But since you're speaking of family..."

Emilio tensed, but a gentle brush from Lena's hand convinced him to hold his tongue. Niklaus, Audrey, and even Grey looked on in surprise and wonder, though none were as flabbergasted as Archie.

"And who might you be?" Steven asked.

"My name is Sumire." She bowed her head and held out the envelope. "And you are...Steven Bauer, are you not?"

"I am." He took the envelope. "Have we met?"

"No." She smiled. "But, strange as it sounds, you knew my great-great-grandmother."

Steven inspected the envelope. His own name, scrawled across the center in familiar script, quickened his pulse. "Your great-*great*-grandmother?"

"Just read the letter, Mr. Bauer. As I understand it, all you need to know and more than I could ever explain waits inside."

Steven carefully tore into the yellowed envelope and pulled out two pages of equally familiar stationery. The tiny script began with a simple salutation in the upper left corner.

He read aloud.

Dearest Steven Bauer,

As I sit here, years after our paths last parted ways, I look back upon our brief crossing (pardon the play on words) and remember you and your friends with the deepest gratitude.

My time on this side of the veil is quickly approaching its end and as someone who understands the siren call of a mystery, I will answer one of many questions that likely remain in your mind, though if you read this at the juncture I intend, you no doubt have many more pressing matters weighing on your thoughts, so I will be brief.

I purposefully kept my identity a secret until such time that you had returned to your point of origin to keep from muddying the waters of time. Were I you, I might have been tempted to seek me out instead of moving forward. If you are reading this, then all the answers I might have provided, you have already discovered on your own, which is best.

Please know that my life since I was very small has been the very definition of conflicting loyalties.

Loyalty to blood versus loyalty to my adoptive father.

Loyalty to that family versus loyalty to those who saved that very family.

Loyalty to the people closest to me versus loyalty to the world at large.

Like your mentor, who I pray is sitting beside you as you read this, my final letter to you, I strive for balance in all things. Fairness. Justice. In this, I went against the wishes of the man you know as the Black King and attempted to aid you in your safe return to your own time. Some would argue that my actions were foreordained and that all I have done was already written somewhere in the stars. But I believe we all make decisions each day that change everything, not the least of which, the balance of good and evil in our own souls.

I love the man that Zed has proven he can be as much as I loved my own father.

I hate the man that Zed has allowed himself to become more than I can fathom.

This war in my heart has been the hardest balance of all to achieve. Trust me on this.

Fight him, Steven Bauer. Do not let his madness engulf the earth.

But fight this battle, this war, not out of hate for the man who raised me to be the very woman writing to you now but out of love for the world that would suffer from the avarice and insanity that has engulfed him.

My request may sound impossible, but I have no doubt the man who risked everything to stop and save my sister, even when the fate of the world was at stake, would understand.

Fare thee well, Steven Bauer. May you and your friends comport

yourselves with honor as you fight for what is right, and in the end, may
goodness prevail, for all our sakes.
   -Kiku

Steven locked gazes with the girl. "You were instructed to seek us out here?"

Sumire checked her phone. "On this date, at this very time." A slight blush colored her cheeks. "I've been waiting for hours." Her eyes glistened, a wellspring of emotion. "That man. Was he my great-great-grandmother's adoptive father?"

She saw him, Steven considered. *Or at least some version of him.*

"In every way that counts." Steven took a breath. "Yes, Sumire. That was Zed."

"All these years I've awaited this day." She shook as tears began to flow. "I never dreamed any of it could be true, much less that I'd see it —him—with my own eyes."

"You know we're destined to fight him, right?" Steven held up Kiku's letter. "To the death, if need be."

"I understand." Sumire turned to leave. "Before I go, though, one last thing?"

Steven laid the letter on the table before him and stood. "Of course."

"This 'Game' you're about to play for the fate of the world..." She crossed her arms, steeling herself for the answer. "What happens if you lose?"

TO BE CONCLUDED

AUTHOR'S NOTE

The whole is greater than the sum of its parts.
Aristotle

Welcome to the end of the second act of this three-part story I've been either writing or preparing to write for as long as I can remember. As we saw at the end of the last chapter, the White stand gathered once more after having been dispersed through time by Zed and his dark machinations. Ready for the battle to come in the final book of this story, we must now take a pause so my heroes can catch their breath, and so I can write another 100,000 words. The coming conflict has been brewing in my head for over three decades and I'm already hard at work at closing this story with the endgame this particular game of chess deserves.

If you enjoyed this middle section of *The Pawn Stratagem*, consider yourself lucky, as the events chronicled herein were not a part of the original story I imagined. In its original conception, the story was basically supposed to involve gathering together all the pieces and then proceed straight into a battle to end all battles in a single volume. That's it. As I was writing *Pawn's Gambit*, however, it became clear very quickly that unless I was going to try to sell a doorstopper as my debut novel (a rarity, though it does happen), I was going to have to break the story up into more than one book. Thus, the first part of *The Pawn Stratagem* became a "gambit" where Steven, against all odds, assembled all the various pieces of the White. This change, in turn, necessitated another book to chronicle the resulting battle.

But, as anyone reading this series likely knows by now, chess games don't involve just a beginning and ending. For the most part— unless you find yourself on the wrong end of a fool's mate—they consist of three parts: an opening, a middle game, and an endgame (a term that is strangely on everyone's tongue here in May of 2019.) If the opening gambit was the first part and the inevitable conflict to decide the fate of the world the third, then I needed to create a middle ground, some additional connective tissue, a place to get to know better all these awesome people we'd just met before sending them off to fight for their lives.

And how better to get to know someone than see what happens when you remove them from their comfort zone and pair them off with someone they don't know all that well?

I have to be honest: writing this book was a ton of fun. Way more fun, in fact, than I imagined it would be. Though everything in this story needed to point back in some way to the main story, sending people anywhere you wanted in American history and then seeing what they did once they got there was extremely freeing, a pantser's dream. As a result of this truly freeform experiment, a lot of connections that would never have been made had we stuck with "Plan A" suddenly sprang to life, bringing new depths to these characters and situations I had never dreamed of. As Steven keeps discovering, sometimes things are simply meant to be.

And now, as always, time for a few acknowledgements.

To my critique group of Matthew Saunders and Caryn Sutorus, thank you for taking the time to always provide such top-notch observations about my writing, characters, and story. I've done my best to incorporate your sage advice at every turn of this twisty maze of a story and the resulting book is the better for your efforts.

To my friends and fellow creators in Charlotte Writers, thank you for ten years of support, for smiles and laughter, and for always being there. Keep writing!

To John Hartness at Falstaff Books, thank you again for taking a chance on this series. I dedicate Book Two to you and everyone at Falstaff for helping me bring the adventures of Steven and his friends to the world.

To Melissa Gilbert, thank you as always for your outstanding editing and proofreading. There is no story so polished that you can't make it shine even more. Also, thank you for the beautiful cover that graces these carefully edited pages...

To the fine folks at Starbucks on East Boulevard in Charlotte, NC, as well as the Park Road Caribou Coffee (the only one left in my immediate vicinity, in fact), thanks for your excellent service, not to mention sustenance, during the countless hours I've spent at your respective establishments as I've pounded out the words found between these covers. They say that writers are strange organisms that consume caffeine and produce words and I appreciate you keeping this particular writer fed and watered over the last decade.

As always, an eternal shout out to all my teachers and professors that helped make me the writer and person I am today. Keep doing what you do. Your noble work grows more important every year.

To my Mom and Dad who just celebrated their 50th wedding anniversary, thanks for always being there and for being the example of how to keep a promise, be it to yourself or another human being. I love you both.

Lastly, to all the many readers who have been waiting a LONG time for this next chapter in the adventures of Steven Bauer and company, enjoy. I hope this book was worth the wait.

ABOUT THE AUTHOR

Darin Kennedy, born and raised in Winston-Salem, North Carolina, is a graduate of Wake Forest University and Bowman Gray School of Medicine. After completing family medicine residency in the mountains of Virginia, he served eight years as a United States Army physician and wrote his first novel in the sands of northern Iraq, a novel that started this very trilogy. He is currently hard at work on the third and final book in the series.

His *Fugue and Fable* trilogy, also available from Falstaff Books, was born from a fusion of two of his lifelong loves: classical music and world mythology. *The Mussorgsky Riddle*, *The Stravinsky Intrigue*, and *The Tchaikovsky Finale*, are the beginning, middle, and end of the closest he will likely ever come to writing his own symphony. His short stories can be found in numerous anthologies and magazines, and the best, particularly those about a certain *Necromancer for Hire*, are collected for your reading pleasure under Darin's imprint, 64Square Publishing.

Doctor by day and novelist by night, he writes and practices medicine in Charlotte, NC. When not engaged in either of the above activities, he has been known to strum the guitar, enjoy a bite of sushi, and, rumor has it, he even sleeps on occasion. Find him online at darinkennedy.com.

ALSO BY DARIN KENNEDY

Fugue & Fable

The Mussorgsky Riddle

The Stravinsky Intrigue

The Tchaikovsky Finale

The Pawn Stratagem

Pawn's Gambit

Queen's Peril

King's Crisis *(forthcoming)*

FRIENDS OF FALSTAFF

The following people graciously support the work we do at Falstaff Books in bringing you the best of genre fiction's Misfit Toys.

Dino Hicks
Samuel Montgomery-Blinn
Scott Norris
Sheryl R. Hayes
Staci-Leigh Santore

You can join them by signing up as a patron at www.patreon.com/falstaffbooks.

Lightning Source UK Ltd.
Milton Keynes UK
UKHW012241161219
355506UK00002B/100/P